MASTERS OF THE MODERN SHORT STORY

Brief Edition

MASTERS OF THE MODERN SHORT STORY

Walter Havighurst

MIAMI UNIVERSITY
OXFORD, OHIO

BRIEF EDITION

HARCOURT, BRACE AND COMPANY, NEW YORK

C.3.56

COPYRIGHTS AND ACKNOWLEDGMENTS

The author and publisher thank the following publishers and copyright holders for their permission to use the selections reprinted in this book:

J. M. DENT AND SONS, LIMITED, for permission to reprint "Youth" by Joseph Conrad.

DOUBLEDAY AND COMPANY, INC., for "He Don't Plant Cotton" from *Prince of Darkness and Other Stories* by J. F. Powers, copyright 1943, by J. F. Powers, reprinted by permission of Doubleday and Company, Inc.

GRAHAM GREENE for Canadian rights to "Across the Bridge" from *Nineteen Stories* by Graham Greene. Copyright 1947, 1949, by Graham Greene.

HARCOURT, BRACE AND COMPANY, INC., for "The Jilting of Granny Weatherall" from *Flowering Judas and Other Stories,* copyright 1930, 1935, by Katherine Anne Porter. Reprinted by permission of Harcourt, Brace and Company, Inc.; for "Livvie" from *The Wide Net and Other Stories,* copyright 1943, by Eudora Welty. Reprinted by permission of Harcourt, Brace and Company, Inc.; for "The New Dress" from *A Haunted House and Other Stories* by Virginia Woolf copyright, 1944. Reprinted by permission of Harcourt, Brace and Company, Inc.

MESSRS. WILLIAM HEINEMANN, LIMITED, for Canadian permission to reprint "Across the Bridge" from *Nineteen Stories* by Graham Greene; for Canadian permission to reprint "Odor of Chrysanthemums" from *The Prussian Officer and Other Stories* by D. H. Lawrence.

ALFRED A. KNOPF, INC., for "The Road from Colonus" reprinted from *The Collected Tales of E. M. Forster,* by permission of Alfred A. Knopf, Inc. Copyright 1947, by Alfred A. Knopf, Inc.; for "The Stranger" reprinted from *The Short Stories of Katherine Mansfield* by permission of Alfred A. Knopf, Inc. Copyright 1922, 1937, by Alfred A. Knopf, Inc.; for "Uprooted" reprinted from *The Stories of Frank O'Connor,* by permission of Alfred A. Knopf, Inc. Copyright 1944, 1952, by Frank O'Connor.

MRS. FRIEDA LAWRENCE for Canadian permission to reprint "Odor of Chrysanthemums" from *The Prussian Officer and Other Stories* by D. H. Lawrence.

JOHN MIDDLETON MURRY for Canadian permission for "The Stranger" reprinted from *The Short Stories of Katherine Mansfield.*

HAROLD OBER ASSOCIATES for permission to reprint "Brother Death" from *Death in the Woods* by Sherwood Anderson, copyright 1933, by Eleanor Anderson.

A. D. PETERS, Literary Agent, for Canadian permission to reprint "Uprooted" from *The Short Stories of Frank O'Connor.*

RANDOM HOUSE, INC., for permission to reprint "Barn Burning" from *Collected Stories of William Faulkner,* copyright 1939, by William Faulkner.

CHARLES SCRIBNER'S SONS, for "The Undefeated" reprinted from *Men Without Women* by Ernest Hemingway; copyright 1926, 1927, by Charles Scribner's Sons; used by permission of the publishers; for "The Madonna of the Future" reprinted from *The Novels of Henry James,* New York Edition; copyright 1908, by Charles Scribner's Sons, 1936, by Henry James; used by permission of the publishers.

SIDGWICK AND JACKSON, LIMITED, Publishers, for Canadian rights to "The Road from Colonus" reprinted from *The Collected Tales of E. M. Forster.*

THE VIKING PRESS, INC., for permission to use "Across the Bridge" from *Nineteen Stories* by Graham Greene. Copyright 1947, 1949, by Graham Greene. Reprinted by permission of The Viking Press, Inc., New York; for permission to reprint "A Little Cloud" from *Dubliners,* included in *The Portable James Joyce.* Copyright 1946, 1947, by The Viking Press, Inc., New York. Reprinted by permission of The Viking Press, Inc., New York; for "Odor of Chrysanthemums" from *The Prussian Officer and Other Stories* by D. H. Lawrence. Reprinted by permission of The Viking Press, Inc., New York.

LEONARD WOOLF for Canadian permission to reprint "The New Dress" by Virginia Woolf, from *A Haunted House and Other Stories* by Virginia Woolf, copyright 1944, by Harcourt, Brace and Company.

PRINTED IN THE UNITED STATES OF AMERICA

Contents

INTRODUCTION

SINCE the original edition of *Masters of the Modern Short Story* ten years ago, the short story in England and America has continued its close examination of people and environment. It mirrors the two worlds of experience, inner and outer, portraying man in his dual role as person and as participant. It shows him in his lonely separateness and in his crushing interdependence; it deals with personal dilemmas and social problems.

In the past decade certain new writers have brought significant observation to contemporary life, while certain of the older writers have come to seem less pertinent. A third of the stories in this new edition are by writers who were not included in the earlier collection but who have in recent years assumed the stature of "masters." Two of the most important older short-story writers have also been added. Several writers who have been retained from the original edition are represented here by new stories. As in the original collection, the stories are almost equally divided between British and American writers. The volume aims to be a collection of the best work of the foremost short-story writers in English at the present time.

There is no reason to alter the definition of the short story which accompanied the original edition of this anthology. That definition was drawn from a statement by Santayana: "Life is the fixation of points of interest in the flux of experience." A short story is an exploration of a point of interest in the course of experience. In the flow of life there are unhurried currents and slowly gathering tides. The short story cannot trace these deliberate movements with the complex play of forces—physical, social, and psychological—that hasten and retard them. But there are points at which experience rises to some crest of interest, like the crest of a sea; here is the moment of the short story. It deals with a point of experience that is crucial and revealing.

Four hundred years ago Sir Philip Sidney spoke of "a tale which holdeth children from play, and old men from the chimney corner." Much has changed in the world since Sidney wrote his *Defence of Poesy*, but stories still have this lifelong spell. Fiction appeals to two ancient and lasting desires: the desire for delight and the desire for meaning. Like all other artists, the short-story writer offers delight; he pictures experience in its endless color and variety. A story has form—beginning, development, outcome—and it has its appropriate mood and atmosphere. These qualities contribute to the pleasure of reading; they give delight. But a story offers something more. It deals with questions of good and evil, of strength and weakness, of success and failure. It contains truth.

The story writer looks at experience with endless curiosity and with constant reflection. He shows where life is well lived and where it is poorly lived, where it contains problems and perplexities, where it finds fulfillment. In the story, meaning is enriched by delight, as delight is increased by the presence of meaning; the two are inseparable. A dull and lifeless story has little chance of making its meaning felt; a skillful and absorbing story needs some significance to make its appeal complete. Conrad once said to Galsworthy: "Whatever you do people look beyond your art to your ideas." The realization of this dual nature of the story, coming to her early in her career, led Katherine Mansfield to say: "They believe I can only write satire, but I'm not a very satiric person really. I believe in something. Let's call it Truth. Truth is a big thing—a very big thing. We have to discover it—that's what the artist is for, to become true by discovering truth. Truth is so important that when you discover it, you forget about everything else—and all about yourself."

The short story, then, is experience portrayed so as to reveal its meaning. Truth is implicit in the story's action, lurking in it, accompanying it like a shadow. The story is a sharply focused glimpse of experience—warm, alive, and urgent. But the picture of life is not complete without its implicit meaning. James Branch Cabell once explained that a writer's task is to take the reader from the blinding confusion of the street into the darkness and quiet of a theater where he tries to explain, concisely and quietly, the meaning of the chaos outside. The story, therefore, is a paradox. It uses clarity to reveal the world's confusion; it employs unity to show life's complexity. It selects and simplifies, making its people and their actions suggest something more general than themselves. The story happens once, in one time and place, to one set of persons, but its meaning widens out to many other situations. The story joins incident and reflection. It tells of a limited happening and of an unlimited meaning which that happening embodies.

The world's first stories were fables—arresting, shrewd, meaningful. Their meaning added to their delight, and the fables with most meaning were best remembered. See the difference in the two primitive stories below—two very short, very simple beast fables.

In the woods of Upper Michigan the Chippewa Indians told a legend: "Once there was a young wolf cub that climbed a hill and stared all around at the horizon. After he had looked awhile he began to wonder how big the world was and what lay at the end of it. Soon he set out. He loped over plains and prairies. He crept through thickets and trotted through forests and climbed the steep sides of mountains. He drank out of rivers and went thirsty in arid places. He pressed on, day after day, season after season, and at last he died of old age. He had not found the end."

What does this story say? It says that America is a huge and varied country. Though the wolf is personified, he does not express human motives and emotions beyond a vague curiosity. He is merely a means of measuring the extent of a wilderness country.

From ancient Persia came this fable: "A fox awoke one morning and saw his shadow huge on the desert sand. He was hungry and he said, 'I shall have a camel for breakfast.' So he set out. He loped over the land, hour after hour, looking for camels. But he never found one. By noon he was tired and he stopped to rest. Looking down, he saw his tiny midday shadow on the sand. He said, 'A mouse will do.' "

What does this story say? It says that youth has bold anticipations which maturity surrenders. It shows intention defeated by effort and hope mocked by reality. It makes an ironical statement about human character and experience. The wolf story is about the huge extent of America: the woods and mountains, the rivers and deserts are literal, and the journey of the wolf is a literal search for the literal limit of the land. In the fox story the details are figurative: morning is youth, noon is maturity, the camel is great expectations, the mouse is reality. It is a wholly symbolic tale.

Every age must write its own books and its own stories, and beast fables are rarely written now. The modern story shows believable people in the midst of recognizable experience, and beyond that verisimilitude the story contains some significant appraisal of the human condition. It is a representation of life accompanied by a reflection about it. Its action casts a shadow of meaning.

A writer makes his story significant by presenting human problems. Always people are perplexed, sometimes they are bewildered and hard-beset, and when he touches these problems a writer touches the reader's interest and concern. The world has an abundance of problems, but not all are equally pertinent at all times. Early in this century Jack London wrote a stark story about an Alaskan miner on the frozen trail, whose numb fingers could not strike a match to make a fire. That elemental problem—how to survive in a hostile world of nature—while of lasting human interest is not a pressing concern of most readers today. Our struggle is not with Arctic cold but with the perverse human self and its social involvement.

The stories in this collection explore various human problems: race prejudice, family strife, economic struggle. But the central problem is personal—the struggle of an individual against the odds of life and his pursuit of fulfillment. It is presented here in many forms: the old bullfighter's struggle for pride and inward victory in Hemingway's "The Undefeated," the artist's pursuit of ideal creation in James's "The Madonna of the Future," a man's search for a whole and harmonious life in Forster's "The Road from Colonus," a woman's struggle for social adequacy and confidence in Virginia Woolf's "The New Dress." These are man's great problems and they do not always end in happiness and success. Glib and shallow stories usually have happy endings, because the problems with which they deal are too easy or because in the solution of the problems the author does not take into account the limitations of human character or the hostility of the world. But significant stories most often deal with the painful dilemmas, with man's desire for fulfillment and with human failure. Half of the stories in this collection show people failing in their endeavors. But it is as important to know of failure as of success, and often it is more enlightening.

In William Faulkner's "Barn Burning" a primitive boy is faced with a profound problem. Deeply, instinctively aware of his allegiance to his father, forcibly reminded of it—"You got to learn to stick to your own blood or you ain't going to have any blood to stick to you"—the Snopes boy is yet aware of another kinship. Some things are hateful and wrong, even if done by one's own father. Some things are right; truth and justice have a claim, even if one's father violates them. There is an inner, unseen kinship more commanding than the ties of blood, but the blood ties have not yielded. So the boy finds himself pulled both ways—"like between two teams of horses." He faces the everlasting dilemma of human nature, with the pull of blood contesting the pull of justice. He must make the hard choice between them.

Another timeless problem appears in J. F. Powers' "He Don't Plant Cotton"—a story of race prejudice within which there is a struggle for personal pride and integrity. In Katherine Mansfield's "The Stranger" a husband tries to cross the gulf of strangeness which separates him from his wife; a somewhat similar problem emerges in D. H. Lawrence's "Odor of Chrysanthemums," where death makes a woman aware of the wall of separation she has raised between herself and her husband. The theme of separateness is common in present-day stories, and is reflected in various ways in this collection.

Long after the incidents of a story are forgotten—the anchoring of a ship in an Australian harbor, the request numbers asked of musicians in a Chicago night club, the preparation of supper in a miner's cottage in Nottinghamshire—we remember the problem around which the story has unfolded. The details of relationship between tenant farmer and landlord may fade from memory, but we do not forget a boy's hard choice between the claims of justice and the blood loyalty to his father. Once James Branch Cabell had a feeling that if he should rise from his study chair and look out the window as far as the Mill Road, he might see, passing away from him and traveling in motley companionship through the gray March weather, all the various people whose lives he had fashioned in his books. They were not all admirable, but all had been at some time of intense interest to him. He understood their joys, and, even more, he understood their struggles and failures—it was his characters who had the hardest problems whom he could best remember.

In presenting human problems a writer enlarges the significance of his story by making it representative. Any writer of fiction knows that all persons are distinct, separate, individual. But he also knows that these separate persons have similar joys and sorrows, hopes and fears, struggles and aspirations. This knowledge leads a story writer to present the experience of an imaginary person so that it resembles the lives of many actual people. Though his characters are distinctly individual, they are at the same time representative.

For example, Sherwood Anderson in "Brother Death" tells of a Virginia farm family in which there were two brothers. The younger brother was frail and could not live to manhood; the older brother was strong, destined for inheritance and possession. The story centers on a struggle between the father and the older son over the felling of two oak trees in the barnyard. In that conflict the son says to his father: "If you cut them down, I will walk off this farm and never come back." The trees come down, and the son walks off. But he comes back, making a surrender of his will. Surrender is the price of his inheritance; at that point he has to submit in order that he may one day come into possession and command. But the frail younger brother, who is going to die anyway, never has to face the subtle and terrible death that has come to his older brother. This human episode occurs once, in a specific family, on a Virginia farm, at a particular season of a particular year. Yet the story is not limited to this single incident; it represents a process ["Something in you must die (some freedom, some innocence, some feeling) before you can possess and command."] that is timeless and universal. These people in the story cast long shadows. The father is all fathers, all authority, all established ownership and command; the older son is all assertive youth, all young and willful ambition; the younger son is all who do not compete and so do not have to surrender. The characters are representative, and the incident also is representative of many situations. The story presents a conflict—the same as that of Absalom and King David three thousand years ago—as old as history and as new as life.

In Ernest Hemingway's "The Undefeated" the veteran bullfighter is a definite character; from the first paragraph of the story he is undeniably distinct and individual. But his experience and attitudes are not unique. His past success, his recent injury, his determination to try again are to be found, in various terms, in many people's experience. Manuel Garcia, with the wounds of his profession and the pigtail that is his proud badge of bullfighting, is any man who chooses to live (and die) on his own terms. A reader cannot fail to see in the life and death of this "undefeated" bullfighter a code of conduct which may belong to persons who have never seen a bull ring. Manuel Garcia's story is dramatic and singular; at the same time it represents the experience of all who face great odds and win an inward victory.

Likewise, the artist in Henry James's "The Madonna of the Future" is both individual and representative. He lives and works in Florence, he has personal memories of America, he suffers his own delusion. But he has the capacity of all artists for seeing the ideal beyond the real, and he represents the artist's aspiration and defeat. His story is not merely the account of a man named Theobald who could not fill the canvas he had reserved for his great work; it is a record of the hopes and despairs of any artist whose conception dwarfs and numbs his powers of expression.

In Eudora Welty's story we see Livvie, significantly, on the first day of spring. She is a distinct and living person, and the day brings to her, while her aged husband sleeps quietly in his unruffled bed, two other persons, also distinct and individual. But the story is full of representative qualities: age and youth, winter and spring, restraint and freedom, duty and instinct. It uses terms which evoke large recognitions; it lets us see the universal in the particular.

Imaginative writing often appeals to a reader on two levels; beneath the literal statement there is a figurative meaning. When a poet says: "We've each a darkening hill to climb," it is clear that he is not talking about topography. Similarly a short-story writer frequently makes use of symbols. It is only a step from the creation of representative character and situation to the creation of symbols. Indeed, a symbol is a specific and pointed representation in which a material object, like a hill, stands for something immaterial, like difficulty; or a specific detail, like morning, conveys an abstract idea, like youth. When old Solomon married his young bride in "Livvie," he used a familiar figure of speech, asking her "if she was choosing winter, would she pine for spring?" Later this seasonal symbolism is recalled by the description of Solomon's hat, "the blackest thing in the world," while young Cash McCord wears a hat as green as April. In "Brother Death" the two felled trees suggest the deaths—of different kinds—of the two brothers. In E. M. Forster's story the Englishman traveling in Greece finds an unexpected green valley on the road from Colonus; this water in a dry land is symbolical of the ardor that his Greek pilgrimage has aroused in Mr. Lucas after his empty life in England. In D. H. Lawrence's story we see a woman standing "insignificantly trapped" between a grimy train of coal cars and a green hedgerow; this is Lawrence's symbolic picture of the modern dilemma, in which people stand immobilized between nature and industrial civilization. Again and again the story writer persuades a reader to see as he sees, to view as symbol what might be regarded as bare fact.

In Frank O'Connor's "Uprooted," Ned Keating is both a representative and a symbolic figure. He has his own personal past, in a farm cottage on the western coast of Ireland where he discovered the spell of books and so outgrew that simple background; he has his own personal present in the barren life of Dublin. He is indisputably distinct and real. But the story emphasizes elements in his experience that are common to many persons who look back at a simple past which they cannot recover, and his visit to his father's cottage illustrates the futility of going "home" to memory. Its meaning extends even, as O'Connor once indicated, to an industrial society or an intellectual culture that cannot reclaim lost simplicities. Ned Keating symbolizes all life that grows complex and worldly and, recalling the charm of a simpler state, tries unsuccessfully to return to the rewarding past.

A story's ultimate symbolism is the story itself—the entire story casting an enlarging shadow of meaning. After reading Stephen Crane's "The Open Boat," Conrad said: "The deep and simple humanity of its presentation seems somehow to illustrate the essentials of life itself, like a symbolic tale." He was not referring to the sea, or the wave-tossed dinghy, or the injured captain, or the oiler who died in the furious surf; he was thinking of the entire story as existing on two levels—real and symbolic. The tale of shipwrecked men struggling to reach shore is a symbolic account of humanity's struggle to endure in the vast and indifferent world. Because he meant his own "Youth" to be such a symbolic tale, Conrad objected to calling it a sea-story. The sea is its circumstance, but the story is a portrayal of the genius of youth for transmuting hardship and peril into glamour and romance. Graham Greene's haunting story "Across the Bridge" can be read as a symbolic account of human guilt and exile; it shows the plight of human nature in a deluding world. In such ways as these the story writer becomes a maker of metaphor.

One of William Faulkner's most familiar stories, the often-reprinted short version of "The Bear," contains an unusually candid statement of the writer's double interest in explicit event and implicit meaning. After the fierce and chivalrous bear hunt, following his encounter with the enormous bear, the boy comes into his father's study. His father crosses the room in the spring twilight and takes down a book from the shelves. "Listen," he says, and in his quiet, deliberate voice he reads the five stanzas of a poem by John Keats about the figures on an antique Grecian urn. The boy waits, and at the end his father says again, "Listen," and he reads again: "She cannot fade, though thou hast not thy bliss; for ever wilt thou love, and she be fair."

That poem seems far indeed from a bear hunt, or anything else that concerns him, and the boy is puzzled. He says, "He's talking about a girl." His father explains: "He had to talk about something." (Something, he seemed to imply, more specific than the unattainable in human experience which forever mocks the attained.) Then the father says, "He was talking about truth. Truth doesn't change. It covers all things which touch the heart—honor and pride and pity and justice and courage and love. Do you see now?"

The boy does not exactly see. He feels it is simpler than that. He prefers to go back to the hunt itself—and this is like going from the theme of a story to its living incident.

"—There was an old bear, fierce and ruthless, not merely just to stay alive, but with the fierce pride of liberty and freedom, proud enough of the liberty and freedom to see it threatened without fear or even alarm; nay who at times seemed even deliberately to put that freedom and liberty in jeopardy in order to savor them, to remind his old strong bones and flesh to keep supple and quick to defend and preserve them. There was an old man, son of a Negro slave and an Indian king, inheritor on one side of the long chronicle of a people who had learned humility through suffering, and pride through the endurance which survived the suffering and injustice, and on the other side, the chronicle of a people even longer in the land than the first, yet who no longer existed in the land at all save in the solitary brotherhood of an old Negro's alien blood and the wild and invincible spirit of an old bear. There was a boy who wished to learn humility and pride in order to become skillful and worthy in the woods, who suddenly found himself becoming so skillful so rapidly that he feared he would never become worthy because he had not learned humility and pride, although he had tried to, until one day and as suddenly he discovered that an old man who could not have defined either had led him, as though by the hand, to that point where an old bear and a little mongrel of a dog showed him that, by possessing one other thing, he would possess them both. . . .

"That was all. It was simple, much simpler than somebody talking in a book about youth and a girl he would never need to grieve over, because he could never approach any nearer her and would never have to get any farther away. He had heard about a bear, and finally got big enough to trail it, and he trailed it four years and at last met it with a gun in his hands and he didn't shoot. Because a little dog—But he could have shot long before the little dog covered the twenty yards to where the bear waited, and Sam Fathers could have shot at any time during that interminable minute while Old Ben stood on his hind feet over them. He stopped. His father was watching him gravely across the spring-rife twilight of the room; when he spoke his words were as quiet as the twilight, too, not loud, because they did not need to be because they would last. 'Courage and honor and pride,' his father said, 'and pity, and love of justice and of liberty. They all touch the heart, and what the heart holds to becomes truth, as far as we know the truth. Do you see now?'

"Sam, and Old Ben, and Nip, he thought. And himself too. He had been all right too. His father had said so. 'Yes, sir,' he said."

So at last the boy does see. The incident has found its meaning, and from this hour the two will be inseparable in his memory.

One reason for the perennial appeal of this story is that here Faulkner has suggested how all literature uses things seen to call up things unseeable. The hunt for the huge, primordial bear is not merely a metaphor in itself; it becomes the occasion for pointing out that all stories "have to talk about something" while they are concerned with something beyond. Truth is not confined to a youth and a girl he could never overtake, or a boy and a bear he could never kill. But it can be glimpsed and grasped only in particular human instances like these.

The stories in this collection contain various glimpses of truth. Incident develops in the foreground; accompanying it, as a man crossing a summer field is accompanied by his shadow, develops the idea which it exemplifies. The story writer embodies truth in people (from which all meaning must come), giving it the warmth and vitality of human experience; he uses specific incidents to symbolize universal conditions of life. That method of conveying truth can be considered indirect, or it can be considered the most concrete and direct method possible. At any rate, it is the storyteller's way.

MASTERS OF THE MODERN SHORT STORY

Brief Edition

Joseph Conrad (1857-1924) was a native of the Polish Ukraine. As a boy he abandoned a prospective professional career in Poland and went to sea as an apprentice seaman. He learned English from his shipmates in British sailing vessels. Though he came to write remarkably pure and expressive English, he never lost a foreign accent in speaking his adopted tongue. During his years at sea he rose to be mate, and then master, of British ships. His first novels were written during long voyages, but in 1894 he came ashore, was naturalized as a British subject, and settled in southern England. For thirty years he wrote distinguished novels and tales, with the sea as background and the study of human character as his essential subject. On a visit to America in 1923 he was received with great enthusiasm by his large reading public in this country. He died in England in 1924 and was buried at historic Canterbury. Among his famous tales and novels are *Lord Jim*, *Nostromo*, *Victory*, and *Typhoon and Other Stories.*

JOSEPH CONRAD

Youth

THIS COULD have occurred nowhere but in England, where men and sea interpenetrate, so to speak—the sea entering into the life of most men, and the men knowing something or everything about the sea, in the way of amusement, of travel, or of breadwinning.

We were sitting round a mahogany table that reflected the bottle, the claret-glasses, and our faces as we leaned on our elbows. There was a director of companies, an accountant, a lawyer, Marlow, and myself. The director had been a *Conway* boy, the accountant had served four years at sea, the lawyer—a fine crusted Tory, High Churchman, the best of old fellows, the soul of honor—had been chief officer in the P. & O. service in the good old days when mail-boats were square-rigged at least on two masts, and used to come down the China Sea before a fair monsoon with stun'sails set alow and aloft. We all began life in the merchant service. Between the five of us there was the strong bond of the sea, and also the fellowship of the craft, which no amount of enthusiasm for yachting, cruising, and so on can give, since one is only the amusement of life and the other is life itself.

Marlow (at least I think that is how he spelled his name) told the story, or rather the chronicle, of a voyage:—

"Yes, I have seen a little of the Eastern seas; but what I remember best is my first voyage there. You fellows know there are those voyages that seem ordered for the illustration of life, that might stand for a symbol of existence. You fight, work, sweat, nearly kill yourself, sometimes do kill yourself, trying to accomplish something—and you can't. Not from any fault of yours. You simply can do nothing, neither great nor little—not a thing in the world—not even marry an old maid, or get a wretched 600-ton cargo of coal to its port of destination.

"It was altogether a memorable affair. It was my first voyage to the East, and my first voyage as second mate; it was also my skipper's first command. You'll admit it was time. He was sixty if a day; a little man, with a broad, not very straight back, with bowed shoulders and one leg more bandy than the other, he had that queer twisted-about appearance you see so often in men who work in the fields. He had a nut-cracker face—chin and nose trying to come together over a sunken mouth—and it was framed in iron-gray fluffy hair, that looked like a chin-strap of cotton-wool sprinkled with coal-dust. And he had blue eyes in that old face of his, which were amazingly like a boy's, with that candid expression some quite common men preserve to the end of their days by a rare internal gift of simplicity of heart and rectitude of soul. What induced him to accept me was a wonder. I had come out of a crack Australian clipper, where I had been third officer, and he seemed to have a prejudice against crack clippers as aristocratic and high-toned. He said to me, 'You know, in this ship you will have to work.' I said I had to work in every ship I had ever been in. 'Ah, but this is different, and you gentlemen out of them big ships; . . . but there! I dare say you will do. Join tomorrow.'

"I joined tomorrow. It was twenty-two years ago; and I was

just twenty. How time passes! It was one of the happiest days of my life. Fancy! Second mate for the first time—a really responsible officer! I wouldn't have thrown up my new billet for a fortune. The mate looked me over carefully. He was also an old chap, but of another stamp. He had a Roman nose, a snow-white, long beard, and his name was Mahon, but he insisted that it should be pronounced Mann. He was well connected; yet there was something wrong with his luck, and he had never got on.

"As to the captain, he had been for years in coasters, then in the Mediterranean, and last in the West Indian trade. He had never been round the Capes. He could just write a kind of sketchy hand, and didn't care for writing at all. Both were thorough good seamen of course, and between those two old chaps I felt like a small boy between two grandfathers.

"The ship also was old. Her name was the *Judea*. Queer name, isn't it? She belonged to a man Wilmer, Wilcox—some name like that; but he has been bankrupt and dead these twenty years or more, and his name don't matter. She had been laid up in Shadwell basin for ever so long. You may imagine her state. She was all rust, dust, grime—soot aloft, dirt on deck. To me it was like coming out of a palace into a ruined cottage. She was about 400 tons, had a primitive windlass, wooden latches to the doors, not a bit of brass about her, and a big square stern. There was on it, below her name in big letters, a lot of scrollwork, with the gilt off, and some sort of a coat of arms, with the motto 'Do or Die' underneath. I remember it took my fancy immensely. There was a touch of romance in it, something that made me love the old thing—something that appealed to my youth!

"We left London in ballast—sand ballast—to load a cargo of coal in a northern port for Bankok. Bankok! I thrilled. I had been six years at sea, but had only seen Melbourne and Sydney, very good places, charming places in their way—but Bankok!

"We worked out of the Thames under canvas, with a North Sea pilot on board. His name was Jermyn, and he dodged all day long about the galley drying his handkerchief before the stove. Apparently he never slept. He was a dismal man, with a perpetual tear sparkling at the end of his nose, who either had been in trouble, or was in trouble, or expected to be in trouble—

couldn't be happy unless something went wrong. He mistrusted my youth, my common sense, and my seamanship, and made a point of showing it in a hundred little ways. I dare say he was right. It seems to me I knew very little then, and I know not much more now; but I cherish a hate for that Jermyn to this day.

"We were a week working up as far as Yarmouth Roads, and then we got into a gale—the famous October gale of twenty-two years ago. It was wind, lightning, sleet, snow, and a terrific sea. We were flying light, and you may imagine how bad it was when I tell you we had smashed bulwarks and a flooded deck. On the second night she shifted her ballast into the lee bow, and by that time we had been blown off somewhere on the Dogger Bank. There was nothing for it but go below with shovels and try to right her, and there we were in that vast hold, gloomy like a cavern, the tallow dips stuck and flickering on the beams, the gale howling above, the ship tossing about like mad on her side; there we all were, Jermyn, the captain, everyone, hardly able to keep our feet, engaged on that gravedigger's work, and trying to toss shovelfuls of wet sand up to windward. At every tumble of the ship you could see vaguely in the dim light men falling down with a great flourish of shovels. One of the ship's boys (we had two), impressed by the weirdness of the scene, wept as if his heart would break. We could hear him blubbering somewhere in the shadows.

"On the third day the gale died out, and by and by a north-country tug picked us up. We took sixteen days in all to get from London to the Tyne! When we got into dock we had lost our turn for loading, and they hauled us off to a tier where we remained for a month. Mrs. Beard (the captain's name was Beard) came from Colchester to see the old man. She lived on board. The crew of runners had left, and there remained only the officers, one boy and the steward, a mulatto who answered to the name of Abraham. Mrs. Beard was an old woman, with a face all wrinkled and ruddy like a winter apple, and the figure of a young girl. She caught sight of me once, sewing on a button, and insisted on having my shirts to repair. This was something different from the captains' wives I had known on board crack clippers. When I brought her the shirts, she said: 'And the socks?

They want mending, I am sure, and John's–Captain Beard's–things are all in order now. I would be glad of something to do.' Bless the old woman. She overhauled my outfit for me, and meantime I read for the first time *Sartor Resartus* and Burnaby's *Ride to Khiva*. I didn't understand much of the first then; but I remember I preferred the soldier to the philosopher at the time; a preference which life has only confirmed. One was a man, and the other was either more–or less. However, they are both dead and Mrs. Beard is dead, and youth, strength, genius, thoughts, achievements, simple hearts–all die. . . . No matter.

"They loaded us at last. We shipped a crew. Eight able seamen and two boys. We hauled off one evening to the buoys at the dock-gates, ready to go out, and with a fair prospect of beginning the voyage next day. Mrs. Beard was to start for home by a late train. When the ship was fast we went to tea. We sat rather silent through the meal–Mahon, the old couple, and I. I finished first, and slipped away for a smoke, my cabin being in a deckhouse just against the poop. It was high water, blowing fresh with a drizzle; the double dock-gates were opened, and the steam-colliers were going in and out in the darkness with their lights burning bright, a great plashing of propellers, rattling of winches, and a lot of hailing on the pierheads. I watched the procession of headlights gliding high and of green lights gliding low in the night, when suddenly a red gleam flashed at me, vanished, came into view again, and remained. The fore-end of a steamer loomed up close. I shouted down the cabin, 'Come up, quick!' and then heard a startled voice saying afar in the dark, 'Stop her, sir.' A bell jingled. Another voice cried warningly, 'We are going right into that barque, sir.' The answer to this was a gruff 'All right,' and the next thing was a heavy crash as the steamer struck a glancing blow with the bluff of her bow about our fore-rigging. There was a moment of confusion, yelling, and running about. Steam roared. Then somebody was heard saying, 'All clear, sir.' . . . 'Are you all right?' asked the gruff voice. I had jumped forward to see the damage, and hailed back, 'I think so.' 'Easy astern,' said the gruff voice. A bell jingled. 'What steamer is that?' screamed Mahon. By that time she was no more to us than a bulky shadow maneuvering a little way off. They shouted at us some name—a woman's name, Miranda or Melissa—or some such thing. 'This means another month in this beastly hole,' said Mahon to me, as we peered with lamps about the splintered bulwarks and broken braces. 'But where's the captain?'

"We had not heard or seen anything of him all that time. We went aft to look. A doleful voice arose hailing somewhere in the middle of the dock, '*Judea* ahoy!' . . . How the devil did he get there? . . . 'Hallo!' we shouted. 'I am adrift in our boat without oars,' he cried. A belated waterman offered his services, and Mahon struck a bargain with him for half a crown to tow our skipper alongside; but it was Mrs. Beard that came up the ladder first. They had been floating about the dock in that mizzly cold rain for nearly an hour. I was never so surprised in my life.

"It appears that when he heard my shout 'Come up' he understood at once what was the matter, caught up his wife, ran on deck, and across, and down into our boat, which was fast to the ladder. Not bad for a sixty-year-old. Just imagine that old fellow saving heroically in his arms that old woman—the woman of his life. He set her down on a thwart, and was ready to climb back on board when the painter came adrift somehow, and away they went together. Of course in the confusion we did not hear him shouting. He looked abashed. She said cheerfully, 'I suppose it does not matter my losing the train now?' 'No, Jenny—you go below and get warm,' he growled. Then to us: 'A sailor has no business with a wife—I say. There I was, out of the ship. Well, no harm done this time. Let's go and look at what that fool of a steamer smashed.'

"It wasn't much, but it delayed us three weeks. At the end of that time, the captain being engaged with his agents, I carried Mrs. Beard's bag to the railway station and put her all comfy into a third-class carriage. She lowered the window to say, 'You are a good young man. If you see John—Captain Beard—without his muffler at night, just remind him from me to keep his throat well wrapped up.' 'Certainly, Mrs. Beard,' I said. 'You are a good young man; I noticed how attentive you are to John—to Captain—' The train pulled out suddenly; I took my cap off to the old woman: I never saw her again. . . . Pass the bottle.

"We went to sea next day. When we made that start for

Bankok we had been already three months out of London. We had expected to be a fortnight or so—at the outside.

"It was January, and the weather was beautiful—the beautiful sunny winter weather that has more charm than in the summer-time, because it is unexpected, and crisp, and you know it won't, it can't, last long. It's like a windfall, like a godsend, like an unexpected piece of luck.

"It lasted all down the North Sea, all down Channel; and it lasted till we were three hundred miles or so to the westward of the Lizards: then the wind went round to the sou'west and began to pipe up. In two days it blew a gale. The *Judea,* hove to, wallowed on the Atlantic like an old candlebox. It blew day after day: it blew with spite, without interval, without mercy, without rest. The world was nothing but an immensity of great foaming waves rushing at us, under a sky low enough to touch with the hand and dirty like a smoked ceiling. In the stormy space surrounding us there was as much flying spray as air. Day after day and night after night there was nothing round the ship but the howl of the wind, the tumult of the sea, the noise of water pouring over her deck. There was no rest for her and no rest for us. She tossed, she pitched, she stood on her head, she sat on her tail, she rolled, she groaned, and we had to hold on while on deck and cling to our bunks when below, in a constant effort of body and worry of mind.

"One night Mahon spoke through the small window of my berth. It opened right into my very bed, and I was lying there sleepless, in my boots, feeling as though I had not slept for years, and could not if I tried. He said excitedly—

" 'You got the sounding-rod in here, Marlow? I can't get the pumps to suck. By God! it's no child's play.'

"I gave him the sounding-rod and lay down again, trying to think of various things—but I thought only of the pumps. When I came on deck they were still at it, and my watch relieved at the pumps. By the light of the lantern brought on deck to examine the sounding-rod I caught a glimpse of their weary, serious faces. We pumped all the four hours. We pumped all night, all day, all the week—watch and watch. She was working herself loose, and leaked badly—not enough to drown us at once, but enough to kill us with the work at the pumps. And while we pumped the ship was going from us piecemeal: the bulwarks went, the stanchions were torn out, the ventilators smashed, the cabin-door burst in. There was not a dry spot in the ship. She was being gutted bit by bit. The long-boat changed, as if by magic, into matchwood where she stood in her gripes. I had lashed her myself, and was rather proud of my handiwork, which had withstood so long the malice of the sea. And we pumped. And there was no break in the weather. The sea was white like a sheet of foam, like a caldron of boiling milk; there was not a break in the clouds, no—not the size of a man's hand—no, not for so much as ten seconds. There was for us no sky, there were for us no stars, no sun, no universe—nothing but angry clouds and an infuriated sea. We pumped watch and watch, for dear life; and it seemed to last for months, for years, for all eternity, as though we had been dead and gone to a hell for sailors. We forgot the day of the week, the name of the month, what year it was, and whether we had ever been ashore. The sails blew away, she lay broadside-on under a weather-cloth, the ocean poured over her, and we did not care. We turned those handles, and had the eyes of idiots. As soon as we had crawled on deck I used to take a round turn with a rope about the men, the pumps, and the mainmast, and we turned, we turned incessantly, with the water to our waists, to our necks, over our heads. It was all one. We had forgotten how it felt to be dry.

"And there was somewhere in me the thought: By Jove! this is the deuce of an adventure—something you read about; and it is my first voyage as second mate—and I am only twenty—and here I am lasting it out as well as any of these men, and keeping my chaps up to the mark. I was pleased. I would not have given up the experience for worlds. I had moments of exultation. Whenever the old dismantled craft pitched heavily with her counter high in the air, she seemed to me to throw up, like an appeal, like a defiance, like a cry to the clouds without mercy, the words written on her stern: '*Judea*, London. Do or Die.'

"O youth! The strength of it, the faith of it, the imagination of it! To me she was not an old rattletrap carting about the world a lot of coal for a freight—to me she was the endeavor, the test, the trial of life. I think of her with pleasure, with affection, with regret—as you would think of someone dead you have loved. I shall never forget her. . . . Pass the bottle.

"One night when tied to the mast, as I explained, we were pumping on, deafened with the wind, and without spirit enough in us to wish ourselves dead, a heavy sea crashed aboard and swept clean over us. As soon as I got my breath I shouted, as in duty bound, 'Keep on, boys!' when suddenly I felt something hard floating on deck strike the calf of my leg. I made a grab at it and missed. It was so dark we could not see each other's faces within a foot—you understand.

"After that thump the ship kept quiet for a while, and the thing, whatever it was, struck my leg again. This time I caught it—and it was a saucepan. At first, being stupid with fatigue and thinking of nothing but the pumps, I did not understand what I had in my hand. Suddenly it dawned upon me, and I shouted, 'Boys, the house on deck is gone. Leave this, and let's look for the cook.'

"There was a deck-house forward, which contained the galley, the cook's berth, and the quarters of the crew. As we had expected for days to see it swept away, the hands had been ordered to sleep in the cabin—the only safe place in the ship. The steward, Abraham, however, persisted in clinging to his berth, stupidly, like a mule—from sheer fright I believe, like an animal that won't leave a stable falling in an earthquake. So we went to look for him. It was chancing death, since once out of our lashings we were as exposed as if on a raft. But we went. The house was shattered as if a shell had exploded inside. Most of it had gone overboard—stove, men's quarters, and their property, all was gone; but two posts, holding a portion of the bulkhead to which Abraham's bunk was attached, remained as if by a miracle. We groped in the ruins and came upon this, and there he was, sitting in his bunk, surrounded by foam and wreckage, jabbering cheerfully to himself. He was out of his mind; completely and forever mad, with this sudden shock coming upon the fag-end of his endurance. We snatched him up, lugged him aft, and pitched him head-first down the cabin companion. You understand there was no time to carry him down with infinite precautions and wait to see how he got on. Those below would pick him up at the bottom of the stairs all right. We were in a hurry to go back to the pumps. That business could not wait. A bad leak is an inhuman thing.

"One would think that the sole purpose of that fiendish gale had been to make a lunatic of that poor devil of a mulatto. It eased before morning, and next day the sky cleared, and as the sea went down the leak took up. When it came to bending a fresh set of sails the crew demanded to put back—and really there was nothing else to do. Boats gone, decks swept clean, cabin gutted, men without a stitch but what they stood in, stores spoiled, ship strained. We put her head for home, and—would you believe it? The wind came east right in our teeth. It blew fresh, it blew continuously. We had to beat up every inch of the way, but she did not leak so badly, the water keeping comparatively smooth. Two hours' pumping in every four is no joke—but it kept her afloat as far as Falmouth.

"The good people there live on casualties of the sea, and no doubt were glad to see us. A hungry crowd of shipwrights sharpened their chisels at the sight of that carcass of a ship. And, by Jove! they had pretty pickings off us before they were done. I fancy the owner was already in a tight place. There were delays. Then it was decided to take part of the cargo out and caulk her topsides. This was done, the repairs finished, cargo reshipped; a new crew came on board, and we went out—for Bankok. At the end of a week we were back again. The crew said they weren't going to Bankok—a hundred and fifty days' passage—in a something hooker that wanted pumping eight hours out of the twenty-four; and the nautical papers inserted again the little paragraph: '*Judea*. Barque. Tyne to Bankok; coals; put back to Falmouth leaky and with crew refusing duty.'

"There were more delays—more tinkering. The owner came down for a day, and said she was as right as a little fiddle. Poor old Captain Beard looked like the ghost of a Geordie skipper—through the worry and humiliation of it. Remember he was sixty, and it was his first command. Mahon said it was a foolish business, and would end badly. I loved the ship more than ever, and wanted awfully to get to Bankok. To Bankok! Magic name, blessed name. Mesopotamia wasn't a patch on it. Remember I was twenty, and it was my first second-mate's billet, and the East was waiting for me.

"We went out and anchored in the outer roads with a fresh crew—the third. She leaked worse than ever. It was as if those confounded shipwrights had actually made a hole in her. This time we did not even go outside. The crew simply refused to man the windlass.

"They towed us back to the inner harbor, and we became a fixture, a feature, an institution of the place. People pointed us out to visitors as 'That 'ere barque that's going to Bankok—has been here six months—put back three times.' On holidays the small boys pulling about in boats would hail, '*Judea*, ahoy!' and if a head showed above the rail shouted, 'Where you bound to?—Bankok?' and jeered. We were only three on board. The poor old skipper mooned in the cabin. Mahon undertook the cooking, and unexpectedly developed all a Frenchman's genius for preparing nice little messes. I looked languidly after the rigging. We became citizens of Falmouth. Every shopkeeper knew us. At the barber's or tobacconist's they asked familiarly, 'Do you think you will ever get to Bankok?' Meantime the owner, the underwriters, and the charterers squabbled amongst themselves in London, and our pay went on. . . . Pass the bottle.

"It was horrid. Morally it was worse than pumping for life. It seemed as though we had been forgotten by the world, belonged to nobody, would get nowhere; it seemed that, as if bewitched, we would have to live for ever and ever in that inner harbor, a derision and a byword to generations of longshore loafers and dishonest boatmen. I obtained three months' pay and a five days' leave, and made a rush for London. It took me a day to get there and pretty well another to come back—but three months' pay went all the same. I don't know what I did with it. I went to a music-hall, I believe, lunched, dined, and supped in a swell place in Regent Street, and was back to time, with nothing but a complete set of Byron's works and a new railway rug to show for three months' work. The boatman who pulled me off to the ship said: 'Hallo! I thought you had left the old thing. *She* will never get to Bankok.' 'That's all *you* know about it,' I said scornfully—but I didn't like that prophecy at all.

"Suddenly a man, some kind of agent to somebody, appeared with full powers. He had grog-blossoms all over his face, an indomitable energy, and was a jolly soul. We leaped into life again. A hulk came alongside, took our cargo, and then we went into dry dock to get our copper stripped. No wonder she leaked. The poor thing, strained beyond endurance by the gale, had, as if in disgust, spat out all the oakum of her lower seams. She was recaulked, new coppered, and made as tight as a bottle. We went back to the hulk and reshipped our cargo.

"Then, on a fine moonlight night, all the rats left the ship.

"We had been infested with them. They had destroyed our sails, consumed more stores than the crew, affably shared our beds and our dangers, and now, when the ship was made seaworthy, concluded to clear out. I called Mahon to enjoy the spectacle. Rat after rat appeared on our rail, took a last look over his shoulder, and leaped with a hollow thud into the empty hulk. We tried to count them, but soon lost the tale. Mahon said: 'Well, well! don't talk to me about the intelligence of rats. They ought to have left before, when we had that narrow squeak from foundering. There you have the proof how silly is the superstition about them. They leave a good ship for an old rotten hulk, where there is nothing to eat, too, the fools! . . . I don't believe they know what is safe or what is good for them, any more than you or I.'

"And after some more talk we agreed that the wisdom of rats had been grossly overrated, being in fact no greater than that of men.

"The story of the ship was known, by this, all up the Channel from Land's End to the Forelands, and we could get no crew on the south coast. They sent us one all complete from Liverpool, and we left once more—for Bankok.

"We had fair breezes, smooth water right into the tropics, and the old *Judea* lumbered along in the sunshine. When she went eight knots everything cracked aloft, and we tied our caps to our heads; but mostly she strolled on at the rate of three miles an hour. What could you expect? She was tired—that old ship.

Her youth was where mine is—where yours is—you fellows who listen to this yarn; and what friend would throw your years and your weariness in your face? We didn't grumble at her. To us aft, at least, it seemed as though we had been born in her, reared in her, had lived in her for ages, had never known any other ship. I would just as soon have abused the old village church at home for not being a cathedral.

"And for me there was also my youth to make me patient. There was all the East before me, and all life, and the thought that I had been tried in that ship and had come out pretty well. And I thought of men of old who, centuries ago, went that road in ships that sailed no better, to the land of palms, and spices, and yellow sands, and of brown nations ruled by kings more cruel than Nero the Roman, and more splendid than Solomon the Jew. The old bark lumbered on, heavy with her age and the burden of her cargo, while I lived the life of youth in ignorance and hope. She lumbered on through an interminable procession of days; and the fresh gilding flashed back at the setting sun, seemed to cry out over the darkening sea the words painted on her stern, '*Judea*, London. Do or Die.'

"Then we entered the Indian Ocean and steered northerly for Java Head. The winds were light. Weeks slipped by. She crawled on, do or die, and people at home began to think of posting us as overdue.

"One Saturday evening, I being off duty, the men asked me to give them an extra bucket of water or so—for washing clothes. As I did not wish to screw on the fresh-water pump so late, I went forward whistling, and with a key in my hand to unlock the forepeak scuttle, intending to serve the water out of a spare tank we kept there.

"The smell down below was as unexpected as it was frightful. One would have thought hundreds of paraffin-lamps had been flaring and smoking in that hole for days. I was glad to get out. The man with me coughed and said, 'Funny smell, sir.' I answered negligently, 'It's good for the health they say,' and walked aft.

"The first thing I did was to put my head down the square of the midship ventilator. As I lifted the lid a visible breath, something like a thin fog, a puff of faint haze, rose from the opening. The ascending air was hot, and had a heavy, sooty, paraffiny smell. I gave one sniff, and put down the lid gently. It was no use choking myself. The cargo was on fire.

"Next day she began to smoke in earnest. You see it was to be expected, for though the coal was of a safe kind, that cargo had been so handled, so broken up with handling, that it looked more like smithy coal than anything else. Then it had been wetted—more than once. It rained all the time we were taking it back from the hulk, and now with this long passage it got heated, and there was another case of spontaneous combustion.

"The captain called us into the cabin. He had a chart spread on the table, and looked unhappy. He said, 'The coast of West Australia is near, but I mean to proceed to our destination. It is the hurricane month, too; but we will just keep her head for Bankok, and fight the fire. No more putting back anywhere, if we all get roasted. We will try first to stifle this 'ere damned combustion by want of air.'

"We tried. We battened down everything, and still she smoked. The smoke kept coming out through imperceptible crevices; it forced itself through bulkheads and covers; it oozed here and there and everywhere in slender threads, in an invisible film, in an incomprehensible manner. It made its way into the cabin, into the forecastle; it poisoned the sheltered places on the deck, it could be sniffed as high as the mainyard. It was clear that if the smoke came out the air came in. This was disheartening. This combustion refused to be stifled.

"We resolved to try water, and took the hatches off. Enormous volumes of smoke, whitish, yellowish, thick, greasy, misty, choking, ascended as high as the trucks. All hands cleared out aft. Then the poisonous cloud blew away, and we went back to work in a smoke that was no thicker now than that of an ordinary factory chimney.

"We rigged the force-pump, got the hose along, and by-and-by it burst. Well, it was as old as the ship—a prehistoric hose, and past repair. Then we pumped with the feeble head-pump, drew water with buckets, and in this way managed in time to pour lots of Indian Ocean into the main hatch. The bright stream flashed in sunshine, fell into a layer of white crawling smoke, and vanished on the black surface of coal. Steam ascended mingling with the smoke. We poured salt water as into a barrel without a bottom. It was our fate to pump in that ship, to pump out of her, to pump into her; and after keeping water out of her to save ourselves from being drowned, we frantically poured water into her to save ourselves from being burned.

"And she crawled on, do or die, in the serene weather. The sky was a miracle of purity, a miracle of azure. The sea was polished, was blue, was pellucid, was sparkling like a precious stone, extending on all sides, all round to the horizon—as if the whole terrestrial globe had been one jewel, one colossal sapphire, a single gem fashioned into a planet. And on the luster of the great calm waters the *Judea* glided imperceptibly, enveloped in languid and unclean vapors, in a lazy cloud that drifted to leeward, light and slow; a pestiferous cloud defiling the splendor of sea and sky.

"All this time of course we saw no fire. The cargo smoldered at the bottom somewhere. Once Mahon, as we were working side by side, said to me with a queer smile: 'Now, if she only would spring a tidy leak—like that time when we first left the Channel—it would put a stopper on this fire. Wouldn't it?' I remarked irrelevantly, 'Do you remember the rats?'

"We fought the fire and sailed the ship too as carefully as though nothing had been the matter. The steward cooked and attended on us. Of the other twelve men, eight worked while four rested. Everyone took his turn, captain included. There was equality, and if not exactly fraternity, then a deal of good feeling. Sometimes a man, as he dashed a bucketful of water down the hatchway, would yell out, 'Hurrah for Bankok!' and the rest laughed. But generally we were taciturn and serious—and thirsty. Oh! how thirsty! And we had to be careful with the water. Strict allowance. The ship smoked, the sun blazed. . . . Pass the bottle.

"We tried everything. We even made an attempt to dig down to the fire. No good, of course. No man could remain more than a minute below. Mahon, who went first, fainted there, and the man who went to fetch him out did likewise. We lugged them out on deck. Then I leaped down to show how easily it could be done. They had learned wisdom by that time, and contented themselves by fishing for me with a chain-hook tied to a broom-handle, I believe. I did not offer to go and fetch up my shovel, which was left down below.

"Things began to look bad. We put the long-boat into the water. The second boat was ready to swing out. We had also another, a 14-foot thing, on davits aft, where it was quite safe.

"Then, behold, the smoke suddenly decreased. We redoubled our efforts to flood the bottom of the ship. In two days there was no smoke at all. Everybody was on the broad grin. This was on a Friday. On Saturday no work but sailing the ship, of course, was done. The men washed their clothes and their faces for the first time in a fortnight, and had a special dinner given them. They spoke of spontaneous combustion with contempt, and implied *they* were the boys to put out combustions. Somehow we all felt as though we each had inherited a large fortune. But a beastly smell of burning hung about the ship. Captain Beard had hollow eyes and sunken cheeks. I had never noticed so much before how twisted and bowed he was. He and Mahon prowled soberly about hatches and ventilators, sniffing. It struck me suddenly poor Mahon was a very, very old chap. As to me, I was as pleased and proud as though I had helped to win a great naval battle. O! Youth!

"The night was fine. In the morning a homeward-bound ship passed us hull down—the first we had seen for months; but we were nearing the land at last, Java Head being about 190 miles off, and nearly due north.

"Next day it was my watch on deck from eight to twelve. At breakfast the captain observed, 'It's wonderful how that smell hangs about the cabin.' About ten, the mate being on the poop, I stepped down on the main-deck for a moment. The carpenter's bench stood abaft the mainmast: I leaned against it sucking at my pipe, and the carpenter, a young chap, came to talk to me. He remarked, 'I think we have done very well, haven't we?' and then I perceived with annoyance the fool was trying to tilt the bench. I said curtly, 'Don't, Chips,' and immediately became aware of a queer sensation, of an absurd delusion,—I seemed somehow to be in the air. I heard all round me like a pent-up breath released—as if a thousand giants simultaneously had said Phoo!—

and felt a dull concussion which made my ribs ache suddenly. No doubt about it—I was in the air, and my body was describing a short parabola. But short as it was, I had the time to think several thoughts in, as far as I can remember, the following order: 'This can't be the carpenter—What is it?—Some accident—Submarine volcano?—Coals, gas!—By Jove! we are being blown up—Everybody's dead—I am falling into the after-hatch—I see fire in it.'

"The coal-dust suspended in the air of the hold had glowed dull-red at the moment of the explosion. In the twinkling of an eye, in an infinitesimal fraction of a second since the first tilt of the bench, I was sprawling full length on the cargo. I picked myself up and scrambled out. It was quick like a rebound. The deck was a wilderness of smashed timber, lying crosswise like trees in a wood after a hurricane; an immense curtain of soiled rags waved gently before me—it was the mainsail blown to strips. I thought, The masts will be toppling over directly; and to get out of the way bolted on all-fours towards the poop-ladder. The first person I saw was Mahon, with eyes like saucers, his mouth open, and the long white hair standing straight on end round his head like a silver halo. He was just about to go down when the sight of the main-deck stirring, heaving up, and changing into splinters before his eyes, petrified him on the top step. I stared at him in unbelief, and he stared at me with a queer kind of shocked curiosity. I did not know that I had no hair, no eyebrows, no eyelashes, that my young moustache was burned off, that my face was black, one cheek laid open, my nose cut, and my chin bleeding. I had lost my cap, one of my slippers, and my shirt was torn to rags. Of all this I was not aware. I was amazed to see the ship still afloat, the poop-deck whole—and, most of all, to see anybody alive. Also the peace of the sky and the serenity of the sea were distinctly surprising. I suppose I expected to see them convulsed with horror. . . . Pass the bottle.

"There was a voice hailing the ship from somewhere—in the air, in the sky—I couldn't tell. Presently I saw the captain—and he was mad. He asked me eagerly, 'Where's the cabin-table?' and to hear such a question was a frightful shock. I had just been blown up, you understand, and vibrated with that experience,—

I wasn't quite sure whether I was alive. Mahon began to stamp with both feet and yelled at him, 'Good God! don't you see the deck's blown out of her?' I found my voice, and stammered out as if conscious of some gross neglect of duty, 'I don't know where the cabin-table is.' It was like an absurd dream.

"Do you know what he wanted next? Well, he wanted to trim the yards. Very placidly, and as if lost in thought, he insisted on having the foreyard squared. 'I don't know if there's anybody alive,' said Mahon, almost tearfully. 'Surely,' he said, gently, 'there will be enough left to square the foreyard.'

"The old chap, it seems, was in his own berth winding up the chronometers, when the shock sent him spinning. Immediately it occurred to him—as he said afterwards—that the ship had struck something, and he ran out into the cabin. There, he saw, the cabin-table had vanished somewhere. The deck being blown up, it had fallen down into the lazarette of course. Where we had our breakfast that morning he saw only a great hole in the floor. This appeared to him so awfully mysterious, and impressed him so immensely, that what he saw and heard after he got on deck were mere trifles in comparison. And, mark, he noticed directly the wheel deserted and his barque off her course—and his only thought was to get that miserable, stripped, undecked, smoldering shell of a ship back again with her head pointing at her port of destination. Bankok! That's what he was after. I tell you this quiet, bowed, bandy-legged, almost deformed little man was immense in the singleness of his idea and in his placid ignorance of our agitation. He motioned us forward with a commanding gesture, and went to take the wheel himself.

"Yes; that was the first thing we did—trim the yards of that wreck! No one was killed, or even disabled, but everyone was more or less hurt. You should have seen them! Some were in rags, with black faces, like coal-heavers, like sweeps, and had bullet heads that seemed closely cropped, but were in fact singed to the skin. Others, of the watch below, awakened by being shot out from their collapsing bunks, shivered incessantly, and kept on groaning even as we went about our work. But they all worked. That crew of Liverpool hard cases had in them the right stuff. It's my experience they always have. It is the sea that gives it—the vastness, the loneliness surrounding their dark stolid souls. Ah! Well! we stumbled, we crept, we fell, we barked our shins on the wreckage, we hauled. The masts stood, but we did not know how much they might be charred down below. It was nearly calm, but a long swell ran from the west and made her roll. They might go at any moment. We looked at them with apprehension. One could not foresee which way they would fall.

"Then we retreated aft and looked about us. The deck was a tangle of planks on edge, of planks on end, of splinters, of ruined woodwork. The masts rose from that chaos like big trees above a matted undergrowth. The interstices of that mass of wreckage were full of something whitish, sluggish, stirring—of something that was like a greasy fog. The smoke of the invisible fire was coming up again, was trailing, like a poisonous thick mist in some valley choked with dead wood. Already lazy wisps were beginning to curl upwards amongst the mass of splinters. Here and there a piece of timber, stuck upright, resembled a post. Half of a fife-rail had been shot through the foresail, and the sky made a patch of glorious blue in the ignobly soiled canvas. A portion of several boards holding together had fallen across the rail, and one end protruded overboard, like a gangway leading upon nothing, like a gangway leading over the deep sea, leading to death—as if inviting us to walk the plank at once and be done with our ridiculous troubles. And still the air, the sky—a ghost, something invisible was hailing the ship.

"Someone had the sense to look over, and there was the helmsman, who had impulsively jumped overboard, anxious to come back. He yelled and swam lustily like a merman, keeping up with the ship. We threw him a rope, and presently he stood amongst us streaming with water and very crestfallen. The captain had surrendered the wheel, and apart, elbow on rail and chin in hand, gazed at the sea wistfully. We asked ourselves, What next? I thought, Now, this is something like. This is great. I wonder what will happen. O youth!

"Suddenly Mahon sighted a steamer far astern. Captain Beard said, 'We may do something with her yet.' We hoisted two flags, which said in the international language of the sea, 'On fire. Want immediate assistance.' The steamer grew bigger rapidly, and by and by spoke with two flags on her foremast, 'I am coming to your assistance.'

"In half an hour she was abreast, to windward, within hail, and rolling slightly, with her engines stopped. We lost our composure, and yelled all together with excitement, 'We've been blown up.' A man in a white helmet, on the bridge, cried, 'Yes! All right! All right!' and he nodded his head, and smiled, and made soothing motions with his hand as though at a lot of frightened children. One of the boats dropped in the water, and walked towards us upon the sea with her long oars. Four Calashes pulled a swinging stroke. This was my first sight of Malay seamen. I've known them since, but what struck me then was their unconcern: they came alongside, and even the bowman standing up and holding to our main-chains with the boat-hook did not deign to lift his head for a glance. I thought people who had been blown up deserved more attention.

"A little man, dry like a chip and agile like a monkey, clambered up. It was the mate of the steamer. He gave one look, and cried, 'Oh, boys–you had better quit.'

"We were silent. He talked apart with the captain for a time, –seemed to argue with him. Then they went away together to the steamer.

"When our skipper came back we learned that the steamer was the *Somerville*, Captain Nash, from West Australia to Singapore via Batavia with mails, and that the agreement was she should tow us to Anjer or Batavia, if possible, where we could extinguish the fire by scuttling, and then proceed on our voyage–to Bankok! The old man seemed excited. 'We will do it yet,' he said to Mahon, fiercely. He shook his fist at the sky. Nobody else said a word.

"At noon the steamer began to tow. She went ahead slim and high, and what was left of the *Judea* followed at the end of seventy fathom of tow-rope,–followed her swiftly like a cloud of smoke with mast-heads protruding above. We went aloft to furl the sails. We coughed on the yards, and were careful about the bunts. Do you see the lot of us there, putting a neat furl on the sails of that ship doomed to arrive nowhere? There was not a man who didn't think that at any moment the masts would topple over. From aloft we could not see the ship for smoke, and they worked carefully, passing the gaskets with even turns. 'Harbor furl—aloft there!' cried Mahon from below.

"You understand this? I don't think one of those chaps expected to get down in the usual way. When we did I heard them saying to each other, 'Well, I thought we would come down overboard, in a lump—sticks and all—blame me if I didn't.' 'That's what I was thinking to myself,' would answer wearily another battered and bandaged scarecrow. And, mind, these were men without the drilled-in habit of obedience. To an onlooker they would be a lot of profane scallywags without a redeeming point. What made them do it—what made them obey me when I, thinking consciously how fine it was, made them drop the bunt of the foresail twice to try and do it better? What? They had no professional reputation—no examples, no praise. It wasn't a sense of duty; they all knew well enough how to shirk, and laze, and dodge—when they had a mind to it—and mostly they had. Was it the two pounds ten a month that sent them there? They didn't think their pay half good enough. No; it was something in them, something inborn and subtle and everlasting. I don't say positively that the crew of a French or German merchantman wouldn't have done it, but I doubt whether it would have been done in the same way. There was a completeness in it, something solid like a principle, and masterful like an instinct—a disclosure of something secret—of that hidden something, that gift of good or evil that makes racial difference, that shapes the fate of nations.

"It was that night at ten that, for the first time since we had been fighting it, we saw the fire. The speed of the towing had fanned the smoldering destruction. A blue gleam appeared forward, shining below the wreck of the deck. It wavered in patches, it seemed to stir and creep like the light of a glowworm. I saw it first, and told Mahon. 'Then the game's up,' he said. 'We had better stop this towing, or she will burst out suddenly fore and aft before we can clear out.' We set up a yell; rang bells to attract their attention; they towed on. At last Mahon and I had to crawl forward and cut the rope with an axe. There was no time to cast off the lashings. Red tongues could be seen licking the wilderness of splinters under our feet as we made our way back to the poop.

"Of course they very soon found out in the steamer that the rope was gone. She gave a loud blast of her whistle, her lights were seen sweeping in a wide circle, she came up ranging close alongside, and stopped. We were all in a tight group on the poop looking at her. Every man had saved a little bundle or a bag. Suddenly a conical flame with a twisted top shot up forward and threw upon the black sea a circle of light, with the two vessels side by side and heaving gently in its centre. Captain Beard had been sitting on the gratings still and mute for hours, but now he rose slowly and advanced in front of us, to the mizzen-shrouds. Captain Nash hailed: 'Come along! Look sharp. I have mail-bags on board. I will take you and your boats to Singapore.'

" 'Thank you! No!' said our skipper. 'We must see the last of the ship.'

" 'I can't stand by any longer,' shouted the other. 'Mails—you know.'

" 'Ay, ay! We are all right.'

" 'Very well! I'll report you in Singapore. . . . Good-bye!'

"He waved his hand. Our men dropped their bundles quietly. The steamer moved ahead, and passing out of the circle of light, vanished at once from our sight, dazzled by the fire which burned fiercely. And then I knew that I would see the East first as commander of a small boat. I thought it fine; and the fidelity to the old ship was fine. We should see the last of her. Oh, the glamour of youth! Oh, the fire of it, more dazzling than the flames of the burning ship, throwing a magic light on the wide earth, leaping audaciously to the sky, presently to be quenched by time, more cruel, more pitiless, more bitter than the sea—and like the flames of the burning ship surrounded by an impenetrable night.

"The old man warned us in his gentle and inflexible way that it was part of our duty to save for the underwriters as much as we could of the ship's gear. Accordingly we went to work aft, while she blazed forward to give us plenty of light. We lugged out a lot of rubbish. What didn't we save? An old barometer fixed with an absurd quantity of screws nearly cost me my life:

a sudden rush of smoke came upon me, and I just got away in time. There were various stores, bolts of canvas, coils of rope; the poop looked like a marine bazaar, and the boats were lumbered to the gunwales. One would have thought the old man wanted to take as much as he could of his first command with him. He was very, very quiet, but off his balance evidently. Would you believe it? He wanted to take a length of old stream-cable and a kedge-anchor with him in the long-boat. We said, 'Ay, ay, sir,' deferentially, and on the quiet let the things slip overboard. The heavy medicine chest went that way, two bags of green coffee, tins of paint—fancy, paint!—a whole lot of things. Then I was ordered with two hands into the boats to make a stowage and get them ready against the time it would be proper for us to leave the ship.

"We put everything straight, stepped the long-boat's mast for our skipper, who was to take charge of her, and I was not sorry to sit down for a moment. My face felt raw, every limb ached as if broken, I was aware of all my ribs, and would have sworn to a twist in the backbone. The boats, fast astern, lay in a deep shadow, and all around I could see the circle of the sea lighted by the fire. A gigantic flame arose forward straight and clear. It flared fierce, with noises like the whirr of wings, with rumbles as of thunder. There were cracks, detonations, and from the cone of flame the sparks flew upwards, as man is born to trouble, to leaky ships, and to ships that burn.

"What bothered me was that the ship, lying broadside to the swell and to such wind as there was—a mere breath—the boats would not keep astern where they were safe, but persisted, in a pig-headed way boats have, in getting under the counter and then swinging alongside. They were knocking about dangerously and coming near the flame, while the ship rolled on them, and, of course, there was always the danger of the masts going over the side at any moment. I and my two boatkeepers kept them off as best we could, with oars and boat-hooks; but to be constantly at it became exasperating, since there was no reason why we should not leave at once. We could not see those on board, nor could we imagine what caused the delay. The boatkeepers were swearing feebly, and I had not only my share of the work but also had to keep at it two men who showed a constant inclination to lay themselves down and let things slide.

"At last I hailed, 'On deck there,' and someone looked over. 'We're ready here,' I said. The head disappeared, and very soon popped up again. 'The captain says, All right, sir, and to keep the boats well clear of the ship.'

"Half an hour passed. Suddenly there was a frightful racket, rattle, clanking of chain, hiss of water, and millions of sparks flew up into the shivering column of smoke that stood leaning slightly above the ship. The cat-heads had burned away, and the two red-hot anchors had gone to the bottom, tearing out after them two hundred fathom of red-hot chain. The ship trembled, the mass of flame swayed as if ready to collapse, and the fore top-gallant-mast fell. It darted down like an arrow of fire, shot under, and instantly leaping up within an oar's-length of the boats, floated quietly, very black on the luminous sea. I hailed the deck again. After some time a man in an unexpectedly cheerful but also muffled tone, as though he had been trying to speak with his mouth shut, informed me, 'Coming directly, sir,' and vanished. For a long time I heard nothing but the whirr and roar of the fire. There were also whistling sounds. The boats jumped, tugged at the painters, ran at each other playfully, knocked their sides together, or, do what we would, swung in a bunch against the ship's side. I couldn't stand it any longer, and swarming up a rope, clambered aboard over the stern.

"It was as bright as day. Coming up like this, the sheet of fire facing me was a terrifying sight, and the heat seemed hardly bearable at first. On a settee cushion dragged out of the cabin Captain Beard, his legs drawn up and one arm under his head, slept with the light playing on him. Do you know what the rest were busy about? They were sitting on deck right aft, round an open case, eating bread and cheese and drinking bottled stout.

"On the background of flames twisting in fierce tongues above their heads they seemed at home like salamanders, and looked like a band of desperate pirates. The fire sparkled in the whites of their eyes, gleamed on patches of white skin seen through the torn shirts. Each had the marks as of a battle about him—bandaged heads, tied-up arms, a strip of dirty rag round a knee—and each man had a bottle between his legs and a chunk of cheese in his hand. Mahon got up. With his handsome and disreputable head, his hooked profile, his long white beard, and with an uncorked bottle in his hand, he resembled one of those reckless sea-robbers of old making merry amidst violence and disaster. 'The last meal on board,' he explained solemnly. 'We had nothing to eat all day, and it was no use leaving all this.' He flourished the bottle and indicated the sleeping skipper. 'He said he couldn't swallow anything, so I got him to lie down,' he went on; and as I stared, 'I don't know whether you are aware, young fellow, the man had no sleep to speak of for days—and there will be dam' little sleep in the boats.' 'There will be no boats by-and-by if you fool about much longer,' I said, indignantly. I walked up to the skipper and shook him by the shoulder. At last he opened his eyes, but did not move. 'Time to leave her, sir,' I said quietly.

"He got up painfully, looked at the flames, at the sea sparkling round the ship, and black, black as ink farther away; he looked at the stars shining dim through a thin veil of smoke in a sky black, black as Erebus.

" 'Youngest first,' he said.

"And the ordinary seaman, wiping his mouth with the back of his hand, got up, clambered over the taffrail, and vanished. Others followed. One, on the point of going over, stopped short to drain his bottle, and with a great swing of his arm flung it at the fire. 'Take this!' he cried.

"The skipper lingered disconsolately, and we left him to commune alone for a while with his first command. Then I went up again and brought him away at last. It was time. The ironwork on the poop was hot to the touch.

"Then the painter of the long-boat was cut, and the three boats, tied together, drifted clear of the ship. It was just sixteen hours after the explosion when we abandoned her. Mahon had charge of the second boat, and I had the smallest—the 14-foot thing. The long-boat would have taken the lot of us; but the skipper said we must save as much property as we could—for the underwriters—and so I got my first command. I had two men with me, a bag of biscuits, a few tins of meat, and a breaker of water. I was ordered to keep close to the long-boat, that in case of bad weather we might be taken into her.

"And do you know what I thought? I thought I would part company as soon as I could. I wanted to have my first command all to myself. I wasn't going to sail in a squadron if there were a chance for independent cruising. I would make land by myself. I would beat the other boats. Youth! All youth! The silly, charming, beautiful youth.

"But we did not make a start at once. We must see the last of the ship. And so the boats drifted about that night, heaving and setting on the swell. The men dozed, waked, sighed, groaned. I looked at the burning ship.

"Between the darkness of earth and heaven she was burning fiercely upon a disc of purple sea shot by the blood-red play of gleams; upon a disc of water glittering and sinister. A high, clear flame, an immense and lonely flame, ascended from the ocean, and from its summit the black smoke poured continuously at the sky. She burned furiously; mournful and imposing like a funeral pile kindled in the night, surrounded by the sea, watched over by the stars. A magnificent death had come like a grace, like a gift, like a reward to that old ship at the end of her laborious days. The surrender of her weary ghost to the keeping of stars and sea was stirring like the sight of a glorious triumph. The masts fell just before daybreak, and for a moment there was a burst and turmoil of sparks that seemed to fill with flying fire the night patient and watchful, the vast night lying silent upon the sea. At daylight she was only a charred shell, floating still under a cloud of smoke and bearing a glowing mass of coal within.

"Then the oars were got out, and the boats forming in a line moved round her remains as if in procession—the long-boat leading. As we pulled across her stern a slim dart of fire shot out viciously at us, and suddenly she went down, head first, in a great hiss of steam. The unconsumed stern was the last to sink; but the paint had gone, had cracked, had peeled off, and there were no letters, there was no word, no stubborn device that was like her soul, to flash at the rising sun her creed and her name.

"We made our way north. A breeze sprang up, and about noon

all the boats came together for the last time. I had no mast or sail in mine, but I made a mast out of a spare oar and hoisted a boat-awning for a sail, with a boat-hook for a yard. She was certainly overmasted, but I had the satisfaction of knowing that with the wind aft I could beat the other two. I had to wait for them. Then we all had a look at the captain's chart, and, after a sociable meal of hard bread and water, got our last instructions. These were simple: steer north, and keep together as much as possible. 'Be careful with that jury-rig, Marlow,' said the captain; and Mahon, as I sailed proudly past his boat, wrinkled his curved nose and hailed, 'You will sail that ship of yours under water, if you don't look out, young fellow.' He was a malicious old man—and may the deep sea where he sleeps now rock him gently, rock him tenderly to the end of time!

"Before sunset a thick rain-squall passed over the two boats, which were far astern, and that was the last I saw of them for a time. Next day I sat steering my cockle-shell—my first command—with nothing but water and sky around me. I did sight in the afternoon the upper sails of a ship far away, but said nothing, and my men did not notice her. You see I was afraid she might be homeward bound, and I had no mind to turn back from the portals of the East. I was steering for Java—another blessed name—like Bankok, you know. I steered many days.

"I need not tell you what it is to be knocking about in an open boat. I remember nights and days of calm, and we pulled, we pulled, and the boat seemed to stand still, as if bewitched within the circle of the sea horizon. I remember the heat, the deluge of rain-squalls that kept us baling for dear life (but filled our water-cask), and I remember sixteen hours on end with a mouth dry as a cinder and a steering-oar over the stern to keep my first command head on to a breaking sea. I did not know how good a man I was till then. I remember the drawn faces, the dejected figures of my two men, and I remember my youth and the feeling that will never come back any more—the feeling that I could last forever, outlast the sea, the earth, and all men; the deceitful feeling that lures us on to joys, to perils, to love, to vain effort—to death; the triumphant conviction of strength, the heat of life in the handful of dust, the glow in the heart that with every year grows dim, grows cold, grows small, and expires -and expires, too soon, too soon—before life itself.

"And this is how I see the East. I have seen its secret places and have looked into its very soul; but now I see it always from a small boat, a high outline of mountains, blue and afar in the morning; like faint mist at noon; a jagged wall of purple at sunset. I have the feel of the oar in my hand, the vision of a scorching blue sea in my eyes. And I see a bay, a wide bay, smooth as glass and polished like ice, shimmering in the dark. A red light burns far off upon the gloom of the land, and the night is soft and warm. We drag at the oars with aching arms, and suddenly a puff of wind, a puff faint and tepid and laden with strange odors of blossoms, of aromatic wood, comes out of the still night—the first sigh of the East on my face. That I can never forget. It was impalpable and enslaving, like a charm, like a whispered promise of mysterious delight.

"We had been pulling this finishing spell for eleven hours. Two pulled, and he whose turn it was to rest sat at the tiller. We had made out the red light in that bay and steered for it, guessing it must mark some small coasting port. We passed two vessels, outlandish and high-sterned, sleeping at anchor, and, approaching the light, now very dim, ran the boat's nose against the end of a jutting wharf. We were blind with fatigue. My men dropped the oars and fell off the thwarts as if dead. I made fast to a pile. A current rippled softly. The scented obscurity of the shore was grouped into vast masses, a density of colossal clumps of vegetation, probably—mute and fantastic shapes. And at their foot the semicircle of a beach gleamed faintly, like an illusion. There was not a light, not a stir, not a sound. The mysterious East faced me, perfumed like a flower, silent like death, dark like a grave.

"And I sat weary beyond expression, exulting like a conqueror, sleepless and entranced as if before a profound, a fateful enigma.

"A splashing of oars, a measured dip reverberating on the level of water, intensified by the silence of the shore into loud claps, made me jump up. A boat, a European boat, was coming in. I invoked the name of the dead; I hailed: *Judea* ahoy! A thin shout answered.

"It was the captain. I had beaten the flagship by three hours, and I was glad to hear the old man's voice again, tremulous and tired. 'Is it you, Marlow?' 'Mind the end of that jetty, sir,' I cried.

"He approached cautiously, and brought up with the deep-sea lead-line which we had saved—for the underwriters. I eased my painter and fell alongside. He sat, a broken figure at the stern, wet with dew, his hands clasped in his lap. His men were asleep already. 'I had a terrible time of it,' he murmured. 'Mahon is behind—not very far.' We conversed in whispers, in low whispers, as if afraid to wake up the land. Guns, thunder, earthquakes would not have awakened the men just then.

"Looking round as we talked, I saw away at sea a bright light traveling in the night. 'There's a steamer passing the bay,' I said. She was not passing, she was entering, and she even came close and anchored. 'I wish,' said the old man, 'you would find out whether she is English. Perhaps they could give us a passage somewhere.' He seemed nervously anxious. So by dint of punching and kicking I started one of my men into a state of somnambulism, and giving him an oar, took another and pulled towards the lights of the steamer.

"There was a murmur of voices in her, metallic hollow clangs of the engine-room, footsteps on the deck. Her ports shone, round like dilated eyes. Shapes moved about, and there was a shadowy man high up on the bridge. He heard my oars.

"And then, before I could open my lips, the East spoke to me, but it was in a Western voice. A torrent of words was poured into the enigmatical, the fateful silence; outlandish, angry words, mixed with words and even whole sentences of good English, less strange but even more surprising. The voice swore and cursed violently; it riddled the solemn peace of the bay by a volley of abuse. It began by calling me Pig, and from that went crescendo into unmentionable adjectives—in English. The man up there raged aloud in two languages, and with a sincerity in his fury that almost convinced me I had, in some way, sinned against the harmony of the universe. I could hardly see him, but began to think he would work himself into a fit.

"Suddenly he ceased, and I could hear him snorting and blowing like a porpoise. I said—

" 'What steamer is this, pray?'

" 'Eh? What's this? And who are you?'

" 'Castaway crew of an English barque burned at sea. We came here tonight. I am the second mate. The captain is in the long-boat, and wishes to know if you would give us a passage somewhere.'

" 'Oh, my goodness! I say. . . . This is the *Celestial* from Singapore on her return trip. I'll arrange with your captain in the morning, . . . and, . . . I say, . . . did you hear me just now?'

" 'I should think the whole bay heard you.'

" 'I thought you were a shore-boat. Now, look here—this infernal lazy scoundrel of a caretaker has gone to sleep again—curse him. The light is out, and I nearly ran foul of the end of this damned jetty. This is the third time he plays me this trick. Now, I ask you, can anybody stand this kind of thing? It's enough to drive a man out of his mind. I'll report him. . . . I'll get the Assistant Resident to give him the sack, by . . . ! See—there's no light. It's out, isn't it! I take you to witness the light's out. There should be a light, you know. A red light on the—'

" 'There was a light,' I said, mildly.

" 'But it's out, man! What's the use of talking like this? You can see for yourself it's out—don't you? If you had to take a valuable steamer along this God-forsaken coast you would want a light, too. I'll kick him from end to end of his miserable wharf. You'll see if I don't. I will—'

" 'So I may tell my captain you'll take us?' I broke in.

" 'Yes, I'll take you. Good-night,' he said, brusquely.

"I pulled back, made fast again to the jetty, and then went to sleep at last. I had faced the silence of the East. I had heard some of its language. But when I opened my eyes again the silence was as complete as though it had never been broken. I was lying in a flood of light, and the sky had never looked so far, so high, before. I opened my eyes and lay without moving.

"And then I saw the men of the East—they were looking at me. The whole length of the jetty was full of people. I saw brown, bronze, yellow faces, the black eyes, the glitter, the color of an Eastern crowd. And all these beings stared without a murmur, without a sigh, without a movement. They stared down at the boats, at the sleeping men who at night had come to them from the sea. Nothing moved. The fronds of palms stood still against the sky. Not a branch stirred along the shore, and the brown roofs of hidden houses peeped through the green foliage, through the big leaves that hung shining and still like leaves forged of heavy metal. This was the East of the ancient navigators, so old, so mysterious, resplendent and somber, living and unchanged, full of danger and promise. And these were the men. I sat up suddenly. A wave of movement passed through the crowd from end to end, passed along the heads, swayed the bodies, ran along the jetty like a ripple on the water, like a breath of wind on a field—and all was still again. I see it now—the wide sweep of the bay, the glittering sands, the wealth of green infinite and varied, the sea blue like the sea of a dream, the crowd of attentive faces, the blaze of vivid color—the water reflecting it all, the curve of the shore, the jetty, the high-sterned outlandish craft floating still, and the three boats with the tired men from the West sleeping, unconscious of the land and the people and of the violence of sunshine. They slept thrown across the thwarts, curled on bottom-boards, in the careless attitudes of death. The head of the old skipper, leaning back in the stern of the long-boat, had fallen on his breast, and he looked as though he would never wake. Farther out old Mahon's face was upturned to the sky, with the long white beard spread out on his breast, as though he had been shot where he sat at the tiller; and a man, all in a heap in the bows of the boat, slept with both arms embracing the stem-head and with his cheek laid on the gunwale. The East looked at them without a sound.

"I have known its fascination since; I have seen the mysterious shores, the still water, the lands of brown nations, where a stealthy Nemesis lies in wait, pursues, overtakes so many of the conquering race, who are proud of their wisdom, of their knowledge, of their strength. But for me all the East is contained in that vision of my youth. It is all in that moment when I opened my young eyes on it. I came upon it from a tussle with the sea—and I was young—and I saw it looking at me. And this is all that is left of it! Only a moment; a moment of strength, of romance, of glamor—of youth! . . . A flick of sunshine upon a strange shore, the time to remember, the time for a sigh, and—good-bye!—Night— Good-bye . . . !"

He drank.

"Ah! The good old time—the good old time. Youth and the sea. Glamor and the sea! The good, strong sea, the salt, bitter sea, that could whisper to you and roar at you and knock your breath out of you."

He drank again.

"By all that's wonderful it is the sea, I believe, the sea itself—or is it youth alone? Who can tell? But you here—you all had something out of life: money, love—whatever one gets on shore—and, tell me, wasn't that the best time, that time when we were young at sea; young and had nothing, on the sea that gives nothing, except hard knocks—and sometimes a chance to feel your strength—that only—what you all regret?"

And we all nodded at him: the man of finance, the man of accounts, the man of law, we all nodded at him over the polished table that like a still sheet of brown water reflected our faces, lined, wrinkled; our faces marked by toil, by deceptions, by success, by love; our weary eyes looking still, looking always, looking anxiously for something out of life, that while it is expected is already gone—has passed unseen, in a sigh, in a flash—together with the youth, with the strength, with the romance of illusions.

Eudora Welty, born in Jackson, Mississippi, in 1909, has remained in her native state except for intervals in the Midwest and in New York City. She was educated at the Mississippi State College for Women and the University of Wisconsin. After two years in New York, where she studied at Columbia University and worked for an advertising agency, she returned to Mississippi. She has made there a career of writing, with gardening, painting, and photography as avocations. Her fiction, full of fresh perception and expression, is rooted in the life of the Deep South. *Delta Wedding* (1946) portrays three generations of a Mississippi plantation family. *The Golden Apples* (1949) covers forty years in a small town in Mississippi. *The Ponder Heart* (1954) is a richly humorous novelette that tells the life story of an eccentric in a Southern town. Eudora Welty's short stories have been collected in *A Curtain of Green* (1941) and *The Wide Net* (1943).

EUDORA WELTY

Livvie

SOLOMON carried Livvie twenty-one miles away from her home when he married her. He carried her away up on the Old Natchez Trace into the deep country to live in his house. She was sixteen—an only girl, then. Once people said he thought nobody would ever come along there. He told her himself that it had been a long time, and a day she did not know about, since that road was a traveled road with *people* coming and going. He was good to her, but he kept her in the house. She had not thought that she could not get back. Where she came from, people said an old man did not want anybody in the world to ever find his wife, for fear they would steal her back from him. Solomon asked her before he took her, "Would she be happy?"—very dignified, for he was a colored man that owned his land and had it written down in the courthouse; and she said, "Yes, sir," since he was an old man and she was young and just listened and answered. He asked her, if she was choosing winter, would she pine for spring, and she said, "No indeed." Whatever she said, always, was because he was an old man . . . while nine years went by. All the time, he got old, and he got so old he gave out. At last he slept the whole day in bed, and she was young still.

It was a nice house, inside and outside both. In the first place, it had three rooms. The front room was papered in holly paper, with green palmettos from the swamp spaced at careful intervals over the walls. There was fresh newspaper cut with fancy borders on the mantel-shelf, on which were propped photographs of old or very young men printed in faint yellow—Solomon's people. Solomon had a houseful of furniture. There was a double settee, a tall scrolled rocker and an organ in the front room, all around a three-legged table with a pink marble top, on which was set a lamp with three gold feet, besides a jelly glass with pretty hen feathers in it. Behind the front room, the other room had the bright iron bed with the polished knobs like a throne, in which Solomon slept all day. There were snow-white curtains of wiry lace at the window, and a lace bedspread belonged on the bed. But what old Solomon slept so sound under was a big feather-stitched piece-quilt in the pattern "Trip Around the World," which had twenty-one different colors, four hundred and forty pieces, and a thousand yards of thread, and that was what Solomon's mother made in her life and old age. There was a table holding the Bible, and a trunk with a key. On the wall were two calendars, and a diploma from somewhere in Solomon's family, and under that Livvie's one possession was nailed, a picture of the little white baby of the family she worked for, back in Natchez before she was married. Going through that room and on to the kitchen, there was a big wood stove and a big round table always with a wet top and with the knives and forks in one jelly glass and the spoons in another, and a cut-glass vinegar bottle between, and going out from those, many shallow dishes of pickled peaches, fig preserves, watermelon pickles and blackberry jam always sitting there. The churn sat in the sun, the doors of the safe were always both shut, and there were four baited mouse-traps in the kitchen, one in every corner.

The outside of Solomon's house looked nice. It was not painted, but across the porch was an even balance. On each side there was one easy chair with high springs, looking out, and a fern basket hanging over it from the ceiling, and a dishpan of zinnia seedlings growing at its foot on the floor. By the door was a plow-wheel, just a pretty iron circle, nailed up on one wall and a square mirror on the other, a turquoise-blue comb stuck up in the frame, with the wash stand beneath it. On the door was a wooden knob with a pearl in the end, and Solomon's black hat hung on that, if he was in the house.

Out front was a clean dirt yard with every vestige of grass patiently uprooted and the ground scarred in deep whorls from the strike of Livvie's broom. Rose bushes with tiny blood-red roses blooming every month grew in threes on either side of the steps. On one side was a peach tree, on the other a pomegranate. Then coming around up the path from the deep cut of the Natchez Trace below was a line of bare crape-myrtle trees with every branch of them ending in a colored bottle, green or blue. There was no word that fell from Solomon's lips to say what they were for, but Livvie knew that there could be a spell put in trees, and she was familiar from the time she was born with the way bottle trees kept evil spirits from coming into the house —by luring them inside the colored bottles, where they cannot get out again. Solomon had made the bottle trees with his own hands over the nine years, in labor amounting to about a tree a year, and without a sign that he had any uneasiness in his heart, for he took as much pride in his precautions against spirits coming in the house as he took in the house, and sometimes in the sun the bottle trees looked prettier than the house did.

It was a nice house. It was in a place where the days would go by and surprise anyone that they were over. The lamplight and the firelight would shine out the door after dark, over the still and breathing country, lighting the roses and the bottle trees, and all was quiet there.

But there was nobody, nobody at all, not even a white person. And if there had been anybody, Solomon would not have let

Livvie look at them, just as he would not let her look at a field hand, or a field hand look at her. There was no house near, except for the cabins of the tenants that were forbidden to her, and there was no house as far as she had been, stealing away down the still, deep Trace. She felt as if she waded a river when she went, for the dead leaves on the ground reached as high as her knees, and when she was all scratched and bleeding she said it was not like a road that went anywhere. One day, climbing up the high bank, she had found a graveyard without a church, with ribbon-grass growing about the foot of an angel (she had climbed up because she thought she saw angel wings), and in the sun, trees shining like burning flames through the great caterpillar nets which enclosed them. Scarey thistles stood looking like the prophets in the Bible in Solomon's house. Indian paint brushes grew over her head, and the mourning dove made the only sound in the world. Oh for a stirring of the leaves, and a breaking of the nets! But not by a ghost, prayed Livvie, jumping down the bank. After Solomon took to his bed, she never went out, except one more time.

Livvie knew she made a nice girl to wait on anybody. She fixed things to eat on a tray like a surprise. She could keep from singing when she ironed, and to sit by a bed and fan away the flies, she could be so still she could not hear herself breathe. She could clean up the house and never drop a thing, and wash the dishes without a sound, and she would step outside to churn, for churning sounded too sad to her, like sobbing, and if it made her home-sick and not Solomon, she did not think of that.

But Solomon scarcely opened his eyes to see her, and scarcely tasted his food. He was not sick or paralyzed or in any pain that he mentioned, but he was surely wearing out in the body, and no matter what nice hot thing Livvie would bring him to taste, he would only look at it now, as if he were past seeing how he could add anything more to himself. Before she could beg him, he would go fast asleep. She could not surprise him any more, if he would not taste, and she was afraid that he was never in the world going to taste another thing she brought him—and so how could he last?

But one morning it was breakfast time and she cooked his eggs and grits, carried them in on a tray, and called his name. He was sound asleep. He lay in a dignified way with his watch beside him, on his back in the middle of the bed. One hand drew the quilt up high, though it was the first day of spring. Through the white lace curtains a little puffy wind was blowing as if it came from round cheeks. All night the frogs had sung out in the swamp, like a commotion in the room, and he had not stirred, though she lay wide awake and saying "Shh, frogs!" for fear he would mind them.

He looked as if he would like to sleep a little longer, and so she put back the tray and waited a little. When she tiptoed and stayed so quiet, she surrounded herself with a little reverie, and sometimes it seemed to her when she was so stealthy that the quiet she kept was for a sleeping baby, and that she had a baby and was its mother. When she stood at Solomon's bed and looked down at him, she would be thinking, "He sleeps so well," and she would hate to wake him up. And in some other way, too, she was afraid to wake him up because even in his sleep he seemed to be such a strict man.

Of course, nailed to the wall over the bed—only she would forget who it was—there was a picture of him when he was young. Then he had a fan of hair over his forehead like a king's crown. Now his hair lay down on his head, the spring had gone out of it. Solomon had a lightish face, with eyebrows scattered but rugged, the way privet grows, strong eyes, with second sight, a strict mouth, and a little gold smile. This was the way he looked in his clothes, but in bed in the daytime he looked like a different and smaller man, even when he was wide awake, and holding the Bible. He looked like somebody kin to himself. And then sometimes when he lay in sleep and she stood fanning the flies away, and the light came in, his face was like new, so smooth and clear that it was like a glass of jelly held to the window, and she could almost look through his forehead and see what he thought.

She fanned him and at length he opened his eyes and spoke her name, but he would not taste the nice eggs she had kept warm under a pan.

Back in the kitchen she ate heartily, his breakfast and hers, and looked out the open door at what went on. The whole day, and the whole night before, she had felt the stir of spring close to her. It was as present in the house as a young man would be. The moon was in the last quarter and outside they were turning the sod and planting peas and beans. Up and down the red fields, over which smoke from the brush-burning hung showing like a little skirt of sky, a white horse and a white mule pulled the plow. At intervals hoarse shouts came through the air and roused her as if she dozed neglectfully in the shade, and they were telling her, "Jump up!" She could see how over each ribbon of field were moving men and girls, on foot and mounted on mules, with hats set on their heads and bright with tall hoes and forks as if they carried streamers on them and were going to some place on a journey—and how as if at a signal now and then they would all start at once shouting, hollering, cajoling, calling and answering back, running, being leaped on and breaking away, flinging to earth with a shout and lying motionless in the trance of twelve o'clock. The old women came out of the cabins and brought them the food they had ready for them, and then all worked together, spread evenly out. The little children came too, like a bouncing stream overflowing the fields, and set upon the men, the women, the dogs, the rushing birds, and the wave-like rows of earth, their little voices almost too high to be heard. In the middle distance like some white-and-gold towers were the haystacks, with black cows coming around to eat their edges. High above everything, the wheel of fields, house, and cabins, and the deep road surrounding like a moat to keep them in, was the turning sky, blue with long, far-flung white mare's-tail clouds, serene and still as high flames. And sound asleep while all this went around him that was his, Solomon was like a little still spot in the middle.

Even in the house the earth was sweet to breathe. Solomon had never let Livvie go any farther than the chicken house and the well. But what if she would walk now into the heart of the fields and take a hoe and work until she fell stretched out and drenched with her efforts, like other girls, and laid her cheek against the laid-open earth, and shamed the old man with her humbleness and delight? To shame him! A cruel wish could come in uninvited and so fast while she looked out the back door. She washed the dishes and scrubbed the table. She could hear the cries of the little lambs. Her mother, that she had not seen since her wedding day, had said one time, "I rather a man be anything, than a woman be mean."

So all morning she kept tasting the chicken broth on the stove, and when it was right she poured off a nice cupful. She carried it in to Solomon, and there he lay having a dream. Now what did he dream about? For she saw him sigh gently as if not to disturb some whole thing he held round in his mind, like a fresh egg. So even an old man dreamed about something pretty. Did he dream of her, while his eyes were shut and sunken, and his small hand with the wedding ring curled close in sleep around the quilt? He might be dreaming of what time it was, for even through his sleep he kept track of it like a clock, and knew how much of it went by, and waked up knowing where the hands were even before he consulted the silver watch that he never let go. He would sleep with the watch in his palm, and even holding it to his cheek like a child that loves a plaything. Or he might dream of journeys and travels on a steamboat to Natchez. Yet she thought he dreamed of her; but even while she scrutinized him, the rods of the foot of the bed seemed to rise up like a rail fence between them, and she could see that people never could be sure of anything as long as one of them was asleep and the other awake. To look at him dreaming of her when he might be going to die frightened her a little, as if he might carry her with him that way, and she wanted to run out of the room. She took hold of the bed and held on, and Solomon opened his eyes and called her name, but he did not want anything. He would not taste the good broth.

Just a little after that, as she was taking up the ashes in the front room for the last time in the year, she heard a sound. It was somebody coming. She pulled the curtains together and looked through the slit.

Coming up the path under the bottle trees was a white lady. At first she looked young, but then she looked old. Marvelous to see, a little car stood steaming like a kettle out in the field-track—it had come without a road.

Livvie stood listening to the long, repeated knockings at the door, and after a while she opened it just a little. The lady came in through the crack, though she was more than middle-sized and wore a big hat.

"My name is Miss Baby Marie," she said.

Livvie gazed respectfully at the lady and at the little suitcase she was holding close to her by the handle until the proper moment. The lady's eyes were running over the room, from palmetto to palmetto, but she was saying, "I live at home . . . out from Natchez . . . and get out and show these pretty cosmetic things to the white people and the colored people both . . . all around . . . years and years. . . . Both shades of powder and rouge. . . . It's the kind of work a girl can do and not go clear 'way from home . . ." And the harder she looked, the more she talked. Suddenly she turned up her nose and said, "It is not Christian or sanitary to put feathers in a vase," and then she took a gold key out of the front of her dress and began unlocking the locks on her suitcase. Her face drew the light, the way it was covered with intense white and red, with a little patty-cake of white between the wrinkles by her upper lip. Little red tassels of hair bobbed under the rusty wires of her picture-hat, as with an air of triumph and secrecy she now drew open her little suitcase and brought out bottle after bottle and jar after jar, which she put down on the table, the mantel-piece, the settee, and the organ.

"Did you ever see so many cosmetics in your life?" cried Miss Baby Marie.

"No'm," Livvie tried to say, but the cat had her tongue.

"Have you ever applied cosmetics?" asked Miss Baby Marie next.

"No'm," Livvie tried to say.

"Then look!" she said, and pulling out the last thing of all, "Try this!" she said. And in her hand was unclenched a golden lipstick which popped open like magic. A fragrance came out of it like incense, and Livvie cried out suddenly, "Chinaberry flowers!"

Her hand took the lipstick, and in an instant she was carried away in the air through the spring, and looking down with a half-drowsy smile from a purple cloud she saw from above a chinaberry tree, dark and smooth and neatly leaved, neat as a guinea hen in the dooryard, and there was her home that she had left. On one side of the tree was her mama holding up her heavy apron, and she could see it was loaded with ripe figs, and on the other side was her papa holding a fish-pole over the pond, and she could see it transparently, the little clear fishes swimming up to the brim.

"Oh, no, not chinaberry flowers—secret ingredients," said Miss Baby Marie. "My cosmetics have secret ingredients—not chinaberry flowers."

"It's purple," Livvie breathed, and Miss Baby Marie said, "Use it freely. Rub it on."

Livvie tiptoed out to the wash stand on the front porch and before the mirror put the paint on her mouth. In the wavery surface her face danced before her like a flame. Miss Baby Marie followed her out, took a look at what she had done, and said, "That's it."

Livvie tried to say "Thank you" without moving her parted lips where the paint lay so new.

By now Miss Baby Marie stood behind Livvie and looked in the mirror over her shoulder, twisting up the tassels of her hair. "The lipstick I can let you have for only two dollars," she said, close to her neck.

"Lady, but I don't have no money, never did have," said Livvie.

"Oh, but you don't pay the first time. I make another trip, that's the way I do. I come back again—later."

"Oh," said Livvie, pretending she understood everything so as to please the lady.

"But if you don't take it now, this may be the last time I'll call at your house," said Miss Baby Marie sharply. "It's far away from anywhere, I'll tell you that. You don't live close to anywhere."

"Yes'm. My husband, he keep the *money*," said Livvie, trembling. "He is strict as he can be. He don't know *you* walk in here—Miss Baby Marie!"

"Where is he?"

"Right now, he in yonder sound asleep, an old man. I wouldn't ever ask him for anything."

Miss Baby Marie took back the lipstick and packed it up. She gathered up the jars for both black and white and got them all inside the suitcase, with the same little fuss of triumph with which she had brought them out. She started away.

"Goodbye," she said, making herself look grand from the back, but at the last minute she turned around in the door. Her old hat wobbled as she whispered, "Let me see your husband."

Livvie obediently went on tiptoe and opened the door to the other room. Miss Baby Marie came behind her and rose on her toes and looked in.

"My, what a little tiny old, old man!" she whispered, clasping her hands and shaking her head over them. "What a beautiful quilt! What a tiny old, old man!"

"He can sleep like that all day," whispered Livvie proudly.

They looked at him awhile so fast asleep, and then all at once they looked at each other. Somehow that was as if they had a secret, for he had never stirred. Livvie then politely, but all at once, closed the door.

"Well! I'd certainly like to leave you with a lipstick!" said Miss Baby Marie vivaciously. She smiled in the door.

"Lady, but I told you I don't have no money, and never did have."

"And never will?" In the air and all around, like a bright halo around the white lady's nodding head, it was a true spring day.

"Would you take eggs, lady?" asked Livvie softly.

"No, I have plenty of eggs—plenty," said Miss Baby Marie.

"I still don't have no money," said Livvie, and Miss Baby Marie took her suitcase and went on somewhere else.

Livvie stood watching her go, and all the time she felt her heart beating in her left side. She touched the place with her hand. It seemed as if her heart beat and her whole face flamed from the pulsing color of her lips. She went to sit by Solomon and when he opened his eyes he could not see a change in her. "He's fixin' to die," she said inside. That was the secret. That was when she went out of the house for a little breath of air.

She went down the path and down the Natchez Trace a way, and she did not know how far she had gone, but it was not far, when she saw a sight. It was a man, looking like a vision—she standing on one side of the Old Natchez Trace and he standing on the other.

As soon as this man caught sight of her, he began to look himself over. Starting at the bottom with his pointed shoes, he began to look up, lifting his peg-top pants the higher to see fully his bright socks. His coat long and wide and leaf-green he opened like doors to see his high-up tawny pants and his pants he smoothed downward from the points of his collar, and he wore a luminous baby-pink satin shirt. At the end, he reached gently above his wide platter-shaped round hat, the color of a plum, and one finger touched at the feather, emerald green, blowing in the spring winds.

No matter how she looked, she could never look so fine as he did, and she was not sorry for that, she was pleased.

He took three jumps, one down and two up, and was by her side.

"My name is Cash," he said.

He had a guinea pig in his pocket. They began to walk along. She stared on and on at him, as if he were doing some daring spectacular thing, instead of just walking beside her. It was not simply the city way he was dressed that made her look at him and see hope in its insolence looking back. It was not only the way he moved along kicking the flowers as if he could break through everything in the way and destroy anything in the world, that made her eyes grow bright. It might be, if he had not appeared the way he did appear that day she would never have looked so closely at him, but the time people come makes a difference.

They walked through the still leaves of the Natchez Trace, the light and the shade falling through trees about them, the white irises shining like candles on the banks and the new ferns shining like green stars up in the oak branches. They came out at Solomon's house, bottle trees and all. Livvie stopped and hung her head.

Cash began whistling a little tune. She did not know what it was, but she had heard it before from a distance, and she had a revelation. Cash was a field hand. He was a transformed field hand. Cash belonged to Solomon. But he had stepped out of his overalls into this. There in front of Solomon's house he laughed. He had a round head, a round face, all of him was young, and he flung his head up, rolled it against the mare's-tail sky in his round hat, and he could laugh just to see Solomon's house sitting there. Livvie looked at it, and there was Solomon's black hat hanging on the peg on the front door, the blackest thing in the world.

"I been to Natchez," Cash said, wagging his head around against the sky. "*I* taken a trip, *I* ready for Easter!"

How was it possible to look so fine before the harvest? Cash must have stolen the money, stolen it from Solomon. He stood in the path and lifted his spread hand high and brought it down again and again in his laughter. He kicked up his heels. A little chill went through her. It was as if Cash was bringing that strong hand down to beat a drum or to rain blows upon a man, such an abandon and menace were in his laugh. Frowning, she went closer to him and his swinging arm drew her in at once and the fright was crushed from her body, as a little match-flame might be smothered out by what it lighted. She gathered the folds of his coat behind him and fastened her red lips to his mouth, and she was dazzled by herself then, the way he had been dazzled at himself to begin with.

In that instant she felt something that could not be told—that Solomon's death was at hand, that he was the same to her as if he were dead now. She cried out, and uttering little cries turned and ran for the house.

At once Cash was coming, following after, he was running behind her. He came close, and halfway up the path he laughed and passed her. He even picked up a stone and sailed it into the bottle trees. She put her hands over her head, and sounds clattered through the bottle trees like cries of outrage. Cash stamped and plunged zigzag up the front steps and in at the door.

When she got there, he had stuck his hands in his pockets and was turning slowly about in the front room. The little guinea pig peeped out. Around Cash, the pinned-up palmettos looked as if a lazy green monkey had walked up and down and around the walls leaving green prints of his hands and feet.

She got through the room and his hands were still in his pockets, and she fell upon the closed door to the other room and pushed it open. She ran to Solomon's bed, calling "Solomon! Solomon!" The little shape of the old man never moved at all, wrapped under the quilt as if it were winter still.

"Solomon!" She pulled the quilt away, but there was another one under that, and she fell on her knees beside him. He made no sound except a sigh, and then she could hear in the silence the light springy steps of Cash walking and walking in the front room, and the ticking of Solomon's silver watch, which came from the bed. Old Solomon was far away in his sleep, his face looked small, relentless, and devout, as if he were walking somewhere where she could imagine the snow falling.

Then there was a noise like a hoof pawing the floor, and the door gave a creak, and Cash appeared beside her. When she looked up, Cash's face was so black it was bright, and so bright and bare of pity that it looked sweet to her. She stood up and held up her head. Cash was so powerful that his presence gave her strength even when she did not need any.

Under their eyes Solomon slept. People's faces tell of things and places not known to the one who looks at them while they sleep, and while Solomon slept under the eyes of Livvie and Cash his face told them like a mythical story that all his life he had built, little scrap by little scrap, respect. A beetle could not have been more laborious or more ingenious in the task of its destiny. When Solomon was young, as he was in his picture overhead, it was the infinite thing with him, and he could see no end to the respect he would contrive and keep in a house. He had built a lonely house, the way he would make a cage, but it grew to be the same with him as a great monumental pyramid and sometimes in his absorption of getting it erected he was like the builder-slaves of Egypt who forgot or never knew the origin and meaning of the thing to which they gave all the strength of their bodies and used up all their days. Livvie and Cash could see that as a man might rest from a life-labor he lay in his bed, and they could hear how, wrapped in his quilt, he sighed to himself comfortably in sleep, while in his dreams he might have been an ant, a beetle, a bird, an Egyptian, assembling and carrying on his back and building with his hands, or he might have been an old man of India or a swaddled baby, about to smile and brush all away.

Then without warning old Solomon's eyes flew wide open under the hedgelike brows. He was wide awake.

And instantly Cash raised his quick arm. A radiant sweat stood on his temples. But he did not bring his arm down—it stayed in the air, as if something might have taken hold.

It was not Livvie—she did not move. As if something said "Wait," she stood waiting. Even while her eyes burned under motionless lids, her lips parted in a stiff grimace, and with her arms stiff at her sides she stood above the prone old man and the panting young one, erect and apart.

Movement when it came came in Solomon's face. It was an old and strict face, a frail face, but behind it, like a covered light, came an animation that could play hide and seek, that would dart and escape, had always escaped. The mystery flickered in him, and invited from his eyes. It was that very mystery that Cash with his quick arm would have to strike, and that Livvie could not weep for. But Cash only stood holding his arm in the air, when the gentlest flick of his great strength, almost a puff of his breath, would have been enough, if he had known how to give it, to send the old man over the obstruction that kept him away from death.

If it could not be that the tiny illumination in the fragile and ancient face caused a crisis, a mystery in the room that would not permit a blow to fall, at least it was certain that Cash, throbbing in his Easter clothes, felt a pang of shame that the vigor of a man would come to such an end that he could not be struck without warning. He took down his hand and stepped back behind Livvie, like a round-eyed schoolboy on whose unsuspecting head the dunce cap has been set.

"Young ones can't wait," said Solomon.

Livvie shuddered violently, and then in a gush of tears she stooped for a glass of water and handed it to him, but he did not see her.

"So here come the young man Livvie wait for. Was no prevention. No prevention. Now I lay eyes on young man and it come to be somebody I know all the time, and been knowing since he were born in a cotton patch, and watched grow up year to year, Cash McCord, growed to size, growed up to come in my house in the end—ragged and barefoot."

Solomon gave a cough of distaste. Then he shut his eyes vigorously, and his lips began to move like a chanter's.

"When Livvie married, her husband were already somebody. He had paid great cost for his land. He spread sycamore leaves over the ground from wagon to door, day he brought her home, so her foot would not have to touch ground. He carried her through his door. Then he growed old and could not lift her, and she were still young."

Livvie's sobs followed his words like a soft melody repeating each thing as he stated it. His lips moved for a little without sound, or she cried too fervently, and unheard he might have been telling his whole life, and then he said, "God forgive Solomon for sins great and small. God forgive Solomon for carrying away too young girl for wife and keeping her away from her people and from all the young people would clamor for her back."

Then he lifted up his right hand toward Livvie where she stood by the bed and offered her his silver watch. He dangled it before her eyes, and she hushed crying; her tears stopped. For a moment the watch could be heard ticking as it always did, precisely in his proud hand. She lifted it away. Then he took hold of the quilt; then he was dead.

Livvie left Solomon dead and went out of the room. Stealthily, nearly without noise, Cash went beside her. He was like a shadow, but his shiny shoes moved over the floor in spangles, and the green downy feather shone like a light in his hat. As they reached the front room, he seized her deftly as a long black cat and dragged her hanging by the waist round and round him, while he turned in a circle, his face bent down to hers. The first moment, she kept one arm and its hand stiff and still, the one that held Solomon's watch. Then the fingers softly let go, all of her was limp, and the watch fell somewhere on the floor. It ticked away in the still room, and all at once there began outside the full song of a bird.

They moved around and around the room and into the brightness of the open door, then he stopped and shook her once. She rested in silence in his trembling arms, unprotesting as a bird on a nest. Outside the redbirds were flying and criss-crossing, the sun was in all the bottles on the prisoned trees, and the young peach was shining in the middle of them with the bursting light of spring.

SHERWOOD ANDERSON

Sherwood Anderson (1876-1941) was a native of the southern Ohio village of Camden, near the Indiana line. As a boy he moved with his family from town to town in Ohio, the state most frequently used as a background for his later stories. He had little schooling but gained a breadth of experience by working on farms and in factories and around fair grounds and race tracks. Briefly he tried the advertising business in Chicago and became manager of a paint factory in Ohio. But all the time he was dominated by an urge to write. The publication in 1919 of *Winesburg, Ohio*, a collection of impressionistic studies of Middle Western life, marked him as a writer of rare insight and compassion. These qualities characterize his many stories and novels. He died in 1941 in Panama while on a good-will mission to South America.

Brother Death

THERE were the two oak stumps, knee high to a not-too-tall man and cut quite squarely across. They became to the two children objects of wonder. They had seen the two trees cut but had run away just as the trees fell. They hadn't thought of the two stumps, to be left standing there; hadn't even looked at them. Afterwards Ted said to his sister Mary, speaking of the stumps: "I wonder if they bled, like legs, when a surgeon cuts a man's leg off." He had been hearing war stories. A man came to the farm one day to visit one of the farm-hands, a man who had been in the World War and lost an arm. He stood in one of the barns talking. When Ted said that Mary spoke up at once. She hadn't been lucky enough to be at the barn when the one-armed man was there talking, and was jealous. "Why not a woman or a girl's leg?" she said, but Ted said the idea was silly. "Women and girls don't get their legs and arms cut off," he declared. "Why not? I'd just like to know why not?" Mary kept saying.

It would have been something if they had stayed, that day the trees were cut. "We might have gone and touched the places," Ted said. He meant the stumps. Would they have been warm? Would they have bled? They did go and touch the places afterwards, but it was a cold day and the stumps were cold. Ted stuck to his point that only men's arms and legs were cut off, but Mary thought of automobile accidents. "You can't think just of wars. There might be an automobile accident," she declared, but Ted wouldn't be convinced.

They were both children, but something had made them both in an odd way old. Mary was fourteen and Ted eleven, but Ted wasn't strong and that rather evened things up. They were the children of a well-to-do Virginia farmer named John Grey in the Blue Ridge country in Southwestern Virginia. There was a wide valley called the "Rich Valley" with a railroad and a small river running through it and high mountains in sight, to the north and south. Ted had some kind of a heart disease, a lesion, something of the sort, the result of a severe attack of diphtheria when he was a child of eight. He was thin and not strong but curiously alive. The doctor said he might die at any moment, might just drop down dead. The fact had drawn him peculiarly close to his sister Mary. It had awakened a strong and determined maternalism in her.

The whole family, the neighbors on neighboring farms in the valley, and even the other children at the schoolhouse where they went to school recognized something as existing between the two children. "Look at them going along there," people said. "They do seem to have good times together, but they are so serious. For such young children they are too serious. Still, I suppose, under the circumstances, it's natural." Of course, everyone knew about Ted. It had done something to Mary. At fourteen she was both a child and a grown woman. The woman side of her kept popping out at unexpected moments.

She had sensed something concerning her brother Ted. It was because he was as he was, having that kind of a heart, a heart likely at any moment to stop beating, leaving him dead, cut down like a young tree. The others in the Grey family, that is to say, the older ones, the mother and father and an older brother, Don, who was eighteen now, recognized something as belonging to the two children, being, as it were, between them, but the recognition wasn't very definite. People in your own family are likely at any moment to do strange, sometimes hurtful things to you. You have to watch them, Ted and Mary had both found that out.

The brother Don was like the father, already at eighteen almost a grown man. He was that sort, the kind people speak of, saying: "He's a good man. He'll make a good solid dependable man." The father, when he was a young man, never drank, never went chasing the girls, was never wild. There had been enough wild young ones in the Rich Valley when he was a lad. Some of them had inherited big farms and had lost them, gambling, drinking, fooling with fast horses and chasing after the women. It had been almost a Virginia tradition, but John Grey was a land man. All the Greys were. There were other large cattle farms owned by Greys up and down the valley.

John Grey, everyone said, was a natural cattle man. He knew beef cattle, of the big so-called export type, how to pick and feed them to make beef. He knew how and where to get the right kind of young stock to turn into his fields. It was the blue-grass country. Big beef cattle went directly off the pastures to market. The Grey farm contained over twelve hundred acres, most of it in blue-grass.

The father was a land man, land hungry. He had begun, as a cattle farmer, with a small place, inherited from his father, some two hundred acres, lying next to what was then the big Aspinwahl place and, after he began, he never stopped getting more land. He kept cutting in on the Aspinwahls who were a rather horsey, fast lot. They thought of themselves as Virginia aristocrats, having, as they weren't so modest about pointing out, a family going back and back, family tradition, guests always being entertained, fast horses kept, money being bet on fast horses. John Grey getting their land, now twenty acres, then thirty, then fifty, until at last he got the old Aspinwahl house, with one of the Aspinwahl girls, not a young one, not one of the best-looking ones, as wife. The Aspinwahl place was down, by that time, to less than a hundred acres, but he went on, year after year, always being careful and shrewd, making every penny count, never wasting a cent, adding and adding to what was now the Grey place. The former Aspinwahl house was a large old brick house with fireplaces in all the rooms and was very comfortable.

People wondered why Louise Aspinwahl had married John Grey, but when they were wondering they smiled. The Aspinwahl girls were all well educated, had all been away to college, but Louise wasn't so pretty. She got nicer after marriage, suddenly almost beautiful. The Aspinwahls were, as everyone knew, naturally sensitive, really first class but the men couldn't hang onto land and the Greys could. In all that section of Virginia, people gave John Grey credit for being what he was. They respected him. "He's on the level," they said, "as honest as a horse. He has cattle sense, that's it." He could run his big hand down over the flank of a steer and say, almost to the pound, what he would weigh on the scales or he could look at a calf or a yearling and say, "He'll do," and he would do. A steer is a steer. He isn't supposed to do anything but make beef.

There was Don, the oldest son of the Grey family. He was so evidently destined to be a Grey, to be another like his father. He had long been a star in the 4H Club of the Virginia county and, even as a lad of nine and ten, had won prizes at steer judging. At twelve he had produced, no one helping him, doing all the work himself, more bushels of corn on an acre of land than any other boy in the State.

It was all a little amazing, even a bit queer to Mary Grey, being as she was a girl peculiarly conscious, so old and young, so aware. There was Don, the older brother, big and strong of body, like the father, and there was the young brother Ted. Ordinarily, in the ordinary course of life, she being what she was—female—it would have been quite natural and right for her to have given her young girl's admiration to Don but she didn't. For some reason, Don barely existed for her. He was outside, not in it, while for her Ted, the seemingly weak one of the family, was everything.

Still there Don was, so big of body, so quiet, so apparently sure of himself. The father had begun, as a young cattle man, with the two hundred acres, and now he had the twelve hundred. What would Don Grey do when he started? Already he knew, although he didn't say anything, that he wanted to start. He wanted to run things, be his own boss. His father had offered to send him away to college, to an agricultural college, but he wouldn't go. "No. I can learn more here," he said.

Already there was a contest, always kept under the surface, between the father and son. It concerned ways of doing things, decisions to be made. As yet the son always surrendered.

It is like that in a family, little isolated groups formed within the larger group, jealousies, concealed hatreds, silent battles secretly going on—among the Greys, Mary and Ted, Don and his father, the mother and the two younger children, Gladys, a girl child of six now, who adored her brother Don, and Harry, a boy child of two.

As for Mary and Ted, they lived within their own world, but their own world had not been established without a struggle. The point was that Ted, having the heart that might at any moment stop beating, was always being treated tenderly by the others. Only Mary understood that—how it infuriated and hurt him.

"No, Ted, I wouldn't do that."

"Now, Ted, do be careful."

Sometimes Ted went white and trembling with anger, Don, the father, the mother, all keeping at him like that. It didn't matter what he wanted to do, learn to drive one of the two family cars, climb a tree to find a bird's nest, run a race with Mary. Naturally, being on a farm, he wanted to try his hand at breaking a colt, beginning with him, getting a saddle on, having it out with him. "No, Ted. You can't." He had learned to swear, picking it up from the farm-hands and from the boys at the country school. "Hell! Goddam!" he said to Mary. Only Mary understood how he felt, and she had not put the matter very definitely into words, not even to herself. It was one of the things that made her old when she was so young. It made her stand aside from the others of the family, aroused in her a curious determination. "They shall not." She caught herself saying the words to herself. "They shall not."

"If he is to have but a few years of life, they shall not spoil what he is to have. Why should they make him die, over and over, day after day?" The thoughts in her mind did not become so definite. She had resentment against the others. She was like a soldier, standing guard over Ted.

The two children drew more and more away, into their own world and only once did what Mary felt come to the surface. That was with the mother.

It was on an early Summer day and Ted and Mary were playing in the rain. They were on a side porch of the house, where the water came pouring down from the eaves. At a corner of the porch there was a great stream, and first Ted and then Mary dashed through it, returning to the porch with clothes soaked and water running in streams from soaked hair. There was something joyous, the feel of the cold water on the body, under clothes, and they were shrieking with laughter when the mother came to the door. She looked at Ted. There was fear and anxiety in her voice. "Oh, Ted, you know you mustn't, you mustn't." Just that. All the rest implied. Nothing said to Mary. There it was. "Oh, Ted, you mustn't. You mustn't run hard, climb trees, ride horses. The least shock to you may do it." It was the old story again, and, of course, Ted understood. He went white and trembled. Why couldn't the rest understand that was a hundred times worse for him? On that day, without answering his mother, he ran off the porch and through the rain toward the barns. He wanted to go hide himself from everyone. Mary knew how he felt.

She got suddenly very old and very angry. The mother and daughter stood looking at each other, the woman nearing fifty and the child of fourteen. It was getting everything in the family reversed. Mary felt that but felt she had to do something. "You should have more sense, Mother," she said seriously. She also had gone white. Her lips trembled. "You mustn't do it any more. Don't you ever do it again."

"What, child?" There was astonishment and half anger in the mother's voice.

"Always making him think of it," Mary said. She wanted to cry but didn't.

The mother understood. There was a queer tense moment before Mary also walked off, toward the barns, in the rain. It wasn't all so clear. The mother wanted to fly at the child, perhaps shake her for daring to be so impudent. A child like that to decide things—to dare to reprove her mother. There was so much implied—even that Ted be allowed to die, quickly, suddenly, rather than that death, danger of sudden death, be brought again and again to his attention. There were values in life, implied by a child's words: "Life, what is it worth? Is death the most terrible thing?" The mother turned and went silently into the house while Mary, going to the barns, presently found Ted. He was in an empty horse stall, standing with his back to the wall, staring. There were no explanations. "Well," Ted said presently, and, "Come on, Ted," Mary replied. It was necessary to do something even perhaps more risky than playing in the rain. The rain was already passing. "Let's take off our shoes," Mary said. Going barefoot was one of the things forbidden Ted. They took their shoes off and, leaving them in the barn, went into an orchard. There was a small creek below the orchard, a creek that went down to the river and now it would be in flood. They went into it and once Mary got swept off her feet so that Ted had to pull her out. She spoke then. "I told Mother," she said, looking serious.

"What?" Ted said. "Gee, I guess maybe I saved you from drowning," he added.

"Sure you did," said Mary. "I told her to let you alone." She grew suddenly fierce. "They've all got to—they've got to let you alone," she said.

There was a bond. Ted did his share. He was imaginative and could think of plenty of risky things to do. Perhaps the mother spoke to the father and to Don, the older brother. There was a new inclination in the family to keep hands off the pair, and the fact seemed to give the two children new room in life. Something seemed to open out. There was a little inner world created, always, every day, being recreated, and in it there was a kind of new security. It seemed to the two children—they could not have put their feelings into words—that, being in their own created world, feeling a security there, they could suddenly look out at the outside world and see, in a new way, what was going on out there in the world that belonged also to others.

It was a world to be thought about, looked at, a world of drama too, the drama of human relations, outside their own world, in a family, on a farm, in a farmhouse. . . . On a farm, calves and yearling steers arriving to be fattened, great heavy steers going off to market, colts being broken to work or to saddle, lambs born in the late Winter. The human side of life was more difficult, to a child often incomprehensible, but after the speech to the mother, on the porch of the house that day when it rained, it seemed to Mary almost as though she and Ted had set up a new family. Everything about the farm, the house and the barns got nicer. There was a new freedom. The two children walked along a country road, returning to the farm from school in the late afternoon. There were other children in the road but they managed to fall behind or they got ahead. There were plans made. "I'm going to be a nurse when I grow up," Mary said. She may have remembered dimly the woman nurse, from the county-seat town, who had come to stay in the house when Ted was so ill. Ted said that as soon as he could–it would be when he was younger yet than Don was now–he intended to leave and go out West . . . far out, he said. He wanted to be a cowboy or a bronco-buster or something, and, that failing, he thought he would be a railroad engineer. The railroad that went down through the Rich Valley crossed a corner of the Grey farm, and, from the road in the afternoon, they could sometimes see trains, quite far away, the smoke rolling up. There was a faint rumbling noise, and on clear days they could see the flying piston rods of the engines.

As for the two stumps in the field near the house, they were what was left of two oak trees. The children had known the trees. They were cut one day in the early Fall.

There was a back porch to the Grey house–the house that had once been the seat of the Aspinwahl family–and from the porch steps a path led down to a stone spring house. A spring came out of the ground just there, and there was a tiny stream that went along the edge of a field, past two large barns and out across a meadow to a creek—called a "branch" in Virginia, and the two trees stood close together beyond the spring house and the fence.

They were lusty trees, their roots down in the rich, always damp soil, and one of them had a great limb that came down near the ground, so that Ted and Mary could climb into it and out another limb into its brother tree, and in the Fall, when other trees, at the front and side of the house, had shed their leaves, blood-red leaves still clung to the two oaks. They were like dry blood on gray days, but on other days, when the sun came out, the trees flamed against the distant hills. The leaves clung, whis pering and talking when the wind blew, so that the trees themselves seemed carrying on a conversation.

John Grey had decided he would have the trees cut. At first it was not a very definite decision. "I think I'll have them cut," he announced.

"But why?" his wife asked. The trees meant a good deal to her. They had been planted, just in that spot, by her grandfather, she said, having in mind just a certain effect. "You see how, in the Fall, when you stand on the back porch, they are so nice against the hills." She spoke of the trees, already quite large, having been brought from a distant woods. Her mother had often spoken of it. The man, her grandfather, had a special feeling for trees. "An Aspinwahl would do that," John Grey said. "There is enough yard, here about the house, and enough trees. They do not shade the house or the yard. An Aspinwahl would go to all that trouble for trees and then plant them where grass might be growing." He had suddenly determined, a half-formed determination in him suddenly hardening. He had perhaps heard too much of the Aspinwahls and their ways. The conversation regarding the trees took place at the table, at the noon hour, and Mary and Ted heard it all.

It began at the table and was carried on afterwards out of doors, in the yard back of the house. The wife had followed her husband out. He always left the table suddenly and silently, getting quickly up and going out heavily, shutting doors with a bang as he went. "Don't, John," the wife said, standing on the porch and calling to her husband. It was a cold day but the sun was out and the trees were like great bonfires against gray distant fields and hills. The older son of the family, young Don, the one so physically like the father and apparently so like him in every other way, had come out of the house with the mother, followed by the two children, Ted and Mary, and at first Don said nothing, but, when the father did not answer the mother's protest but started toward the barn, he also spoke. What he said was obviously the determining thing, hardening the father.

To the two other children—they had walked a little aside and stood together watching and listening—there was something. There was their own child's world. "Let us alone and we'll let you alone." It wasn't as definite as that. Most of the definite thoughts about what happened in the yard that afternoon came to Mary Grey long afterwards, when she was a grown woman. At the moment there was merely a sudden sharpening of the feeling of isolation, a wall between herself and Ted and the others. The father, even then perhaps, seen in a new light, Don and the mother seen in a new light.

There was something, a driving destructive thing in life, in all relationships between people. All of this felt dimly that day—she always believed both by herself and Ted—but only thought out long afterwards, after Ted was dead. There was the farm her father had won from the Aspinwahls—greater persistence, greater shrewdness. In a family, little remarks dropped from time to time, an impression slowly built up. The father, John Grey, was a successful man. He had acquired. He owned. He was the commander, the one having power to do his will. And the power had run out and covered, not only other human lives, impulses in others, wishes, hungers in others . . . he himself might not have, might not even understand . . . but it went far out beyond that. It was, curiously, the power also of life and death. Did Mary Grey think such thoughts at that moment? . . . She couldn't have. . . . Still there was her own peculiar situation, her relationship with her brother Ted, who was to die.

Ownership that gave curious rights, dominances—fathers over children, men and women over lands, houses, factories in cities, fields. "I will have the trees in that orchard cut. They produce apples but not of the right sort. There is no money in apples of that sort any more."

"But, Sir . . . you see . . . look . . . the trees there against that hill, against the sky."

"Nonsense. Sentimentality."

Confusion.

It would have been such nonsense to think of the father of Mary Grey as a man without feeling. He had struggled hard all his life, perhaps, as a young man, gone without things wanted, deeply hungered for. Someone has to manage things in this life. Possessions mean power, the right to say "Do this" or "Do that." If you struggle long and hard for a thing it becomes infinitely sweet to you.

Was there a kind of hatred between the father and the older son of the Grey family? "You are one also who has this thing—the impulse to power, so like my own. Now you are young and I am growing old." Admiration mixed with fear. If you would retain power it will not do to admit fear.

The young Don was so curiously like the father. There were the same lines about the jaws, the same eyes. They were both heavy men. Already the young man walked like the father, slammed doors as did the father. There was the same curious lack of delicacy of thought and touch—the heaviness that plows through, gets things done. When John Grey had married Louise Aspinwahl he was already a mature man, on his way to success. Such men do not marry young and recklessly. Now he was nearing sixty and there was the son—so like himself, having the same kind of strength.

Both land lovers, possession lovers. "It is my farm, my house, my horses, cattle, sheep." Soon now, another ten years, fifteen at the most, and the father would be ready for death. "See, already my hand slips a little. All of this to go out of my grasp." He, John Grey, had not got all of these possessions so easily. It had taken much patience, much persistence. No one but himself would ever quite know. Five, ten, fifteen years of work and saving, getting the Aspinwahl farm piece by piece. "The fools!" They had liked to think of themselves as aristocrats, throwing the land away, now twenty acres, now thirty, now fifty.

Raising horses that could never plow an acre of land.

And they had robbed the land too, had never put anything

back, doing nothing to enrich it, build it up. Such a one thinking: "I'm an Aspinwahl, a gentleman. I do not soil my hands at the plow."

"Fools who do not know the meaning of land owned, possessions, money—responsibility. It is they who are second-rate men."

He had got an Aspinwahl for a wife and, as it had turned out, she was the best, the smartest and, in the end, the best-looking one of the lot.

And now there was his son, standing at the moment near the mother. They had both come down off the porch. It would be natural and right for this one—he being what he already was, what he would become—for him, in his turn, to come into possession, to take command.

There would be, of course, the rights of the other children. If you have the stuff in you (John Grey felt that his son Don had) there is a way to manage. You buy the others out, make arrangements. There was Ted—he wouldn't be alive—and Mary and the two younger children. "The better for you if you have to struggle."

All of this, the implication of the moment of sudden struggle between a father and son, coming slowly afterwards to the man's daughter, as yet little more than a child. Does the drama take place when the seed is put into the ground or afterwards when the plant has pushed out of the ground and the bud breaks open, or still later, when the fruit ripens? There were the Greys with their ability—slow, saving, able, determined, patient. Why had they superseded the Aspinwahls in the Rich Valley? Aspinwahl blood also in the two children, Mary and Ted.

There was an Aspinwahl man—called "Uncle Fred," a brother to Louise Grey—who came sometimes to the farm. He was a rather striking-looking, tall old man with a gray Vandyke beard and a mustache, somewhat shabbily dressed but always with an indefinable air of class. He came from the county-seat town, where he lived now with a daughter who had married a merchant, a polite courtly old man who always froze into a queer silence in the presence of the sister's husband.

The son Don was standing near the mother on the day in the Fall, and the two children, Mary and Ted, stood apart.

"Don't, John," Louise Grey said again. The father, who had started toward the barns, stopped.

"Well, I guess I will."

"No, you won't," said young Don, speaking suddenly. There was a queer fixed look in his eyes. It had flashed into life—something that was between the two men: "I possess" . . . "I will possess." The father wheeled and looked sharply at the son and then ignored him.

For a moment the mother continued pleading.

"But why, why?"

"They make too much shade. The grass does not grow."

"But there is so much grass, so many acres of grass."

John Grey was answering his wife, but now again he looked at his son. There were unspoken words flying back and forth.

"I possess. I am in command here. What do you mean by telling me that I won't?"

"Ha! So! You possess now but soon I will possess."

"I'll see you in hell first."

"You fool! Not yet! Not yet!"

None of the words, set down above, was spoken at the moment, and afterwards the daughter Mary never did remember the exact words that had passed between the two men. There was a sudden quick flash of determination in Don—even perhaps sudden determination to stand by the mother—even perhaps something else—a feeling in the young Don out of the Aspinwahl blood in him—for the moment tree love superseding grass love—grass that would fatten steers. . . .

Winner of 4H Club prizes, champion young corn-raiser, judge of steers, land lover, possession lover.

"You won't," Don said again.

"Won't what?"

"Won't cut those trees."

The father said nothing more at the moment but walked away from the little group toward the barns. The sun was still shining brightly. There was a sharp cold little wind. The two trees were like bonfires lighted against distant hills.

It was the noon hour and there were two men, both young, employees on the farm, who lived in a small tenant house beyond the barns. One of them, a man with a harelip, was married and the other, a rather handsome silent young man, boarded with him. They had just come from the midday meal and were going toward one of the barns. It was the beginning of the Fall corn-cutting time and they would be going together to a distant field to cut corn.

The father went to the barn and returned with the two men. They brought axes and a long cross-cut saw. "I want you to cut those two trees." There was something, a blind, even stupid determination in the man, John Grey. And at that moment his wife, the mother of his children . . . There was no way any of the children could ever know how many moments of the sort she had been through. She had married John Grey. He was her man.

"If you do, Father . . ." Don Grey said coldly.

"Do as I tell you! Cut those two trees!" This addressed to the two workmen. The one who had a harelip laughed. His laughter was like the bray of a donkey.

"Don't," said Louise Grey, but she was not addressing her husband this time. She stepped to her son and put a hand on his arm.

"Don't.

"Don't cross him. Don't cross my man." Could a child like Mary Grey comprehend? It takes time to understand things that happen in life. Life unfolds slowly to the mind. Mary was standing with Ted, whose young face was white and tense. Death at his elbow. At any moment. At any moment.

"I have been through this a hundred times. That is the way this man I married has succeeded. Nothing stops him. I married him; I have had my children by him.

"We women choose to submit.

"This is my affair, more than yours, Don, my son."

A woman hanging onto her things—the family, created about her.

The son not seeing things with her eyes. He shook off his mother's hand, lying on his arm. Louise Grey was younger than her husband, but, if he was now nearing sixty, she was drawing near fifty. At the moment she looked very delicate and fragile.

There was something, at the moment, in her bearing . . . Was there, after all, something in blood, the Aspinwahl blood?

In a dim way perhaps, at the moment the child Mary did comprehend. Women and their men. For her then, at that time, there was but one male, the child Ted. Afterwards she remembered how he looked at that moment, the curiously serious old look on his young face. There was even, she thought later, a kind of contempt for both the father and brother, as though he might have been saying to himself—he couldn't really have been saying it—he was too young: "Well, we'll see. This is something. These foolish ones—my father and my brother. I myself haven't long to live. I'll see what I can, while I do live."

The brother Don stepped over near to where his father stood. "If you do, Father . . ." he said again.

"Well?"

"I'll walk off this farm and I'll never come back."

"All right. Go then."

The father began directing the two men who had begun cutting the trees, each man taking a tree. The young man with the harelip kept laughing, the laughter like the bray of a donkey. "Stop that," the father said sharply, and the sound ceased abruptly. The son Don walked away, going rather aimlessly toward the barn. He approached one of the barns and then stopped. The mother, white now, half ran into the house.

The son returned toward the house, passing the two younger children without looking at them, but did not enter. The father did not look at him. He went hesitatingly along a path at the front of the house and through a gate and into a road. The road ran for several miles down through the valley and then, turning, went over a mountain to the county-seat town.

As it happened, only Mary saw the son Don when he returned to the farm. There were three or four tense days. Perhaps, all the time, the mother and son had been secretly in touch. There was a telephone in the house. The father stayed all day in the fields, and when he was in the house was silent.

Mary was in one of the barns on the day when Don came back and when the father and son met. It was an odd meeting.

The son came, Mary always afterwards thought, rather sheepishly. The father came out of a horse's stall. He had been throwing corn to work horses. Neither the father nor the son saw Mary. There was a car parked in the barn and she had crawled into the driver's seat, her hands on the steering wheel, pretending she was driving.

"Well," the father said. If he felt triumphant, he did not show his feeling.

"Well," said the son, "I have come back."

"Yes, I see," the father said. "They are cutting corn." He walked toward the barn door and then stopped. "It will be yours soon now," he said. "You can be boss then."

He said no more and both men went away, the father toward the distant fields and the son toward the house. Mary was afterwards quite sure that nothing more was ever said.

What had the father meant?

"When it is yours you can be the boss." It was too much for the child. Knowledge comes slowly. It meant:

"You will be in command; and for you, in your turn, it will be necessary to assert.

"Such men as we are cannot fool with delicate stuff. Some men are meant to command and others must obey. You can make them obey in your turn.

"There is a kind of death.

"Something in you must die before you can possess and command."

There was, so obviously, more than one kind of death. For Don Grey one kind and for the younger brother Ted, soon now perhaps, another.

Mary ran out of the barn that day, wanting eagerly to get out into the light, and afterwards, for a long time, she did not try to think her way through what had happened. She and her brother Ted did, however, afterwards, before he died, discuss quite often the two trees. They went on a cold day and put their fingers on the stumps, but the stumps were cold. Ted kept asserting that only men get their legs and arms cut off, and she protested. They continued doing things that had been forbidden Ted to do, but no one protested, and, a year or two later, when he died, he died during the night in his bed.

But while he lived, there was always, Mary afterwards thought, a curious sense of freedom, something that belonged to him that made it good, a great happiness, to be with him. It was, she finally thought, because having to die his kind of death, he never had to make the surrender his brother had made—to be sure of possessions, success, his time to command—would never have to face the more subtle and terrible death that had come to his older brother.

WILLIAM FAULKNER

William Faulkner is a native of Mississippi, the scene of most of his fiction. Soon after his birth in 1897, he was taken to live in the university town of Oxford, Mississippi, which has been his home ever since. His schooling at the University of Mississippi was interrupted when he joined the Canadian Flying Corps in World War I. After rising to the rank of lieutenant and being wounded in combat flying over France, he returned to Mississippi and worked as a newspaper reporter and free-lance writer. Soon he turned to fiction, beginning a remarkable sequence of stories and novels that sketch the social, economic, and psychological history of the Deep South. In 1949 he was awarded the Nobel Prize for Literature. Notable among his novels are *The Sound and the Fury*, *Light in August*, and *Intruder in the Dust*. In 1954 he published a novel called *A Fable*. A distinguished volume of *Collected Stories of William Faulkner* appeared in 1950.

Barn Burning

THE STORE in which the Justice of the Peace's court was sitting smelled of cheese. The boy, crouched on his nail keg at the back of the crowded room, knew he smelled cheese, and more: from where he sat he could see the ranked shelves close-packed with the solid, squat, dynamic shapes of tin cans whose labels his stomach read, not from the lettering which meant nothing to his mind but from the scarlet devils and the silver curve of fish—this, the cheese which he knew he smelled and the hermetic meat which his intestines believed he smelled coming in intermittent gusts momentary and brief between the other constant one, the smell and sense just a little of fear because mostly of despair and grief, the old fierce pull of blood. He could not see the table where the Justice sat and before which his father and his father's enemy (*our enemy* he thought in that despair;

ourn! mine and hisn both! He's my father!) stood, but he could hear them, the two of them that is, because his father had said no word yet:

"But what proof have you, Mr. Harris?"

"I told you. The hog got into my corn. I caught it up and sent it back to him. He had no fence that would hold it. I told him so, warned him. The next time I put the hog in my pen. When he came to get it I gave him enough wire to patch up his pen. The next time I put the hog up and kept it. I rode down to his house and saw the wire I gave him still rolled on to the spool in his yard. I told him he could have the hog when he paid me a dollar pound fee. That evening a nigger came with the dollar and got the hog. He was a strange nigger. He said, 'He say to tell you wood and hay kin burn.' I said, 'What?' 'That whut he say to tell you,' the nigger said. 'Wood and hay kin burn.' That night my barn burned. I got the stock out but I lost the barn."

"Where is the nigger? Have you got him?"

"He was a strange nigger, I tell you. I don't know what became of him."

"But that's not proof. Don't you see that's not proof?"

"Get that boy up here. He knows." For a moment the boy thought too that the man meant his older brother until Harris said, "Not him. The little one. The boy," and, crouching, small for his age, small and wiry like his father, in patched and faded jeans even too small for him, with straight, uncombed, brown hair and eyes gray and wild as storm scud, he saw the men between himself and the table part and become a lane of grim faces, at the end of which he saw the Justice, a shabby, collarless, graying man in spectacles, beckoning him. He felt no floor under his bare feet; he seemed to walk beneath the palpable weight of the grim turning faces. His father, stiff in his black Sunday coat donned not for the trial but for the moving, did not even look at him. *He aims for me to lie*, he thought, again with that frantic grief and despair. *And I will have to do hit.*

"What's your name, boy?" the Justice said.

"Colonel Sartoris Snopes," the boy whispered.

"Hey?" the Justice said. "Talk louder. Colonel Sartoris? I reckon anybody named for Colonel Sartoris in this country can't help but tell the truth, can they?" The boy said nothing. *Enemy! Enemy!* he thought; for a moment he could not even see, could not see that the Justice's face was kindly nor discern that his voice was troubled when he spoke to the man named Harris: "Do you want me to question this boy?" But he could hear, and during those subsequent long seconds while there was absolutely no sound in the crowded little room save that of quiet and intent breathing it was as if he had swung outward at the end of a grape vine, over a ravine, and at the top of the swing had been caught in a prolonged instant of mesmerized gravity, weightless in time.

"No!" Harris said violently, explosively. "Damnation! Send him out of here!" Now time, the fluid world, rushed beneath him again, the voices coming to him again through the smell of cheese and sealed meat, the fear and despair and the old grief of blood:

"This case is closed. I can't find against you, Snopes, but I can give you advice. Leave this country and don't come back to it."

His father spoke for the first time, his voice cold and harsh, level, without emphasis: "I aim to. I don't figure to stay in a country among people who . . ." he said something unprintable and vile, addressed to no one.

"That'll do," the Justice said. "Take your wagon and get out of this country before dark. Case dismissed."

His father turned, and he followed the stiff black coat, the wiry figure walking a little stiffly from where a Confederate provost's man's musket ball had taken him in the heel on a stolen horse thirty years ago, followed the two backs now, since his older brother had appeared from somewhere in the crowd, no taller than the father but thicker, chewing tobacco steadily, between the two lines of grim-faced men and out of the store and across the worn gallery and down the sagging steps and among the dogs and half-grown boys in the mild May dust, where as he passed a voice hissed:

"Barn burner!"

Again he could not see, whirling; there was a face in a red haze, moonlike, bigger than the full moon, the owner of it half again his size, he leaping in the red haze toward the face, feeling no blow, feeling no shock when his head struck the earth, scrabbling up and leaping again, feeling no blow this time either and tasting no blood, scrabbling up to see the other boy in full flight and himself already leaping into pursuit as his father's hand jerked him back, the harsh, cold voice speaking above him: "Go get in the wagon."

It stood in a grove of locusts and mulberries across the road. His two hulking sisters in their Sunday dresses and his mother and her sister in calico and sunbonnets were already in it, sitting on and among the sorry residue of the dozen and more movings which even the boy could remember—the battered stove, the broken beds and chairs, the clock inlaid with mother-of-pearl, which would not run, stopped at some fourteen minutes past two o'clock of a dead and forgotten day and time, which had been his mother's dowry. She was crying, though when she saw him she drew her sleeve across her face and began to descend from the wagon. "Get back," the father said.

"He's hurt. I got to get some water and wash his . . ."

"Get back in the wagon," his father said. He got in too, over the tail-gate. His father mounted to the seat where the older brother already sat and struck the gaunt mules two savage blows with the peeled willow, but without heat. It was not even sadistic; it was exactly that same quality which in later years would cause his descendants to over-run the engine before putting a motor car into motion, striking and reining back in the same movement. The wagon went on, the store with its quiet crowd of grimly watching men dropped behind; a curve in the road hid it. *Forever* he thought. *Maybe he's done satisfied now, now that he has . . .* stopping himself, not to say it aloud even to himself. His mother's hand touched his shoulder.

"Does hit hurt?" she said.

"Naw," he said. "Hit don't hurt. Lemme be."

"Can't you wipe some of the blood off before hit dries?"

"I'll wash tonight," he said. "Lemme be, I tell you."

The wagon went on. He did not know where they were going. None of them ever did or ever asked, because it was always somewhere, always a house of sorts waiting for them a day or two days or even three days away. Likely his father had already arranged to make a crop on another farm before he . . . Again he had to stop himself. He (the father) always did. There was something about his wolflike independence and even courage when the advantage was at least neutral which impressed strangers, as if they got from his latent ravening ferocity not so much a sense of dependability as a feeling that his ferocious conviction in the rightness of his own actions would be of advantage to all whose interest lay with his.

That night they camped, in a grove of oaks and beeches where a spring ran. The nights were still cool and they had a fire against it, of a rail lifted from a near-by fence and cut into lengths—a small fire, neat, niggard almost, a shrewd fire; such fires were his father's habit and custom always, even in freezing weather. Older, the boy might have remarked this and wondered why not a big one; why should not a man who had not only seen the waste and extravagance of war, but who had in his blood an inherent voracious prodigality with material not his own, have burned everything in sight? Then he might have gone a step farther and thought that that was the reason: that niggard blaze was the living fruit of nights passed during those four years in the woods hiding from all men, blue or gray, with his strings of horses (captured horses, he called them). And older still, he might have divined the true reason: that the element of fire spoke to some deep mainspring of his father's being, as the element of steel or of powder spoke to other men, as the one weapon for the preservation of integrity, else breath were not worth the breathing, and hence to be regarded with respect and used with discretion.

But he did not think this now and he had seen those same niggard blazes all his life. He merely ate his supper beside it and was already half asleep over his iron plate when his father called him, and once more he followed the stiff back, the stiff and ruthless limp, up the slope and on to the starlit road where, turning, he could see his father against the stars but without face or depth—a shape black, flat, and bloodless as though cut from tin in the iron folds of the frock coat which had not been made for him, the voice harsh like tin and without heat like tin:

"You were fixing to tell them. You would have told him." He didn't answer. His father struck him with the flat of his hand on the side of the head, hard but without heat, exactly as he had struck the two mules at the store, exactly as he would strike either of them with any stick in order to kill a horse fly, his voice still without heat or anger: "You're getting to be a man. You got to learn. You got to learn to stick to your own blood or you ain't going to have any blood to stick to you. Do you think either of them, any man there this morning, would? Don't you know all they wanted was a chance to get at me because they knew I had them beat? Eh?" Later, twenty years later, he was to tell himself, "If I had said they wanted only truth, justice, he would have hit me again." But now he said nothing. He was not crying. He just stood there. "Answer me," his father said.

"Yes," he whispered. His father turned.

"Get on to bed. We'll be there tomorrow."

Tomorrow they were there. In the early afternoon the wagon stopped before a paintless two-room house identical almost with the dozen others it had stopped before even in the boy's ten years, and again, as on the other dozen occasions, his mother and aunt got down and began to unload the wagon, although his two sisters and his father and brother had not moved.

"Likely hit ain't fitten for hawgs," one of the sisters said.

"Nevertheless, fit it will and you'll hog it and like it," his father said. "Get out of them chairs and help your Ma unload."

The two sisters got down, big, bovine, in a flutter of cheap ribbons; one of them drew from the jumbled wagon bed a battered lantern, the other a worn broom. His father handed the reins to the older son and began to climb stiffly over the wheel. "When they get unloaded, take the team to the barn and feed them." Then he said, and at first the boy thought he was still speaking to his brother: "Come with me."

"Me?" he said.

"Yes," his father said. "You."

"Abner," his mother said. His father paused and looked back—the harsh level stare beneath the shaggy, graying, irascible brows.

"I reckon I'll have a word with the man that aims to begin tomorrow owning me body and soul for the next eight months."

They went back up the road. A week ago—or before last night, that is—he would have asked where they were going, but not now. His father had struck him before last night but never before had he paused afterward to explain why; it was as if the blow and the following calm, outrageous voice still rang, repercussed, divulging nothing to him save the terrible handicap of being young, the light weight of his few years, just heavy enough to prevent his soaring free of the world as it seemed to be ordered but not heavy enough to keep him footed solid in it, to resist it and try to change the course of its events.

Presently he could see the grove of oaks and cedars and the other flowering trees and shrubs where the house would be, though not the house yet. They walked beside a fence massed with honeysuckle and Cherokee roses and came to a gate swinging open between two brick pillars, and now, beyond a sweep of drive, he saw the house for the first time and at that instant he forgot his father and the terror and despair both, and even when he remembered his father again (who had not stopped) the terror and despair did not return. Because, for all the twelve movings, they had sojourned until now in a poor country, a land of small farms and fields and houses, and he had never seen a house like this before. *Hit's big as a courthouse* he thought quietly, with a surge of peace and joy whose reason he could not have thought into words, being too young for that: *They are safe from him. People whose lives are a part of this peace and dignity are beyond his touch, he no more to them than a buzzing wasp: capable of stinging for a little moment but that's all; the spell of this peace and dignity rendering even the barns and stable and cribs which belong to it impervious to the puny flames he might contrive* . . . this, the peace and joy, ebbing for an instant as he looked again at the stiff black back, the stiff and implacable limp of the figure which was not dwarfed by the house, for the reason that it had never looked big anywhere and which now, against the serene columned backdrop, had more than ever that impervious quality of something cut ruthlessly from tin, depthless, as though, sidewise to the sun, it would cast no shadow. Watching him, the boy remarked the absolutely undeviating course which his father held and saw the stiff foot come squarely down in a pile of fresh droppings where a horse had stood in the drive and which his father could have avoided by a simple change of stride. But it ebbed only for a moment, though he could not have thought this into words either, walking on in the spell of the house, which he could even want but without envy, without sorrow, certainly never with that ravening and jealous rage which unknown to him walked in the ironlike black coat before him: *Maybe he will feel it too. Maybe it will even change him now from what maybe he couldn't help but be.*

They crossed the portico. Now he could hear his father's stiff foot as it came down on the boards with clocklike finality, a sound out of all proportion to the displacement of the body it bore and which was not dwarfed either by the white door before it, as though it had attained to a sort of vicious and ravening minimum not to be dwarfed by anything—the flat, wide, black hat, the formal coat of broadcloth which had once been black but which had now that friction-glazed greenish cast of the bodies of old house flies, the lifted sleeve which was too large, the lifted hand like a curled claw. The door opened so promptly that the boy knew the Negro must have been watching them all the time, an old man with neat grizzled hair, in a linen jacket, who stood barring the door with his body, saying, "Wipe yo foots, white man, fo you come in here. Major ain't home nohow."

"Get out of my way, nigger," his father said, without heat too, flinging the door back and the Negro also and entering, his hat still on his head. And now the boy saw the prints of the stiff foot on the doorjamb and saw them appear on the pale rug behind the machinelike deliberation of the foot which seemed to bear (or transmit) twice the weight which the body compassed. The Negro was shouting "Miss Lula! Miss Lula!" somewhere behind them, then the boy, deluged as though by a warm wave by a suave turn of carpeted stair and a pendant glitter of chandeliers and a mute gleam of gold frames, heard the swift feet and saw her too, a lady—perhaps he had never seen her like before either—in a gray, smooth gown with lace at the throat and an apron tied at the waist and the sleeves turned back, wiping cake or biscuit dough from her hands with a towel as she came up the hall, looking not at his father at all but at the tracks on the blond rug with an expression of incredulous amazement.

"I tried," the Negro cried. "I tole him to . . ."

"Will you please go away?" she said in a shaking voice. "Major de Spain is not at home. Will you please go away?"

His father had not spoken again. He did not speak again. He did not even look at her. He just stood stiff in the center of the rug, in his hat, the shaggy iron-gray brows twitching slightly above the pebble-colored eyes as he appeared to examine the house with brief deliberation. Then with the same deliberation he turned; the boy watched him pivot on the good leg and saw the stiff foot drag round the arc of the turning, leaving a final long and fading smear. His father never looked at it, he never once looked down at the rug. The Negro held the door. It closed behind them, upon the hysteric and indistinguishable woman-wail. His father stopped at the top of the steps and scraped his boot clean on the edge of it. At the gate he stopped again. He stood for a moment, planted stiffly on the stiff foot, looking back at the house. "Pretty and white, ain't it?" he said. "That's sweat. Nigger sweat. Maybe it ain't white enough yet to suit him. Maybe he wants to mix some white sweat with it."

Two hours later the boy was chopping wood behind the house within which his mother and aunt and the two sisters (the mother and aunt, not the two girls, he knew that; even at this distance and muffled by walls the flat loud voices of the two girls emanated an incorrigible idle inertia) were setting up the stove to prepare a meal, when he heard the hooves and saw the linen-clad man on a fine sorrel mare, whom he recognized even before he saw the rolled rug in front of the Negro youth following on a fat bay carriage horse—a suffused, angry face vanishing, still at full gallop, beyond the corner of the house where his father and brother were sitting in the two tilted chairs; and a moment later, almost before he could have put the axe down, he heard the hooves again and watched the sorrel mare go back out of the yard, already galloping again. Then his father began to shout one of the sisters' names, who presently emerged backward from the kitchen door dragging the rolled rug along the ground by one end while the other sister walked behind it.

"If you ain't going to tote, go on and set up the wash pot," the first said.

"You, Sarty!" the second shouted. "Set up the wash pot!" His father appeared at the door, framed against that shabbiness, as he had been against that other bland perfection, impervious to either, the mother's anxious face at his shoulder.

"Go on," the father said. "Pick it up." The two sisters stooped, broad, lethargic; stooping, they presented an incredible expanse of pale cloth and a flutter of tawdry ribbons.

"If I thought enough of a rug to have to git hit all the way from France I wouldn't keep hit where folks coming in would have to tromp on hit," the first said. They raised the rug.

"Abner," the mother said. "Let me do it."

"You go back and git dinner," his father said. "I'll tend to this."

From the woodpile through the rest of the afternoon the boy watched them, the rug spread flat in the dust beside the bubbling wash-pot, the two sisters stooping over it with that profound and lethargic reluctance, while the father stood over them in turn, implacable and grim, driving them though never raising his voice again. He could smell the harsh homemade lye they were using; he saw his mother come to the door once and look toward them with an expression not anxious now but very like despair; he saw his father turn, and he fell to with the axe and saw from the corner of his eye his father raise from the ground a flattish fragment of field stone and examine it and return to the pot, and this time his mother actually spoke: "Abner. Abner. Please don't. Please, Abner."

Then he was done too. It was dusk; the whippoorwills had already begun. He could smell coffee from the room where they would presently eat the cold food remaining from the mid-afternoon meal, though when he entered the house he realized they were having coffee again probably because there was a fire on the hearth, before which the rug now lay spread over the backs of the two chairs. The tracks of his father's foot were gone. Where they had been were now long, water-cloudy scoriations resembling the sporadic course of a lilliputian mowing machine.

It still hung there while they ate the cold food and then went to bed, scattered without order or claim up and down the two rooms, his mother in one bed, where his father would later lie, the older brother in the other, himself, the aunt, and the two sisters on pallets on the floor. But his father was not in bed yet. The last thing the boy remembered was the depthless, harsh silhouette of the hat and coat bending over the rug and it seemed to him that he had not even closed his eyes when the silhouette was standing over him, the fire almost dead behind it, the stiff foot prodding him awake. "Catch up the mule," his father said.

When he returned with the mule his father was standing in the black door, the rolled rug over his shoulder. "Ain't you going to ride?" he said.

"No. Give me your foot."

He bent his knee into his father's hand, the wiry, surprising power flowed smoothing, rising, he rising with it, onto the mule's bare back (they had owned a saddle once; the boy could remember it though not when or where) and with the same effortlessness his father swung the rug up in front of him. Now in the starlight they retraced the afternoon's path, up the dusty road rife with honeysuckle, through the gate and up the black tunnel of the drive to the lightless house, where he sat on the mule and felt the rough warp of the rug drag across his thighs and vanish.

"Don't you want me to help?" he whispered. His father did not answer and now he heard again that stiff foot striking the hollow portico with that wooden and clocklike deliberation, that outrageous overstatement of the weight it carried. The rug, hunched, not flung (the boy could tell that even in the darkness) from his father's shoulder struck the angle of wall and floor with a sound unbelievably loud, thunderous, then the foot again, unhurried and enormous; a light came on in the house and the boy sat, tense, breathing steadily and quietly and just a little fast, though the foot itself did not increase its beat at all, descending the steps now; now the boy could see him.

"Don't you want to ride now?" he whispered. "We kin both ride now," the light within the house altering now, flaring up and sinking. *He's coming down the stairs now,* he thought. He had already ridden the mule up beside the horse block; presently his father was up behind him and he doubled the reins over and slashed the mule across the neck, but before the animal could begin to trot the hard, thin arm came round him, the hard, knotted hand jerking the mule back to a walk.

In the first red rays of the sun they were in the lot, putting plow gear on the mules. This time the sorrel mare was in the lot before he heard it at all, the rider collarless and even bareheaded, trembling, speaking in a shaking voice as the woman in the house had done, his father merely looking up once before stooping again to the hame he was buckling, so that the man on the mare spoke to his stooping back:

"You must realize you have ruined that rug. Wasn't there anybody here, any of your women . . ." he ceased, shaking, the boy watching him, the older brother leaning now in the stable door, chewing, blinking slowly and steadily at nothing apparently. "It cost a hundred dollars. But you never had a hundred dollars. You never will. So I'm going to charge you twenty bushels of corn against your crop. I'll add it in your contract and when you come to the commissary you can sign it. That won't keep Mrs. de Spain quiet but maybe it will teach you to wipe your feet off before you enter her house again."

Then he was gone. The boy looked at his father, who still had not spoken or even looked up again, who was now adjusting the logger-head in the hame.

"Pap," he said. His father looked at him—the inscrutable face, the shaggy brows beneath which the gray eyes glinted coldly. Suddenly the boy went toward him, fast, stopping as suddenly. "You done the best you could!" he cried. "If he wanted hit done different why didn't he wait and tell you how? He won't git no twenty bushels! He won't git none! We'll gether hit and hide hit! I kin watch . . ."

"Did you put the cutter back in that straight stock like I told you?"

"No, sir," he said.

"Then go do it."

That was Wednesday. During the rest of that week he worked steadily, at what was within his scope and some which was beyond it, with an industry that did not need to be driven nor even commanded twice; he had this from his mother, with the difference that some at least of what he did he liked to do, such as splitting wood with the half-size axe which his mother and aunt had earned, or saved money somehow, to present him with at Christmas. In company with the two older women (and on one afternoon, even one of the sisters), he built pens for the shoat and the cow which were a part of his father's contract with the landlord, and one afternoon, his father being absent, gone somewhere on one of the mules, he went to the field.

They were running a middle-buster now, his brother holding the plow straight while he handled the reins, and walking beside the straining mule, the rich black soil shearing cool and damp against his bare ankles, he thought *Maybe this is the end of it. Maybe even that twenty bushels that seems hard to have to pay for just a rug will be a cheap price for him to stop forever and always from being what he used to be;* thinking, dreaming now, so that his brother had to speak sharply to him to mind the mule: *Maybe he even won't collect the twenty bushels. Maybe it will all add up and balance and vanish—corn, rug, fire; the terror and grief, the being pulled two ways like between two teams of horses—gone, done with for ever and ever.*

Then it was Saturday; he looked up from beneath the mule he was harnessing and saw his father in the black coat and hat. "Not that," his father said. "The wagon gear." And then, two hours later, sitting in the wagon bed behind his father and brother on the seat, the wagon accomplished a final curve, and he saw the weathered paintless store with its tattered tobacco- and patent-medicine posters and the tethered wagons and saddle animals below the gallery. He mounted the gnawed steps behind his father and brother, and there again was the lane of quiet, watching faces for the three of them to walk through. He saw the man in spectacles sitting at the plank table and he did not need to be told this was a Justice of the Peace; he sent one glare of fierce, exultant, partisan defiance at the man in collar and cravat now, whom he had seen but twice before in his life, and that on a galloping horse, who now wore on his face an expression not of rage but of amazed unbelief which the boy could not have known was at the incredible circumstance of being sued by one of his own tenants, and came and stood against his father and cried at the Justice: "He ain't done it! He ain't burnt . . ."

"Go back to the wagon," his father said.

"Burnt?" the Justice said. "Do I understand this rug was burned too?"

"Does anybody here claim it was?" his father said. "Go back to the wagon." But he did not, he merely retreated to the rear of the room, crowded as that other had been, but not to sit down this time, instead, to stand pressing among the motionless bodies, listening to the voices:

"And you claim twenty bushels of corn is too high for the damage you did to the rug?"

"He brought the rug to me and said he wanted the tracks washed out of it. I washed the tracks out and took the rug back to him."

"But you didn't carry the rug back to him in the same condition it was in before you made the tracks on it."

His father did not answer, and now for perhaps half a minute there was no sound at all save that of breathing, the faint, steady suspiration of complete and intent listening.

"You decline to answer that, Mr. Snopes?" Again his father did not answer. "I'm going to find against you, Mr. Snopes. I'm going to find that you were responsible for the injury to Major de Spain's rug and hold you liable for it. But twenty bushels of corn seems a little high for a man in your circumstances to have to pay. Major de Spain claims it cost a hundred dollars. October corn will be worth about fifty cents. I figure that if Major de Spain can stand a ninety-five-dollar loss on something he paid cash for, you can stand a five-dollar loss you haven't earned yet. I hold you in damages to Major de Spain to the amount of ten bushels of corn over and above your contract with him, to be paid to him out of your crop at gathering time. Court adjourned."

It had taken no time hardly, the morning was but half begun. He thought they would return home and perhaps back to the field, since they were late, far behind all other farmers. But instead his father passed on behind the wagon, merely indicating with his hand for the older brother to follow with it, and crossed the road toward the blacksmith shop opposite, pressing on after his father, overtaking him, speaking, whispering up at the harsh, calm face beneath the weathered hat: "He won't git no ten bushels neither. He won't git one. We'll . . ." until his father glanced for an instant down at him, the face absolutely calm, the grizzled eyebrows tangled above the cold eyes, the voice almost pleasant, almost gentle:

"You think so? Well, we'll wait till October anyway."

The matter of the wagon—the setting of a spoke or two and the tightening of the tires—did not take long either, the business of the tires accomplished by driving the wagon into the spring branch behind the shop and letting it stand there, the mules nuzzling into the water from time to time, and the boy on the seat with the idle reins, looking up the slope and through the sooty tunnel of the shed where the slow hammer rang and where his father sat on an upended cypress bolt, easily, either talking or listening, still sitting there when the boy brought the dripping wagon up out of the branch and halted it before the door.

"Take them on to the shade and hitch," his father said. He did so and returned. His father and the smith and a third man squatting on his heels inside the door were talking, about crops and animals; the boy, squatting too in the ammoniac dust and hoof-parings and scales of rust, heard his father tell a long and unhurried story out of the time before the birth of the older brother even when he had been a professional horsetrader. And then his father came up beside him where he stood before a tattered last year's circus poster on the other side of the store, gazing rapt and quiet at the scarlet horses, the incredible poisings and convolutions of tulle and tights and the painted leers of comedians, and said, "It's time to eat."

But not at home. Squatting beside his brother against the front wall, he watched his father emerge from the store and produce from a paper sack a segment of cheese and divide it carefully and deliberately into three with his pocket knife and produce crackers from the same sack. They all three squatted on the gallery and ate, slowly, without talking; then in the store again, they drank from a tin dipper tepid water smelling of the cedar bucket and of living beech trees. And still they did not go home. It was a horse lot this time, a tall rail fence upon and along which men stood and sat and out of which one by one horses were led, to be walked and trotted and then cantered back and forth along the road while the slow swapping and buying went on and the sun began to slant westward, they—

the three of them—watching and listening, the older brother with his muddy eyes and his steady, inevitable tobacco, the father commenting now and then on certain of the animals, to no one in particular.

It was after sundown when they reached home. They ate supper by lamplight, then, sitting on the doorstep, the boy watched the night fully accomplished, listening to the whip-poorwills and the frogs, when he heard his mother's voice: "Abner! No! No! Oh, God. Oh, God. Abner!" and he rose, whirled, and saw the altered light through the door where a candle stub now burned in a bottle neck on the table and his father, still in the hat and coat, at once formal and burlesque as though dressed carefully for some shabby and ceremonial violence, emptying the reservoir of the lamp back into the five-gallon kerosene can from which it had been filled, while the mother tugged at his arm until he shifted the lamp to the other hand and flung her back, not savagely or viciously, just hard, into the wall, her hands flung out against the wall for balance, her mouth open and in her face the same quality of hopeless despair as had been in her voice. Then his father saw him standing in the door.

"Go to the barn and get that can of oil we were oiling the wagon with," he said. The boy did not move. Then he could speak.

"What . . ." he cried. "What are you . . ."

"Go get that oil," his father said. "Go."

Then he was moving, running, outside the house, toward the stable: this the old habit, the old blood which he had not been permitted to choose for himself, which had been bequeathed him willy-nilly and which had run for so long (and who knew where, battening on what of outrage and savagery and lust) before it came to him. *I could keep on,* he thought. *I could run on and on and never look back, never need to see his face again. Only I can't. I can't,* the rusted can in his hand now, the liquid sploshing in it as he ran back to the house and into it, into the sound of his mother's weeping in the next room, and handed the can to his father.

"Ain't you going to even send a nigger?" he cried. "At least you sent a nigger before!"

This time his father didn't strike him. The hand came even faster than the blow had, the same hand which had set the can on the table with almost excruciating care flashing from the can toward him too quick for him to follow it, gripping him by the back of his shirt and on to tiptoe before he had seen it quit the can, the face stooping at him in breathless and frozen ferocity, the cold, dead voice speaking over him to the older brother who leaned against the table, chewing with that steady, curious, sidewise motion of cows:

"Empty the can into the big one and go on. I'll catch up with you."

"Better tie him up to the bedpost," the brother said.

"Do like I told you," the father said. Then the boy was moving, his bunched shirt and the hard, bony hand between his shoulder-blades, his toes just touching the floor, across the room and into the other one, past the sisters sitting with spread heavy thighs in the two chairs over the cold hearth, and to where his mother and aunt sat side by side on the bed, the aunt's arms about his mother's shoulders.

"Hold him," the father said. The aunt made a startled movement. "Not you," the father said. "Lennie. Take hold of him. I want to see you do it." His mother took him by the wrist. "You'll hold him better than that. If he gets loose don't you know what he is going to do? He will go up yonder." He jerked his head toward the road. "Maybe I'd better tie him."

"I'll hold him," his mother whispered.

"See you do then." Then his father was gone, the stiff foot heavy and measured upon the boards, ceasing at last.

Then he began to struggle. His mother caught him in both arms, he jerking and wrenching at them. He would be stronger in the end, he knew that. But he had no time to wait for it. "Lemme go!" he cried. "I don't want to have to hit you!"

"Let him go!" the aunt said. "If he don't go, before God, I am going up there myself!"

"Don't you see I can't?" his mother cried. "Sarty! Sarty! No! No! Help me, Lizzie!"

Then he was free. His aunt grasped at him but it was too late. He whirled, running, his mother stumbled forward onto her knees behind him, crying to the nearer sister: "Catch him, Net! Catch him!" But that was too late too, the sister (the sisters were twins, born at the same time, yet either of them now gave the impression of being, encompassing as much living meat and volume and weight as any other two of the family) not yet having begun to rise from the chair, her head, face, alone merely turned, presenting to him in the flying instant an astonishing expanse of young female features untroubled by any surprise even, wearing only an expression of bovine interest. Then he was out of the room, out of the house, in the mild dust of the starlit road and the heavy rifeness of honeysuckle, the pale ribbon unspooling with terrific slowness under his running feet, reaching the gate at last and turning in, running, his heart and lungs drumming, on up the drive toward the lighted house, the lighted door. He did not knock, he burst in, sobbing for breath, incapable for the moment of speech; he saw the astonished face of the Negro in the linen jacket without knowing when the Negro had appeared.

"De Spain!" he cried, panted. "Where's . . ." then he saw the white man too emerging from a white door down the hall. "Barn!" he cried. "Barn!"

"What?" the white man said. "Barn?"

"Yes!" the boy cried. "Barn!"

"Catch him!" the white man shouted.

But it was too late this time too. The Negro grasped his shirt, but the entire sleeve, rotten with washing, carried away, and he was out that door too and in the drive again, and had actually never ceased to run even while he was screaming into the white man's face.

Behind him the white man was shouting, "My horse! Fetch my horse!" and he thought for an instant of cutting across the park and climbing the fence into the road, but he did not know the park nor how high the vine-massed fence might be and he dared not risk it. So he ran on down the drive, blood and breath roaring; presently he was in the road again though he could not see it. He could not hear either: the galloping mare was almost upon him before he heard her, and even then he held his course, as if the very urgency of his wild grief and need must in a moment more find him wings, waiting until the ultimate instant to hurl himself aside and into the weed-choked roadside ditch as the horse thundered past and on, for an instant in furious silhouette against the stars, the tranquil early summer night sky which, even before the shape of the horse and rider vanished, stained abruptly and violently upward: a long, swirling roar incredible and soundless, blotting the stars, and he springing up and into the road again, running again, knowing it was too late yet still running even after he heard the shot and, an instant later, two shots, pausing now without knowing he had ceased to run, crying "Pap! Pap!", running again before he knew he had begun to run, stumbling, tripping over something and scrabbling up again without ceasing to run, looking backward over his shoulder at the glare as he got up, running on among the invisible trees, panting, sobbing, "Father! Father!"

At midnight he was sitting on the crest of a hill. He did not know it was midnight and he did not know how far he had come. But there was no glare behind him now and he sat now, his back toward what he had called home for four days anyhow, his face toward the dark woods which he would enter when breath was strong again, small, shaking steadily in the chill darkness, hugging himself into the remainder of his thin, rotten shirt, the grief and despair now no longer terror and fear but just grief and despair. *Father. My father,* he thought. "He was brave!" he cried suddenly, aloud but not loud, no more than a whisper: "He was! He was in the war! He was in Colonel Sartoris' cav'ry!" not knowing that his father had gone to that war a private in the fine old European sense, wearing no uniform, admitting the authority of and giving fidelity to no man or army or flag, going to war as Malbrouck himself did: for booty–it meant nothing and less than nothing to him if it were enemy booty or his own.

The slow constellations wheeled on. It would be dawn and then sun-up after a while and he would be hungry. But that would be tomorrow and now he was only cold, and walking would cure that. His breathing was easier now and he decided to get up and go on, and then he found that he had been asleep because he knew it was almost dawn, the night almost over. He could tell that from the whippoorwills. They were everywhere now among the dark trees below him, constant and inflectioned and ceaseless, so that, as the instant for giving over to the day birds drew nearer and nearer, there was no interval at all between them. He got up. He was a little stiff, but walking would cure that too as it would the cold, and soon there would be the sun. He went on down the hill, toward the dark woods within which the liquid silver voices of the birds called unceasing—the rapid and urgent beating of the urgent and quiring heart of the late spring night. He did not look back.

E. M. Forster was born in southern England in 1879. He attended Tonbridge School and King's College, Cambridge, becoming a fellow of King's College after taking his degree. During World War I he was stationed in Egypt; both before and after the war he traveled widely. His most famous novel, *A Passage to India* (1924), was written after two years' residence in India. In 1927 appeared his acute critical study, *Aspects of the Novel.* In recent years Forster has led a quiet life, reading and writing, in a Surrey village in the south of England. His short stories, collected under the titles *The Celestial Omnibus, The Story of the Siren,* and *The Eternal Moment,* show marked originality of mind and feeling. *The Hill of Devi* (1953) is an account of his early experiences in India.

E. M. FORSTER

The Road from Colonus

FOR NO very intelligible reason, Mr. Lucas had hurried ahead of his party. He was perhaps reaching the age at which independence becomes valuable, because it is so soon to be lost. Tired of attention and consideration, he liked breaking away from the younger members, to ride by himself, and to dismount unassisted. Perhaps he also relished that more subtle pleasure of being kept waiting for lunch, and of telling the others on their arrival that it was of no consequence.

So, with childish impatience, he battered the animal's sides with his heels, and made the muleteer bang it with a thick stick and prick it with a sharp one, and jolted down the hillsides through clumps of flowering shrubs and stretches of anemones and asphodel, till he heard the sound of running water, and came in sight of the group of plane trees where they were to have their meal.

Even in England those trees would have been remarkable, so

huge were they, so interlaced, so magnificently clothed in quivering green. And here in Greece they were unique, the one cool spot in that hard brilliant landscape, already scorched by the heat of an April sun. In their midst was hidden a tiny Khan or country inn, a frail mud building with a broad wooden balcony in which sat an old woman spinning, while a small brown pig, eating orange peel, stood beside her. On the wet earth below squatted two children, playing some primeval game with their fingers; and their mother, none too clean either, was messing with some rice inside. As Mrs. Forman would have said, it was all very Greek, and the fastidious Mr. Lucas felt thankful that they were bringing their food with them, and should eat it in the open air.

Still, he was glad to be there—the muleteer had helped him off—and glad that Mrs. Forman was not there to forestall his opinions—glad even that he should not see Ethel for quite half an hour. Ethel was his youngest daughter, still unmarried. She was unselfish and affectionate, and it was generally understood that she was to devote her life to her father, and be the comfort of his old age. Mrs. Forman always referred to her as Antigone, and Mr. Lucas tried to settle down to the role of Oedipus, which seemed the only one that public opinion allowed him.

He had this in common with Oedipus, that he was growing old. Even to himself it had become obvious. He had lost interest in other people's affairs, and seldom attended when they spoke to him. He was fond of talking himself but often forgot what he was going to say, and even when he succeeded, it seldom seemed worth the effort. His phrases and gestures had become stiff and set, his anecdotes, once so successful, fell flat, his silence was as meaningless as his speech. Yet he had led a healthy, active life, had worked steadily, made money, educated his children. There was nothing and no one to blame: he was simply growing old.

At the present moment, here he was in Greece, and one of the dreams of his life was realized. Forty years ago he had caught the fever of Hellenism, and all his life he had felt that could he but visit that land, he would not have lived in vain. But Athens had been dusty, Delphi wet, Thermopylae flat, and he had listened with amazement and cynicism to the rapturous explanations of his companions. Greece was like England: it was a man who was growing old, and it made no difference whether that man looked at the Thames or the Eurotas. It was his last hope of contradicting that logic of experience, and it was failing.

Yet Greece had done something for him, though he did not know it. It had made him discontented, and there are stirrings of life in discontent. He knew that he was not the victim of continual ill-luck. Something great was wrong, and he was pitted against no mediocre or accidental enemy. For the last month a strange desire had possessed him to die fighting.

"Greece is the land for young people," he said to himself as he stood under the plane trees, "but I will enter into it, I will possess it. Leaves shall be green again, water shall be sweet, the sky shall be blue. They were so forty years ago, and I will win them back. I do mind being old, and I will pretend no longer."

He took two steps forward, and immediately cold waters were gurgling over his ankle.

"Where does the water come from?" he asked himself. "I do not even know that." He remembered that all the hillsides were dry; yet here the road was suddenly covered with flowing streams.

He stopped still in amazement, saying: "Water out of a tree—out of a hollow tree? I never saw nor thought of that before."

For the enormous plane that leaned toward the Khan was hollow—it had been burned out for charcoal—and from its living trunk there gushed an impetuous spring, coating the bark with fern and moss, and flowing over the mule track to create fertile meadows beyond. The simple country folk had paid to beauty and mystery such tribute as they could, for in the rind of the tree a shrine was cut, holding a lamp and a little picture of the Virgin, inheritor of the Naiad's and Dryad's joint abode.

"I never saw anything so marvellous before," said Mr. Lucas. "I could even step inside the trunk and see where the water comes from."

For a moment he hesitated to violate the shrine. Then he remembered with a smile his own thought—"the place shall be mine; I will enter it and possess it"—and leaped almost aggressively onto a stone within.

The water pressed up steadily and noiselessly from the hollow roots and hidden crevices of the plane, forming a wonderful amber pool ere it spilled over the lip of bark onto the earth outside. Mr. Lucas tasted it and it was sweet, and when he looked up the black funnel of the trunk he saw sky which was blue, and some leaves which were green; and he remembered, without smiling, another of his thoughts.

Others had been before him—indeed he had a curious sense of companionship. Little votive offerings to the presiding Power were fastened onto the bark—tiny arms and legs and eyes in tin, grotesque models of the brain or the heart—all tokens of some recovery of strength or wisdom or love. There was no such thing as the solitude of nature, for the sorrows and joys of humanity had pressed even into the bosom of a tree. He spread out his arms and steadied himself against the soft charred wood, and then slowly leaned back, till his body was resting on the trunk behind. His eyes closed, and he had the strange feeling of one who is moving, yet at peace—the feeling of the swimmer, who, after long struggling with chopping seas, finds that after all the tide will sweep him to his goal.

So he lay motionless, conscious only of the stream below his feet, and that all things were a stream, in which he was moving.

He was aroused at last by a shock—the shock of an arrival perhaps, for when he opened his eyes, something unimagined, indefinable, had passed over all things, and made them intelligible and good.

There was meaning in the stoop of the old woman over her work, and in the quick motions of the little pig, and in her diminishing globe of wool. A young man came singing over the streams on a mule, and there was beauty in his pose and sincerity in his greeting. The sun made no accidental patterns upon the spreading roots of the trees, and there was intention in the nodding clumps of asphodel, and in the music of the water. To Mr. Lucas, who, in a brief space of time, had discovered not only Greece, but England and all the world and life, there seemed nothing ludicrous in the desire to hang within the tree another votive offering—a little model of an entire man.

"Why, here's papa, playing at being Merlin."

All unnoticed they had arrived—Ethel, Mrs. Forman, Mr. Graham, and the English-speaking dragoman. Mr. Lucas peered out at them suspiciously. They had suddenly become unfamiliar, and all that they did seemed strained and coarse.

"Allow me to give you a hand," said Mr. Graham, a young man who was always polite to his elders.

Mr. Lucas felt annoyed. "Thank you, I can manage perfectly well by myself," he replied. His foot slipped as he stepped out of the tree, and went into the spring.

"Oh papa, my papa!" said Ethel, "what are you doing? Thank goodness I have got a change for you on the mule."

She tended him carefully, giving him clean socks and dry boots, and then sat him down on the rug beside the lunch basket, while she went with the others to explore the grove.

They came back in ecstasies, in which Mr. Lucas tried to join. But he found them intolerable. Their enthusiasm was superficial, commonplace, and spasmodic. They had no perception of the coherent beauty that was flowering around them. He tried at least to explain his feelings, and what he said was:

"I am altogether pleased with the appearance of this place. It impresses me very favorably. The trees are fine, remarkably fine for Greece, and there is something very poetic in the spring of clear running water. The people too seem kindly and civil. It is decidedly an attractive place."

Mrs. Forman upbraided him for his tepid praise.

"Oh, it is a place in a thousand!" she cried. "I could live and die here! I really would stop if I had not to be back at Athens! It reminds me of the Colonus of Sophocles."

"Well, I must stop," said Ethel. "I positively must."

"Yes, do! You and your father! Antigone and Oedipus. Of course you must stop at Colonus."

Mr. Lucas was almost breathless with excitement. When he stood within the tree, he had believed that his happiness would be independent of locality. But these few minutes' conversation had undeceived him. He no longer trusted himself to journey through the world, for old thoughts, old wearinesses might be waiting to rejoin him as soon as he left the shade of the planes, and the music of the virgin water. To sleep in the Khan with the gracious, kind-eyed country people, to watch the bats flit about within the globe of shade, and see the moon turn the golden patterns into silver—one such night would place him beyond relapse, and confirm him forever in the kingdom he had regained. But all his lips could say was: "I should be willing to put in a night here."

"You mean a week, papa! It would be sacrilege to put in less."

"A week then, a week," said his lips, irritated at being corrected, while his heart was leaping with joy. All through lunch he spoke to them no more, but watched the place he should know so well, and the people who would so soon be his companions and friends. The inmates of the Khan only consisted of an old woman, a middle-aged woman, a young man and two children, and to none of them had he spoken, yet he loved them as he loved everything that moved or breathed or existed beneath the benedictory shade of the planes.

"En route!" said the shrill voice of Mrs. Forman. "Ethel! Mr. Graham! The best of things must end."

"Tonight," thought Mr. Lucas, "they will light the little lamp by the shrine. And when we all sit together on the balcony, perhaps they will tell me which offerings they put up."

"I beg your pardon, Mr. Lucas," said Graham, "but they want to fold up the rug you are sitting on."

Mr. Lucas got up, saying to himself: "Ethel shall go to bed first, and then I will try to tell them about my offering too—for it is a thing I must do. I think they will understand if I am left with them alone."

Ethel touched him on the cheek. "Papa! I've called you three times. All the mules are here."

"Mules? What mules?"

"Our mules. We're all waiting. Oh, Mr. Graham, do help my father on."

"I don't know what you're talking about, Ethel."

"My dearest papa, we must start. You know we have to get to Olympia tonight."

Mr. Lucas in pompous, confident tones replied: "I always did wish, Ethel, that you had a better head for plans. You know perfectly well that we are putting in a week here. It is your own suggestion."

Ethel was startled into impoliteness. "What a perfectly ridiculous idea. You must have known I was joking. Of course I meant I wished we could."

"Ah! if we could only do what we wished!" sighed Mrs. Forman, already seated on her mule.

"Surely," Ethel continued in calmer tones, "you didn't think I meant it."

"Most certainly I did. I have made all plans on the supposition that we are stopping here, and it will be extremely inconvenient, indeed, impossible for me to start."

He delivered this remark with an air of great conviction, and Mrs. Forman and Mr. Graham had to turn away to hide their smiles.

"I am sorry I spoke so carelessly; it was wrong of me. But, you know, we can't break up our party, and even one night here would make us miss the boat at Patras."

Mrs. Forman, in an aside, called Mr. Graham's attention to the excellent way in which Ethel managed her father.

"I don't mind about the Patras boat. You said that we should stop here, and we are stopping."

It seemed as if the inhabitants of the Khan had divined in some mysterious way that the altercation touched them. The old woman stopped her spinning, while the young man and the two children stood behind Mr. Lucas, as if supporting him.

Neither arguments nor entreaties moved him. He said little, but he was absolutely determined, because for the first time he saw his daily life aright. What need had he to return to England? Who would miss him? His friends were dead or cold. Ethel loved him in a way, but, as was right, she had other interests. His other children he seldom saw. He had only one other relative, his sister Julia, whom he both feared and hated. It was no effort to struggle. He would be a fool as well as a coward if he stirred from the place which brought him happiness and peace.

At last Ethel, to humor him, and not disinclined to air her modern Greek, went into the Khan with the astonished dragoman to look at the rooms. The woman inside received them with loud welcomes, and the young man, when no one was looking, began to lead Mr. Lucas' mule to the stable.

"Drop it, you brigand!" shouted Graham, who always declared that foreigners could understand English if they chose. He was right, for the man obeyed, and they all stood waiting for Ethel's return.

She emerged at last, with close-gathered skirts, followed by the dragóman bearing the little pig, which he had bought at a bargain.

"My dear papa, I will do all I can for you, but stop in that Khan—no."

"Are there—fleas?" asked Mrs. Forman.

Ethel intimated that "fleas" was not the word.

"Well, I am afraid that settles it," said Mrs. Forman, "I know how particular Mr. Lucas is."

"It does not settle it," said Mr. Lucas. "Ethel, you go on, I do not want you. I don't know why I ever consulted you. I shall stop here alone."

"That is absolute nonsense," said Ethel, losing her temper. "How can you be left alone at your age? How would you get your meals or your bath? All your letters are waiting for you at Patras. You'll miss the boat. That means missing the London operas, and upsetting all your engagements for the month. And as if you could travel by yourself!"

"They might knife you," was Mr. Graham's contribution.

The Greeks said nothing; but whenever Mr. Lucas looked their way, they beckoned him towards the Khan. The children would even have drawn him by the coat, and the old woman on the balcony stopped her almost completed spinning, and fixed him with mysterious appealing eyes. As he fought, the issue assumed gigantic proportions, and he believed that he was not merely stopping because he had regained youth or seen beauty or found happiness, but because in that place and with those people a supreme event was awaiting him which would transfigure the face of the world. The moment was so tremendous that he abandoned words and arguments as useless, and rested on the strength of his mighty unrevealed allies: silent men, murmuring water, and whispering trees. For the whole place called with one voice, articulate to him, and his garrulous opponents became every minute more meaningless and absurd. Soon they would be tired and go chattering away into the sun, leaving him to the cool grove and the moonlight and the destiny he foresaw.

Mrs. Forman and the dragoman had indeed already started, amid the piercing screams of the little pig, and the struggle might have gone on indefinitely if Ethel had not called in Mr. Graham.

"Can you help me?" she whispered. "He is absolutely unmanageable."

"I'm no good at arguing—but if I could help you in any other way—" and he looked down complacently at his well-made figure.

Ethel hesitated. Then she said: "Help me in any way you can. After all, it is for his good that we do it."

"Then have his mule led up behind him."

So when Mr. Lucas thought he had gained the day, he suddenly felt himself lifted off the ground, and sat sideways on the saddle, and at the same time the mule started off at a trot. He said nothing, for he had nothing to say, and even his face showed little emotion as he felt the shade pass and heard the sound of the water cease. Mr. Graham was running at his side, hat in hand, apologizing.

"I know I had no business to do it, and I do beg your pardon awfully. But I do hope that some day you too will feel that I was—damn!"

A stone had caught him in the middle of the back. It was thrown by the little boy, who was pursuing them along the mule track. He was followed by his sister, also throwing stones.

Ethel screamed to the dragoman, who was some way ahead with Mrs. Forman, but before he could rejoin them, another adversary appeared. It was the young Greek, who had cut them off in front, and now dashed down at Mr. Lucas' bridle. Fortunately Graham was an expert boxer, and it did not take him a moment to beat down the youth's feeble defence, and to send him sprawling with a bleeding mouth into the asphodel. By this time the dragoman had arrived, the children, alarmed at the fate of their brother, had desisted, and the rescue party, if such it is to be considered, retired in disorder to the trees.

"Little devils!" said Graham, laughing with triumph. "That's the modern Greek all over. Your father meant money if he stopped, and they consider we were taking it out of their pocket."

"Oh, they are terrible—simple savages! I don't know how I shall ever thank you. You've saved my father."

"I only hope you didn't think me brutal."

"No," replied Ethel with a little sigh. "I admire strength."

Meanwhile the cavalcade re-formed, and Mr. Lucas, who, as Mrs. Forman said, bore his disappointment wonderfully well, was put comfortably on to his mule. They hurried up the opposite hillside, fearful of another attack, and it was not until they had left the eventful place far behind that Ethel found an opportunity to speak to her father and ask his pardon for the way she had treated him.

"You seemed so different, dear father, and you quite frightened me. Now I feel that you are your old self again."

He did not answer, and she concluded that he was not unnaturally offended at her behavior.

By one of those curious tricks of mountain scenery, the place they had left an hour before suddenly reappeared far below them. The Khan was hidden under the green dome, but in the open there still stood three figures, and through the pure air rose up a faint cry of defiance or farewell.

Mr. Lucas stopped irresolutely, and let the reins fall from his hand.

"Come, father dear," said Ethel gently.

He obeyed, and in another moment a spur of the hill hid the dangerous scene for ever.

II

It was breakfast time, but the gas was alight, owing to the fog. Mr. Lucas was in the middle of an account of a bad night he had spent. Ethel, who was to be married in a few weeks, had her arms on the table, listening.

"First the door bell rang, then you came back from the theater. Then the dog started, and after the dog the cat. And at three in the morning a young hooligan passed by singing. Oh yes: then there was the water gurgling in the pipe above my head."

"I think that was only the bath water running away," said Ethel, looking rather worn.

"Well, there's nothing I dislike more than running water. It's perfectly impossible to sleep in the house. I shall give it up. I shall give notice next quarter. I shall tell the landlord plainly, 'The reason I am giving up the house is this: it is perfectly impossible to sleep in it.' If he says—says—well, what has he got to say?"

"Some more toast, father?"

"Thank you, my dear." He took it, and there was an interval of peace.

But he soon recommenced. "I'm not going to submit to the practicing next door as tamely as they think. I wrote and told them so—didn't I?"

"Yes," said Ethel, who had taken care that the letter should not reach. "I have seen the governess, and she has promised to arrange it differently. And Aunt Julia hates noise. It is sure to be all right."

Her aunt, being the only unattached member of the family, was coming to keep house for her father when she left him. The reference was not a happy one, and Mr. Lucas commenced a series of half-articulate sighs, which was only stopped by the arrival of the post.

"Oh, what a parcel!" cried Ethel. "For me! What can it be! Greek stamps. This is most exciting!"

It proved to be some asphodel bulbs sent by Mrs. Forman from Athens for planting in the conservatory.

"Doesn't it bring it all back! You remember the asphodels, father. And all wrapped up in Greek newspapers. I wonder if I can read them still. I used to be able to, you know."

She rattled on, hoping to conceal the laughter of the children next door—a favorite source of querulousness at breakfast time.

"Listen to me! 'A rural disaster.' Oh, I've hit on something sad. But never mind. 'Last Tuesday at Platansite, in the province of Messenia, a shocking tragedy occurred. A large tree'—aren't I getting on well?—'blew down in the night and'—wait a minute —oh, dear! 'crushed to death the five occupants of the little Khan there, who had apparently been sitting in the balcony. The bodies of Maria Rhomaides, the aged proprietress, and of her daughter, aged forty-six, were easily recognizable, whereas that of her grandson'—oh, the rest is really too horrid; I wish I had never tried it, and what's more I feel to have heard the name Plataniste before. We didn't stop there, did we, in the spring?"

"We had lunch," said Mr. Lucas, with a faint expression of trouble on his vacant face. "Perhaps it was where the dragoman bought the pig."

"Of course," said Ethel in a nervous voice. "Where the dragoman bought the little pig. How terrible!"

"Very terrible!" said her father, whose attention was wandering to the noisy children next door. Ethel suddenly started to her feet with genuine interest.

"Good gracious!" she exclaimed. "This is an old paper. It happened not lately but in April—the night of Tuesday the eighteenth—and we—we must have been there in the afternoon."

"So we were," said Mr. Lucas. She put her hand to her heart, scarcely able to speak.

"Father, dear father, I must say it: you wanted to stop there. All those people, those poor half-savage people, tried to keep you, and they're dead. The whole place, it says, is in ruins, and even the stream has changed its course. Father, dear, if it had not been for me, and if Arthur had not helped me, you must have been killed."

Mr. Lucas waved his hand irritably. "It is not a bit of good speaking to the governess, I shall write to the landlord and say, 'The reason I am giving up the house is this: the dog barks, the children next door are intolerable, and I cannot stand the noise of running water.' "

Ethel did not check his babbling. She was aghast at the narrowness of the escape, and for a long time kept silence. At last she said: "Such a marvelous deliverance does make one believe in Providence."

Mr. Lucas, who was still composing his letter to the landlord, did not reply.

"Frank O'Connor" is the pseudonym of Michael O'Donovan, who was born in Ireland in 1903. His parents were poor, and he has stated that much of his education was acquired "haphazard in a public library." After attending the College of the Christian Brothers at Cork, he became a professional librarian. For several years he served as a director of the Abbey Theater in Dublin. Recently he has made extended visits to the United States and has taught a course in the short story at Northwestern University and at Harvard. All of O'Connor's writing has been done in the short-story form. His stories range over the whole of Irish life—rural and urban, religious and secular—and though carefully planned and revised they seem written with spontaneous exuberance and vitality. In 1952 he published *The Stories of Frank O'Connor*.

FRANK O'CONNOR

Uprooted

SPRING had only come and already he was tired to death; tired of the city, tired of his job. He had come up from the country intending to do wonders, but he was as far as ever from that. He would be lucky if he could carry on, be at school each morning at half-past nine and satisfy his half-witted principal.

He lodged in a small red-brick house in Rathmines that was kept by a middle-aged brother and sister who had been left a bit of money and thought they would end their days enjoyably in a city. They did not enjoy themselves, regretted their little farm in Kerry, and were glad of Ned Keating because he could talk to them about all the things they remembered and loved.

Keating was a slow, cumbrous young man with dark eyes and a dark cow's-lick that kept tumbling into them. He had a slight stammer and ran his hand through his long limp hair from pure nervousness. He had always been dreamy and serious. Sometimes on market days you saw him standing for an hour in Nolan's shop, turning the pages of a schoolbook. When he could not afford it he put it back with a sigh and went off to find his father in a pub, just raising his eyes to smile at Jack Nolan. After his elder brother Tom had gone for the church he and his father had constant rows. Nothing would do Ned now but to be a teacher. Hadn't he all he wanted now? his father asked. Hadn't he the place to himself? What did he want going teaching? But Ned was stubborn. With an obstinate, almost despairing determination he had fought his way through the training college into a city job. The city was what he had always wanted. And now the city had failed him. In the evenings you could still see him poking round the second-hand bookshops on the quays, but his eyes were already beginning to lose their eagerness.

It had all seemed so clear. But then he had not counted on his own temper. He was popular because of his gentleness, but how many concessions that involved! He was hesitating, good-natured, slow to see guile, slow to contradict. He felt he was constantly underestimating his own powers. He even felt he lacked spontaneity. He did not drink, smoked little, and saw dangers and losses everywhere. He blamed himself for avarice and cowardice. The story he liked best was about the country boy and the letter box. "Indeed, what a fool you think I am! Put me letther in a pump!"

He was in no danger of putting his letter in a pump or anywhere else for the matter of that. He had only one friend, a nurse in Vincent's Hospital, a wild, light-hearted, light-headed girl. He was very fond of her and supposed that some day when he had money enough he would ask her to marry him; but not yet: and at the same time something that was both shyness and caution kept him from committing himself too far. Sometimes he planned excursions beside the usual weekly walk or visit to the pictures but somehow they seldom came to anything.

He no longer knew why he had come to the city, but it was not for the sake of the bed-sitting-room in Rathmines, the oblong of dusty garden outside the window, the trams clanging up and down, the shelf full of second-hand books, or the occasional visit to the pictures. Half humorously, half despairingly, he would sometimes clutch his head in his hands and admit to himself that he had no notion of what he wanted. He would have liked to leave it all and go to Glasgow or New York as a laborer, not because he was romantic, but because he felt that only when he had to work with his hands for a living and was no longer sure of his bed would he find out what all his ideals and emotions meant and where he could fit them into the scheme of his life.

But no sooner did he set out for school next morning, striding slowly along the edge of the canal, watching the trees become green again and the tall claret-colored houses painted on the quiet surface of the water, than all his fancies took flight. Put his letter in a pump indeed! He would continue to be submissive and draw his salary and wonder how much he could save and when he would be able to buy a little house to bring his girl into; a nice thing to think of on a spring morning: a house of his own and a wife in the bed beside him. And his nature would continue to contract about him, every ideal, every generous impulse another mesh to draw his head down tighter to his knees till in ten years time it would tie him hand and foot.

II

Tom who was a curate in Wicklow wrote and suggested that they might go home together for the long week-end, and on Saturday morning they set out in Tom's old Ford. It was Easter weather, pearly and cold. They stopped at several pubs on the way and Tom ordered whiskies. Ned was feeling expansive and joined him. He had never quite grown used to his brother, partly because of old days when he felt that Tom was getting the education he should have got, partly because his ordination seemed to have shut him off from the rest of the family, and now it was as though he were trying to surmount it by his boisterous manner and affected bonhomie. He was like a man shouting to his comrades across a great distance. He was different from Ned; lighter in color of hair and skin; fat-headed, fresh-complexioned, deep-voiced, and autocratic; an irascible, humorous, friendly man who was well liked by those he worked for. Ned, who was shy and all tied up within himself, envied him his way with men in garages and barmaids in hotels.

It was nightfall when they reached home. Their father was in his shirtsleeves at the gate waiting to greet them, and immediately their mother rushed out as well. The lamp was standing in the window and threw its light as far as the whitewashed gateposts. Little Brigid, the girl from up the hill who helped their mother now she was growing old, stood in the doorway in half-silhouette. When her eyes caught theirs she bent her head in confusion.

Nothing was changed in the tall, bare, whitewashed kitchen. The harness hung in the same place on the wall, the rosary on the same nail in the fireplace, by the stool where their mother usually sat; table under the window, churn against the back door, stair without banisters mounting straight to the attic door that yawned in the wall—all seemed as unchanging as the sea outside. Their mother sat on the stool, her hands on her knees, a colored shawl tied tightly about her head, like a gipsy woman with her battered yellow face and loud voice. Their father, fresh-complexioned like Tom, stocky and broken-bottomed, gazed out the front door, leaning with one hand on the dresser in the pose of an orator while Brigid wet the tea.

"I said ye'd be late," their father proclaimed triumphantly, twisting his moustache. "Didn't I, woman? Didn't I say they'd be late?"

"He did, he did," their mother assured them. " 'Tis true for him."

"Ah, I knew ye'd be making halts. But damn it, if I wasn't put astray by Thade Lahy's car going east!"

"And was that Thade Lahy's car?" their mother asked in a shocked tone.

"I told ye 'twas Thade Lahy's," piped Brigid, plopping about in her long frieze gown and bare feet.

"Sure I should know it, woman," old Tomas said with chagrin. "He must have gone into town without us noticing him."

"Oye, and how did he do that?" asked their mother.

"Leave me alone now," Tomas said despairingly. "I couldn't tell you, I could not tell you."

"My goodness, I was sure that was the Master's car," their

mother said wonderingly, pulling distractedly at the tassels of her shawl.

"I'd know the rattle of Thade Lahy's car anywhere," little Brigid said very proudly and quite unregarded.

It seemed to Ned that he was interrupting a conversation that had been going on since his last visit, and that the road outside and the sea beyond it, and every living thing that passed before them, formed a pantomime that was watched endlessly and passionately from the darkness of the little cottage.

"Wisha, I never asked if ye'd like a drop of something," their father said with sudden vexation.

"Is it whisky?" boomed Tom.

"Why? Would you sooner whisky?"

"Can't you pour it out first and ask us after?" growled Tom.

"The whisky, is it?"

" 'Tis not. I didn't come all the ways to this place for what I can get better at home. You'd better have a bottle ready for me to take back."

"Coleen will have it. Damn it, wasn't it only last night I said to Coleen that you'd likely want a bottle? Some way it struck me you would. Oh, he'll have it, he'll have it."

"Didn't they catch that string of misery yet?" asked Tom with the cup to his lips.

"Ah, man alive, you'd want to be a greyhound to catch him. God Almighty, hadn't they fifty police after him last November, scouring the mountains from one end to the other and all they caught was a glimpse of the white of his ass. Ah, but the priest preached a terrible sermon against him—by name, Tom, by name!"

"Is old Murphy blowing about it still?" growled Tom.

"Oh, let me alone now!" Tomas threw his hands to heaven and strode to and fro in his excitement, his bucket-bottom wagging. Ned knew to his sorrow that his father could be prudent, silent, and calculating; he knew only too well the cock of the head, the narrowing of the eyes, but, like a child, the old man loved innocent excitement and reveled in scenes of the wildest passion, all about nothing. Like an old actor he turned everything to drama. "The like of it for abuse was never heard, never heard, never heard! How Coleen could ever raise his head again after it! And where the man got the words from! Tom, my treasure, my son, you'll never have the like."

"I'd spare my breath to cool my porridge," Tom replied scornfully. "I dare say you gave up your own still so?"

"I didn't, Tom, I didn't. The drop I make, 'twould harm no one. Only a drop for Christmas and Easter."

The lamp was in its own place on the rear wall, and made a circle of brightness on the fresh lime wash. Their mother was leaning over the fire with joined hands, lost in thought. The front door was open and night thickening outside, the colored night of the west; and as they ate their father walked to and fro in long ungainly strides, pausing each time at the door to give a glance up and down the road and at the fire to hoist his broken bottom to warm. Ned heard steps come up the road from the west. His father heard them too. He returned to the door and glued his hand to the jamb. Ned covered his eyes with his hands and felt that everything was as it had always been. He could hear the noise of the strand as a background to the voices.

"God be with you, Tomas," the voice said.

"God and Mary be with you, Teig." (In Irish they were speaking.) "What way are you?"

"Well, honor and praise be to God. 'Tis a fine night."

" 'Tis, 'tis, 'tis so indeed. A grand night, praise be to God."

"Musha, who is it?" their mother asked, looking round.

" 'Tis young Teig," their father replied, looking after him.

"Shemus's young Teig?"

" 'Tis, 'tis, 'tis."

"But where would Shemus's young Teig be going at this hour of night? 'Tisn't to the shop?"

"No, woman, no, no, no. Up to the uncle's I suppose."

"Is it Ned Willie's?"

"He's sleeping at Ned Willie's," Brigid chimed in in her high-pitched voice, timid but triumphant. " 'Tis since the young teacher came to them."

There was no more to be said. Everything was explained and Ned smiled. The only unfamiliar voice, little Brigid's, seemed the most familiar of all.

III

Tom said first Mass next morning and the household, all but Brigid, went. They drove, and Tomas in high glee sat in front with Tom, waving his hand and shouting greetings at all they met. He was like a boy, so intense was his pleasure. The chapel was perched high above the road. Outside the morning was gray and beyond the windy edge of the cliff was the sea. The wind blew straight in, setting cloaks and petticoats flying.

After dinner as the two boys were returning from a series of visits to the neighbors' houses their father rushed down the road to meet them, shaking them passionately by the hand and asking were they well. When they were seated in the kitchen he opened up the subject of his excitement.

"Well," he said, "I arranged a grand little outing for ye to-morrow, thanks be to God," and to identify further the source of his inspiration he searched at the back of his neck for the peak of his cap and raised it solemnly.

"Musha, what outing are you talking about?" their mother asked angrily.

"I arranged for us to go over the bay to your brother's."

"And can't you leave the poor boys alone?" she bawled. "Haven't they only the one day? Isn't it for the rest they came?"

"Even so, even so, even so," Tomas said with mounting passion. "Aren't their own cousins to lay eyes on them?"

"I was in Carriganassa for a week last summer," said Tom.

"Yes, but I wasn't, and Ned wasn't. 'Tis only decent."

" 'Tisn't decency is worrying you at all but drink," growled Tom.

"Oh!" gasped his father, fishing for the peak of his cap to swear with, "that I might be struck dead!"

"Be quiet, you old heathen!" crowed his wife. "That's the truth, Tom my pulse. Plenty of drink is what he wants where he won't be under my eye. Leave ye stop at home."

"I can't stop at home, woman," shouted Tomas. "Why do you be always picking at me? I must go whether they come or not. I must go, I must go, and that's all there is about it."

"Why must you?" asked his wife.

"Because I warned Red Pat and Dempsey," he stormed. "And

the woman from the island is coming as well to see a daughter of hers that's married there. And what's more, I borrowed Cassidy's boat and he lent it at great inconvenience, and 'twould be very bad manners for me to throw his kindness back in his face. I must go."

"Oh, we may as well all go," said Tom.

It blew hard all night and Tomas, all anxiety, was out at break of day to watch the whitecaps on the water. While the boys were at breakfast he came in and, leaning his arms on the table with hands joined as though in prayer, he announced in a caressing voice that it was a beautiful day, thank God, a pet day with a moist gentle little bit of a breezheen that would only blow them over. His voice would have put a child to sleep, but his wife continued to nag and scold, and he stumped out again in a fury and sat on the wall with his back to the house and his legs crossed, chewing his pipe. He was dressed in his best clothes, a respectable blue tailcoat and pale frieze trousers with only one patch on the seat. He had turned his cap almost right way round so that the peak covered his right ear.

He was all over the boat like a boy. Dempsey, a haggard, pockmarked, melancholy man with a soprano voice of astounding penetration, took the tiller and Red Patrick the sail. Tomas clambered into the bows and stood there with one knee up, leaning forward like a figurehead. He knew the bay like a book. The island woman was perched on the ballast with her rosary in her hands and her shawl over her eyes to shut out the sight of the waves. The cumbrous old boat took the sail lightly enough and Ned leaned back on his elbows against the side, rejoicing in it all.

"She's laughing," his father said delightedly when her bows ran white.

"Whose boat is that, Dempsey?" he asked, screwing up his eyes as another brown sail tilted ahead of them.

" 'Tis the island boat," shrieked Dempsey.

" 'Tis not, Dempsey. 'Tis not indeed, my love. That's not the island boat."

"Whose boat is it then?"

"It must be some boat from Carriganassa, Dempsey."

" 'Tis the island boat I tell you."

"Ah, why will you be contradicting me, Dempsey, my treasure? 'Tis not the island boat. The island boat has a dark brown sail; 'tis only a month since 'twas tarred, and that's an old tarred sail, and what proves it out and out, Dempsey, the island-boat sail has a patch in the corner."

He was leaning well over the bows, watching the rocks that fled beneath them, a dark purple. He rested his elbow on his raised knee and looked back at them, his brown face sprinkled with spray and lit from below by the accumulated flickerings of the water. His flesh seemed to dissolve, to become transparent, while his blue eyes shone with extraordinary brilliance. Ned half-closed his eyes and watched sea and sky slowly mount and sink behind the red-brown, sun-filled sail and the poised and eager figure.

"Tom!" shouted his father, and the battered old face peered at them from under the arch of the sail, with which it was almost one in tone, the silvery light filling it with warmth.

"Well?" Tom's voice was an inexpressive boom.

"You were right last night, Tom, my boy. My treasure, my son, you were right. 'Twas for the drink I came."

"Ah, do you tell me so?" Tom asked ironically.

" 'Twas, 'twas, 'twas," the old man said regretfully. " 'Twas for the drink. 'Twas so, my darling. They were always decent people, your mother's people, and 'tis her knowing how decent they are makes her so suspicious. She's a good woman, a fine woman, your poor mother, may the Almighty God bless her and keep her and watch over her."

"Aaaa-men," Tom chanted irreverently as his father shook his old cap piously toward the sky.

"But, Tom! Are you listening, Tom?"

"Well, what is it now?"

"I had another reason."

"Had you indeed?" Tom's tone was not encouraging.

"I had, I had, God's truth, I had. God blast the lie I'm telling you, Tom, I had."

" 'Twas boasting out of the pair of ye," shrieked Dempsey from the stern, the wind whipping the shrill notes from his lips and scattering them wildly like scraps of paper.

" 'Twas so, Dempsey, 'twas so. You're right, Dempsey. You're always right. The blessing of God on you, Dempsey, for you always had the true word." Tomas's laughing leprechaun countenance gleamed under the bellying, tilting, chocolate-colored sail and his powerful voice beat Dempsey's down. "And would you blame me?"

"The O'Donnells hadn't the beating of them in their own hand," screamed Dempsey.

"Thanks be to God for all His goodness and mercy," shouted Tomas, again waving his cap in a gesture of recognition toward the spot where he felt the Almighty might be listening, "they have not. They have not so, Dempsey. And they have a good hand. The O'Donnells are a good family and an old family and a kind family, but they never had the like of my two sons."

"And they were stiff enough with you when you came for the daughter," shrieked Dempsey.

"They were, Dempsey, they were. They were stiff. They were so. You wouldn't blame them, Dempsey. They were an old family and I was nothing only a landless man." With a fierce gesture the old man pulled his cap still further over his ear, spat, gave his moustache a tug and leaned at a still more precarious angle over the bow, his blue eyes dancing with triumph. "But I had the gumption, Dempsey. I had the gumption, my love."

The islands slipped past; the gulf of water narrowed and grew calmer, and white cottages could be seen scattered under the tall ungainly church. It was a wild and rugged coast, the tide was full, and they had to pull in as best they could among the rocks. Red Patrick leaped lightly ashore to draw in the boat. The others stepped after him into several inches of water and Red Patrick, himself precariously poised, held them from slipping. Rather shamefastly, Ned and Tom took off their shoes.

"Don't do that!" shrieked their father. "We'll carry ye up. Mother of God, yeer poor feet!"

"Will you shut your old gob?" Tom said angrily.

They halted for a moment at the stile outside Caheragh's. Old Caheragh had a red beard and a broad, smiling face. Then they went on to O'Donnell's who had two houses, modern and old, separated by a yard. In one lived Uncle Maurice and his family and in the other Maurice's married son, Sean. Ned and Tom remained with Sean and his wife. Tom and he were old friends. When he spoke he rarely looked at Tom, merely giving him a sidelong glance that just reached to his chin and then dropped his eyes with a peculiar timid smile. " 'Twas," Ned heard him say, and then: "He did," and after that: "Hardly." Shuvaun was tall, nervous and matronly. She clung to their hands with an excess of eagerness as though she couldn't bear to let them go, uttering ejaculations of tenderness, delight, astonishment, pity, and admiration. Her speech was full of diminutives: "childeen," "handeen," "boateen." Three young children scrambled about the floor with a preoccupation scarcely broken by the strangers. Shuvaun picked her way through them, filling the kettle and cutting the bread, and then, as though afraid of neglecting Tom, she clutched his hand again. Her feverish concentration gave an impression that its very intensity bewildered her and made it impossible for her to understand one word they said. In three days' time it would all begin to drop into place in her mind and then she would begin quoting them.

Young Niall O'Donnell came in with his girl; one of the Deignans from up the hill. She was plump and pert; she had been in service in town. Niall was a well-built boy with a soft, wild-eyed, sensuous face and a deep mellow voice of great power. While they were having a cup of tea in the parlor where the three or four family photos were skyed, Ned saw the two of them again through the back window. They were standing on the high ground behind the house with the spring sky behind them and the light in their faces. Niall was asking her something but she, more interested in the sitting-room window, only shook her head.

"Ye only just missed yeer father," said their Uncle Maurice when they went across to the other house for dinner. Maurice was a tight-lipped little man with a high bald forehead and a snappy voice. "He went off to Owney Pat's only this minute."

"The devil!" said Tom. "I knew he was out to dodge me. Did you give him whisky?"

"What the hell else could I give him?" snapped Maurice. "Do you think 'twas tea the old coot was looking for?"

Tom took the place of honor at the table. He was the favorite. Through the doorway into the bedroom could be seen a big canopy bed and on the whiteness of a raised pillow a skeleton face in a halo of smoke-blue hair surmounted with what looked suspiciously like a mauve tea-cosy. Sometimes the white head would begin to stir and everyone fell silent while Niall, the old man's pet, translated the scarcely audible whisper. Sometimes Niall would go in with his stiff ungainly swagger and repeat one of Tom's jokes in his drawling, powerful bass. The hens stepped daintily about their feet, poking officious heads between them, and rushing out the door with a wild flutter and shriek when one of the girls hooshed them. Something timeless, patriarchal and restful about it made Ned notice everything. It was as though he had never seen his mother's house before.

"Tell me," Tom boomed with mock concern, leaning over confidentially to his uncle and looking under his brows at young Niall, "speaking as a clergyman and for the good of the family and so on, is that son of yours coorting Delia Deignan?"

"Why? Was the young blackguard along with her again?" snapped Maurice in amusement.

"Of course I might be mistaken," Tom said doubtfully.

"You wouldn't know a Deignan, to be sure," Sean said dryly.

"Isn't any of them married yet?" asked Tom.

"No, by damn, no," said Maurice. "Isn't it a wonder?"

"Because," Tom went on in the same solemn voice, "I want someone to look after this young brother of mine. Dublin is a wild sort of place and full of temptations. Ye wouldn't know a decent little girl I could ask?"

"Cait! Cait!" they all shouted, Niall's deep voice loudest of all.

"Now all the same, Delia looks a smart little piece," said Tom.

"No, Cait! Cait! Delia isn't the same since she went to town. She has notions of herself. Leave him marry Cait!"

Niall rose gleefully and shambled in to the old man. With a gamesome eye on the company Tom whispered:

"Is she a quiet sort of girl? I wouldn't like Ned to get anyone rough."

"She is, she is," they said, "a grand girl!"

Sean rose quietly and went to the door with his head bowed.

"God knows, if anyone knows he should know and all the times he manhandled her."

Tom sat bolt upright with mock indignation while the table rocked. Niall shouted the joke into his grandfather's ear. The mauve tea-cosy shook; it was the only indication of the old man's amusement.

IV

The Deignans' house was on top of a hill high over the road and commanded a view of the countryside for miles. The two brothers with Sean and the O'Donnell girls reached it by a long winding boreen that threaded its way uncertainly through little gray rocky fields and walls of unmortared stone which rose against the sky along the edges of the hill like lacework. On their way they met another procession coming down the hill. It was headed by their father and the island woman, arm in arm, and behind came two locals with Dempsey and Red Patrick. All the party except the island woman were well advanced in liquor. That was plain when their father rushed forward to shake them all by the hand and ask them how they were. He said that divil such honorable and kindly people as the people of Carriganassa were to be found in the whole world, and of these there was no one a patch on the O'Donnells; kings and sons of kings as you could see from one look at them. He had only one more call to pay and promised to be at Caheragh's within a quarter of an hour.

They looked over the Deignans' half-door. The kitchen was empty. The girls began to titter. They knew the Deignans must have watched them coming from Maurice's door. The kitchen was a beautiful room; woodwork and furniture, homemade and shapely, were painted a bright red-brown and the painted dresser shone with pretty ware. They entered and looked about them. Nothing was to be heard but the tick of the cheap alarm-clock on the dresser. One of the girls began to giggle hysterically. Sean raised his voice.

"Are ye in or are ye out, bad cess to ye!"

For a moment there was no reply. Then a quick step sounded in the attic and a girl descended the stairs at a run, drawing a black knitted shawl tighter about her shoulders. She was perhaps twenty-eight or thirty, with a narrow face, sharp like a ferret's, and blue nervous eyes. She entered the kitchen awkwardly sideways, giving the customary greetings but without looking at anyone.

"A hundred welcomes. . . . How are ye? . . . 'Tis a fine day."

The O'Donnell girls giggled again. Nora Deignan looked at them in astonishment, biting nervously at the tassel of her shawl. She had tiny sharp white teeth.

"What is it, aru?" she asked.

"Musha, will you stop your old cimeens," boomed Tom, "and tell us where's Cait from you? You don't think 'twas to see your ugly puss that we came up here?"

"Cait!" Nora called in a low voice.

"What is it?" another voice replied from upstairs.

"Damn well you know what it is," bellowed Tom, "and you cross-eyed expecting us since morning. Will you come down out of that or will I go up and fetch you?"

There was the same hasty step and a second girl descended the stairs. It was only later that Ned was able to realize how beautiful she was. She had the same narrow pointed face as her sister, the same slight features sharpened by a sort of animal instinct, the same blue cyes with their startled brightness; but all seemed to have been differently composed, and her complexion had a transparency as though her whole nature were shining through it. "Child of Light, thy limbs are burning through the veil which seems to hide them," Ned found himself murmuring. She came on them in the same hostile way, blushing furiously. Tom's eyes rested on her; soft, bleary, emotional eyes incredibly unlike her own.

"Have you nothing to say to me, Cait?" he boomed, and Ned thought his very voice was soft and clouded.

"Oh, a hundred welcomes." Her blue eyes rested for a moment on him with what seemed a fierce candor and penetration and went past him to the open door. Outside a soft rain was beginning to fall; heavy clouds crushed down the gray landscape, which grew clearer as it merged into one common plane: the little gray bumpy fields with the walls of gray unmortared stone that drifted hither and over across them like blown sand, the whitewashed farmhouses lost to the sun sinking back into the brown-gray hillsides.

"Nothing else, my child?" he growled, pursing his lips.

"How are you?"

"The politeness is suffocating you. Where's Delia?"

"Here I am," said Delia from the doorway immediately behind him. In her furtive way she had slunk round the house. Her bland impertinence raised a laugh.

"The reason we called," said Tom, clearing his throat, "is this young brother of mine that's looking for a wife."

Everyone laughed again. Ned knew the oftener a joke was repeated the better they liked it, but for him this particular joke was beginning to wear thin.

"Leave him take me," said Delia with an arch look at Ned who smiled and gazed at the floor.

"Be quiet, you slut!" said Tom. "There are your two sisters before you."

"Even so, I want to go to Dublin. . . . Would you treat me to lemonade, mister?" she asked Ned with her impudent smile. "This is a rotten hole. I'd go to America if they left me."

"America won't be complete without you," said Tom. "Now, don't let me hurry ye, ladies, but my old fellow will be waiting for us in Johnny Kit's."

"We'll go along with you," said Nora, and the three girls took down three black shawls from inside the door. Some tension seemed to have gone out of the air. They laughed and joked between themselves.

"Ye'll get wet," said Sean to the two brothers.

"Cait will make room for me under her shawl," said Tom.

"Indeed I will not," she cried, starting back with a laugh.

"Very shy you're getting," said Sean with a good-natured grin.

" 'Tisn't that at all but she'd sooner the young man," said Delia.

"What's strange is wonderful," said Nora.

Biting her lip with her tiny front teeth, Cait looked angrily at her sisters and Sean, and then began to laugh. She glanced at Ned and smilingly held out her shawl in invitation, though at the same moment angry blushes chased one another across her forehead like squalls across the surface of a lake. The rain was a mild, persistent drizzle and a strong wind was blowing. Everything had darkened and grown lonely and, with his head in the blinding folds of the shawl, which reeked of turf-smoke, Ned felt as if he had dropped out of Time's pocket.

They waited in Caheragh's kitchen. The bearded old man sat in one chimney corner and a little barelegged boy in the other. The dim blue light poured down the wide chimney on their heads in a shower with the delicacy of light on old china, picking out surfaces one rarely saw; and between them the fire burned a bright orange in the great whitewashed hearth with the black, swinging bars and pothook. Outside the rain fell softly, almost soundlessly, beyond the half door. Delia, her black shawl trailing from her shoulders, leaned over it, acting the part of watcher as in a Greek play. Their father's fifteen minutes had strung themselves out to an hour and two little barefooted boys had already been sent to hunt him down.

"Where are they now, Delia?" one of the O'Donnells would ask.

"Crossing the fields from Patsy Kit's."

"He wasn't there so."

"He wouldn't be," the old man said. "They'll likely go on to Ned Kit's now."

"That's where they're making for," said Delia. "Up the hill at the far side of the fort."

"They'll find him there," the old man said confidently.

Ned felt as though he were still blanketed by the folds of the turf-reeking shawl. Something seemed to have descended on him that filled him with passion and loneliness. He could scarcely take his eyes off Cait. She and Nora sat on the form against the back wall, a composition in black and white, the black shawl drawn tight under the chin, the cowl of it breaking the curve of her dark hair, her shadow on the gleaming wall behind. She did not speak except to answer some question of Tom's about her brother, but sometimes Ned caught her looking at him with naked eyes. Then she smiled swiftly and secretly and turned her eyes again to the door, sinking back into pensiveness. Pensiveness or vacancy? he wondered. While he gazed at her face with the animal instinctiveness of its overdelicate features it seemed like a mirror in which he saw again the falling rain, the rocks and hills and angry sea.

The first announced by Delia was Red Patrick. After him came the island woman. Each had last seen his father in a different place. Ned chuckled at a sudden vision of his father, eager and impassioned and aflame with drink, stumping with his broken bottom across endless fields through pouring rain with a growing procession behind him. Dempsey was the last to come. He doubted if Tomas would be in a condition to take the boat at all.

"What matter, aru?" said Delia across her shoulder. "We can find room for the young man."

"And where would we put him?" gaped Nora.

"He can have Cait's bed," Delia said innocently.

"Oye, and where would Cait sleep?" Nora asked and then skitted and covered her face with her shawl. Delia scoffed. The men laughed and Cait, biting her lip furiously, looked at the floor. Again Ned caught her eyes on him and again she laughed and turned away.

Tomas burst in unexpected on them all like a sea-wind that scattered them before him. He wrung Tom's hand and asked him how he was. He did the same to Ned. Ned replied gravely that he was very well.

"In God's holy name," cried his father, waving his arms like a windmill, "what are ye all waiting for?"

The tide had fallen. Tomas grabbed an oar and pushed the boat onto a rock. Then he raised the sail and collapsed under it and had to be extricated from its drenching folds, glauming and swearing at Cassidy's old boat. A little group stood on a naked rock against a gray background of drifting rain. For a long time Ned continued to wave back to the black shawl that was lifted to him. An extraordinary feeling of exultation and loss enveloped him. Huddled up in his overcoat he sat with Dempsey in the stern, not speaking.

"It was a grand day," his father declared, swinging himself to and fro, tugging at his Viking moustache, dragging the peak of his cap farther over his ear. His gestures betrayed a certain lack of rhythmical cohesion; they began and ended abruptly. "Dempsey, my darling, wasn't it a grand day?"

" 'Twas a grand day for you," shrieked Dempsey as if his throat would burst.

" 'Twas, my treasure, 'twas a beautiful day. I got an honorable reception and my sons got an honorable reception."

By this time he was flat on his belly, one leg completely over the edge of the boat. He reached back a clammy hand to his sons.

" 'Twas the best day I ever had," he said. "I got porter and I got whisky and I got poteen. I did so, Tom, my calf. Ned, my brightness, I went to seven houses and in every house I got seven drinks and with every drink I got seven welcomes. And your mother's people are a hand of trumps. It was no slight they put on me at all even if I was nothing but a landless man. No slight, Tom. No slight at all."

Darkness had fallen, the rain had cleared, the stars came out of a pitch-black sky under which the little tossing, nosing boat seemed lost beyond measure. In all the waste of water nothing could be heard but the splash of the boat's sides and their father's voice raised in tipsy song.

"*The evening was fair and the sunlight was yellow,*
I halted, beholding a maiden bright
Coming to me by the edge of the mountain,
Her cheeks had a berry-bright rosy light."

V

Ned was the first to wake. He struck a match and lit the candle. It was time for them to be stirring. It was just after dawn, and at half past nine he must be in his old place in the schoolroom before the rows of pinched little city-faces. He lit a cigarette and closed his eyes. The lurch of the boat was still in his blood, the face of Cait Deignan in his mind, and as if from far away he heard a line of the wild love-song his father had been singing: "And we'll drive the geese at the fall of night."

He heard his brother mumble something and nudged him. Tom looked big and fat and vulnerable with his fair head rolled sideways and his heavy mouth dribbling onto the sleeve of his pajamas. Ned slipped quietly out of bed, put on his trousers, and went to the window. He drew the curtains and let in the thin cold daylight. The bay was just visible and perfectly still. Tom began to mumble again in a frightened voice and Ned shook him. He started out of his sleep with a cry of fear, grabbing at the bedclothes. He looked first at Ned, then at the candle and drowsily rubbed his eyes.

"Did you hear it too?" he asked.

"Did I hear what?" asked Ned with a smile.

"In the room," said Tom.

"There was nothing in the room," replied Ned. "You were ramaishing so I woke you up."

"Was I? What was I saying?"

"You were telling no secrets," said Ned with a quiet laugh.

"Hell!" Tom said in disgust and stretched out his arm for a cigarette. He lit it at the candle flame, his drowsy red face puckered and distraught. "I slept rotten."

"Oye!" Ned said quietly, raising his eyebrows. It wasn't often Tom spoke in that tone. He sat on the edge of the bed, joined his hands and leaned forward, looking at Tom with wide gentle eyes.

"Is there anything wrong?" he asked.

"Plenty."

"You're not in trouble?" Ned asked without raising his voice.

"Not that sort of trouble. The trouble is in myself."

Ned gave him a look of intense sympathy and understanding. The soft emotional brown eyes were searching him for a judgment. Ned had never felt less like judging him.

"Ay," he said gently and vaguely, his eyes wandering to the other side of the room while his voice took on its accustomed stammer, "the trouble is always in ourselves. If we were contented in ourselves the other things wouldn't matter. I suppose we must only leave it to time. Time settles everything."

"Time will settle nothing for me," Tom said despairingly. "You have something to look forward to. I have nothing. It's the loneliness of my job that kills you. Even to talk about it would be a relief but there's no one you can talk to. People come to you with their troubles but there's no one you can go to with your own."

Again the challenging glare in the brown eyes and Ned realized with infinite compassion that for years Tom had been living in the same state of suspicion and fear, a man being hunted down by his own nature; and that for years to come he would continue to live in this way, and perhaps never be caught again as he was now.

"A pity you came down here," stammered Ned flatly. "A pity we went to Carriganassa. 'Twould be better for both of us if we went somewhere else."

"Why don't you marry her, Ned?" Tom asked earnestly.

"Who?" asked Ned.

"Cait."

"Yesterday," said Ned with the shy smile he wore when he confessed something, "I nearly wished I could."

"But you can, man," Tom said eagerly, sitting upon his elbow. Like all men with frustration in their hearts he was full of schemes for others. "You could marry her and get a school down here. That's what I'd do if I was in your place."

"No," Ned said gravely. "We made our choice a long time ago. We can't go back on it now."

Then with his hands in his trouser pockets and his head bowed he went out to the kitchen. His mother, the colored shawl about her head, was blowing the fire. The bedroom door was open and he could see his father in shirtsleeves kneeling beside the bed, his face raised reverently toward a holy picture, his braces hanging down behind. He unbolted the half-door, went through the garden and out on to the road. There was a magical light on everything. A boy on a horse rose suddenly against the sky, a startling picture. Through the apple-green light over Carriganassa ran long streaks of crimson, so still they might have been enameled. Magic, magic, magic! He saw it as in a children's picture-book with all its colors intolerably bright; something he had outgrown and could never return to, while the world he aspired to was as remote and intangible as it had seemed even in the despair of youth.

It seemed as if only now for the first time was he leaving home; for the first time and forever saying good-bye to it all.

JAMES JOYCE

James Joyce (1882-1941), a native of Dublin, was educated for the priesthood. While still in his teens, however, he shifted his interest to literature, music, and medicine. Restlessly he left Ireland for Paris and then went on to Switzerland and Italy where he supported himself by teaching languages. He lived in Zurich during World War I, afterwards moving to Paris, which became his permanent home. Though most of his writing was done in Paris, the scene of his novels and stories is his native city of Dublin. His experimental novel *Ulysses*, for years banned in Great Britain and the United States, has exerted a powerful influence on contemporary literature. His short stories are limited to the single volume *Dubliners*, in which with marked objectivity he portrays the life of the city of his boyhood. His final novel, *Finnegans Wake*, has caused extensive controversy among its readers.

A Little Cloud

EIGHT years before he had seen his friend off at the North Wall and wished him godspeed. Gallaher had got on. You could tell that at once by his traveled air, his well-cut tweed suit, and fearless accent. Few fellows had talents like his and fewer still could remain unspoiled by such success. Gallaher's heart was in the right place and he had deserved to win. It was something to have a friend like that.

Little Chandler's thoughts ever since lunch-time had been of his meeting with Gallaher, of Gallaher's invitation and of the great city London where Gallaher lived. He was called Little Chandler because, though he was but slightly under the average stature, he gave one the idea of being a little man. His hands were white and small, his frame was fragile, his voice was quiet and his manners were refined. He took the greatest care of his fair silken hair and moustache and used perfume discreetly on his handkerchief. The half-moons of his nails were perfect and when he smiled you caught a glimpse of a row of childish white teeth.

As he sat at his desk in the King's Inns he thought what changes those eight years had brought. The friend whom he had known under a shabby and necessitous guise had become a brilliant figure on the London Press. He turned often from his tiresome writing to gaze out of the office window. The glow of a late autumn sunset covered the grass plots and walks. It cast a shower of kindly golden dust on the untidy nurses and decrepit old men who drowsed on the benches; it flickered upon all the moving figures —on the children who ran screaming along the gravel paths and on everyone who passed through the gardens. He watched the scene and thought of life; and (as always happened when he thought of life) he became sad. A gentle melancholy took possession of him. He felt how useless it was to struggle against fortune, this being the burden of wisdom which the ages had bequeathed to him.

He remembered the books of poetry upon his shelves at home. He had bought them in his bachelor days and many an evening, as he sat in the little room off the hall, he had been tempted to take one down from the bookshelf and read out something to his wife. But shyness had always held him back; and so the books had remained on their shelves. At times he repeated lines to himself and this consoled him.

When his hour had struck he stood up and took leave of his desk and of his fellow-clerks punctiliously. He emerged from under the feudal arch of the King's Inns, a neat modest figure, and walked swiftly down Henrietta Street. The golden sunset was waning and the air had grown sharp. A horde of grimy children populated the street. They stood or ran in the roadway or crawled up the steps before the gaping doors or squatted like mice upon the thresholds. Little Chandler gave them no thought. He picked his way deftly through all that minute vermin-like life and under the shadow of the gaunt spectral mansions in which the old nobility of Dublin had roistered. No memory of the past touched him, for his mind was full of a present joy.

He had never been in Corless's but he knew the value of the name. He knew that people went there after the theater to eat oysters and drink liqueurs; and he had heard that the waiters there spoke French and German. Walking swiftly by at night he had seen cabs drawn up before the door and richly dressed ladies, escorted by cavaliers, alight and enter quickly. They wore noisy dresses and many wraps. Their faces were powdered and they caught up their dresses, when they touched earth, like alarmed Atalantas. He had always passed without turning his head to look. It was his habit to walk swiftly in the street even by day and whenever he found himself in the city late at night he hurried on his way apprehensively and excitedly. Sometimes, however, he courted the causes of his fear. He chose the darkest and narrowest streets and, as he walked boldly forward, the silence that was spread about his footsteps troubled him, the wandering, silent figures troubled him; and at times a sound of low fugitive laughter made him tremble like a leaf.

He turned to the right toward Capel Street. Ignatius Gallaher on the London Press! Who would have thought it possible eight years before? Still, now that he reviewed the past, Little Chandler could remember many signs of future greatness in his friend. People used to say that Ignatius Gallaher was wild. Of course, he did mix with a rakish set of fellows at that time, drank freely and borrowed money on all sides. In the end he had got mixed up in some shady affair, some money transaction; at least, that was one version of his flight. But nobody denied him talent. There was always a certain . . . something in Ignatius Gallaher that impressed you in spite of yourself. Even when he was out at elbows and at his wit's end for money he kept up a bold face. Little Chandler remembered (and the remembrance brought a slight flush of pride to his cheek) one of Ignatius Gallaher's sayings when he was in a tight corner:

"Half time now, boys," he used to say lightheartedly. "Where's my considering cap?"

That was Ignatius Gallaher all out; and, damn it, you couldn't but admire him for it.

Little Chandler quickened his pace. For the first time in his life he felt himself superior to the people he passed. For the first time his soul revolted against the dull inelegance of Capel Street. There was no doubt about it: if you wanted to succeed you had to go away. You could do nothing in Dublin. As he crossed Grattan

Bridge he looked down the river towards the lower quays and pitied the poor stunted houses. They seemed to him a band of tramps, huddled together along the river-banks, their old coats covered with dust and soot, stupefied by the panorama of sunset and waiting for the first chill of night to bid them arise, shake themselves and be gone. He wondered whether he could write a poem to express his idea. Perhaps Gallaher might be able to get it into some London paper for him. Could he write something original? He was not sure what idea he wished to express but the thought that a poetic moment had touched him took life within him like an infant hope. He stepped onward bravely.

Every step brought him nearer to London, farther from his own sober inartistic life. A light began to tremble on the horizon of his mind. He was not so old—thirty-two. His temperament might be said to be just at the point of maturity. There were so many different moods and impressions that he wished to express in verse. He felt them within him. He tried to weigh his soul to see if it was a poet's soul. Melancholy was the dominant note of his temperament, he thought, but it was a melancholy tempered by recurrences of faith and resignation and simple joy. If he could give expression to it in a book of poems perhaps men would listen. He would never be popular: he saw that. He could not sway the crowd but he might appeal to a little circle of kindred minds. The English critics, perhaps, would recognize him as one of the Celtic school by reason of the melancholy tone of his poems; besides that, he would put in allusions. He began to invent sentences and phrases from the notice which his book would get. "*Mr. Chandler has the gift of easy and graceful verse.*" . . . "*A wistful sadness pervades these poems.*" . . . "*The Celtic note.*" It was a pity his name was not more Irish-looking. Perhaps it would be better to insert his mother's name before the surname: Thomas Malone Chandler, or better still: T. Malone Chandler. He would speak to Gallaher about it.

The light and noise of the bar held him at the doorway for a few moments. He looked about him, but his sight was confused by the shining of many red and green wine-glasses. The bar seemed to him to be full of people and he felt that the people were observing him curiously. He glanced quickly to right and left (frowning slightly to make his errand appear serious), but when his sight cleared a little he saw that nobody had turned to look at him: and there, sure enough, was Ignatius Gallaher leaning with his back against the counter and his feet planted far apart.

"Hallo, Tommy, old hero, here you are! What is it to be? What will you have? I'm taking whisky: better stuff than we get across the water. Soda? Lithia? No mineral? I'm the same. Spoils the flavor. . . . Here, garçon, bring us two halves of malt whisky, like a good fellow. . . . Well, and how have you been pulling along since I saw you last? Dear God, how old we're getting! Do you see any signs of aging in me—eh, what? A little gray and thin on the top—what?"

Ignatius Gallaher took off his hat and displayed a large closely cropped head. His face was heavy, pale and clean-shaven. His eyes, which were of bluish slate-color, relieved his unhealthy pallor and shone out plainly above the vivid orange tie he wore. Between these rival features the lips appeared very long and shapeless and colorless. He bent his head and felt with two sympathetic fingers the thin hair at the crown. Little Chandler shook his head as a denial. Ignatius Gallaher put on his hat again.

"It pulls you down," he said. "Press life. Always hurry and scurry, looking for copy and sometimes not finding it: and then, always to have something new in your stuff. Damn proofs and printers, I say, for a few days. I'm deuced glad, I can tell you, to get back to the old country. Does a fellow good, a bit of a holiday. I feel a ton better since I landed again in dear dirty Dublin. . . . Here you are, Tommy. Water? Say when."

Little Chandler allowed his whisky to be very much diluted.

"You don't know what's good for you, my boy," said Gallaher. "I drink mine neat."

"I drink very little as a rule," said Little Chandler modestly. "An odd half-one or so when I meet any of the old crowd: that's all."

"Ah, well," said Ignatius Gallaher, cheerfully, "here's to us and to old times and old acquaintance."

They clinked glasses and drank the toast.

"I met some of the old gang today," said Ignatius Gallaher. "O'Hara seems to be in a bad way. What's he doing?"

"Nothing," said Little Chandler. "He's gone to the dogs."

"But Hogan has a good sit, hasn't he?"

"Yes; he's in the Land Commission."

"I met him one night in London and he seemed to be very flush. . . . Poor O'Hara! Booze, I suppose?"

"Other things, too," said Little Chandler shortly.

Ignatius Gallaher laughed.

"Tommy," he said, "I see you haven't changed an atom. You're the very same serious person that used to lecture me on Sunday mornings when I had a sore head and a fur on my tongue. You'd want to knock about a bit in the world. Have you never been anywhere even for a trip?"

"I've been to the Isle of Man," said Little Chandler.

Ignatius Gallaher laughed.

"The Isle of Man!" he said. "Go to London or Paris: Paris, for choice. That'd do you good."

"Have you seen Paris?"

"I should think I have! I've knocked about there a little."

"And is it really so beautiful as they say?" asked Little Chandler.

He sipped a little of his drink while Ignatius Gallaher finished his boldly.

"Beautiful?" said Ignatius Gallaher, pausing on the word and on the flavor of his drink. "It's not so beautiful, you know. Of course, it is beautiful. . . . But it's the life of Paris; that's the thing. Ah, there's no city like Paris for gaiety, movement, excitement. . . ."

Little Chandler finished his whisky and, after some trouble, succeeded in catching the barman's eye. He ordered the same again.

"I've been to the Moulin Rouge," Ignatius Gallaher continued when the barman had removed their glasses, "and I've been to all the Bohemian cafés. Hot stuff! Not for a pious chap like you, Tommy."

Little Chandler said nothing until the barman returned with two glasses: then he touched his friend's glass lightly and reciprocated the former toast. He was beginning to feel somewhat disillusioned. Gallaher's accent and way of expressing himself did not please him. There was something vulgar in his friend which he had not observed before. But perhaps it was only the result of living in London amid the bustle and competition of the Press. The old personal charm was still there under this new gaudy manner. And, after all, Gallaher had lived, he had seen the world. Little Chandler looked at his friend enviously.

"Everything in Paris is gay," said Ignatius Gallaher. "They believe in enjoying life—and don't you think they're right? If you want to enjoy yourself properly you must go to Paris. And, mind you, they've a great feeling for the Irish there. When they heard I was from Ireland they were ready to eat me, man."

Little Chandler took four or five sips from his glass.

"Tell me," he said, "is it true that Paris is so . . . immoral as they say?"

"Every place is immoral," he said. "Of course you do find spicy bits in Paris. Go to one of the students' balls, for instance. That's lively, if you like, when the *cocottes* begin to let themselves loose. You know what they are, I suppose?"

"I've heard of them," said Little Chandler.

Ignatius Gallaher drank off his whisky and shook his head.

"Ah," he said, "you may say what you like. There's no woman like the Parisienne—for style, for go."

"Then it is an immoral city," said Little Chandler, with timid insistence—"I mean, compared with London or Dublin?"

"London!" said Ignatius Gallaher. "It's six of one and half-a-dozen of the other. You ask Hogan, my boy. I showed him a bit about London when he was over there. He'd open your eye. . . . I say, Tommy, don't make punch of that whisky: liquor up."

"No, really. . . ."

"Oh, come on, another one won't do you any harm. What is it? The same again, I suppose?"

"Well . . . all right."

"*François*, the same again. . . . Will you smoke, Tommy?"

Ignatius Gallaher produced his cigar case. The two friends lit their cigars and puffed at them in silence until their drinks were served.

"I'll tell you my opinion," said Ignatius Gallaher, emerging after some time from the clouds of smoke in which he had taken refuge, "it's a rum world. Talk of immorality! I've heard of cases —what am I saying?—I've known them: cases of . . . immorality. . . ."

Ignatius Gallaher puffed thoughtfully at his cigar and then in a calm historian's tone he proceeded to sketch for his friend some pictures of the corruption which was rife abroad. He summarized the vices of many capitals and seemed inclined to award the palm to Berlin. Some things he could not vouch for (his friends had told him), but of others he had had personal experience. He spared neither rank nor caste. He revealed many of the secrets of religious houses on the Continent and described some of the practices which were fashionable in high society and ended by telling, with details, a story about an English duchess—a story which he knew to be true. Little Chandler was astonished.

"Ah, well," said Ignatius Gallaher, "here we are in old jog-along Dublin where nothing is known of such things."

"How dull you must find it," said Little Chandler, "after all the other places you've seen!"

"Well," said Ignatius Gallaher, "it's a relaxation to come over here, you know. And, after all, it's the old country, as they say, isn't it? You can't help having a certain feeling for it. That's human nature. . . . But tell me something about yourself. Hogan told me you had . . . tasted the joys of connubial bliss. Two years ago, wasn't it?"

Little Chandler blushed and smiled.

"Yes," he said. "I was married last May twelve months."

"I hope it's not too late in the day to offer my best wishes," said Ignatius Gallaher. "I didn't know your address or I'd have done so at the time."

He extended his hand, which Little Chandler took.

"Well, Tommy," he said, "I wish you and yours every joy in life, old chap, and tons of money, and may you never die till I shoot you. And that's the wish of a sincere friend, an old friend. You know that?"

"I know that," said Little Chandler.

"Any youngsters?" said Ignatius Gallaher.

Little Chandler blushed again.

"We have one child," he said.

"Son or daughter?"

"A little boy."

Ignatius Gallaher slapped his friend sonorously on the back.

"Bravo," he said, "I wouldn't doubt you, Tommy."

Little Chandler smiled, looked confusedly at his glass and bit his lower lip with three childishly white front teeth.

"I hope you'll spend an evening with us," he said, "before you go back. My wife will be delighted to meet you. We can have a little music and–"

"Thanks awfully, old chap," said Ignatius Gallaher. "I'm sorry we didn't meet earlier. But I must leave tomorrow night."

"Tonight, perhaps . . . ?"

"I'm awfully sorry, old man. You see I'm over here with another fellow, clever young chap he is too, and we arranged to go to a little card-party. Only for that . . ."

"Oh, in that case . . ."

"But who knows?" said Ignatius Gallaher considerately. "Next year I may take a little skip over here now that I've broken the ice. It's only a pleasure deferred."

"Very well," said Little Chandler, "the next time you come we must have an evening together. That's agreed now, isn't it?"

"Yes, that's agreed," said Ignatius Gallaher. "Next year if I come, *parole d'honneur*."

"And to clinch the bargain," said Little Chandler, "we'll just have one more now."

Ignatius Gallaher took out a large gold watch and looked at it.

"Is it to be the last?" he said. "Because you know, I have an a.p."

"Oh, yes, positively," said Little Chandler.

"Very well, then," said Ignatius Gallaher, "let us have one as a *deoc an doruis*–that's good vernacular for a small whisky, I believe."

Little Chandler ordered the drinks. The blush which had risen to his face a few moments before was establishing itself. A trifle made him blush at any time: and now he felt warm and excited. Three small whiskies had gone to his head and Gallaher's strong cigar had confused his mind, for he was a delicate and abstinent person. The adventure of meeting Gallaher after eight years, of finding himself with Gallaher in Corless's surrounded by lights and noise, of listening to Gallaher's stories and of sharing for a brief space Gallaher's vagrant and triumphant life, upset the equipoise of his sensitive nature. He felt acutely the contrast between his own life and his friend's, and it seemed to him unjust. Gallaher was his inferior in birth and education. He was sure that he could do something better than his friend had ever done, or could ever do, something higher than mere tawdry journalism if he only got the chance. What was it that stood in his way? His unfortunate timidity! He wished to vindicate himself in some way, to assert his manhood. He saw behind Gallaher's refusal of his invitation. Gallaher was only patronizing him by his friendliness just as he was patronizing Ireland by his visit.

treat with condescension

The barman brought their drinks. Little Chandler pushed one glass toward his friend and took up the other boldly.

"Who knows?" he said, as they lifted their glasses. "When you come next year I may have the pleasure of wishing long life and happiness to Mr. and Mrs. Ignatius Gallaher."

Ignatius Gallaher in the act of drinking closed one eye expressively over the rim of his glass. When he had drunk he smacked his lips decisively, set down his glass and said:

"No blooming fear of that, my boy. I'm going to have my fling first and see a bit of life and the world before I put my head in the sack—if I ever do."

"Some day you will," said Little Chandler calmly.

Ignatius Gallaher turned his orange tie and slate-blue eyes full upon his friend.

"You think so?" he said.

"You'll put your head in the sack," repeated Little Chandler stoutly, "like everyone else if you can find the girl."

He had slightly emphasized his tone and he was aware that he had betrayed himself; but, though the color had heightened in his cheek, he did not flinch from his friend's gaze. Ignatius Gallaher watched him for a few moments and then said:

"If ever it occurs, you may bet your bottom dollar there'll be no mooning and spooning about it. I mean to marry money.

She'll have a good fat account at the bank or she won't do for me."

Little Chandler shook his head.

"Why, man alive," said Ignatius Gallaher, vehemently, "do you know what it is? I've only to say the word and tomorrow I can have the woman and the cash. You don't believe it? Well, I know it. There are hundreds—what am I saying?—thousands of rich Germans and Jews, rotten with money, that'd only be too glad. . . . You wait a while, my boy. See if I don't play my cards properly. When I go about a thing I mean business, I tell you. You just wait."

He tossed his glass to his mouth, finished his drink and laughed loudly. Then he looked thoughtfully before him and said in a calmer tone:

"But I'm in no hurry. They can wait. I don't fancy tying myself up to one woman, you know."

He imitated with his mouth the act of tasting and made a wry face.

"Must get a bit stale, I should think," he said.

Little Chandler sat in the room off the hall, holding a child in his arms. To save money they kept no servant but Annie's young sister Monica came for an hour or so in the morning and an hour or so in the evening to help. But Monica had gone home long ago. It was a quarter to nine. Little Chandler had come home late for tea and, moreover, he had forgotten to bring Annie home the parcel of coffee from Bewley's. Of course she was in a bad humor and gave him short answers. She said she would do without any tea but when it came near the time at which the shop at the corner closed she decided to go out herself for a quarter of a pound of tea and two pounds of sugar. She put the sleeping child deftly in his arms and said:

"Here. Don't waken him."

A little lamp with a white china shade stood upon the table and its light fell over a photograph which was enclosed in a frame of crumpled horn. It was Annie's photograph. Little Chandler looked at it, pausing at the thin tight lips. She wore the pale blue summer blouse which he had brought her home as a present one Saturday. It had cost him ten and eleven pence; but what an agony of nervousness it had cost him! How he had suffered that day, waiting at the shop door until the shop was empty, standing at the counter and trying to appear at his ease while the girl piled ladies' blouses before him, paying at the desk and forgetting to take up the odd penny of his change, being called back by the cashier, and finally striving to hide his blushes as he left the shop by examining the parcel to see if it was securely tied. When he brought the blouse home Annie kissed him and said it was very pretty and stylish; but when she heard the price she threw the blouse on the table and said it was a regular swindle to charge ten and elevenpence for it. At first she wanted to take it back but when she tried it on she was delighted with it, especially with the make of the sleeves, and kissed him and said he was very good to think of her.

Hm!

He looked coldly into the eyes of the photograph and they answered coldly. Certainly they were pretty and the face itself was pretty. But he found something mean in it. Why was it so unconscious and ladylike? The composure of the eyes irritated him. They repelled him and defied him: there was no passion in them, no rapture. He thought of what Gallaher had said about rich Jewesses. Those dark Oriental eyes, he thought, how full they are of passion, of voluptuous longing! . . . Why had he married the eyes in the photograph?

He caught himself up at the question and glanced nervously round the room. He found something mean in the pretty furniture which he had bought for his house on the hire system. Annie had chosen it herself and it reminded him of her. It was too prim and pretty. A dull resentment against his life awoke within him. Could he not escape from his little house? Was it too late for him to try to live bravely like Gallaher? Could he go to London? There was the furniture still to be paid for. If he could only write a book and get it published, that might open the way for him.

A volume of Byron's poems lay before him on the table. He opened it cautiously with his left hand lest he should waken the child and began to read the first poem in the book:

Hushed are the winds and still the evening gloom,
Not e'en a Zephyr wanders through the grove,
Whilst I return to view my Margaret's tomb
And scatter flowers on the dust I love.

He paused. He felt the rhythm of the verse about him in the room. How melancholy it was! Could he, too, write like that, express the melancholy of his soul in verse? There were so many things he wanted to describe: his sensation of a few hours before on Grattan Bridge, for example. If he could get back again into that mood. . . .

The child awoke and began to cry. He turned from the page and tried to hush it: but it would not be hushed. He began to rock it to and fro in his arms but its wailing cry grew keener. He rocked it faster while his eyes began to read the second stanza:

Within this narrow cell reclined her clay,
That clay where once . . .

It was useless. He couldn't read. He couldn't do anything. The wailing of the child pierced the drum of his ear. It was useless, useless! He was a prisoner for life. His arms trembled with anger and suddenly bending to the child's face he shouted:

"Stop!"

The child stopped for an instant, had a spasm of fright and began to scream. He jumped up from his chair and walked hastily up and down the room with the child in his arms. It began to sob piteously, losing its breath for four or five seconds, and then bursting out anew. The thin walls of the room echoed the sound. He tried to soothe it but it sobbed more convulsively. He looked at the contracted and quivering face of the child and began to be alarmed. He counted seven sobs without a break between them and caught the child to his breast in fright. If it died! . . .

The door was burst open and a young woman ran in, panting.

"What is it? What is it?" she cried.

The child, hearing its mother's voice, broke out into a paroxysm of sobbing.

"It's nothing, Annie . . . it's nothing. . . . He began to cry. . . ."

She flung her parcels on the floor and snatched the child from him.

"What have you done to him?" she cried, glaring into his face.

Little Chandler sustained for one moment the gaze of her eyes and his heart closed together as he met the hatred in them. He began to stammer:

"It's nothing. . . . He . . . he began to cry. . . . I couldn't . . . I didn't do anything. . . . What?"

Giving no heed to him she began to walk up and down the room, clasping the child tightly in her arms and murmuring:

"My little man! My little mannie! Was 'ou frightened, love? . . . There now, love! There now! Lambabaun! Mamma's little lamb of the world! . . . There now!"

Little Chandler felt his cheeks suffused with shame and he stood back out of the lamplight. He listened while the paroxysm of the child's sobbing grew less and less; and tears of remorse started to his eyes.

HENRY JAMES

Henry James (1843-1916), a pre-eminent figure in modern fiction, was born in New York City and was privately educated in America and Europe. Before he began writing he was familiar with the languages and literatures of England, France, Italy, and Germany. He early developed a conception of his role as a detached observer of life, and he found inexhaustible literary material in the "international theme"—a comparative study of the temperament and character of Americans and Europeans. After 1866 he chose to spend most of his time abroad, in Italy, France, and England, because he found America materialistic in spirit, crass and empty. He became a British subject in 1915 and died in London a year later. All his fiction, long and short, is distinguished by sensitive psychological insight, careful and complex structure, and a subtle and involved prose style. The New York Edition of *The Novels and Tales of Henry James* (1907-1917) contains illuminating prefaces which discuss his artistic methods and purposes.

The Madonna of the Future

WE HAD been talking about the masters who had achieved but a single masterpiece—the artists and poets who but once in their lives had known the divine afflatus and touched the high level of perfection. Our host had shown us a charming little cabinet picture by a painter whose name we had never heard, and who, after this single spasmodic bid for fame, had appeared to relapse into obscurity and mediocrity. There was some discussion as to the frequency of this inconsequence; during which I noted H—— sit silent, finishing his cigar with a meditative air and looking at the picture, which was being handed round the table. "I don't know how common a case it is," he said at last, "but I've seen it. I've known a poor fellow who painted his one masterpiece, and who"—he added with a smile—"didn't even paint that. He made his bid for fame and missed it." We all knew

H—— for a clever man who had seen much of men and manners and had a great stock of reminiscences. Someone immediately questioned him further, and while I was engrossed with the raptures of my neighbor over the precious object in circulation he was induced to tell his tale. If I were to doubt whether it would bear repeating, I should only have to remember how that charming woman our hostess, who had left the table, ventured back, in rustling rose color, to pronounce our lingering a want of gallantry, and, then finding us under the spell, sank into her chair in spite of our cigars and heard the story out so graciously that when the catastrophe was reached she glanced across and showed me a tear in each of her beautiful eyes.

It relates to my youth and to Italy: two very fine things! (H—— began.) I had arrived late in the evening at Florence and, while I finished my bottle of wine at supper, had fancied that, tired traveler though I was, I might pay such a place a finer compliment than by going vulgarly to bed. A narrow passage wandered darkly away out of the little square before my hotel and looked as if it bored into the heart of Florence. I followed it and at the end of ten minutes emerged upon a great piazza filled only with the mild autumn moonlight. Opposite rose the Palazzo Vecchio, like some huge civic fortress, with the great bell tower springing from its embattled verge even as a mountain pine from the edge of a cliff. At the base, in the great projected shadow, gleamed certain dim sculptures which I wonderingly approached. One of the images, on the left of the palace door, was a magnificent colossus who shone through the dusky air like a sentinel roused by some alarm and in whom I at once recognized Michelangelo's famous David. I turned with a certain relief from his heroic sinister strength to a slender figure in bronze poised beneath the high, light loggia which opposes the free and elegant span of its arches to the dead masonry of the palace; a figure supremely shapely and graceful, markedly gentle almost, in spite of his holding out with his light nervous arm the snaky head of the slaughtered Gorgon. His name—as, unlike the great David, he still stands there—is Perseus, and you may read his story not in the Greek mythology but in the memoirs of Benvenuto Cellini. Glancing from one of these fine fellows to the other, I probably uttered some irrepressible commonplace of praise, for, as if provoked by my voice, a man rose from the steps of the loggia, where he had been sitting in the shadow, and addressed me in proper English—a small slim personage clad in some fashion of black velvet tunic (as it seemed) and with a mass of auburn hair, which shimmered in the moonlight, escaping from a little biretta of the *cinquecento*. In a tone of the most insinuating deference he proceeded to appeal to me for my "impressions." He was romantic; fantastic, slightly unreal. Hovering in that consecrated neighborhood he might have passed for the genius of aesthetic hospitality—if the genius of aesthetic hospitality wasn't commonly some shabby little *custode* who flourishes a calico pocket handkerchief and openly resents the divided franc. This analogy was made none the less complete by his breaking into discourse as I threw myself diffidently back upon silence.

"I've known Florence long, sir, but I've never known her so lovely as tonight. It's as if the ghosts of her past were abroad in the empty streets. The present is sleeping; the past hovers about us like a dream made visible. Fancy the old Florentines strolling up in couples to pass judgment on the last performance of Michael, of Benvenuto! We should come in for a precious lesson if we might overhear what they say. The plainest burgher of them, in his cap and gown, had a taste in the matter. That was the prime of art, sir. The sun stood high in heaven, and his broad and equal blaze made the darkest places bright and the dullest eyes clear. We live in the evening of time. We grope in the gray dusk, carrying each our poor little taper of selfish and painful wisdom, holding it up to the great models and to the dim idea, and seeing nothing but overwhelming greatness and dimness. The days of illumination are gone. But do you take my refreshing idea"—and he grew suddenly almost familiar in this visionary fervor—"my idea that the light of that time rests upon us here for an hour? I've never seen the David so grand, the Perseus so fair! Even the inferior productions of John of Bologna and of Baccio Bandinelli seem to realize the artist's dream. I feel as if the moonlit air were charged with the secrets of the masters, and as if, standing here in religious attention, we might—well, witness a revelation!" Perceiving at this moment, I suppose, my halting comprehension reflected in my puzzled face, this interesting rhapsodist paused and blushed. Then with a melancholy smile: "You think me a moonstruck charlatan, I suppose. It's not my habit to hang about the piazza and pounce upon innocent tourists. But tonight, I confess, I'm under the charm. And then, somehow, I seemed to take you too for an artist!"

"I'm not an artist, I'm sorry to say, as you must understand the term. But pray make no apologies. I *am* also under the charm, and your eloquent remarks," I declared, "have only deepened it."

"If you're not an artist, you're worthy to be one!" he returned with flattering frankness. "A young man who arrives at Florence late in the evening and, instead of going prosaically to bed or hanging over the travelers' book at his hotel, walks forth without loss of time to render homage to these blest objects is a young man after my own heart!"

The mystery was suddenly solved; my friend was the most characteristic of compatriots. He would *have* to be one of "us," of the famished race—for we were at least a pair—to take the situation so to heart. "None the less so, I trust," I answered, "if the young man is a sordid New Yorker."

"New Yorkers have often been munificent patrons of art!" he answered urbanely.

For a moment I was alarmed. Was his irrepressible passion mere Yankee enterprise?—was he simply a desperate brother of the brush who had posted himself here to extort an "order" from a sauntering tourist? But I wasn't called to defend myself. A great brazen note broke suddenly from the far-off summit of the bell tower above us and sounded the first stroke of midnight. My companion started, apologized for detaining me, and prepared to retire. But he seemed to offer so lively a promise of further entertainment that I was loath to part with him and suggested we should proceed homeward together. He cordially assented; so we turned out of the Piazza, passed down before the statued arcade of the Uffizi, and came out upon the Arno. What course we took I hardly remember, but we roamed far and wide for an hour, my companion delivering by snatches a positively moon-touched aesthetic lecture. I listened in puzzled fascination, wondering who the deuce he might be. He confessed with a melancholy but all-respectful headshake to an origin identical with my own. "We're the disinherited of Art! We're condemned to be superficial! We're excluded from the magic circle! The soil of American perception is a poor little barren artificial deposit! Yes, we're wedded to imperfection! An American, to excel, has just ten times as much to learn as a European! We lack the deeper sense! We have neither taste nor tact nor force! How *should* we have them? Our crude and garish climate, our silent past, our deafening present, the constant pressure about us of unlovely conditions, are as void of all that nourishes and prompts and inspires the artist as my sad heart is void of bitterness in saying so! We poor aspirants must live in perpetual exile."

"You seem fairly at home in exile," I made answer, "and Florence seems to me a very easy Siberia. But do you know my own thought? Nothing is so idle as to talk about our want of a nursing air, of a kindly soil, of opportunity, of inspiration, of the things that help. The only thing that helps is to do something fine. There's no law in our glorious Constitution against that. Invent, create, achieve. No matter if you've to study fifty times as much as one of these. What else are you an artist for? Be you our Moses," I added, laughing and laying my hand on his shoulder, "and lead us out of the house of bondage!"

"Golden words, golden words, young man!"—my friend rose to it beautifully. " 'Invent, create, achieve!' Yes, that's our business; I know it well. Don't take me, in heaven's name, for one of your barren complainers, of the falsely fastidious, who have neither talent nor faith! I'm at work!"—and he glanced about him and lowered his voice as if this were quite a peculiar secret—"I'm at work night and day. I've undertaken, believe me, a creation. I'm no Moses; I'm only a poor patient artist; but it would be a fine thing if I were to cause some slender stream of beauty to flow in our thirsty land! Don't think me a monster of conceit," he went on as he saw me smile at the avidity with which he adopted my illustration; "I confess that I *am* in one of those moods when great things seem possible! This is one of my—shall I say inspired?—nights: I dream waking! When the south wind blows over Florence at midnight it seems to coax the soul from all the fair things locked away in her churches and galleries; it comes into my own little studio with the moonlight; it sets my heart beating too deeply for rest. You see I'm always adding a thought to my conception. This evening I felt I couldn't sleep unless I had communed with the genius of Buonarotti!"

He seemed really to know his Florence through and through and had no need to tell me he loved her. I saw he was an old devotee and had taken her even from the first to his heart. "I owe her everything," he put it—"it's only since I came here that I've really lived, intellectually and aesthetically speaking. One by one all profane desires, all mere worldly aims, have dropped away from me and left me nothing but my pencil, my little notebook"—he tapped his breast pocket—"and the worship of the pure masters, those who were pure because they were innocent and those who were pure because they were strong!"

"And have you been very productive all this time?" I found myself too interested to keep from asking.

He was silent a while before replying. "Not in the vulgar sense! I've chosen never to manifest myself by imperfection. The good in every performance I've reabsorbed into the generative force of new creations; the bad—there's always plenty of that—I've religiously destroyed. I may say with some satisfaction that I've not added a grain to the rubbish of the world. As a proof of my conscientiousness"—and he stopped short, eyeing me with extraordinary candor, as if the proof were to be overwhelming—"I've never sold a picture! 'At least no merchant traffics in my heart!' Do you remember that divine line in Browning? My little studio has never been profaned by superficial feverish mercenary work. It's a temple of labor but of leisure! Art is long. If we work for ourselves, of course, we must hurry. If we work for *her* we must often pause. She can wait!"

This had brought us to my hotel door, somewhat to my relief, I confess, for I had begun to feel unequal to the society of a genius of this heroic strain. I left him, however, not without expressing a friendly hope that we should meet again. The next morning my curiosity had not abated; I was anxious to see him by common daylight. I counted on meeting him in one of the many art haunts of the so rich little city, and I was gratified without delay. I found him in the course of the morning in the Tribune of the Uffizi—that little treasure chamber of world-famous things. He had turned his back on the Venus de' Medici and, with his arms resting on the rail that protects the pictures and his head buried in his hands, was lost in the contemplation of that superb neighboring triptych of Andrea Mantegna—a work which has neither the material splendor nor the commanding force of some of its neighbors, but which, glowing there with the loveliness of patient labor, suits possibly a more constant need of the soul. I looked at the picture for some time over his shoulder; at last, with a heavy sigh, he turned away and our eyes met. As he recognized me he colored for the consciousness of what I brought back: he recalled perhaps that he had made a fool of himself overnight. But I offered him my hand with a frankness that assured him I was no scoffer. I knew him by his great nimbus of red hair; otherwise he was much altered. His midnight mood was over, and he looked as haggard as an actor by daylight. He was much older than I had supposed, and had less bravery of costume and attitude. He seemed quite the poor patient artist he had proclaimed himself, and the fact that he had never sold a picture was more conceivable doubtless than commendable. His velvet coat was threadbare and his short, slouched hat, of an antique pattern, revealed a rustiness that marked it an "original" and not one of the picturesque reproductions that members of his craft sometimes affect. His eye was mild and heavy, and his expression singularly gentle and acquiescent; the more so for a certain pale facial spareness which I hardly knew whether to refer to the consuming fire of genius or to a meager diet. A very little talk, however, cleared his brow and brought back his flow.

"And this is your first visit to these enchanted halls?" he cried. "Happy, thrice happy youth!"—with which, taking me by the arm, he prepared to lead me to each of the pre-eminent works in turn and show me the flower of the array. Before we left the Mantegna, however, I felt him squeeze me and give it a loving look. "*He* was not in a hurry," he murmured. "*He* knew nothing of 'raw Haste, half sister to Delay'!" How sound a critic he might have been didn't seem to me even then to concern me—it so served that he was an amusing one; overflowing with opinions and theories, sympathies and aversions, with disquisition and gossip and anecdote. He inclined more than I approved to the sentimental proposition, was too fond, I thought, of superfine shades and of discovering subtle intentions and extracting quintessences. At moments too he plunged into the sea of metaphysics and floundered a while in waters that were not for my breasting. But his abounding knowledge and frequent felicities told a touching story of long attentive hours in all such worshipful companies; there was a reproach to my wasteful saunterings in his systematic and exhaustive attack. "There are two moods," I remember his saying, "in which we may walk through galleries—the critical and the ideal. They seize us at their pleasure, and we can never tell which is to take its turn. The critical, oddly, is the genial one, the friendly, the condescending. It relishes the pretty trivialities of art, its vulgar cleverness, its conscious graces. It has a kindly greeting for anything which looks as if, according to his light, the painter had enjoyed doing it—for the little Dutch cabbages and kettles, for the taper fingers and breezy mantles of late-coming Madonnas, for the little blue-hilled, broken-bridged, pastoral, classical landscapes. Then there are the days of fierce, fastidious longing—solemn church feasts of the taste or the faith—when all vulgar effort and all petty success is a weariness and everything but the best, the best of the best, disgusts. In these hours we're relentless aristocrats of attitude. We'll not take Michael for granted, we'll not swallow Raphael whole!"

The gallery of the Uffizi is not only rich in its possessions, but peculiarly fortunate in that fine architectural accident or privilege which unites it—with the breadth of river and city between them—to the princely extent of the Pitti. The Louvre and the Vatican hardly give you such a sense of sustained enclosure as those long passages projected over street and stream to establish an inviolate transition between the two palaces of art. We paced the clear tunnel in which those precious drawings by eminent hands hang chaste and gray above the swirl and murmur of the yellow Arno, and reached the grand-ducal, the palatial saloons. Grand-ducal as they are, they must be pronounced imperfect showrooms, since, thanks to their deep-set windows and their massive moldings, it is rather a broken light that reaches the pictured walls. But here the masterpieces hang thick, so that you see them in a deep diffused luster of their own. And the great chambers, with their superb dim ceilings, their outer wall in splendid shadow and the somber opposite glow of toned canvas and gleaming gold, make themselves almost as fine a picture as the Titians and Raphaels they imperfectly reveal. We lingered briefly before many a Raphael and Titian; but I saw my friend was impatient and I suffered him at last to lead me directly to the goal of our journey—the most tenderly fair of Raphael's virgins, the "Madonna of the Chair." Of all the fine pictures of the world, it was to strike me at once as the work with which criticism has least to do. None betrays less effort, less of the mechanism of success and of the irrepressible discord between conception and result that sometimes faintly invalidates noble efforts. Graceful, human, near to our sympathies as it is, it has nothing of manner, of method, nothing almost of style; it blooms there in a softness as rounded and as instinct with harmony as if it were an immediate exhalation of genius. The figure imposes on the spectator a spell of submission which he scarce knows whether he has given to heavenly purity or to earthly charm. He is intoxicated with the fragrance of the tenderest blossom of maternity that ever bloomed among men.

"That's what I call a fine picture," said my companion after we had gazed a while in silence. "I've a right to say so, for I've copied it so often and so carefully that I could repeat it now with my eyes shut. Other works are of Raphael: this *is* Raphael himself. Others you can praise, you can qualify, you can measure, explain, account for: this you can only love and admire. I don't know in what seeming he walked here below while this divine mood was upon him; but after it surely he could do nothing but die—this world had nothing more to teach him. Think of it a while, my friend, and you'll admit that I'm not raving. Think of his seeing that spotless image not for a moment, for a day, in a happy dream or a restless fever fit, not as a poet in a five minutes' frenzy—time to snatch his phrase and scribble his immortal stanza; but for days together, while the slow labor of the brush went on, while the foul vapors of life interposed and the fancy ached with tension, fixed, radiant, distinct, as we see it now! What a master, certainly! But ah, what a seer!"

"Don't you imagine," I fear I profanely asked, "that he had a model, and that some pretty young woman—"

"As pretty a young woman as you please! It doesn't diminish the miracle. He took his hint of course, and the young woman possibly sat smiling before his canvas. But meanwhile the painter's idea had taken wings. No lovely human outline could charm it to vulgar fact. He saw the fair form made perfect; he rose to the vision without tremor, without effort of wing; he communed with it face to face and resolved into finer and lovelier truth the purity which completes it as the fragrance completes the rose. That's what they call idealism; the word's vastly abused, but the thing's good. It's my own creed at any rate. Lovely Madonna, model at once and muse, I call you to witness that I too am an idealist!"

"An idealist then"—and I really but wanted to draw him further out—"an idealist is a gentleman who says to Nature in the person of a beautiful girl: 'Go to, you're all wrong! Your fine's coarse, your bright's dim, your grace is gaucherie. This is the way you should have done it!' Isn't the chance against him?"

He turned on me at first almost angrily—then saw that I was but sowing the false to reap the true. "Look at that picture," he said, "and cease your irreverent mockery! Idealism is *that!* There's no explaining it; one must feel the flame. It says nothing to Nature, or to any beautiful girl, that they won't both forgive. It says to the fair woman: 'Accept me as your artist friend, lend me your beautiful face, trust me, help me, and your eyes shall be half my masterpiece.' No one so loves and respects the rich realities of nature as the artist whose imagination intensifies them. He knows what a fact may hold—whether Raphael knew, you may judge by his inimitable portrait, behind us there, of Tommaso Inghirami—but his fancy hovers above it as Ariel in the play hovers above the sleeping prince. There's only one Raphael, but an artist may still be an artist. As I said last night, the days of illumination are gone; visions are rare; we've to look long to have them. But in meditation we may still cultivate the ideal; round it, smooth it, perfect it. The result, the result"—here his voice faltered suddenly and he fixed his eyes for a moment on the picture; when they met my own again they were full of tears —"the result may be less than this, but still it may be good, it may be *great!*" he cried with vehemence. "It may hang somewhere, through all the years, in goodly company, and keep the artist's memory warm. Think of being known to mankind after some such fashion as this; of keeping pace with the restless centuries and the changing world; of living on and on in the cunning of an eye and a hand that belong to the dust of ages, a delight and a law to remote generations; of making beauty more and more a force and purity more and more an example!"

"Heaven forbid," I smiled, "that I should take the wind out of your sails! But doesn't it occur to you that besides being strong in his genius Raphael was happy in a certain good faith of which we've lost the trick? There are people, I know, who deny that his spotless Madonnas are anything more than pretty blondes of that period, enhanced by the Raphaelesque touch, which they declare to be then as calculating and commercial as any other. Be that as it may, people's religious and aesthetic needs went arm in arm, and there was, as I may say, a demand for the Blessed Virgin, visible and adorable, which must have given firmness to the artist's hand. I'm afraid there's no demand now."

My friend momentarily stared—he shivered and shook his ears under this bucketful of cold water. But he bravely kept up his high tone. "There's always a demand—that ineffable type is one of the eternal needs of man's heart; only pious souls long for it in silence, almost in shame. Let it appear and their faith grows brave. How *should* it appear in this corrupt generation? It can't be made to order. It could indeed when the order came trumpet-toned from the lips of the Church herself and was addressed to genius panting with inspiration. But it can spring now only from the soil of passionate labor and culture. Do you really fancy that while from time to time a man of complete artistic vision is born into the world such an image can perish? The man who paints it has painted everything. The subject admits of every perfection —form, color, expression, composition. It can be as simple as you please and yet as rich; as broad and free and yet as full of delicate detail. Think of the chance for flesh in the little naked, nestling child, irradiating divinity; of the chance for drapery in the chaste and ample garment of the mother. Think of the great story you compress into that simple theme. Think above all of the mother's face and its ineffable suggestiveness, of the mingled burden of joy and trouble, the tenderness turned to worship and the worship turned to far-seeing pity. Then look at it all in perfect line and lovely color, breathing truth and beauty and mastery."

"*Anch' io son pittore!*" I laughed. "Unless I'm mistaken *you* have a masterpiece on the stocks. If you put all that in, you'll do more than Raphael himself did. Let me know when your picture's finished, and wherever in the wide world I may be I'll post back to Florence and pay my respects to—the *Madonna of the future!*"

His face, at this, had a flush of consciousness, and he seemed to sigh half in protest, half in resignation. "I don't often mention my picture by name. I detest this modern custom of premature publicity. A great work needs silence, privacy, mystery. And then, do you know, people are so cruel, so frivolous, so unable to imagine a man's wishing to paint a Madonna at this time of day, that I've been laughed at, positively laughed at, sir!"—and his poor, guilty blush deepened. "I don't know what has prompted me to be so frank and trustful with you. You look as if you wouldn't laugh at me. My dear young man"—and he laid his hand on my arm—"I'm worthy of respect. Whatever my limitations may be, I'm honest. There's nothing grotesque in a pure ambition or in a life devoted to it."

II

There was something so admirably candid in his look and tone that further questions seemed to savor just then of indiscretion. I had repeated opportunity to put as many as I would, however, for after this we spent much time together. Daily, for a fortnight, we met under agreement that he should help me to intimacy with the little treasure city. He knew it so well and had studied it with so pious a patience, he was so deeply versed both in its greater and its minor memories, he had become in short so fond and familiar a Florentine, that he was an ideal *valet de place* and I was glad enough to leave dryer documents at home and learn what I wanted from his lips and his example. He talked of Florence as a devoted old lover might still speak of an old incomparable mistress who remained proof against time; he liked to describe how he had lost his heart to her at first sight. "It's the fashion to make all cities of the feminine gender, but as a rule it's a monstrous mistake. Is Florence of the same sex as New York, as Chicago, as London, as Liverpool? She's the sole perfect lady of them all; one feels toward her as some sensitive, aspiring youth feels to some beautiful older woman with a 'history.' She fills you with a presumptuous gallantry." This disinterested passion seemed to stand my friend instead of the common social ties; he led a lonely life and cared for nothing but his work. I was duly flattered by his having taken my uninstructed years into his favor and by his generous sacrifice of precious hours to my society. We spent them in historic streets and consecrated nooks, in churches and convents and galleries, spent them above all in study of those early paintings in which Florence is so rich, returning ever and anon, with restless sympathies, to find in these tender blossoms of art a fragrance and savor more precious than the full-fruited knowledge of the later works. We lingered often in the mortuary chapel of San Lorenzo, where we watched Michelangelo's dim-visaged warrior sit like some awful Genius of Doubt and brood behind his eternal mask upon the mysteries of life. We stood more than once in the little convent chambers where Fra Angelico wrought as if an angel indeed had held his hand, and gathered that sense of scattered dews and early bird notes which makes an hour among his relics resemble a morning stroll in some monkish garden. We did all this and much more—wandered into obscure shrines, damp courts, and dusty palace rooms, in quest of lingering hints of fresco and lurking treasures of sculpture.

I was more and more impressed with my companion's remarkable singleness of purpose. Everything became a pretext for one of his high-flown excursions. Nothing could be seen or said that didn't lead him sooner or later to a glowing discourse on the true, the beautiful, and the good. If my friend was not a genius, he was certainly a natural rhapsodist, or even a harmless madman;

and I found the play of his temper, his humor, and his candid and unworldly character as quaint as if he had been a creature from another planet. He seemed indeed to know very little of this one, and lived and moved altogether in his boundless province of art. A creature more unsullied by the accidents of life it's impossible to conceive, and I sometimes questioned the reality of an artistic virtue, an aesthetic purity, on which some profane experience hadn't rubbed off a little more. It was hard to have to accept him as of our own hard-headed stock; but after all there could be no better sign of his American star than the completeness of his reaction in favor of vague profits. The very heat of his worship was a mark of conversion; those born within sight of the temple take their opportunities more for granted. He had, moreover, all our native mistrust for intellectual discretion and our native relish for sonorous superlatives. As a critic he rather ignored proportion and degree; his recognitions had a generous publicity, his discriminations were all discoveries. The small change of appreciation seemed to him in fine no coin for a gentleman to handle; and yet with all this overflow of opinion and gesture he remained in himself a mystery. His professions were practically, somehow, all masks and screens, and his personal allusions, as to his ambiguous background, mere wavings of the dim lantern. He was modest and proud, in other words, and never spoke of his domestic matters. He was evidently poor, and yet must have had some slender independence, since he could afford to make so merry over the fact that his culture of ideal beauty had never brought him a penny. His poverty, I supposed, was his motive for neither inviting me to his lodging nor mentioning its whereabouts. We met either in some public place or at my hotel, where I entertained him as freely as I might without appearing to be prompted by charity. He appeared for the most part hungry, and this was his nearest approach to human grossness. I made a point of never seeming to cross a certain line with him, but, each time we met, I ventured to make some respectful allusion to the *magnum opus*, to inquire, if I might, as to its health and progress. "We're getting on, with the Lord's help," he would say with a bravery that never languished; "I think we can't be said not to be doing well. You see I've the grand advantage that I lose no time. These hours I spend with you are pure profit. They bring me in a harvest of incentives. Just as the truly religious soul is always at worship, the genuine artist is always in labor. He takes his property wherever he finds it—he learns some precious secret from every object that stands up in the light. If you but knew—in connection with something to be done—of the rapture of observing and remembering, of applying one's notes. I take in at every glance some hint for light, for color, for style. When I get home I pour out my treasures into the lap of my Madonna. Oh, I'm not idle! *Nulla dies sine linea.*"

III

I had been introduced meanwhile to an American lady whose drawing room had long formed an attractive place of reunion for strangers of supposed distinction. She lived on a fourth floor and was not rich; but she offered her visitors very good tea, little cakes at option, and conversation not quite to match. Her conversation had mainly a high aesthetic pitch, for Mrs. Coventry was famously "artistic." Her apartment was a sort of miniature Pitti Palace. She possessed "early masters" by the dozen—a cluster of Peruginos in her dining room, a Giotto in her boudoir, an Andrea del Sarto over her drawing-room chimney piece. Surrounded by these treasures and by innumerable bronzes, mosaics, majolica dishes, and little worm-eaten diptychs covered with angular saints on gilded backgrounds, she enjoyed the dignity of a social high priestess of the arts. She always wore on her bosom a huge, if reduced, copy of the "Madonna della Seggiola." Gaining her ear quietly one evening I asked her whether she knew among our compatriots in the place a certain eccentric but charming Mr. Theobald.

"Know him, know poor Theobald?"—her answer was as public as if I had owed it to the bell crier. "All Florence knows him, his flame-colored locks, his black velvet coat, his interminable harangues on the Beautiful and his wondrous Madonna that mortal eye has never seen and that mortal patience has quite given up expecting."

"Really," I asked, "you don't believe in his wondrous Madonna?"

"My dear ingenuous youth," rejoined my shrewd friend, "has

he made a convert of you? Well, we all believed in him once; he came down upon Florence—that is, on our little colony here—and took the town by storm. Another Raphael, at the very least, had been born among men, and our poor, dear, barbarous country was to have the credit of him. Hadn't he the very hair of Raphael flowing down on his shoulders? The hair, alas—it's his difficulty—appears to have to do duty for the head! We swallowed him whole, however; we hung on his lips and proclaimed his genius from the house tops. The women were dying to sit to him for their portraits and be made immortal like Leonardo's Gioconda. We decided that his manner was a good deal like Leonardo's—'esoteric' and indescribable and fascinating. Well, it has all remained esoteric, and nobody can describe what nobody has ever seen. The months, the years have passed and the miracle has hung fire; our master has never produced his masterpiece. He has passed hours in the galleries and churches, posturing, musing, and gazing; he has talked more about his subject—about every subject—than any human being before has ever talked about anything, but has never put brush to canvas. We had all subscribed, as it were, to the great performance; but as it never came off people began to ask for their money again. I was one of the last of the faithful; I carried devotion so far as to sit to him for my head. If you could have seen the horrible creature he made of me, you'd recognize that even a woman with no more vanity than will tie her bonnet straight must have cooled off then. The man didn't know the very alphabet of drawing. His strong point, he intimated, was his sentiment; but is it a consolation, when one has been painted a fright, to know that the man has particularly enjoyed doing it? One by one, I confess, we fell away from the faith, and Mr. Theobald didn't lift his little finger to preserve us. At the first hint that we were tired of waiting and that we should like the show to begin he was off in a huff. 'Great work requires time, contemplation, privacy, mystery! O ye of little faith!' We answered that we didn't insist on a great work; that the five-act tragedy might come at his convenience; that we merely asked for something to keep us from yawning, some light little *lever de rideau*. On that the poor, dear man took his stand as a genius misconceived and persecuted, a martyr to his opinions, and washed his hands of us from that hour! No, I believe he does me the honor to consider me the head and front of the conspiracy formed to nip his glory in the bud—a bud that has taken twenty years to blossom. Ask him if he knows me, and he'll tell you I'm a horribly ugly old woman who has vowed his destruction because he doesn't see his way to paint her in the style of Titian's Flora. I'm afraid that since then he has had none but chance followers, innocent strangers like yourself, who have taken him at his word. The mountain's still in labor; I haven't heard that the mouse has been born. I pass him once in a while in the galleries, and he fixes his great dark eyes on me with a sublimity of indifference, as if I were a bad copy of a Sassoferrato! It's ever so long now since I heard that he was making studies for a Madonna who was to be a résumé of all the other Madonnas of the Italian school—like that antique Venus who borrowed a nose from one great image and an ankle from another. It's certainly a grand idea. The parts may be fine, but when I think of my unhappy portrait I tremble for the whole. He has communicated this *trouvaille*, under pledge of solemn secrecy, to fifty chosen spirits, to everyone he has ever been able to buttonhole for five minutes. I suppose he wants to get an order for it, and he's not to blame; for goodness knows how he lives. I see by your blush" —my friend freely proceeded—"that you've been honored with his confidence. You needn't be ashamed, my dear young man; a man of your age is none the worse for a certain generous credulity. Only allow me this word of advice: keep your credulity out of your pockets! Don't pay for the picture till it's delivered. You haven't been treated to a peep at it, I imagine? No more have your fifty predecessors in the faith. There are people who doubt there's any picture to be seen. I shouldn't myself be surprised if, when one runs him to earth, one finds scarce more than in that terrible little tale of Balzac's—a mere mass of incoherent scratches and daubs, a jumble of dead paint!"

I listened to this bold sketch in silent wonder. It had a painfully plausible sound, it set the seal on shy suspicions of my own. My hostess was satirical, but was neither unveracious nor vindictive. I determined to let my judgment wait upon events. Possibly she was right, but if she was wrong she was cruelly wrong. Her version of my friend's eccentricities made me impatient to see him again and examine him in the light of public opinion. On our next meeting I at once asked him if he knew Mrs. Coventry. He laid his hand on my arm with a sadder, though perhaps sharper, look than had ever yet come into his face. "Has she got *you* into training? She's a most vain woman. She's empty and scheming, and she pretends to be serious and kind. She prattles about Giotto's second manner and Vittoria Colonna's liaison with 'Michael'—one would suppose Michael lived across the way and was expected in to take a hand at whist—but she knows as little about art, and about the conditions of production, as I know about the stock market. She profanes sacred things," he more vehemently went on. "She cares for you only as someone to hand teacups in that horrible humbugging little parlor with its trumpery Peruginos! If you can't dash off a new picture every three day and let her hand it round among her guests, she tells them you're a low fraud and that they must have nothing to do with you."

This attempt of mine to test Mrs. Coventry's understanding of our poor friend was made in the course of a late afternoon walk to the quiet old church of San Miniato, on one of the hilltops which directly overlook the city, from whose gates you are guided to it by a stony and cypress-bordered walk, the most fitting of avenues to a shrine. No spot is more propitious to rest and thought than the broad terrace in front of the church, where, lounging against the parapet, you may glance in slow alternation from the black and yellow marbles of the church façade, seamed and cracked with time and wind-sown with a tender flora of their own, down to the full domes and slender towers of Florence and over to the blue sweep of the wide-mouthed cup of mountains in whose hollow this choicest handful of the spoils of time has been stored away for keeping. I had proposed, as a diversion from the painful memories evoked by Mrs. Coventry's name, that Theobald should go with me the next evening to the opera, where some work rarely played was to be given. He declined, as I half expected, for I had noted that he regularly kept his evenings in reserve and never alluded to his manner of passing them. "You've reminded me before," I put to him, "of that charming speech of the Florentine painter in Alfred de Musset's *Lorenzaccio*: '*I do no harm to anyone. I pass my days in my studio. On Sunday I go to the Annunziata or to Santa Maria; the monks think I have a voice; they dress me in a white gown and a red cap, and I take a share in the choruses; sometimes I do a little solo: these are the only times I go into public. In the evening, I visit my sweetheart; when the night is fine, we pass it on her balcony.*' I don't know whether you've a sweetheart or whether she has a balcony. But if you *are* so happy it's certainly better than trying to hold out against a third-rate prima donna."

He made no immediate answer, but at last he turned to me solemnly. "Can you look upon a beautiful woman with reverent eyes?"

"Really," I said, "I don't pretend to be sheepish, but I should be sorry to think myself impudent." And I asked him what in the world he meant. When at last I had assured him that if the question was of his giving me such an exhibition I would accept it on the terms he should impose, he made known to me—with an air of religious mystery—that it was in his power to introduce me to the most beautiful woman in Italy: "A beauty with a beautiful soul."

"Upon my word," I said, "you're extremely fortunate. I'm not less so, but you do keep cards up your sleeve."

"This woman's beauty," he returned, "is a revelation, a lesson, a morality, a poem! It's my daily study." Of course after this I lost no time in reminding him of what, before we parted, had taken the shape of a promise. "I feel somehow," he had said, "as if it were a violation of that privacy in which I've always studied and admired her. Therefore what I'm doing for you—well, my friend, is friendship. No hint of her existence has ever fallen from my lips. But with too great a familiarity we're apt to lose a sense of the real value of things, and you'll perhaps throw some new light on what I show you and offer a fresher appreciation."

We went accordingly by appointment to a certain ancient house in the heart of Florence—the precinct of the Mercato Vecchio—and climbed a dark, steep staircase to its highest flight. Theobald's worshiped human type seemed hung as far above the line of common vision as his artistic ideal was lifted over the usual practice of men. He passed without knocking into the dark vestibule of a small apartment where, opening an inner door, he ushered me into a small saloon. The room affected me as mean and somber, though I caught a glimpse of white curtains swaying gently at an open window. At a table, near a lamp, sat a woman dressed in black, working at a piece of embroidery. As my guide entered she looked up with a serene smile; then, seeing me, she made a movement of surprise and rose with stately grace. He stepped nearer, taking her hand and kissing it with an indescribable air of immemorial usage. As he bent his head she looked at me askance and had, I thought, a perfectly human change of color.

"This is the sublime Serafina!"—Theobald frankly waved me forward. "And this is a friend and a lover of the arts," he added, introducing me. I received a smile, a curtsey, and a request to be seated.

The most beautiful woman in Italy was a person of a generous Italian type and of a great simplicity of demeanor. Seated again at her lamp with her embroidery, she seemed to have nothing whatever to say. Theobald, bending to her in a sort of Platonic ecstasy, asked her a dozen paternally tender questions about her health, her state of mind, her occupations and the progress of her needlework, which he examined minutely and summoned me to admire. It was one of the pieces of some ecclesiastical vestment—ivory satin wrought with an elaborate design of silver and gold. She made answer in a full rich voice, but with a brevity I couldn't know whether to attribute to native reserve or to the profane constraint of my presence. She had been that morning to confession; she had also been to market and had bought a chicken for dinner. She felt very happy; she had nothing to complain of except that the people for whom she was making her vestment and who furnished her materials should be willing to put such rotten silver thread into the garment, as one might say, of the Lord. From time to time, as she took her slow stitches, she raised her eyes and covered me with a glance which seemed at first to express but a placid curiosity, but in which, as I saw it repeated, I thought I perceived the dim glimmer of an attempt to establish an understanding with me at the expense of our companion. Meanwhile, as mindful as possible of Theobald's injunction of reverence, I considered the lady's personal claims to the fine compliment he had paid her.

That she was indeed a beautiful woman I recognized as soon as I had recovered from the surprise of finding her without the freshness of youth. Her appearance was of the sort which, in losing youth, loses little of its greater merit, expressed for the most part as it was in form and structure and, as Theobald would have said, in "composition." She was broad and ample, low-browed and large-eyed, dark and pale. Her thick brown hair hung low beside her cheek and ear and seemed to drape her head with a covering as chaste and formal as the veil of a nun. The poise and carriage of this head were admirably free and noble, and all the more effective that their freedom was at moments discreetly corrected by a little sanctimonious droop which harmonized admirably with the level gaze of her dark and quiet eye. A strong, serene, physical nature, with the placid temper which comes of no nerves and no troubles, seemed this lady's comfortable portion. She was dressed in plain, dull black, save for a dark-blue kerchief which was folded across her bosom and exposed a glimpse of her massive throat. Over this kerchief was suspended a little silver cross. I admired her greatly, yet with a considerable reserve. A certain mild intellectual apathy was the very mark of her complexion and form, and always seemed to round and enrich them; but this bourgeoise Egeria, if I viewed her right, betrayed rather a vulgar stagnation of mind. There might have once been a dim spiritual light in her face, but it had long since begun to wane. And furthermore, in plain prose, she was growing stout. My disappointment amounted very nearly to complete disenchantment when Theobald, as if to facilitate my covert inspection, declaring that the lamp was very dim and that she would ruin her eyes without more light, rose and addressed himself to a couple of candles on the mantelpiece, which he lighted and transferred to the table. In this improved clearness I made our hostess out a very mature person. She was neither haggard nor worn nor gray, but she was thick and coarse. The beautiful soul my friend had promised me seemed scarce worth making such a point of; it dwelt in no deeper principle than some accident of quietude, some matronly mildness of lip and brow. I should have been ready even to pronounce her sanctified bend of the head nothing more inward than the trick of a person always working at embroidery. It might have been even a slightly more sinister symptom, for in spite of her apparently admirable dullness this object of our all-candid homage practically dropped a hint that she took the situation rather less seriously than her friend. When he rose to light the candles, she looked across at me with a quick intelligent smile and tapped her forehead with her forefinger; then, as from a sudden feeling of compassionate loyalty to poor Theobald I preserved a blank face, she gave a little shrug and resumed her work.

What was the relation of this singular couple? Was he the most ardent of friends or the most discreet of lovers? Did she regard him as an eccentric swain whose benevolent admiration of her beauty she was not ill-pleased to humor at the small cost of having him climb into her little parlor and gossip of summer nights? With her decent and somber dress, her simple gravity, and that fine piece of priestly stitching, she looked like some pious lay member of a sisterhood living by special permission outside her convent walls. Or was she maintained here aloft by her admirer in comfortable leisure, so that he might have before him the perfect eternal type, uncorrupted and untarnished by the struggle for existence? Her shapely hands, I observed, were very fair and white; they lacked the traces of what is called honest toil.

"And the pictures, how do they come on?" she asked of Theobald after a long pause.

"Oh, in their own fine, quiet way! I've here a friend whose sympathy and encouragement give me new faith and ardor."

Our hostess turned to me, gazed at me a moment rather inscrutably, and then, repeating the vivid reference to the contents of our poor friend's head she had used a minute before, "He has a magnificent genius!" she said with perfect gravity.

"I'm inclined to think so"—I was amused in spite of myself.

"Eh, why do you smile?" she cried. "If you doubt what I say, you must see the *santo bambino!*" And she took the lamp and conducted me to the other side of the room, where, on the wall, in a plain black frame, hung a large drawing in red chalk. Beneath it was attached a little bowl for holy water. The drawing represented a very young child, entirely naked, half-nestling back against his mother's gown, but with his two little arms outstretched as in the act of benediction. It had been thrown off with singular freedom and directness, but was none the less vivid with the sacred bloom of infancy. A dimpled elegance and grace, which yet didn't weaken its expression, recalled the touch of Correggio. "That's what he can do!" said my hostess. "It's the blessed little boy I lost. It's his very image, and the Signor Teobaldo, a generous person if there ever was one, gave it me as a gift. He has given me many things besides!"

I looked at the picture for some time—certainly it had a charm. Turning back to our friend I assured him that if it were hung amid the drawings in the Uffizi and labeled with a glorious name it would bravely hold its own. My praise seemed to give him joy; he pressed my hands—his eyes filled with tears. I had apparently quickened his desire to expatiate on the history of the drawing, for he rose and took leave of our companion, kissing her hand with the same mild ardor as before. It occurred to me that the offer of a similar piece of gallantry on my own part might help me to know what manner of woman she was. When she felt my intention she withdrew her hand, dropped her eyes solemnly, and made me a severe curtsey. Theobald took my arm and led me rapidly into the street.

"And what do you think of the sublime Serafina?" he cried with anxiety.

"She's certainly a fine figure of a woman," I answered without ceremony.

He eyed me an instant askance and then seemed hurried along by the current of remembrance. "You should have seen the mother and the child together, seen them as I first saw them—the mother with her head draped in a shawl, a divine trouble in her face, and the bambino pressed to her bosom. You'd have said, I'm sure, that Raphael had found his match in common chance. I was coming back one summer night from a long walk in the country when I met this apparition at the city gate. The woman held out her hand and I hardly knew whether to say 'What do you want?'

or to fall down and worship. She asked for a little money and received what I gave her with the holy sweetness with which the Santissima Vergine receives the offerings of the faithful. I saw she was beautiful and pale—she might have stepped out of the stable of Bethlehem! I gave her money and helped her on her way into the town. I had guessed her story. She too was a maiden mother, but she had been turned out into the world in her shame. I felt in all my pulses that here was my subject marvelously realized. It was as if I had had like one of the monkish artists of old a miraculous vision. I rescued the poor creatures, cherished them, watched them as I would have done some precious work of art, some lovely fragment of fresco discovered in a moldering cloister. In a month—as if to deepen and sanctify the sadness and sweetness of it all—the poor little child died. When she felt he was going, she lifted him up to me for ten minutes—so as not to lose him *all*—and I made that sketch. You saw a feverish haste in it, I suppose; I wanted to spare the poor little mortal the pain of his position. After that I doubly valued the mother. She's the simplest, sweetest, most natural creature that ever bloomed in this brave old land of Italy. She lives in the memory of her child, in her gratitude for the scanty kindness I've been able to show her, and in her simple, instinctive, imperturbable piety. She's not even conscious of her beauty; my admiration has never made her vain. Heaven yet knows that I've made no secret what I think of it. You must have taken in the extraordinary clearness and modesty of her look. Was there ever such a truly virginal brow, such a natural classic elegance in the wave of the hair and the arch of the forehead? I've studied her; I may say I know her. I've absorbed her little by little, I've made her my own, my mind's stamped and imbued, and I've determined now to clinch the impression. I shall at last invite her to sit for me!"

" 'At last—at last'?" I repeated in amazement. "Do you mean she has never done so yet?"

"I've not really—since that first time—made her *pose*," he said with a shade of awkwardness. "I've taken notes, you know; I've got my grand fundamental impression. That's the great thing! But I've not actually put her to the inconvenience—so to call it—to which I'd have put a common model."

What had become for the moment of my perception and my tact I'm at a loss to say; in their absence I was unable to repress a headlong exclamation. I was destined to regret it. We had stopped at a turning and beneath a lamp. "My poor friend," I exclaimed, laying my hand on his shoulder, "you've *dawdled!* She's an old, old woman—for a maiden mother."

It was as if I had brutally struck him; I shall never forget the long slow almost ghastly look of pain with which he answered me. "Dawdled?—old, old?" he stammered. "Are you joking?"

"Why, my dear fellow, I suppose you don't take her for anything *but* mature?"

He drew a long breath and leaned against a house, looked at me with questioning, protesting, reproachful eyes. At last starting forward and grasping my arm: "Answer me solemnly: does she seem to you really and truly old? Is she wrinkled, is she faded—and I blind?" he demanded.

Then at last I understood the immensity of his illusion; how, one by one, the noiseless years had ebbed away and left him brooding in charmed inaction, forever preparing for a work forever deferred. It struck me almost as a kindness now to tell him the plain truth. "I should be sorry to say you're blind," I returned, "but I think you're rather unfortunately deceived. You've lost time in effortless contemplation. Your friend was once young and fresh and virginal; but you see that must have been some years ago. Still, she has fine things left. By all means make her sit for you." But I broke down; his face was too horribly reproachful.

He took off his hat and stood passing his handkerchief mechanically over his forehead. " 'Fine things left'?" he stared. "Do you speak as if other people had helped themselves—?"

"Why, my dear man," I smiled, "the years have helped themselves! But she has what the French call—don't they?—*de beaux restes?*"

Oh, how he gaped and how something seemed to roll over him! "I must make my Madonna out of *de beaux restes!* What a masterpiece she'll be! Old—old! Old—old!" he re-echoed.

"Never mind her age," I cried, revolted by what I had done; "never mind my impression of her! You have your memory, your notes, your genius. Finish your picture in a month. I pronounce it beforehand a masterpiece and hereby offer you for it any sum you may choose to ask."

He kept staring, but seemed scarce to understand me. "Old—old!" he kept stupidly repeating. "If she's old what am I? If her beauty has faded where, where is my strength? Has life been a dream? Have I worshiped too long? Have I loved too well?" The charm in truth was broken. That the chord of illusion should have snapped at my light accidental touch showed how it had been weakened by excessive tension. The poor fellow's sense of wasted time, of vanished opportunity, surged in upon his soul in waves of darkness. He suddenly dropped his head and burst into tears.

I led him homeward with all possible tenderness, but I attempted neither to check his grief, to restore his equanimity, nor to unsay the hard truth. When we reached my hotel I tried to induce him to come in. "We'll drink a glass of wine," I smiled, "to the completion of the Madonna."

With a violent effort he held up his head, mused for a moment with a formidably somber frown and then, giving me his hand, "I'll finish it," he vowed, "in a month! No, no, in a fortnight! After all I have it *here!*" And he smote his forehead. "Of course she's old! She can afford to have it said of her—a woman who has made twenty years pass like a twelvemonth! Old—old! Why, sir, she shall be eternal!"

I wished to see him safely to his own door, but he waved me back and walked away with an air of resolution, whistling and swinging his cane. I waited a moment—then followed him at a distance and saw him proceed to cross the Santa Trinità Bridge. When he reached the middle he suddenly paused, as if his strength had deserted him, and leaned upon the parapet gazing over into the Arno. I was careful to keep him in sight; I confess I passed ten very nervous minutes. He recovered himself at last and went his way slowly and with hanging head.

That I had really startled him into a bolder use of his long-garnered stores of knowledge and taste, into the vulgar effort and hazard of production, seemed at first reason enough for his continued silence and absence; but as day followed day without his either calling or sending me a line and without my meeting him in his customary haunts, in the galleries, in the chapel at San Lorenzo, or even strolling between the Arno-side and the great hedge screen of verdure which, along the drive of the Cascine, throws the fair occupants of the open carriages into such becoming relief—as for more than a week I got neither tidings nor sight of him, I began to fear I might have fatally offended him and that instead of giving a wholesome push to his talent, or at least to his faith, I had done it a real harm. I had a wretched suspicion I might have made him ill. My stay at Florence was drawing to a close, and it was important that before resuming my journey I should assure myself of the truth. Theobald had to the last kept his lodging a secret, and I was at a loss how to follow him up. The simplest course was to make inquiry of the object of his homage who neighbored with the Mercato Vecchio, and I confess that unsatisfied curiosity as to the lady herself counseled it as well. Perhaps I had done her injustice, perhaps she was as immortally fresh and fair as he conceived her. I was at any rate anxious to set eyes once more on the ripe enchantress who had made twenty years, as he had said, pass like a twelvemonth. I repaired accordingly one morning to her abode, climbed the interminable staircase, and reached her door. It stood ajar, and, while I hesitated to enter, a little serving maid came clattering out with an empty cooking pot, as if she had just performed some savory errand. The inner door too was open; so I crossed the little vestibule and reached the room in which I had formerly been received. It hadn't its evening aspect. The table, or one end of it, was spread for a late breakfast, before which sat a gentleman—an individual at least of the male sex—doing execution upon a beefsteak and onions and a bottle of wine. At his elbow, in intimate nearness, was placed the lady of the house. Her attitude, as I arrived, was not that of an enchantress. With one hand she held in her lap a plate of smoking macaroni; with the other she had lifted high in air one of the pendulous filaments of this succulent compound and was in the act of slipping it gently down her throat. On the uncovered end of the table, facing her companion, were ranged half-a-dozen small statuettes, of some snuff-colored substance resembling terra cotta.

He, brandishing his knife with ardor, was apparently descanting on their merits.

Evidently I darkened the door. My hostess dropped her macaroni—into her mouth, and rose hastily with a harsh exclamation and a flushed face. I forthwith felt sure that the sublime Serafina's secret was still better worth knowing than I had supposed, and that the way to learn it was to take it for granted. I summoned my best Italian, I smiled and bowed and apologized for my intrusion; and in a moment, whether or no I had dispelled the lady's irritation, I had at least made her prudent. I must put myself at my ease; I must take a seat. This was another friend of hers—also an artist, she declared with a smile that had turned to the gracious. Her companion wiped his mustache and bowed with great civility. I saw at a glance that he was equal to the situation. He was presumably the author of the statuettes on the table and knew a money-spending *forestière* when he saw one. He was a small active man, with a clever, impudent tossed-up nose, a sharp, little black eye, conscious of many things at once, and the cocked-up mustache of a trooper. On the side of his head he wore jauntily one of the loose velvet caps affected by sculptors in damp studios, and I observed that his feet were encased in bright "worked" slippers. On Serafina's remarking with dignity that I was the friend of Mr. Theobald he broke out into that fantastic French of which Italians are sometimes so insistently lavish, declaring without reserve that Mr. Theobald was a magnificent genius.

"I am sure I don't know," I answered with a shrug. "If you're in a position to affirm it you've the advantage of me. I've seen nothing from his hand but the bambino yonder, which certainly is fine."

He had it that the bambino was a masterpiece—in the *maniera Correggiesca*. It was only a pity, he added with a knowing laugh, that the sketch hadn't been made on some good bit of honeycombed old panel. The sublime Serafina hereupon protested that Mr. Theobald was the soul of honor and didn't lend himself to that style of manufacture. "I'm not a judge of genius," she said, "and I know nothing of pictures. I'm a poor, simple widow; but I'm sure *nostro signore* has the heart of an angel and the virtue of a saint. He's my great benefactor," she made no secret of it. The afterglow of the somewhat sinister flush with which she had greeted me still lingered in her cheek and perhaps didn't favor her beauty; I couldn't but judge it a wise custom of Theobald's to visit her only by candlelight. She was coarse and her poor adorer a poet.

"I've the greatest esteem for him," I stated; "it's for that reason I've been so uneasy at not seeing him for ten days. Have you seen him? Is he perhaps ill?"

"Ill? Heaven forbid!" cried Serafina with genuine vehemence.

Her companion uttered a rapid expletive and reproached her with not having been to see him. She hesitated a moment, then simpered the least bit and bridled. "He comes to see me—without reproach! But it wouldn't be the same for me to go to him, though indeed you may almost call him a man of holy life."

"He has the greatest admiration for you," I said. "He'd have been honored by your visit."

She looked at me a moment sharply. "More admiration than you. Admit that!" Of course I protested with all the eloquence at my command, and my ambiguous hostess then confessed that she had taken no fancy to me on my former visit and that, our friend not having returned, she believed I had poisoned his mind against her. "It would be no kindness to the poor gentleman, I can tell you that," she said. "He has come to see me every evening for years. It's a long friendship! No one knows him as I do."

"I don't pretend to know him or to understand him. I can only esteem and—I think I may say—love him. Nevertheless he seems to me a little—!" And I touched my forehead and waved my hand in the air.

Serafina glanced at her companion as for inspiration. He contented himself with shrugging his shoulders while he filled his glass again. The *padrona* hereupon treated me to a look of more meaning than quite consorted with her noble blankness. "Ah, but it's for that that *I* love him! The world has so little kindness for such persons. It laughs at them and despises them and cheats them. He's too good for this wicked life. It's his blest imagination that he finds a little Paradise up here in my poor apartment. If he thinks so, how can I help it? He has a strange belief—really I ought to be ashamed to tell you—that I resemble the Madonna Santissima, heaven forgive me! I let him think what he pleases so long as it makes him happy. He was very kind to me once and I'm not one who forgets a favor. So I receive him every evening civilly, and ask after his health, and let him look at me on this side and that. For that matter, I may say it without vanity, I was worth looking at once. And he's not always amusing, *poveretto!* He sits sometimes for an hour without speaking a word, or else he talks away, without stopping, about art and nature and beauty and duty, about fifty fine things that are all so much Latin to me. I beg you to understand that he has never said a word to me I mightn't honorably listen to. He may be a little cracked, but he's one of the blessed saints."

"Eh, eh," cried the man, "the blessed saints were all a little cracked!"

Serafina, I surmised, left part of her story untold; what she said sufficed to make poor Theobald's own statement still more affecting than I had already found its strained simplicity. "It's a strange fortune, certainly," she went on, "to have such a friend as this dear man—a friend who's less than a lover, yet more than a brother." I glanced at her comrade, who continued to smirk in a mystifying manner while he twisted the ends of his mustache between his copious mouthfuls. Was *he* less than a lover? "But what will you have?" Serafina pursued. "In this hard world one mustn't ask too many questions; one must take what comes and keep what one gets. I've kept my *amoroso* for twenty years, and I do hope that, at this time of day, signore, you've not come to turn him against me!"

I assured her I had no such intention, and that I should vastly regret disturbing Mr. Theobald's habits or convictions. On the contrary I was alarmed about him and would at once go in search of him. She gave me his address and a florid account of her sufferings at his nonappearance. She had not been to him for various reasons; chiefly because she was afraid of displeasing him, as he had always made such a mystery of his home. "You might have sent this gentleman!" I however ventured to suggest.

"Ah," cried the gentleman, "he admires Madonna Serafina, but he wouldn't admire me whom he doesn't take for Saint Joseph!"

And then confidentially, his finger on his nose: "His taste's terribly severe!"

I was about to withdraw after having promised that I would inform our hostess of my friend's condition, when her companion, who had risen from table and girded his loins apparently for the onset, grasped me gently by the arm and led me before the row of statuettes. "I perceive by your conversation, signore, that you're a patron of the arts. Allow me to request your honorable attention for these modest products of my own ingenuity. They are brand-new, fresh from my atelier, and have never been exhibited in public. I have brought them here to receive the verdict of this dear lady, who's a good critic, for all she may pretend to the contrary. I'm the inventor of this peculiar style of statuette—of subject, manner, material, everything. Touch them, I pray you; handle them freely—you needn't fear. Delicate as they look, it's impossible they should break! My various creations have met with great success. They're especially admired by the American *conoscenti*. I've sent them all over Europe—to London, Paris, Vienna! You may have noticed some little specimens in Paris, on the *grand boulevard*"—he aimed at the French sound of the words—"in a shop of which they constitute the specialty. There's always a crowd about the window. They form a very pleasing ornament for the mantelshelf of a gay young bachelor, for the boudoir of a pretty woman. You couldn't make a prettier present to a person with whom you should wish to exchange a harmless joke. It's not classic art, signore, of course; but, between ourselves, isn't classic art sometimes rather a bore? Caricature, burlesque, *la charge*, has hitherto been confined to paper, to the pen and pencil. Now it has been my inspiration to introduce it into statuary. For this purpose I've invented a peculiar plastic compound which you will permit me not to divulge. That's my secret, signore! It's as light, you perceive, as cork, and yet firm as alabaster! I frankly confess that I really pride myself as much on this little stroke of chemical ingenuity as upon the other element of novelty in my creations—my types. What do you say to my types, signore? The idea's bold; does it strike you as happy? Cats and monkeys—monkeys and cats—all human life is there! Human life, of course I mean, viewed with the eye of the satirist! To combine sculpture and satire, signore, has been my unprecedented ambition. I flatter myself I've not egregiously failed."

As this jaunty Juvenal of the chimney piece thus persuasively proceeded, he took up his little groups successively from the table, held them aloft, turned them about, rapped them with his knuckles and gazed at them lovingly, his head on one side. They consisted each, with a vengeance, of a cat and a monkey, occasionally draped, in some preposterously sentimental conjunction. They exhibited a certain sameness of motive and illustrated chiefly the different phases of what, in fine terms, might have been called the amorous advance and the amorous alarm; but they were strikingly clever and expressive, and were at once very dreadful little beasts and very natural men and women. I confess, however, that they failed to amuse me. I was doubtless not in a mood to enjoy them, for they seemed to me peculiarly cynical and vulgar. Their imitative felicity was revolting. As I looked askance at the complacent little artist, brandishing them between finger and thumb and caressing them with the fondest eye, he struck me as himself little more than an exceptionally intelligent ape. I mustered an admiring grin, however, and he blew another blast. "My figures are studied from life! I've a little menagerie of monkeys whose frolics I follow by the hour. As for the cats, one has only to look out of one's back window! Since I've begun to examine these expressive little brutes I've made many profound observations. Speaking, signore, to a man of imagination, I may say that my little designs are not without a philosophy of their own. Truly, I don't know whether the cats and monkeys imitate us, or whether it's we who imitate them." I congratulated him on his philosophy, and he resumed: "You'll do me the honor to admit that I've handled my subjects with delicacy. Eh, it was needed, *signore mio*. I've been just a bit free, but not too free—eh, *dica?* Just a scrap of a hint, you know! You may see as much or as little as you please. These little groups, however, are no measure of my invention. If you'll favor me with a call at my studio, I think you'll admit that my combinations are really infinite. I likewise execute figures to command. You've perhaps some little motive—the fruit of your philosophy of life, signore—which you'd like to have interpreted. I can promise to work it up to your satisfaction; it shall have as many high lights and sharp accents as you please! Allow me to present you with my card and to remind you that my prices are moderate. Only sixty francs for a little group like that. My statuettes are as durable as bronze —*aere perennius*, signore—and, between ourselves, I think they're more amusing!"

As I pocketed his card I turned an eye on Madonna Serafina, wondering whether she had a sense for contrasts. She had picked up one of the little couples and was tenderly dusting it with a feather broom.

What I had just seen and heard had so deepened my compassionate interest in my deluded friend that I took a summary leave, making my way directly to the house designated by this remarkable woman. It was in an obscure corner of the opposite side of the town and presented a somber and squalid appearance. A withered crone, in the doorway, on my inquiring for Theobald, welcomed me with a mumbled blessing and an expression of relief at the poor gentleman's having at last a caller. His lodging appeared to consist of a single room at the top of the house. On getting no answer to my knock I opened the door, supposing him absent; so that it gave me a certain shock to find him but seated helpless and dumb. His chair was near the single window, facing an easel which supported a large canvas. On my entering he looked up at me blankly, without changing his position, which was that of absolute lassitude and dejection, his arms loosely folded, his legs stretched before him, his head hanging on his breast. Advancing into the room I saw how vividly his face answered to his attitude. He was pale, haggard, and unshaven, and his dull and sunken eye gazed at me without a spark of recognition. My fear had been that he would greet me with fierce reproaches, as the cruelly officious patron who had turned his contentment to bitterness, and I was relieved to find my appearance excite no visible resentment. "Don't you know me?"—I put out my hand. "Have you already forgotten me?"

He made no response, but kept his position stupidly, and left me staring about the room. It spoke, the poor place, all plaintively for itself. Shabby, sordid, naked, it contained, beyond the wretched bed, but the scantiest provision for personal comfort.

It was bedroom at once and studio—a grim ghost of a studio. A few dusty casts and prints on the walls, three or four old canvases turned face inward and a rusty-looking color box formed, with the easel at the window, the sum of its appurtenances. The whole scene savored horribly of indigence. Its only wealth was the picture on the easel, presumably the famous Madonna. Averted as this was from the door, I was unable to see its face; but at last, sickened by my impression of vacant misery, I passed behind Theobald eagerly and tenderly. I can scarcely say I was surprised at what I found—a canvas that was a mere dead blank cracked and discolored by time. This was his immortal work! Though not surprised, I confess I was powerfully moved, and I think that for five minutes I couldn't have trusted myself to speak. At last my silent nearness affected him; he stirred and turned and then rose, looking at me with a slow return of intelligence. I murmured some kind ineffective nothings about his being ill and needing advice and care, but he seemed absorbed in the effort to recall distinctly what had last passed between us. "You were right," he said with a pitiful smile, "I'm a dawdler! I'm a failure! I shall do nothing more in this world. You opened my eyes, and though the truth is bitter I bear you no grudge. Amen! I've been sitting here for a week face to face with it, the terrible truth, face to face with the past, with my weakness and poverty and nullity. I shall never touch a brush! I believe I've neither eaten nor slept. Look at that canvas!" he went on as I relieved my emotion by an urgent request that he would come home with me and dine. "That was to have contained my masterpiece! Isn't it a promising foundation? The elements of it are all *here*." And he tapped his forehead with that mystic confidence which had so often marked the gesture for me before. "If I could only transpose them into some brain that has the hand, the will! Since I've been sitting here taking stock of my intellects, I've come to believe that I've the material for a hundred masterpieces. But my hand's paralyzed now and they'll never be painted. I never began! I waited and waited to be worthier to begin—I wasted my life in preparation. While I fancied my creation was growing it was only dying. I've taken the whole business too hard. Michelangelo didn't when he went at the Lorenzo. He did his best at a venture, and his venture's immortal. *That's* mine!" And he pointed with a gesture I shall never forget at the empty canvas. "I suppose we're a genus by ourselves in the providential scheme—we talents that can't act, that can't do nor dare! We take it out in talk, in study, in plans and promises, in visions! But our visions, let me tell you," he cried with a toss of his head, "have a way of being brilliant, and a man has not lived in vain who has seen the things *I've* seen! Of course you won't believe in them when that bit of worm-eaten cloth is all I have to show for them; but to convince you, to enchant and astound the world, I need only the hand of Raphael. His brain I already have. A pity, you'll say, that I haven't his modesty! Ah, let me boast and babble now—it's all I have left! I'm the half of a genius! Where in the wide world is my other half? Lodged perhaps in the vulgar soul, the cunning ready fingers of some dull copyist or some trivial artisan who turns out by the dozen his easy prodigies of touch! But it's not for me to sneer at him; he at least does something. He's not a dawdler. Well for me if I had been vulgar and clever and reckless, if I could have shut my eyes and taken my leap."

What to say to the poor fellow, what to do for him, seemed hard to determine; I chiefly felt I must break the spell of his present inaction and draw him out of the haunted air of the little room it was such cruel irony to call a studio. I can't say I persuaded him to come forth with me; he simply suffered himself to be led, and when we began to walk in the warm light of day I was able to appreciate his great weakness. Nevertheless he seemed in a manner to revive; he even murmured to me at last that he should like to go to the Pitti Gallery. I shall never forget our melancholy stroll through those gorgeous halls, every picture on whose walls glowed, to my stricken sight, with an insolent renewal of strength and luster. The eyes and lips of the great portraits reflected for me a pitying scorn of the dejected pretender who had dreamed of competing with their triumphant authors. The celestial candor even of the "Madonna of the Chair," as we paused in perfect silence before her, broke into the strange smile of the women of Leonardo. Perfect silence indeed marked our whole progress—the silence of a deep farewell; for I felt in all my pulses, as Theobald, leaning on my arm, dragged one heavy foot after the other, that he was looking his last. When we came out he was so exhausted that instead of taking him to my hotel to dine I called a cab and drove him straight to his own poor lodging. He had sunk into the deepest lethargy; he lay back in the vehicle with his eyes closed, as pale as death, his faint breathing interrupted at intervals by a gasp like a smothered sob or a vain attempt to speak. With the help of the old woman who had admitted me before and who emerged from a dark back court I contrived to lead him up the long, steep staircase and lay him on his wretched bed. To her I gave him in charge while I prepared in all haste to call in a doctor. But she followed me out of the room with a pitiful clasping of her hands.

"Poor, dear, blessed gentleman," she wailed—"is he dying?"

"Possibly. How long has he been so bad?"

"Since a certain night he passed ten days ago. I came up in the morning to make his poor bed, and found him sitting up in his clothes before that great dirty canvas he keeps there. Poor, dear, strange man, he says his prayers to it! He hadn't been to bed—nor even since then, as you may say. What has happened to him? Has he found out about *quella cattiva donna?*" she panted with a glittering eye and a toothless grin.

"Prove at least that one old woman can be faithful," I said, "and watch him well till I come back." My return was delayed through the absence of the English physician, who was away on a round of visits and whom I vainly pursued from house to house before I overtook him. I brought him to Theobald's bedside none too soon. A violent fever had seized our patient, whose case was evidently grave. A couple of hours later on I knew he had brain fever. From this moment I was with him constantly, but I am far from wishing fully to report his illness. Excessively painful to witness, it was happily brief. Life burned out in delirium. One night in particular that I passed at his pillow, listening to his wild snatches of regret, of aspiration, of rapture and awe at the phantasmal pictures with which his brain seemed to swarm, comes back to my memory now like some stray page from a lost masterpiece of tragedy. Before a week was over we had buried him in the little Protestant cemetery on the way to Fiesole. Madonna Serafina, whom I had caused to be informed of his state, had come in person, I was told, to inquire about its progress; but she was absent from his funeral, which was attended but by a scanty concourse of mourners. Half-a-dozen old Florentine sojourners, in spite of the prolonged estrangement that had preceded his death, had felt the kindly impulse to honor his grave. Among them was my friend Mrs. Coventry, whom I found, on my departure, waiting in her carriage at the gate of the cemetery.

"Well," she said, relieving at last with a significant smile the solemnity of our immediate greeting, "and the greatest of all Madonnas? Have you seen her after all?"

"I've seen her," I said; "she's mine—by bequest. But I shall never show her to you."

"And why not, pray?"

"Because you wouldn't understand her!"

She rather glared at me. "Upon my word you're polite!"

"Pardon me—I'm sad and vexed and bitter." And with reprehensible rudeness I marched away. I was impatient to leave Florence; my friend's blighted spirit met my eyes in all aspects. I had packed my trunk to start for Rome that night, and meanwhile, to beguile my unrest, I aimlessly paced the streets. Chance led me at last to the church of San Lorenzo. Remembering poor Theobald's phrase about Michelangelo—"He did his best at a venture"—I went in and turned my steps to the chapel of the tombs. Viewing in sadness the sadness of its immortal treasures, I could say to myself while I stood there that they needed no ampler commentary than those simple words. As I passed through the church again to leave it, a woman, turning away from one of the side altars, met me face to face. The black shawl depending from her head draped becomingly the handsome face of Madonna Serafina. She stopped as she recognized me, and I saw she wished to speak. Her brow was lighted and her ample bosom heaved in a way that seemed to portend a certain sharpness of reproach. But some expression of my own then drew the sting from her resentment, and she addressed me in a tone in which bitterness was tempered by an acceptance of the anticlimax that had been after all so long and so wondrously postponed. "I know it was you. now, who separated us," she said. "It was a pity he ever brought you to see me! Of course, you couldn't think of me as he did. Well, the Lord gave him, the Lord has taken him. I've just paid for a nine days' mass for his soul. And I can tell you this, signore—I never deceived him. Who put it into his head that I was made to live on holy thoughts and fine phrases? It was his own imagination, and it pleased him to think so. Did he suffer much?" she added more softly and after a pause.

"His sufferings were great, but they were short."

"And did he speak of me?" She had hesitated and dropped her eyes; she raised them with her question, and revealed in their somber stillness a gleam of feminine confidence which for the moment revived and enhanced her beauty. Poor Theobald! Whatever name he had given his passion it was still her fine eyes that had charmed him.

"Be contented, madam," I answered gravely.

She lowered her lids again and was silent. Then exhaling a full, rich sigh as she gathered her shawl together: "He was a magnificent genius!"

I bowed assent and we separated.

Passing through a narrow side street on my way back to my hotel, I noted above a doorway a sign that it seemed to me I had read before. I suddenly remembered it for identical with the superscription of a card that I had carried for an hour in my waistcoat pocket. On the threshold stood the ingenious artist whose claims to public favor were thus distinctly signalized, smoking a pipe in the evening air and giving the finishing polish with a bit of rag to one of his inimitable "combinations." I caught the expressive curl of a couple of tails. He recognized me, removed his little red cap with an obsequious bow, and motioned me to enter his studio. I returned his salute and passed on, vexed with the apparition. For a week afterwards, whenever I was seized among the ruins of triumphant Rome with some peculiarly poignant memory of Theobald's transcendent illusions and deplorable failure, I seemed to catch the other so impertinent and so cynical echo: "Cats and monkeys, monkeys and cats—all human life is there!"

Ernest Hemingway, born in the Chicago suburb of Oak Park in 1898, received most of his education from experience. After a year as reporter on the Kansas City *Star* he went to Europe and served as a volunteer in an American ambulance unit. In 1917 he joined the Italian Arditi and was wounded on the Italian front. Following the war he became an American newspaper correspondent in Paris, where he wrote his first stories. France and Spain had a great appeal for him and became the setting for much of his fiction. He once observed that a writer's greatest single difficulty is in knowing truly what he really feels, rather than what he is supposed to feel. This aim of honest and direct portrayal of experience has marked his stories of soldiers, bullfighters, hunters, and fishermen. The Spanish Civil War gave him the material for his novel *For Whom the Bell Tolls.* During World War II he served as a magazine correspondent on various fronts. His novelette *The Old Man and the Sea*, telling of a Cuban fisherman and his struggle with a giant marlin, was awarded a Pulitzer Prize in 1953. His most notable stories appear in *The Fifth Column and the First Forty-Nine Stories.*

ERNEST HEMINGWAY

The Undefeated

MANUEL GARCIA climbed the stairs to Don Miguel Retana's office. He set down his suitcase and knocked on the door. There was no answer. Manuel, standing in the hallway, felt there was someone in the room. He felt it through the door.

"Retana," he said, listening.

There was no answer.

He's there, all right, Manuel thought.

"Retana," he said and banged the door.

"Who's there?" said someone in the office.

"Me, Manolo," Manuel said.

"What do you want?" asked the voice.

"I want to work," Manuel said.

Something in the door clicked several times and it swung open. Manuel went in, carrying his suitcase.

A little man sat behind a desk at the far side of the room. Over his head was a bull's head, stuffed by a Madrid taxidermist; on the walls were framed photographs and bullfight posters.

The little man sat looking at Manuel.

"I thought they'd kill you," he said.

Manuel knocked with his knuckles on the desk. The little man sat looking at him across the desk.

"How many corridas you had this year?" Retana asked.

"One," he answered.

"Just that one?" the little man asked.

"That's all."

"I read about it in the papers," Retana said. He leaned back in the chair and looked at Manuel.

Manuel looked up at the stuffed bull. He had seen it often before. He felt a certain family interest in it. It had killed his brother, the promising one, about nine years ago. Manuel remembered the day. There was a brass plate on the oak shield the bull's head was mounted on. Manuel could not read it, but he imagined it was in memory of his brother. Well, he had been a good kid.

The plate said: "The Bull 'Mariposa' of the Duke of Veragua, which accepted 9 varas for 7 caballos, and caused the death of Antonio Garcia, Novillero, April 27, 1909."

Retana saw him looking at the stuffed bull's head.

"The lot the Duke sent me for Sunday will make a scandal," he said. "They're all bad in the legs. What do they say about them at the Café?"

"I don't know," Manuel said. "I just got in."

"Yes," Retana said. "You still have your bag."

He looked at Manuel, leaning back behind the big desk.

"Sit down," he said. "Take off your cap."

Manuel sat down; his cap off, his face was changed. He looked pale, and his coleta pinned forward on his head, so that it would not show under the cap, gave him a strange look.

"You don't look well," Retana said.

"I just got out of the hospital," Manuel said.

"I heard they'd cut your leg off," Retana said.

"No," said Manuel. "It got all right."

Retana leaned forward across the desk and pushed a wooden box of cigarettes toward Manuel.

"Have a cigarette," he said.

"Thanks."

Manuel lit it.

"Smoke?" he said, offering the match to Retana.

"No," Retana waved his hand, "I never smoke."

Retana watched him smoking.

"Why don't you get a job and go to work?" he said.

"I don't want to work," Manuel said. "I am a bullfighter."

"There aren't any bullfighters any more," Retana said.

"I'm a bullfighter," Manuel said.

"Yes, while you're in there," Retana said.

Manuel laughed.

Retana sat, saying nothing and looking at Manuel.

"I'll put you in a nocturnal if you want," Retana offered.

"When?" Manuel asked.

"Tomorrow night."

"I don't like to substitute for anybody," Manuel said. That was the way they all got killed. That was the way Salvator got killed. He tapped with his knuckles on the table.

"It's all I've got," Retana said.

"Why don't you put me on next week?" Manuel suggested.

"You wouldn't draw," Retana said. "All they want is Litri and Rubito and La Torre. Those kids are good."

"They'd come to see me get it," Manuel said, hopefully.

"No, they wouldn't. They don't know who you are any more."

"I've got a lot of stuff," Manuel said.

"I'm offering to put you on tomorrow night," Retana said. "You can work with young Hernandez and kill two novillos after the Charlots."

"Whose novillos?" Manuel asked.

"I don't know. Whatever stuff they've got in the corrals. What the veterinaries won't pass in the daytime."

"I don't like to substitute," Manuel said.

"You can take it or leave it," Retana said. He leaned forward over the papers. He was no longer interested. The appeal that Manuel had made to him for a moment when he thought of the old days was gone. He would like to get him to substitute for Larita because he could get him cheaply. He could get others cheaply too. He would like to help him though. Still he had given him the chance. It was up to him.

"How much do I get?" Manuel asked. He was still playing with the idea of refusing. But he knew he could not refuse.

"Two hundred and fifty pesetas," Retana said. He had thought of five hundred, but when he opened his mouth it said two hundred and fifty.

"You pay Villalta seven thousand," Manuel said

"You're not Villalta," Retana said.

"I know it," Manuel said.

"He draws it, Manolo," Retana said in explanation.

"Sure," said Manuel. He stood up. "Give me three hundred, Retana."

"All right," Retana agreed. He reached in the drawer for a paper.

"Can I have fifty now?" Manuel asked.

"Sure," said Retana. He took a fifty-peseta note out of his pocketbook and laid it, spread out flat, on the table.

Manuel picked it up and put it in his pocket.

"What about a cuadrilla?" he asked.

"There's the boys that always work for me nights," Retana said. "They're all right."

"How about picadors?" Manuel asked.

"They're not much," Retana admitted.

"I've got to have one good pic," Manuel said.

"Get him then," Retana said. "Go and get him."

"Not out of this," Manuel said. "I'm not paying for any cuadrilla out of sixty duros."

Retana said nothing but looked at Manuel across the big desk.

"You know I've got to have one good pic," Manuel said.

Retana said nothing but looked at Manuel from a long way off.

"It isn't right," Manuel said.

Retana was still considering him, leaning back in his chair, considering him from a long way away.

"There're the regular pics," he offered.

"I know," Manuel said. "I know your regular pics."

Retana did not smile. Manuel knew it was over.

"All I want is an even break," Manuel said reasoningly. "When I go out there I want to be able to call my shots on the bull. It only takes one good picador."

He was talking to a man who was no longer listening.

"If you want something extra," Retana said, "go and get it. There will be a regular cuadrilla out there. Bring as many of your own pics as you want. The charlotada is over by 10:30."

"All right," Manuel said. "If that's the way you feel about it."

"That's the way," Retana said.

"I'll see you tomorrow night," Manuel said.

"I'll be out there," Retana said.

Manuel picked up his suitcase and went out.

"Shut the door," Retana called.

Manuel looked back. Retana was sitting forward looking at some papers. Manuel pulled the door tight until it clicked.

He went down the stairs and out of the door into the hot brightness of the street. It was very hot in the street and the light on the white buildings was sudden and hard on his eyes. He walked down the shady side of the steep street toward the Puerta del Sol. The shade felt solid and cool as running water. The heat came suddenly as he crossed the intersecting streets. Manuel saw no one he knew in all the people he passed.

Just before the Puerta del Sol he turned into a café.

It was quiet in the café. There were a few men sitting at tables against the wall. At one table four men played cards. Most of the men sat against the wall smoking, empty coffee-cups and liqueur-glasses before them on the tables. Manuel went through the long room to a small room in back. A man sat at a table in the corner asleep. Manuel sat down at one of the tables.

A waiter came in and stood beside Manuel's table.

"Have you seen Zurito?" Manuel asked him.

"He was in before lunch," the waiter answered. "He won't be back before five o'clock.

"Bring me some coffee and milk and a shot of the ordinary," Manuel said.

The waiter came back into the room carrying a tray with a big coffee-glass and a liqueur-glass on it. In his left hand he held a bottle of brandy. He swung these down to the table and a boy who had followed him poured coffee and milk into the glass from two shiny, spouted pots with long handles.

Manuel took off his cap and the waiter noticed his pigtail pinned forward on his head. He winked at the coffee-boy as he poured out the brandy into the little glass beside Manuel's coffee. The coffee-boy looked at Manuel's pale face curiously.

"You fighting here?" asked the waiter, corking up the bottle.

"Yes," Manuel said. "Tomorrow."

The waiter stood there, holding the bottle on one hip.

"You in the Charlie Chaplins?" he asked.

The coffee-boy looked away, embarrassed.

"No. In the ordinary."

"I thought they were going to have Chaves and Hernandez," the waiter said.

"No. Me and another."

"Who? Chaves or Hernandez?"

"Hernandez, I think."

"What's the matter with Chaves?"

"He got hurt."

"Where did you hear that?"

"Retana."

"Hey, Looie," the waiter called to the next room, "Chaves got cogida."

Manuel had taken the wrapper off the lumps of sugar and dropped them into his coffee. He stirred it and drank it down, sweet, hot, and warming in his empty stomach. He drank off the brandy.

"Give me another shot of that," he said to the waiter.

The waiter uncorked the bottle and poured the glass full, slopping another drink into the saucer. Another waiter had come up in front of the table. The coffee-boy was gone.

"Is Chaves hurt bad?" the second waiter asked Manuel.

"I don't know," Manuel said, "Retana didn't say."

"A hell of a lot he cares," the tall waiter said. Manuel had not seen him before. He must have just come up.

"If you stand in with Retana in this town, you're a made man," the tall waiter said. "If you aren't in with him, you might just as well go out and shoot yourself."

"You said it," the other waiter who had come in said. "You said it then."

"You're right I said it," said the tall waiter. "I know what I'm talking about when I talk about that bird."

"Look what he's done for Villalta," the first waiter said.

"And that ain't all," the tall waiter said. "Look what he's done for Marcial Lalanda. Look what he's done for Nacional."

"You said it, kid," agreed the short waiter.

Manuel looked at them, standing talking in front of his table. He had drunk his second brandy. They had forgotten about him. They were not interested in him.

"Look at that bunch of camels," the tall waiter went on. "Did you ever see this Nacional II?"

"I seen him last Sunday, didn't I?" the original waiter said.

"He's a giraffe," the short waiter said.

"What did I tell you?" the tall waiter said. "Those are Retana's boys."

"Say, give me another shot of that," Manuel said. He had poured the brandy the waiter had slopped over in the saucer into his glass and drank it while they were talking.

The original waiter poured his glass full mechanically, and the three of them went out of the room talking.

In the far corner the man was still asleep, snoring slightly on the intaking breath, his head back against the wall.

Manuel drank his brandy. He felt sleepy himself. It was too hot to go out into the town. Besides there was nothing to do. He wanted to see Zurito. He would go to sleep while he waited. He kicked his suitcase under the table to be sure it was there. Perhaps it would be better to put it back under the seat, against the wall. He leaned down and shoved it under. Then he leaned forward on the table and went to sleep.

When he woke there was someone sitting across the table from him. It was a big man with a heavy brown face like an Indian. He had been sitting there some time. He had waved the waiter away and sat reading the paper and occasionally looking down at Manuel, asleep, his head on the table. He read the paper laboriously, forming the words with his lips as he read. When it tired him he looked at Manuel. He sat heavily in the chair, his black Cordoba hat tipped forward.

Manuel sat up and looked at him.

"Hello, Zurito," he said.

"Hello, kid," the big man said.

"I've been asleep." Manuel rubbed his forehead with the back of his fist.

"I thought maybe you were."

"How's everything?"

"Good. How is everything with you?"

"Not so good."

They were both silent. Zurito, the picador, looked at Manuel's white face. Manuel looked down at the picador's enormous hands folding the paper to put away in his pocket.

"I got a favor to ask you, Manos," Manuel said.

Manosduros was Zurito's nickname. He never heard it without thinking of his huge hands. He put them forward on the table self-consciously.

"Let's have a drink," he said.

"Sure," said Manuel.

The waiter came and went and came again. He went out of the room looking back at the two men at the table.

"What's the matter, Manolo?" Zurito set down his glass.

"Would you pic two bulls for me tomorrow night?" Manuel asked, looking up at Zurito across the table.

"No," said Zurito. "I'm not pic-ing."

Manuel looked down at his glass. He had expected that answer; now he had it. Well, he had it.

"I'm sorry, Manolo, but I'm not pic-ing." Zurito looked at his hands.

"That's all right," Manuel said.

"I'm too old," Zurito said.

"I just asked you," Manuel said.

"Is it the nocturnal tomorrow?"

"That's it. I figured if I had just one good pic, I could get away with it."

"How much are you getting?"

"Three hundred pesetas."

"I get more than that for pic-ing."

"I know," said Manuel. "I didn't have any right to ask you."

"What do you keep on doing it for?" Zurito asked. "Why don't you cut off your coleta, Manolo?"

"I don't know," Manuel said.

"You're pretty near as old as I am," Zurito said.

"I don't know," Manuel said. "I got to do it. If I can fix it so that I get an even break, that's all I want. I got to stick with it, Manos."

"No, you don't."

"Yes, I do. I've tried keeping away from it."

"I know how you feel. But it isn't right. You ought to get out and stay out."

"I can't do it. Besides, I've been going good lately."

Zurito looked at his face.

"You've been in the hospital."

"But I was going great when I got hurt."

Zurito said nothing. He tipped the cognac out of his saucer into his glass.

"The papers said they never saw a better faena," Manuel said.

Zurito looked at him.

"You know when I get going I'm good," Manuel said.

"You're too old," the picador said.

"No," said Manuel. "You're ten years older than I am."

"With me it's different."

"I'm not too old," Manuel said.

They sat silent, Manuel watching the picador's face.

"I was going great till I got hurt," Manuel offered.

"You ought to have seen me, Manos," Manuel said, reproachfully.

"I don't want to see you," Zurito said. "It makes me nervous."

"You haven't seen me lately."

"I've seen you plenty."

Zurito looked at Manuel, avoiding his eyes.

"You ought to quit it, Manolo."

"I can't," Manuel said. "I'm going good now, I tell you."

Zurito leaned forward, his hands on the table.

"Listen. I'll pic for you and if you don't go big tomorrow night, you'll quit. See? Will you do that?"

"Sure."

Zurito leaned back, relieved.

"You got to quit," he said. "No monkey business. You got to cut the coleta."

"I won't have to quit," Manuel said. "You watch me. I've got the stuff."

Zurito stood up. He felt tired from arguing.

"You got to quit," he said. "I'll cut your coleta myself."

"No, you won't," Manuel said. "You won't have a chance."

Zurito called the waiter.

"Come on," said Zurito. "Come on up to the house."

Manuel reached under the seat for his suitcase. He was happy. He knew Zurito would pic for him. He was the best picador living. It was all simple now.

"Come on up to the house and we'll eat," Zurito said.

Manuel stood in the patio de caballos waiting for the Charlie Chaplins to be over. Zurito stood beside him. Where they stood it was dark. The high door that led into the bull-ring was shut. Above them they heard a shout, then another shout of laughter. Then there was silence. Manuel liked the smell of the stables about the patio de caballos. It smelled good in the dark. There was another roar from the arena and then applause, prolonged applause, going on and on.

"You ever seen these fellows?" Zurito asked, big and looming beside Manuel in the dark.

"No," Manuel said.

"They're pretty funny," Zurito said. He smiled to himself in the dark.

The high, double, tight-fitting door into the bull-ring swung open and Manuel saw the ring in the hard light of the arc-lights, the plaza, dark all the way around, rising high; around the edge of the ring were running and bowing two men dressed like tramps, followed by a third in the uniform of a hotel bell-boy who stooped and picked up the hats and canes thrown down onto the sand and tossed them back up into the darkness.

The electric light went on in the patio.

"I'll climb onto one of those ponies while you collect the kids," Zurito said.

Behind them came the jingle of the mules, coming out to go into the arena and be hitched onto the dead bull.

The members of the cuadrilla, who had been watching the burlesque from the runway between the barrera and the seats, came walking back and stood in a group talking, under the electric light in the patio. A good-looking lad in a silver-and-orange suit came up to Manuel and smiled.

"I'm Hernandez," he said and put out his hand.

Manuel shook it.

"They're regular elephants we've got tonight," the boy said cheerfully.

"They're big ones with horns," Manuel agreed.

"You drew the worst lot," the boy said.

"That's all right," Manuel said. "The bigger they are, the more meat for the poor."

"Where did you get that one?" Hernandez grinned.

"That's an old one," Manuel said. "You line up your cuadrilla, so I can see what I've got."

"You've got some good kids," Hernandez said. He was very cheerful. He had been on twice before in nocturnals and was beginning to get a following in Madrid. He was happy the fight would start in a few minutes.

"Where are the pics?" Manuel asked.

"They're back in the corrals fighting about who gets the beautiful horses," Hernandez grinned.

The mules came through the gate in a rush, the whips snapping, bells jangling and the young bull ploughing a furrow of sand.

They formed up for the paseo as soon as the bull had gone through.

Manuel and Hernandez stood in front. The youths of the cuadrillas were behind, their heavy capes furled over their arms. In back, the four picadors, mounted, holding their steel-tipped push-poles erect in the half-dark of the corral.

"It's a wonder Retana wouldn't give us enough light to see the horses by," one picador said.

"He knows we'll be happier if we don't get too good a look at these skins," another pic answered.

"This thing I'm on barely keeps me off the ground," the first picador said.

"Well, they're horses."

"Sure, they're horses."

They talked, sitting their gaunt horses in the dark.

Zurito said nothing. He had the only steady horse of the lot. He had tried him, wheeling him in the corrals and he responded to the bit and the spurs. He had taken the bandage off his right eye and cut the strings where they had tied his ears tight shut at the base. He was a good, solid horse, solid on his legs. That was all he needed. He intended to ride him all through the corrida. He had already, since he had mounted, sitting in the half-dark in the big, quilted saddle, waiting for the paseo, pic-ed through the whole corrida in his mind. The other picadors went on talking on both sides of him. He did not hear them.

The two matadors stood together in front of their three peones, their capes furled over their left arms in the same fashion. Manuel was thinking about the three lads in back of him. They were all three Madrilenos, like Hernandez, boys about nineteen. One of them, a gypsy, serious, aloof, and dark-faced, he liked the look of. He turned.

"What's your name, kid?" he asked the gypsy.

"Fuentes," the gypsy said.

"That's a good name," Manuel said.

The gypsy smiled, showing his teeth.

"You take the bull and give him a little run when he comes out," Manuel said.

"All right," the gypsy said. His face was serious. He began to think about just what he would do.

"Here she goes," Manuel said to Hernandez.

"All right. We'll go."

Heads up, swinging with the music, their right arms swinging free, they stepped out, crossing the sanded arena under the arc-lights, the cuadrillas opening out behind, the picadors riding after; behind came the bull-ring servants and the jingling mules. The crowd applauded Hernandez as they marched across the arena. Arrogant, swinging, they looked straight ahead as they marched.

They bowed before the president, and the procession broke up into its component parts. The bullfighters went over to the barrera and changed their heavy mantles for the light fighting capes. The mules went out. The picadors galloped jerkily around the ring, and two rode out the gate they had come in by. The servants swept the sand smooth.

Manuel drank a glass of water poured for him by one of Retana's deputies, who was acting as his manager and sword-handler. Hernandez came over from speaking with his own manager.

"You got a good hand, kid," Manuel complimented him.

"They like me," Hernandez said happily.

"How did the paseo go?" Manuel asked Retana's man.

"Like a wedding," said the handler. "Fine. You came out like Joselito and Belmonte."

Zurito rode by, a bulky equestrian statue. He wheeled his horse and faced him toward the toril on the far side of the ring where the bull would come out. It was strange under the arc-light. He pic-ed in the hot afternoon sun for big money. He didn't like this arc-light business. He wished they would get started.

Manuel went up to him.

"Pic him, Manos," he said. "Cut him down to size for me."

"I'll pic him, kid." Zurito spat on the sand. "I'll make him jump out of the ring."

"Lean on him, Manos," Manuel said.

"I'll lean on him," Zurito said. "What's holding it up?"

"He's coming now," Manuel said.

Zurito sat there, his feet in the box-stirrups, his great legs in the buckskin-covered armor gripping the horse, the reins in his left hand, the long pic held in his right hand, his broad hat well down over his eyes to shade them from the lights, watching the distant door of the toril. His horse's ears quivered. Zurito patted him with his left hand.

The red door of the toril swung back and for a moment Zurito looked into the empty passageway far across the arena. Then the bull came out in a rush, skidding on his four legs as he came out under the lights, then charging in a gallop, moving softly in a fast gallop, silent except as he woofed through wide nostrils as he charged, glad to be free after the dark pen.

In the first row of seats, slightly bored, leaning forward to write on the cement wall in front of his knees, the substitute bullfight critic of *El Heraldo* scribbled: "Campagnero, Negro, 42, came out at 90 miles an hour with plenty of gas—"

Manuel, leaning against the barrera, watching the bull, waved his hand and the gypsy ran out, trailing his cape. The bull, in full gallop, pivoted and charged the cape, his head down, his tail rising. The gypsy moved in a zigzag, and as he passed, the bull caught sight of him and abandoned the cape to charge the man. The gyp sprinted and vaulted the red fence of the barrera as the bull struck it with his horns. He tossed into it twice with his horns, banging into the wood blindly.

The critic of *El Heraldo* lit a cigarette and tossed the match at the bull, then wrote in his note-book, "large and with enough horns to satisfy the cash customers, Campagnero showed a tendency to cut into the terrain of the bullfighters."

Manuel stepped out on the hard sand as the bull banged into the fence. Out of the corner of his eye he saw Zurito sitting the white horse close to the barrera, about a quarter of the way around the ring to the left. Manuel held the cape close in front of him, a fold in each hand, and shouted at the bull. "Huh! Huh!" The bull turned, seemed to brace against the fence as he charged in a scramble, driving into the cape as Manuel side-stepped, pivoted on his heels with the charge of the bull, and swung the cape just ahead of the horns. At the end of the swing he was facing the bull again and held the cape in the same position close in front of his body, and pivoted again as the bull recharged. Each time, as he swung, the crowd shouted.

Four times he swung with the bull, lifting the cape so it billowed full, and each time bringing the bull around to charge again. Then, at the end of the fifth swing, he held the cape against his hip and pivoted, so the cape swung out like a ballet dancer's skirt and wound the bull around himself like a belt, to step clear, leaving the bull facing Zurito on the white horse, come up and planted firm, the horse facing the bull, its ears forward, its lips nervous, Zurito, his hat over his eyes, leaning forward, the long pole sticking out before and behind in a sharp angle under his right arm, held half-way down, the triangular iron point facing the bull.

El Heraldo's second-string critic, drawing on his cigarette, his eyes on the bull, wrote: "The veteran Manolo designed a series of acceptable veronicas, ending in a very Belmontistic recorte that earned applause from the regulars, and we entered the tercio of the cavalry."

Zurito sat his horse, measuring the distance between the bull and the end of the pic. As he looked, the bull gathered himself together and charged, his eyes on the horse's chest. As he lowered his head to hook, Zurito sunk the point of the pic in the swelling hump of muscle above the bull's shoulder, leaned all his weight on the shaft, and with his left hand pulled the white horse into the air, front hoofs pawing, and swung him to the right as he pushed the bull under and through so the horns passed safely under the horse's belly and the horse came down, quivering, the bull's tail brushing his chest as he charged the cape Hernandez offered him.

Hernandez ran sideways, taking the bull out and away with the cape, toward the other picador. He fixed him with a swing of the cape, squarely facing the horse and rider, and stepped back. As the bull saw the horse he charged. The picador's lance slid along his back, and as the shock of the charge lifted the horse, the picador was already halfway out of the saddle, lifting his right leg clear as he missed with the lance and falling to the left side to keep the horse between him and the bull. The horse, lifted and gored, crashed over with the bull driving into him, the picador gave a shove with his boots against the horse and lay clear, waiting to be lifted and hauled away and put on his feet.

Manuel let the bull drive into the fallen horse; he was in no hurry, the picador was safe; besides, it did a picador like that good to worry. He'd stay on longer next time. Lousy pics! He looked across the sand at Zurito a little way out from the barrera, his horse rigid, waiting.

"Huh!" he called to the bull, "Tomar!" holding the cape in both hands so it would catch his eye. The bull detached himself from the horse and charged the cape, and Manuel, running sideways and holding the cape spread wide, stopped, swung on his heels, and brought the bull sharply around facing Zurito.

"Campagnero accepted a pair of varas for the death of one rosinante, with Hernandez and Manolo at the quites," *El Heraldo's* critic wrote. "He pressed on the iron and clearly showed he was no horse-lover. The veteran Zurito resurrected some of his old stuff with the pike-pole, notably the suerte—"

"Olé! Olé!" the man sitting beside him shouted. The shout was lost in the roar of the crowd, and he slapped the critic on the back. The critic looked up to see Zurito, directly below him, leaning far out over his horse, the length of the pic rising in a sharp angle under his armpit, holding the pic almost by the point, bearing down with all his weight, holding the bull off, the bull pushing and driving to get at the horse, and Zurito, far out, on top of him, holding him, holding him, and slowly pivoting the horse against the pressure, so that at last he was clear. Zurito felt the moment when the horse was clear and the bull could come past, and relaxed the absolute steel lock of his resistance, and the triangular steel point of the pic ripped in the bull's hump of shoulder muscle as he tore loose to find Hernandez's cape before his muzzle. He charged blindly into the cape and the boy took him out into the open arena.

Zurito sat patting his horse and looking at the bull charging the cape that Hernandez swung for him out under the bright light while the crowd shouted.

"You see that one?" he said to Manuel.

"It was a wonder," Manuel said.

"I got him that time," Zurito said. "Look at him now."

At the conclusion of a closely turned pass of the cape the bull slid to his knees. He was up at once, but far out across the sand

Manuel and Zurito saw the shine of the pumping flow of blood, smooth against the black of the bull's shoulder.

"I got him that time," Zurito said.

"He's a good bull," Manuel said.

"If they gave me another shot at him, I'd kill him," Zurito said.

"They'll change the thirds on us," Manuel said.

"Look at him now," Zurito said.

"I got to go over there," Manuel said, and started on a run for the other side of the ring, where the monos were leading a horse out by the bridle toward the bull, whacking him on the legs with rods and all, in a procession, trying to get him toward the bull, who stood, dropping his head, pawing, unable to make up his mind to charge.

Zurito, sitting his horse, walking him toward the scene, not missing any detail, scowled.

Finally the bull charged, the horse leaders ran for the barrera, the picador hit too far back, and the bull got under the horse, lifted him, threw him onto his back.

Zurito watched. The monos, in their red shirts, running out to drag the picador clear. The picador, now on his feet, swearing and flopping his arms. Manuel and Hernandez standing ready with their capes. And the bull, the great, black bull, with a horse on his back, hooves dangling, the bridle caught in the horns. Black bull with a horse on his back, staggering short-legged, then arching his neck and lifting, thrusting, charging to slide the horse off, horse sliding down. Then the bull into a lunging charge at the cape Manuel spread for him.

The bull was slower now, Manuel felt. He was bleeding badly. There was a sheen of blood all down his flank.

Manuel offered him the cape again. There he came, eyes open, ugly, watching the cape. Manuel stepped to the side and raised his arms, tightening the cape ahead of the bull for the veronica.

Now he was facing the bull. Yes, his head was going down a little. He was carrying it lower. That was Zurito.

Manuel flopped the cape; there he comes; he side-stepped and swung in another veronica. He's shooting awfully accurately, he thought. He's had enough fight, so he's watching now. He's hunting now. Got his eye on me. But I always give him the cape.

He shook the cape at the bull; there he comes; he side-stepped. Awful close that time. I don't want to work that close to him.

The edge of the cape was wet with blood where it had swept along the bull's back as he went by.

All right, here's the last one.

Manuel, facing the bull, having turned with him each charge, offered the cape with his two hands. The bull looked at him. Eyes watching, horns straight forward, the bull looked at him, watching.

"Huh!" Manuel said, "Toro!" and leaning back, swung the cape forward. Here he comes. He side-stepped, swung the cape in back of him, and pivoted, so the bull followed a swirl of cape and then was left with nothing, fixed by the pass, dominated by the cape. Manuel swung the cape under his muzzle with one hand, to show the bull was fixed, and walked away.

There was no applause.

Manuel walked across the sand toward the barrera, while Zurito rode out of the ring. The trumpet had blown to change the act to the planting of the banderillos while Manuel had been working with the bull. He had not consciously noticed it. The monos were spreading canvas over the two dead horses and sprinkling sawdust around them.

Manuel came up to the barrera for a drink of water. Retana's man handed him the heavy porous jug.

Fuentes, the tall gypsy, was standing holding a pair of banderillos, holding them together, slim, red sticks, fish-hook points out. He looked at Manuel.

"Go on out there," Manuel said.

The gypsy trotted out. Manuel set down the jug and watched. He wiped his face with his handkerchief.

The critic of *El Heraldo* reached for the bottle of warm champagne that stood between his feet, took a drink, and finished his paragraph.

"—the aged Manolo rated no applause for a vulgar series of lances with the cape and we entered the third of the palings."

Alone in the center of the ring the bull stood, still fixed. Fuentes, tall, flat-backed, walking toward him arrogantly, his arms spread out, the two slim, red sticks, one in each hand, held by the fingers, points straight forward. Fuentes walked forward. Back of him and to one side was a peon with a cape. The bull looked at him and was no longer fixed.

His eyes watched Fuentes, now standing still. Now he leaned back, calling to him. Fuentes twitched the two banderillos and the light on the steel points caught the bull's eye.

His tail went up and he charged.

He came straight, his eyes on the man. Fuentes stood still, leaning back, the banderillos pointing forward. As the bull lowered his head to hook, Fuentes leaned backward, his arms came together and rose, his two hands touching, the banderillos two descending red lines, and leaning forward drove the points into the bull's shoulder, leaning far in over the bull's horns and pivoting on the two upright sticks, his legs tight together, his body curving to one side to let the bull pass.

"Olé!" from the crowd.

The bull was hooking wildly, jumping like a trout, all four feet off the ground. The red shaft of the banderillos tossed as he jumped.

Manuel, standing at the barrera, noticed that he looked always to the right.

"Tell him to drop the next pair on the right," he said to the kid who started to run out to Fuentes with the new banderillos.

A heavy hand fell on his shoulder. It was Zurito.

"How do you feel, kid?" he asked.

Manuel was watching the bull.

Zurito leaned forward on the barrera, leaning the weight of his body on his arms. Manuel turned to him.

"You're going good," Zurito said.

Manuel shook his head. He had nothing to do now until the next third. The gypsy was very good with the banderillos. The bull would come to him in the next third in good shape. He was a good bull. It had all been easy up to now. The final stuff with the sword was all he worried over. He did not really worry. He did not even think about it. But standing there he had a heavy sense of apprehension. He looked out at the bull, planning his faena, his work with the red cloth that was to reduce the bull, to make him manageable.

The gypsy was walking out toward the bull again, walking heel-and-toe, insultingly, like a ballroom dancer, the red shafts of the banderillos twitching with his walk. The bull watched him, not fixed now, hunting him, but waiting to get close enough so he could be sure of getting him, getting the horns into him.

As Fuentes walked forward the bull charged. Fuentes ran across the quarter of a circle as the bull charged and, as he passed running backward, stopped, swung forward, rose on his toes, arm straight out, and sunk the banderillos straight down into the tight of the big shoulder muscles as the bull missed him.

The crowd were wild about it.

"That kid won't stay in this night stuff long," Retana's man said to Zurito.

"He's good," Zurito said.

"Watch him now."

They watched.

Fuentes was standing with his back against the barrera. Two of the cuadrilla were back of him, with their capes ready to flop over the fence to distract the bull.

The bull, with his tongue out, his barrel heaving, was watching the gypsy. He thought he had him now. Back against the red planks. Only a short charge away. The bull watched him.

The gypsy bent back, drew back his arms, the banderillos pointing at the bull. He called to the bull, stamped one foot. The bull was suspicious. He wanted the man. No more barbs in the shoulder.

Fuentes walked a little closer to the bull. Bent back. Called again. Somebody in the crowd shouted a warning.

"He's too damn close," Zurito said.

"Watch him," Retana's man said.

Leaning back, inciting the bull with the banderillos, Fuentes jumped, both feet off the ground. As he jumped the bull's tail rose and he charged. Fuentes came down on his toes, arms straight out, whole body arching forward, and drove the shafts straight down as he swung his body clear of the right horn.

The bull crashed into the barrera where the flopping capes had attracted his eye as he lost the man.

The gypsy came running along the barrera toward Manuel,

taking the applause of the crowd. His vest was ripped where he had not quite cleared the point of the horn. He was happy about it, showing it to the spectators. He made the tour of the ring. Zurito saw him go by, smiling, pointing at his vest. He smiled.

Somebody else was planting the last pair of banderillos. Nobody was paying any attention.

Retana's man tucked a baton inside the red cloth of a muleta, folded the cloth over it, and handed it over the barrera to Manuel. He reached in the leather sword-case, took out a sword, and holding it by its leather scabbard, reached it over the fence to Manuel. Manuel pulled the blade out by the red hilt and the scabbard fell limp.

He looked at Zurito. The big man saw he was sweating.

"Now you get him, kid," Zurito said.

Manuel nodded.

"He's in good shape," Zurito said.

"Just like you want him," Retana's man assured him.

Manuel nodded.

The trumpeter, up under the roof, blew for the final act, and Manuel walked across the arena toward where, up in the dark boxes, the president must be.

In the front row of seats the substitute bullfight critic of *El Heraldo* took a long drink of the warm champagne. He had decided it was not worth while to write a running story and would write up the corrida back in the office. What the hell was it anyway? Only a nocturnal. If he missed anything he would get it out of the morning papers. He took another drink of the champagne. He had a date at Maxim's at twelve. Who were these bullfighters anyway? Kids and bums. A bunch of bums. He put his pad of paper in his pocket and looked over toward Manuel, standing very much alone in the ring, gesturing with his hat in a salute toward a box he could not see high up in the dark plaza. Out in the ring the bull stood quiet, looking at nothing.

"I dedicate this bull to you, Mr. President, and to the public of Madrid, the most intelligent and generous of the world," was what Manuel was saying. It was a formula. He said it all. It was a little long for nocturnal use.

He bowed at the dark, straightened, tossed his hat over his

shoulder, and, carrying the muleta in his left hand and the sword in his right, walked out toward the bull.

Manuel walked toward the bull. The bull looked at him; his eyes were quick. Manuel noticed the way the banderillos hung down on his left shoulder and the steady sheen of blood from Zurito's pic-ing. He noticed the way the bull's feet were. As he walked forward, holding the muleta in his left hand and the sword in his right, he watched the bull's feet. The bull could not charge without gathering his feet together. Now he stood square on them, dully.

Manuel walked toward him, watching his feet. This was all right. He could do this. He must work to get the bull's head down, so he could go in past the horns and kill him. He did not think about the sword, not about killing the bull. He thought about one thing at a time. The coming things oppressed him, though. Walking forward, watching the bull's feet, he saw successively his eyes, his wet muzzle, and the wide, forward-pointing spread of his horns. The bull had light circles about his eyes. His eyes watched Manuel. He felt he was going to get this little one with the white face.

Standing still now and spreading the red cloth of the muleta with the sword, pricking the point into the cloth so that the sword, now held in his left hand, spread the red flannel like the jib of a boat, Manuel noticed the points of the bull's horns. One of them was splintered from banging against the barrera. The other was sharp as a porcupine quill. Manuel noticed while spreading the muleta that the white base of the horn was stained red. While he noticed these things he did not lose sight of the bull's feet. The bull watched Manuel steadily.

He's on the defensive now, Manuel thought. He's reserving himself. I've got to bring him out of that and get his head down. Always get his head down. Zurito had his head down once, but he's come back. He'll bleed when I start him going and that will bring it down.

Holding the muleta, with the sword in his left hand widening it in front of him, he called to the bull.

The bull looked at him.

He leaned back insultingly and shook the wide-spread flannel.

The bull saw the muleta. It was a bright scarlet under the arc-light. The bull's legs tightened.

Here he comes. Whoosh! Manuel turned as the bull came and raised the muleta so that it passed over the bull's horns and swept down his broad back from head to tail. The bull had gone clean up in the air with the charge. Manuel had not moved.

At the end of the pass the bull turned like a cat coming around a corner and faced Manuel.

He was on the offensive again. His heaviness was gone. Manuel noted the fresh blood shining down the black shoulder and dripping down the bull's leg. He drew the sword out of the muleta and held it in his right hand. The muleta held low down in his left hand, leaning toward the left, he called to the bull. The bull's legs tightened, his eyes on the muleta. Here he comes, Manuel thought. Yuh!

He swung with the charge, sweeping the muleta ahead of the bull, his feet firm, the sword following the curve, a point of light under the arcs.

The bull recharged as the pase natural finished and Manuel raised the muleta for a pase de pecho. Firmly planted, the bull came by his chest under the raised muleta. Manuel leaned his head back to avoid the clattering banderillo shafts. The hot, black bull body touched his chest as it passed.

Too damn close, Manuel thought. Zurito, leaning on the barrera, spoke rapidly to the gypsy, who trotted out toward Manuel with a cape. Zurito pulled his hat down low and looked out across the arena at Manuel.

Manuel was facing the bull again, the muleta held low and to the left. The bull's head was down as he watched the muleta.

"If it was Belmonte doing that stuff, they'd go crazy," Retana's man said.

Zurito said nothing. He was watching Manuel out in the center of the arena.

"Where did the boss dig this fellow up?" Retana's man asked.

"Out of the hospital," Zurito said.

"That's where he's going damn quick," Retana's man said.

Zurito turned on him.

"Knock on that," he said, pointing to the barrera.

"I was just kidding, man," Retana's man said.

"Knock on the wood."

Retana's man leaned forward and knocked three times on the barrera.

"Watch the faena," Zurito said.

Out in the center of the ring, under the lights, Manuel was kneeling, facing the bull, and as he raised the muleta in both hands the bull charged, tail up.

Manuel swung his body clear and, as the bull recharged, brought around the muleta in a half-circle that pulled the bull to his knees.

"Why, that one's a great bullfighter," Retana's man said.

"No, he's not," said Zurito.

Manuel stood up and, the muleta in his left hand, the sword in his right, acknowledged the applause from the dark plaza.

The bull had humped himself up from his knees and stood waiting, his head hung low.

Zurito spoke to two of the other lads of the cuadrilla and they ran out to stand back of Manuel with their capes. There were four men back of him now. Hernandez had followed him since he first came out with the muleta. Fuentes stood watching, his cape held against his body, tall, in repose, watching lazy-eyed. Now the two came up. Hernandez motioned them to stand one at each side. Manuel stood alone, facing the bull.

Manuel waved back the men with the capes. Stepping back cautiously, they saw his face was white and sweating.

Didn't they know enough to keep back? Did they want to catch the bull's eye with the capes after he was fixed and ready? He had enough to worry about without that kind of thing.

The bull was standing, his four feet square, looking at the muleta. Manuel furled the muleta in his left hand. The bull's eyes watched it. His body was heavy on his feet. He carried his head low, but not too low.

Manuel lifted the muleta at him. The bull did not move. Only his eyes watched.

He's all lead, Manuel thought. He's all square. He's framed right. He'll take it.

He thought in bullfight terms. Sometimes he had a thought and the particular piece of slang would not come into his mind and he could not realize the thought. His instincts and his knowledge worked automatically, and his brain worked slowly and in words. He knew all about bulls. He did not have to think about them. He just did the right thing. His eyes noted things and his body performed the necessary measures without thought. If he thought about it, he would be gone.

Now, facing the bull, he was conscious of many things at the same time. There were the horns, the one splintered, the other smoothly sharp, the need to profile himself toward the left horn, lance himself short and straight, lower the muleta so the bull would follow it, and, going in over the horns, put the sword all the way into a little spot about as big as a five-peseta piece straight in back of the neck, between the sharp pitch of the bull's shoulders. He must do all this and must then come out from between the horns. He was conscious he must do all this, but his only thought was in words: "Corto y derecho."

"Corto y derecho," he thought, furling the muleta. Short and straight. Corto y derecho, he drew the sword out of the muleta, profiled on the splintered left horn, dropped the muleta across his body, so his right hand with the sword on the level with his eye made the sign of the cross, and, rising on his toes, sighted along the dipping blade of the sword at the spot high up between the bull's shoulders.

Corto y derecho he launched himself on the bull.

There was a shock, and he felt himself go up in the air. He pushed on the sword as he went up and over, and it flew out of his hand. He hit the ground and the bull was on him. Manuel, lying on the ground, kicked at the bull's muzzle with his slippered feet. Kicking, kicking, the bull after him, missing him in his excitement, bumping him with his head, driving the horns into the sand. Kicking like a man keeping a ball in the air, Manuel kept the bull from getting a clean thrust at him.

Manuel felt the wind on his back from the capes flopping at the bull, and then the bull was gone, gone over him in a rush. Dark, as his belly went over. Not even stepped on.

Manuel stood up and picked up the muleta. Fuentes handed him the sword. It was bent where it had struck the shoulder-blade. Manuel straightened it on his knee and ran toward the bull, standing now beside one of the dead horses. As he ran, his jacket flopped where it had been ripped under his arm pit.

"Get him out of there," Manuel shouted to the gypsy. The bull had smelled the blood of the dead horse and ripped into the canvas-cover with his horns. He charged Fuentes's cape, with the canvas hanging from his splintered horn, and the crowd laughed. Out in the ring, he tossed his head to rid himself of the canvas. Hernandez, running up from behind him, grabbed the end of the canvas and neatly lifted it off the horn.

The bull followed it in a half-charge and stopped still. He was on the defensive again. Manuel was walking toward him with the sword and muleta. Manuel swung the muleta before him. The bull would not charge.

Manuel profiled toward the bull, sighting along the dipping blade of the sword. The bull was motionless, seemingly dead on his feet, incapable of another charge.

Manuel rose to his toes, sighting along the steel, and charged.

Again there was the shock and he felt himself being borne back in a rush, to strike hard on the sand. There was no chance of kicking this time. The bull was on top of him. Manuel lay as though dead, his head on his arms, and the bull bumped him. Bumped his back, bumped his face in the sand. He felt the horn go into the sand between his folded arms. The bull hit him in the small of the back. His face drove into the sand. The horn drove through one of his sleeves and the bull ripped it off. Manuel was tossed clear and the bull followed the capes.

Manuel got up, found the sword and muleta, tried the point of the sword with his thumb, and then ran toward the barrera for a new sword.

Retana's man handed him the sword over the edge of the barrera.

"Wipe off your face," he said.

Manuel, running again toward the bull, wiped his bloody face with his handkerchief. He had not seen Zurito. Where was Zurito?

The cuadrilla had stepped away from the bull and waited with their capes. The bull stood, heavy and dull again after the action.

Manuel walked toward him with the muleta. He stopped and shook it. The bull did not respond. He passed it right and left, left and right before the bull's muzzle. The bull's eyes watched it and turned with the swing, but he would not charge. He was waiting for Manuel.

Manuel was worried. There was nothing to do but go in. Corto y derecho. He profiled close to the bull, crossed the muleta in front of his body and charged. As he pushed in the sword, he jerked his body to the left to clear the horn. The bull passed him and the sword shot up in the air, twinkling under the arc-lights, to fall red-hilted on the sand.

Manuel ran over and picked it up. It was bent and he straightened it over his knee.

As he came running toward the bull, fixed again now, he passed Hernandez standing with his cape.

"He's all bone," the boy said encouragingly.

Manuel nodded, wiping his face. He put the bloody handkerchief in his pocket.

There was the bull. He was close to the barrera now. Damn him. Maybe he was all bone. Maybe there was not any place for the sword to go in. The hell there wasn't! He'd show them.

He tried a pass with the muleta and the bull did not move. Manuel chopped the muleta back and forth in front of the bull. Nothing doing.

He furled the muleta, drew the sword out, profiled and drove in on the bull. He felt the sword buckle as he shoved it in, leaning his weight on it, and then it shot high in the air, end-over-ending into the crowd. Manuel had jerked clear as the sword jumped.

The first cushions thrown down out of the dark missed him. Then one hit him in the face, his bloody face looking toward the crowd. They were coming down fast. Spotting the sand. Somebody threw an empty champagne-bottle from close range. It hit Manuel on the foot. He stood there watching the dark, where the things were coming from. Then something whished through the air and struck by him. Manuel leaned over and picked it up. It was his sword. He straightened it over his knee and gestured with it to the crowd.

"Thank you," he said. "Thank you."

Oh, the dirty bastards! Dirty bastards! Oh, the lousy, dirty bastards! He kicked into a cushion as he ran.

There was the bull. The same as ever. All right, you dirty, lousy bastard!

Manuel passed the muleta in front of the bull's black muzzle. Nothing doing.

You won't! All right. He stepped close and jammed the sharp peak of the muleta into the bull's damp muzzle.

The bull was on him as he jumped back and as he tripped on a cushion he felt the horn go into him, into his side. He grabbed the horn with his two hands and rode backward, holding tight onto the place. The bull tossed him and he was clear. He lay still. It was all right. The bull was gone.

He got up coughing and feeling broken and gone. The dirty bastards!

"Give me the sword," he shouted. "Give me the stuff."

Fuentes came up with the muleta and the sword.

Hernandez put his arm around him.

"Go on to the infirmary, man," he said. "Don't be a damn fool."

"Get away from me," Manuel said. "Get to hell away from me."

He twisted free. Hernandez shrugged his shoulders. Manuel ran toward the bull.

There was the bull standing, heavy, firmly planted.

All right, you bastard! Manuel drew the sword out of the muleta, sighted with the same movement, and flung himself onto the bull. He felt the sword go in all the way. Right up to the guard. Four fingers and his thumb into the bull. The blood was hot on his knuckles, and he was on top of the bull.

The bull lurched with him as he lay on, and seemed to sink; then he was standing clear. He looked at the bull going down slowly over on his side, then suddenly four feet in the air.

Then he gestured at the crowd, his hand warm from the bull blood.

All right, you bastards! He wanted to say something, but he started to cough. It was hot and choking. He looked down for the muleta. He must go over and salute the president. President, hell! He was sitting down looking at something. It was the bull. His four feet up. Thick tongue out. Things crawling around on his belly and under his legs. Crawling where the hair was thin. Dead bull. To hell with the bull! To hell with them all! He started to get to his feet and commenced to cough. He sat down again, coughing. Somebody came and pushed him up.

They carried him across the ring to the infirmary, running with him across the sand, standing blocked at the gate as the mules came in, then around under the dark passageway, men grunting as they took him up the stairway, and then laid him down.

The doctor and two men in white were waiting for him. They laid him out on the table. They were cutting away his shirt. Manuel felt tired. His whole chest felt scalding inside. He started to cough and they held something to his mouth. Everybody was very busy.

There was an electric light in his eyes. He shut his eyes.

He heard someone coming very heavily up the stairs. Then he did not hear it. Then he heard a noise far off. That was the crowd. Well, somebody would have to kill his other bull. They had cut away all his shirt. The doctor smiled at him. There was Retana.

"Hello, Retana!" Manuel said. He could not hear his voice.

Retana smiled at him and said something. Manuel could not hear it.

Zurito stood beside the table, bending over where the doctor was working. He was in his picador clothes, without his hat.

Zurito said something to him. Manuel could not hear it.

Zurito was speaking to Retana. One of the men in white smiled and handed Retana a pair of scissors. Retana gave them to Zurito. Zurito said something to Manuel. He could not hear it.

To hell with this operating-table. He'd been on plenty of operating-tables before. He was not going to die. There would be a priest if he was going to die.

Zurito was saying something to him. Holding up the scissors.

That was it. They were going to cut off his coleta. They were going to cut off his pigtail.

Manuel sat up on the operating-table. The doctor stepped back, angry. Someone grabbed him and held him.

"You couldn't do a thing like that, Manos," he said.

He heard suddenly, clearly, Zurito's voice.

"That's all right," Zurito said. "I won't do it. I was joking."

"I was going good," Manuel said. "I didn't have any luck. That was all."

Manuel lay back. They had put something over his face. It was all familiar. He inhaled deeply. He felt very tired. He was very, very tired. They took the thing away from his face.

"I was going good," Manuel said weakly. "I was going great."

Retana looked at Zurito and started for the door.

"I'll stay here with him," Zurito said.

Retana shrugged his shoulders.

Manuel opened his eyes and looked at Zurito.

"Wasn't I going good, Manos?" he asked, for confirmation.

"Sure," said Zurito. "You were going great."

The doctor's assistant put the cone over Manuel's face and he inhaled deeply. Zurito stood awkwardly, watching.

J. F. Powers was born in Jacksonville, Illinois, in 1911. His later boyhood was spent in southern Minnesota where he was educated under the direction of Franciscan Friars. He has taught at St. John's Benedictine Monastery in Minnesota and at Marquette University in Milwaukee. His short stories, published in *Prince of Darkness and Other Stories* (1947) portray such disparate scenes as monastery life and the slums of Chicago. Though Powers uses Midwestern settings, his stories reveal universal problems of human feelings and relationships. He was awarded a Guggenheim Fellowship for creative writing in 1948.

J. F. POWERS

He Don't Plant Cotton

SPRING entered the black belt in ashes, dust, and drabness, without benefit of the saving green. The seasons were known only by the thermometer and the clothing of the people. There were only a few nights in the whole year when the air itself told you. Perhaps a night in April or May might escape the plague of smells, achieve a little of the enchantment, be the diminished echo of spring happening ardently in the suburbs, but it was all over in a night and the streets were filled with summer, as a hollow mouth with bad breath, and even the rain could not wash it away. And winter . . .

The beginning snow swirled in from the lake, dusting the streets with white. Baby squinted down the lonesome tracks. The wind twisted snow into his eyes, the flakes as sharp as sand, grinding, and his eyeballs were coated with cold tears. Baby worked his hands in his overcoat pockets to make heat. He saw a woman cross the street to catch the Big Red, which was coming now, but the woman refused stiffly to run for it. The wind went off hooting down the tracks ahead. Baby got on. The conductor held out one hand for the fare and yanked a cord twice with the other, prodding the red monster into motion.

Baby sat down inside. A cold breeze swept the floor, rattling old transfers and gum wrappers. Baby placed his feet uneasily on the heater to make the meager warmth funnel up his pants' legs. The dark flesh beneath the tuxedo was chilled to chalky gray at the joints. He listened to the wheels bump over the breaks in the track, and the warmth from the heater rose higher on his legs. He became warm and forgetful of the weather, except as scenery. The streets were paved evenly with snow twinkling soft and clean and white under the lights, and velvet red and green from the neon signs.

New York may be all right, he hummed to himself, but Beale Street's paved with gold. That's a lie, he thought; I been down on Beale. And Chicago, same way. All my life playing jobs in Chicago, and I still got to ride the Big Red. And that's no lie. Jobs were getting harder and harder to find. What they wanted was Mickey Mouse sound effects, singing strings, electric guitars, neon violins, even organs and accordions and harmonica teams. Hard to find a spot to play in, and when you did it was always a white place with drunken advertising men wanting to hear "a old song"—"My Wild Irish Rose" or "I Love You Truly." So you played it, of course, and plenty of schmaltz. And the college kids who wanted swing—any slick popular song. So you played that, too. And always you wanted to play the music you were born to, blue or fast, music that had no name. You managed somehow to play that, too, when there was a lull or the place was empty and you had to stay until 4 A.M. anyway.

Baby got off the streetcar and walked the same two blocks he saw every night except Tuesday. The wind had died down almost entirely and the snow whirled in big flakes end over end. Padding along, Baby told himself he liked winter better than summer. Then he came to the place, said, "How's it, Chief?" to the doorman, an Indian passing for Negro, went down three steps, and forgot all about winter and summer. It was always the same here. It was not so much a place of temperatures as a place of lights and shades and chromium, pastel mirrors, the smell of beer, rum, whisky, smoke—a stale blend of odors and shadows, darkness and music. It was a place of only one climate and that was it.

Baby's overcoat, hat, and scarf went into a closet and settled familiarly on hooks. His old tuxedo walked over to the traps. Its black hands rubbed together briskly, driving out the chill. One hand fumbled in the dark at the base of the big drum, and a second later a watery blue light winked on dully and flooded the drumhead, staring like a blind blue eye. Immediately the tuxedo sat down and worked its feet with a slight rasping noise into the floor. The fingers thumped testingly on the hide, tightened the snare. They knew, like the ears, when it was right. Gingerly, as always, the right foot sought the big drum's pedal. The tuxedo was not ready yet. It had to fidget and massage its seat around on the chair, stretch out its arms, and hug the whole outfit a fraction of an inch this way and that. Then the eyes glanced at the piano player, signaling ready. The drumsticks paused a moment tensely, slid into the beat, barely heard, accenting perfectly the shower of piano notes. Everything worked together for two choruses. Then the piano player tapered his solo gently, so that at a certain point Baby knew it was his. He brought the number to a lifeless close, run down. Too early in the evening.

"Dodo," Baby said to the piano player, "Libby come in yet?"

Dodo sent a black hand up, slow as smoke, toward the ceiling. "Upstairs," he said, letting the hand fall to the keyboard with a faint, far-off chord. It stirred there, gently worming music from the battered upright. Notes drew nearer, riding on ships and camels through a world of sand and water, till they came forthright from the piano, taking on patterns, as the other black hand came to life on the bass keys, dear to Dodo. Baby picked up his sticks, recognizing the number. He called it "Dodo's Blues," though he knew Dodo called it nothing. Every night about this time, when there was no crowd and Dodo hadn't yet put on the white coat he wore servicing the bar, they would play it. Baby half closed his eyes. With pleasure he watched Dodo through the clouds of rhythm he felt shimmering up like heat from his drums. Baby's eyes were open only enough to frame Dodo like a picture; everything else was out. It was a picture of many dimensions; music was only one of them.

Here was a man, midgety, hunchbacked, black, and proud—mostly all back and music. A little man who, when he was fixing to play, had to look around for a couple of three-inch telephone directories. Piling them on top of the piano bench, he sat down, with all their names and streets and numbers and exchanges under him. He had very little of thighs and stomach—mostly just back, which threw a round shadow on the wall. When he leaned farther away from the piano, so the light slanted through his hands, his shadow revealed him walking on his hands down the keyboard, dancing on the tips of fingery toes. Sometimes it seemed to Baby through half-closed eyes, when Dodo's body was bobbing on the wall and his hands were feet dancing on the keyboard, as though the dim light shaped him into a gigantic, happy spider. When he became a spider you could forget he was a man, hunchbacked, runtish, black; and he, too, could forget perhaps that he had to be careful and proud. Perhaps he could be happy always if his back and size and color and pride were not always standing in the way. The piano made him whole. The piano taught him to find himself and jump clean over the moon. When he played, his feet never touched the pedals.

People were beginning to fill the place. They finished off the number, Baby smiling his admiration, Dodo scrupulously expressionless.

"For a young man . . ." Baby said.

Dodo got down off the telephone directories and threw them under the piano at the bass end, beyond the blue glow of the big drum. He had seen Libby come down the steps from the dressing room—a red dress, a gardenia. Dodo went behind the bar and put on his white service coat. Libby sat down at the piano.

Helplessly attracted, several men came over from the bar and leaned on the piano. They stared, burdening Libby's body with calculations. Singly at first and then, gathering unity, together. Libby sang a popular song. The men went back to the bar to get their drinks, which they brought over and set on top of the upright. Libby sang the words about lost love, and the men licked their lips vacantly. At the end of the song they clapped fiercely. Libby ignored them with a smile.

"Say, that was just fine," one man said. "Where you from anyhow?"

With a little grin Libby acknowledged Baby. Baby, beaming his veteran admiration of a fine young woman, nodded.

"Where you from? Huh?"

"New Orleans."

"Well, you don't say!" the man blurted out joyfully. "We're from down South, too . . . Mississippi, matter of fact!"

Icily, Libby smiled her appreciation of this coincidence. She looked at Baby, who was also registering appropriately. Just think of that! Small world! And welcome to our city!

"Well, what do you know!" crowed the gentleman from Mississippi. "So you're from down South!" He was greatly pleased and already very drunk. He eyed his friends, four or five of them, distributing his discovery equally among them.

"You never know," he explained. Then he appeared to suffer a pang of doubt. He turned quickly to Libby again, as though to make sure she was still there. His eyes jellied blearily and in them an idea was born.

"I know," he said. "Sing . . . sing–sing 'Ol' Man River' for the boys. They all'd sure like that."

Without responding, Libby looked down at her hands, smiling. She measured chords between her thumbs and little fingers, working her amusement into the keys. Baby stared at the mottled hide of his snare drum, at the big one's rim worn down from playing "Dixieland." The gentleman from Mississippi got worried.

"Aw, sing it," he pleaded. So Libby sang a chorus. The gentlemen from Mississippi were overwhelmed. They loved the song, they loved the South, the dear old Southland. Land of cotton, cinnamon seed, and sandy bottom. Look away! Look away! They loved themselves. Look away! Look away! There was the tiniest touch of satire in Libby's voice, a slightly overripe fervor. Baby caught it and behind the bar Dodo caught it, but the gentlemen did not. Dodo had put down the martini glass he was polishing and look away! look away!–good.

At the bridge of the second chorus, Libby nodded "Take it!" to Baby. He stood up, staggering from the heat of the fields, clenching his black, toilworn fists. In profound anguish, he hollered, giving the white folks his all, really knocking himself out.

Tote that bar!
Lift that bale!
Git a little drunk–

Baby grimaced in torment and did his best to look like ol' Uncle Tom out snatchin' cotton.

Behind the bar, unnoticed, Dodo's sad black face had turned beatific. "–And you land in jail!" Dodo could not see the other faces, the big white ones, but he could imagine them, the heads fixed and tilted. It was too dark in the place, and he could make out only blurrily the outlines of the necks. Ordinarily he was capable only of hating them. Now he had risen to great unfamiliar heights and was actually enjoying them. Surprised at this capacity in himself, yet proud he could feel this way, he was confused. He went further and started to pity them. But his memory stood up outraged at his forgetfulness and said, Kill that pity dead. Then he remembered he was really alone in the place. It was different with Libby and Baby, though they were black, too. He did not understand why. Say their skin was thicker–only that was not why. Probably this was not the first time they had jived white folks to death and them none the wiser. Dodo was not like that; he had to wait a long time for his kicks. From his heart no pity went out for the white men. He kept it all to himself, where it was needed. But he had to smile inside of him with Libby and Baby. Only more. Look at that fool Baby! Jam up!

Bend your knees!
Bow your head!
And pick that cotton!
Tiiilllll you're dead!

Baby sat down with a thud, exhausted. The gentlemen from Mississippi brayed their pleasure. My, it was good to see that black boy all sweatin' and perspirin' that way. They clapped furiously, called for drinks, gobbled. . . .

"And bring some for the darkies!"

Baby swallowed some of his drink. He looked at the beaten

rim of the big drum, then at the sticks. He took out his pocketknife and scraped the rough, splintery places smooth. He glanced at Libby and ventured the kind of smile he felt and knew she did. He finished his drink. The gentlemen from Mississippi hung around the piano, getting drunker, shouting in one another's faces. Nervously Libby lighted a cigarette. A college boy tried to make conversation with her while his honey-haired girl assumed an attitude of genuine concern.

"Can you play 'Hot Lips'?" He was the real American Boy.

"Don't know it," Libby lied. She wished she didn't.

"Can you play 'Sugar Blues'?" Right back.

"Don't know it."

One of the Mississippi gentlemen, who had been hanging back, crowded up to the piano, making his move. He drained his drink and pushed closer to the piano so as to brush Libby's left hand with the front of his trousers. Libby moved her hand, sounding a chord that Baby caught. The gentleman, grinning lewdly, tried to follow her hand up the keyboard.

"That's all right," he snickered. "Play lots of bass, honey."

The first gentleman from Mississippi, drink in hand, stumbled over from the bar. He told Libby to play that "Ol' Man River" song some more. Libby hesitated. Then she lit into it, improvising all around it, and it was a pleasure for Baby, but the first gentleman from Mississippi was not happy. He said if that was the best she could do she had better try singing. Libby sang only one chorus. The gentlemen from Mississippi, though they applauded, were not gratified. There was an air of petulance among them. They remembered another time they heard the song, but it was not clear now what had made it different and better. They saw Baby all right, but they did not remember that he was the one who had sung before, the good one that toted their bars, lifted their bales, and landed drunk in their jails. Something was wrong, but they saw no remedy. Each gentleman suspected the fault was personal, what with him drinking so heavy and all.

Dodo, behind the bar, had not enjoyed the song the last time, hating the coercion the white men worked on Libby and Baby, and feared his advantage was slipping away. In a minute he would be hating them to pieces again.

"Can you play 'Tiger Rag'?" The American Boy was back.

"No." Libby made a face and then managed to turn it into a smile for him. He held his drink up for the world to see on the night before the big game.

The honey-haired girl wrenched her face into a winning smile and hit the jack pot. "Can you play 'St. Louis Blues'?"

"How you want it?" Libby said. She put out her cigarette. "Blues, rhumba . . . what kind a way?"

"Oh, play it low down. The way *you people* play it." So Libby would understand, she executed a ponderous wink, narrowed her eyes, and made them glitter wantonly behind the lashes. "*You* know," she said.

Libby knew. She played "St. Louis," losing herself in it with Baby. She left the college boy and the honey-haired girl behind. She forgot she knew. She gazed at Baby with her eyes dreamy, unseeing, blind with the blue drum, her head nodding in that wonderful, graceful way. Baby saw his old tuxedo in the mirror, its body shimmying on the chair, and he was pleased. The drums, beating figures, rocked with a steady roll. They were playing "Little Rock Getaway" now, the fine, young-woman music.

And Libby was pleased, watching Baby. And then, somehow, he vanished for her into the blue drum. The sticks still danced at an oblique angle on the snare, but there were no hands to them and Libby could not see Baby on the chair. She could only feel him somewhere in the blue glow. Abandoning herself, she lost herself in the piano. Now, still without seeing him, she could feel him with a clarity and warmth beyond vision. Miniature bell notes, mostly blue, blossomed ecstatically, perished *affettuoso*, weaving themselves down into the dark beauty of the lower keys, because it was closer to the drum, and multiplied. They came back to "St. Louis" again.

"Stop." The first gentleman from Mississippi touched Libby on the arm. "When I do that to you, that means 'Stop,'" he said. Libby chorded easily. "Some of the boys like to hear that 'Ol' Man River' some more." He straightened up, turning to the other gentleman, his smile assuring them it would not be long now.

"Kick off," Baby sighed.

But Libby broke into "St. Louis" again. Baby, with a little

whoop, came clambering after, his sticks slicing into the drum rim, a staccato "Dixieland."

The first gentleman frowned, touching Libby's arm. "Remember what that means? Means 'Ol' Man River,' " he said calmly, as though correcting a slight error. "Toot sweet. Know what that means? That's French. Means right now." No harm done, however. Just that his friends here, a bunch of boys from down South, were dying to hear that song again—up to him to see that they got satisfaction—knew there would be no trouble about it.

"We'll play it for you later on," Libby said quickly. "We got some other requests besides yours. How many you got now, Baby?"

Baby held up eight fingers, very prompt.

"Coming up," he said.

The first gentleman was undecided. "Well . . ." he drawled. Libby began a popular song. The first gentleman faced his friends. His eyes more or less met theirs and found no agreement. The boys looked kind of impatient, like a bunch of boys out for a little fun and not doing so well. He turned to Libby again.

"We just gotta have that 'Ol' Man River' some more. Boys all got their hearts set on it," he said. "Right away! Toot sweet! Toot—away!" There he'd gone and made a joke, and the boys all laughed and repeated it to each other. Libby played on, as though she had not heard. The first gentleman took hold of her arm. She gazed steadily up into his bleary eyes.

"Not now. Later."

"No, you don't. You gotta play it right now. For a bunch of boys from down South. They all got a hankerin' to hear that 'Ol' Man River' some more."

"So you best play it," another gentleman said, leaning down hard on the old upright piano. "On account of I'm gonna take and give ear. We kinda like how that old song sounds up North. Whatcha all need. The drummer will sing," he said, and looked at Baby. Baby looked back, unsmiling.

Libby chorded lightly, waiting for the gentlemen from Mississippi to get tired. They could not see how it was with her and Baby—never.

"You ain't gonna play?"

Baby's eyes strained hard in their sockets.

"We ain't comin'," Libby said.

Baby's eyes relaxed and he knew the worst part was over. They felt the same way about it. They had made up their minds. The rest was easy. Baby was even a little glad it had happened. A feeling was growing within him that he had wanted to do this for a long time—for years and years, in a hundred different places he had played.

Secretly majestic, Baby sat at his drums, the goal of countless uplifted eyes—beseeching him. For it seemed that hordes of white people were far below him, making their little commotions and noises, asking favors of him, like Lord, please bring the rain, or Lord, please take it away. Lord Baby. Waves of warm exhilaration washed into him, endearing him to himself. No, he smiled, I am sorry, no favors today. Yes, Lord, they all said, if that's the way it is, so be it.

But somebody objected. The manager's voice barked, far below, scarcely audible to Baby in his new eminence. ". . . honoring requests," he heard, and ". . . trouble with the local," and ". . . wanting to get a sweet-swing trio in this place a long time now." And the manager, strangely small, an excited, pale pygmy, explaining to the gentlemen from Mississippi, also small, how it was, "That's all I can do in the circumstances," and them saying, "Well, I guess so; well, I guess so all right; don't pay to pamper 'em, to give 'em an inch."

Baby noticed Libby had got up from the piano and put on her coat, the long dress hanging out at the bottom, red.

"I won't change," she said, and handed Baby the canvas cover for the snare drum.

"Huh?" Baby said foggily. He set about taking his traps apart. Dodo, not wearing his white service coat, came over to help.

"You don't have to," Baby said.

Chief, freezing outside in his long, fancy maroon coat, opened the door for them. "You all through, Baby?"

"Yeah, Chief. You told that right."

They walked down the street toward the car line. Baby, going first, plowed a path for Libby and Dodo in the snow. Window sills, parked cars, and trees were padded with it. The wind was dead and buried. Baby bore the big drum on his shoulder and felt the sticks pressing tight and upright in his vest pockets, two on each side. Libby had her purse and street clothes rolled up under her arm. Dodo carried the snare drum.

Softly as snow, Libby laughed. "That's all I can do in the circumstances," she said.

"I got your old circumstances," Baby said.

Then they were silent, tramping in the snow.

At the corner they waited in a store entrance for a southbound streetcar. Libby raised a foot now and then, shuddering with cold. Dead still, Dodo breathed down inside the collar of his overcoat, retarding his breath, frowning at the little smoke trickling out, as though it were the only thing left in the world to remind him he was alive. Baby talked of taking a cab and finally did go out into the street to hail one approaching. It slowed up, pulled over to the curb, hesitated . . . and lurched away, with Baby's hand reaching for the door. Baby watched the cab speed down the snowy street, following it for a few steps, speechless. There was nothing to do. Without looking, he saw Libby and Dodo shivering in the store entrance. They had seen the cab come and go. They had not moved an inch. They waited unfooled, as before, for the Big Red.

"What's wrong with you, Baby?" Libby called out. A tiny moment of silence, and she was laughing, gradually louder, mellow octaves of it, mounting, pluming . . .

Like her piano, it seemed to Baby—that fine, young-woman laughter.

"Why you laugh so much, woman?" he inquired plaintively from the street. Then he moved to join them, a few steps only, dallying at the curb to temper the abruptness of his retreat. Like her piano on "Little Rock"—that fine, young-woman laughter.

VIRGINIA WOOLF

Virginia Woolf (1882-1941), the daughter of Sir Leslie Stephen and the descendant of two of England's most distinguished intellectual families, was born in London and educated entirely at home. In 1912 she was married to Leonard Woolf, a literary journalist and leader of the noted Bloomsbury Group in London. With her husband she founded the Hogarth Press, which after World War I developed into an important publishing house. In her short stories and novels Virginia Woolf was a restless experimenter, constantly trying new techniques to replace the conventional flow of narrative which she thought an undue simplification of experience. Some of her experiments, as in *To the Lighthouse*, *The Waves*, and *The Years*, have had an extended influence on contemporary writing. Her death by suicide in 1941 was a result of the nervous strain of war. *A Writer's Diary*, giving an intimate account of her aims and methods and of her attitude toward her own work, was published in 1954.

The New Dress

MABEL had her first serious suspicion that something was wrong as she took her cloak off and Mrs. Barnet, while handing her the mirror and touching the brushes and thus drawing her attention, perhaps rather markedly, to all the appliances for tidying and improving hair, complexion, clothes, which existed on the dressing table, confirmed the suspicion—that it was not right, not quite right, which growing stronger as she went upstairs and springing at her with conviction as she greeted Clarissa Dalloway, she went straight to the far end of the room, to a shaded corner where a looking-glass hung and looked. No! It was not right. And at once the misery which she always tried to hide, the profound dissatisfaction—the sense she had had, ever since she was a child, of being inferior to other people—set upon her, relentlessly, remorselessly, with an intensity which she could not beat off, as she would when she woke at night at home, by reading Borrow or Scott; for, oh, these men, oh, these women, all were thinking—"What's Mabel wearing? What a fright she looks! What a hideous new dress!"—their eyelids flickering as they came up and then their lids shutting rather tight. It was her own appalling inadequacy; her cowardice; her mean, water-sprinkled blood that depressed her. And at once the whole of the room where, for ever so many hours, she had planned with the little dressmaker how it was to go, seemed sordid, repulsive; and her own drawing-room so shabby, and herself, going out, puffed up with vanity as she touched the letters on the hall table and said: "How dull!" to show off—all this now seemed unutterably silly, paltry, and provincial. All this had been absolutely destroyed, shown up, exploded, the moment she came into Mrs. Dalloway's drawing-room.

What she had thought that evening when, sitting over the tea-cups, Mrs. Dalloway's invitation came, was that, of course, she could not be fashionable. It was absurd to pretend to even—fashion meant cut, meant style, meant thirty guineas at least—but why not be original? Why not be herself, anyhow? And, getting up, she had taken that old fashion book of her mother's, a Paris fashion book of the time of the Empire, and had thought how much prettier, more dignified, and more womanly, they were then, and so set herself—oh, it was foolish—trying to be like them, pluming herself in fact upon being modest and old-fashioned and very charming, giving herself up, no doubt about it, to an orgy of self-love which deserved to be chastised, and so rigged herself out like this.

But she dared not look in the glass. She could not face the whole horror—the pale yellow, idiotically old-fashioned silk dress with its long skirt and its high sleeves and its waist and all the things that looked so charming in the fashion book, but not on her, not among all these ordinary people. She felt like a dress-maker's dummy standing there for young people to stick pins into.

"But, my dear, it's perfectly charming!" Rose Shaw said, looking her up and down with that little satirical pucker of the lips which she expected—Rose herself being dressed in the height of the fashion, precisely like everybody else, always.

"We are all like flies trying to crawl over the edge of the saucer," Mabel thought, and repeated the phrase as if she were crossing herself, as if she were trying to find some spell to annul this pain, to make this agony endurable. Tags of Shakespeare, lines from books she had read ages ago, suddenly came to her when she was in agony, and she repeated them over and over again. "Flies trying to crawl," she repeated. If she could say that over often enough and make herself see the flies, she would become numb, chill, frozen, dumb. Now she could see flies crawling slowly out of a saucer of milk with their wings stuck together; and she strained and strained (standing in front of the looking-glass, listening to Rose Shaw) to make herself see Rose Shaw and all the other people there as flies, trying to hoist themselves out of something, or into something, meager, insignificant, toiling flies. But she could not see them like that, not other people. She saw herself like that—she was a fly, but the others were dragonflies, butterflies, beautiful insects, dancing, fluttering, skimming, while she alone dragged herself up out of the saucer. (Envy and spite, the most detestable of the vices, were her chief faults.)

"I feel like some dowdy, decrepit, horribly dingy old fly," she said, making Robert Haydon stop just to hear her say that, just to reassure herself by furbishing up a poor weak-kneed phrase and so showing how detached she was, how witty, that she did not feel in the least out of anything. And, of course, Robert Haydon answered something quite polite, quite insincere, which she saw through instantly, and said to herself, directly he went (again from some book), "Lies, lies, lies!" For a party makes things either much more real or much less real, she thought; she saw in a flash to the bottom of Robert Haydon's heart; she saw through everything. She saw the truth. This was true, this drawing-room, this self, and the other false. Miss Milan's little work-room was really terribly hot, stuffy, sordid. It smelt of clothes and cabbage cooking; and yet, when Miss Milan put the glass in her hand, and she looked at herself with the dress on, finished, an extraordinary bliss shot through her heart. Suffused with light, she sprang into existence. Rid of cares and wrinkles, what she had dreamed of herself was there—a beautiful woman. Just for a second (she had not dared look longer, Miss Milan wanted to know about the length of the skirt), there looked at her, framed in the scrolloping mahogany, a gray-white, mysteriously smiling, charming girl, the core of herself, the soul of herself; and it was not vanity only, not only self-love that made her think it good, tender, and true. Miss Milan said that the skirt could not well be longer; if anything the skirt, said Miss Milan, puckering her forehead, considering with all her wits about her, must be shorter; and she felt, suddenly, honestly, full of love for Miss Milan, much, much fonder of Miss Milan than of anyone in the whole world, and could have cried for pity that she should be crawling on the floor with her mouth full of pins and her face red and her eyes bulging —that one human being should be doing this for another, and she saw them all as human beings merely, and herself going off to her party, and Miss Milan pulling the cover over the canary's cage, or letting him pick a hemp-seed from between her lips, and the thought of it, of this side of human nature and its patience and its endurance and its being content with such miserable, scanty, sordid, little pleasures filled her eyes with tears.

And now the whole thing had vanished. The dress, the room, the love, the pity, the scrolloping looking-glass, and the canary's cage—all had vanished, and here she was in a corner of Mrs. Dalloway's drawing-room, suffering tortures, woken wide awake to reality.

But it was all so paltry, weak-blooded, and petty-minded to care so much at her age with two children, to be still so utterly dependent on people's opinions and not have principles or convictions, not to be able to say as other people did, "There's Shakespeare! There's death! We're all weevils in a captain's biscuit"—or whatever it was that people did say.

She faced herself straight in the glass; she pecked at her left shoulder; she issued out into the room, as if spears were thrown at her yellow dress from all sides. But instead of looking fierce or tragic, as Rose Shaw would have done—Rose would have looked like Boadicea—she looked foolish and self-conscious and simpered like a schoolgirl and slouched across the room, positively slinking, as if she were a beaten mongrel, and looked at a picture, an engraving. As if one went to a party to look at a picture! Everybody knew why she did it—it was from shame, from humiliation.

"Now the fly's in the saucer," she said to herself, "right in the middle, and can't get out, and the milk," she thought, rigidly staring at the picture, "is sticking its wings together."

"It's so old-fashioned," she said to Charles Burt, making him stop (which by itself he hated) on his way to talk to someone else.

She meant, or she tried to make herself think that she meant, that it was the picture and not her dress, that was old-fashioned. And one word of praise, one word of affection from Charles would have made all the difference to her at the moment. If he had only said, "Mabel, you're looking charming tonight!" it would have changed her life. But then she ought to have been truthful and direct. Charles said nothing of the kind, of course. He was malice itself. He always saw through one, especially if one were feeling particularly mean, paltry, or feeble-minded.

"Mabel's got a new dress!" he said, and the poor fly was absolutely shoved into the middle of the saucer. Really, he would like her to drown, she believed. He had no heart, no fundamental kindness, only a veneer of friendliness. Miss Milan was much more real, much kinder. If only one could feel that and stick to it, always. "Why," she asked herself—replying to Charles much too pertly, letting him see that she was out of temper, or "ruffled" as he called it ("Rather ruffled?" he said and went on to laugh at her with some woman over there)—"Why," she asked herself, "can't I feel one thing always, feel quite sure that Miss Milan is right, and Charles wrong and stick to it, feel sure about the canary and pity and love and not be whipped all round in a second by coming into a room full of people?" It was her odious, weak, vacillating character again, always giving at the critical moment and not being seriously interested in conchology, etymology, botany, archeology, cutting up potatoes and watching them fructify like Mary Dennis, like Violet Searle.

Then Mrs. Holman, seeing her standing there, bore down upon her. Of course a thing like a dress was beneath Mrs. Holman's notice, with her family always tumbling downstairs or having the scarlet fever. Could Mabel tell her if Elmthorpe was ever let for August and September? Oh, it was a conversation that bored her unutterably!—it made her furious to be treated like a house agent or a messenger boy, to be made use of. Not to have value, that was it, she thought, trying to grasp something hard, something real, while she tried to answer sensibly about the bathroom and the south aspect and the hot water to the top of the house; and all the time she could see little bits of her yellow dress in the round looking-glass which made them all the size of boot-buttons or tadpoles; and it was amazing to think how much humiliation and agony and self-loathing and effort and passionate ups and downs of feeling were contained in a thing the size of a threepenny bit. And what was still odder, this thing, this Mabel Waring, was separate, quite disconnected; and though Mrs. Holman (the black button) was leaning forward and telling her how her eldest boy had strained his heart running, she could see her, too, quite detached in the looking-glass, and it was impossible that the black dot, leaning forward, gesticulating, should make the yellow dot, sitting solitary, self-centered, feel what the black dot was feeling, yet they pretended.

"So impossible to keep boys quiet"—that was the kind of thing one said.

And Mrs. Holman, who could never get enough sympathy and snatched what little there was greedily, as if it were her right (but she deserved much more for there was her little girl who had come down this morning with a swollen knee-joint), took this miserable offering and looked at it suspiciously, grudgingly, as if it were a halfpenny when it ought to have been a pound and put it away in her purse, must put up with it, mean and miserly though it was, times being hard, so very hard; and on she went, creaking, injured Mrs. Holman, about the girl with the swollen joints. Ah, it was tragic, this greed, this clamor of human beings, like a row of cormorants, barking and flapping their wings for sympathy—it was tragic, could one have felt it and not merely pretended to feel it!

But in her yellow dress tonight she could not wring out one drop more; she wanted it all, all for herself. She knew (she kept on looking into the glass, dipping into that dreadfully showing-up blue pool) that she was condemned, despised, left like this in a backwater, because of her being like this—a feeble, vacillating creature; and it seemed to her that the yellow dress was a penance which she had deserved, and if she had been dressed like Rose Shaw, in lovely, clinging green with a ruffle of swansdown, she would have deserved that; and she thought that there was no escape for her—none whatever. But it was not her fault altogether, after all. It was being one of a family of ten; never having money enough, always skimping and paring; and her mother carrying great cans, and the linoleum worn on the stair edges, and one sordid little domestic tragedy after another—nothing catastrophic, the sheep farm failing, but not utterly; her eldest brother marrying beneath him but not very much—there was no romance, nothing extreme about them all. They petered out respectably in seaside resorts; every watering-place had one of her aunts even now asleep in some lodging with the front windows not quite facing the sea. That was so like them—they had to squint at things always. And she had done the same—she was just like her aunts. For all her dreams of living in India, married to some hero like Sir Henry Lawrence, some empire builder (still the sight of a native in a turban filled her with romance), she had failed utterly. She had married Hubert, with his safe, permanent underling's job in the Law Courts, and they managed tolerably in a smallish house, without proper maids, and hash when she was alone or just bread and butter, but now and then—Mrs. Holman was off, thinking her the most dried-up, unsympathetic twig she had ever met, absurdly dressed, too, and would tell everyone about Mabel's fantastic appearance—now and then, thought Mabel Waring, left alone on the blue sofa, punching the cushion in order to look occupied, for she would not join Charles Burt and Rose Shaw, chattering like magpies and perhaps laughing at her by the fireplace—now and then, there did come to her delicious moments, reading the other night in bed, for instance, or down by the sea on the sand in the sun, at Easter—let her recall it—a great tuft of pale sand-grass, standing all twisted like a shock of spears against the sky, which was blue like a smooth china egg, so firm, so hard, and then the melody of the waves—"Hush, hush," they said, and the children's shouts paddling—yes, it was a divine moment, and there she lay, she felt, in the hand of the Goddess who was the world; rather a hard-hearted, but very beautiful Goddess, a little lamb laid on the altar (one did think these silly things, and it didn't matter so long as one never said them). And also with Hubert sometimes she had quite unexpectedly—carving the mutton for Sunday lunch, for no reason, opening a letter, coming into a room—divine moments, when she said to herself (for she would never say this to anybody else), "This is it. This has happened. This is it!" And the other way about it was equally surprising—that is, when everything was arranged—music, weather, holidays, every reason for happiness was there—then nothing happened at all. One wasn't happy. It was flat, just flat, that was all.

Her wretched self again, no doubt! She had always been a fretful, weak, unsatisfactory mother, a wobbly wife, lolling about in a kind of twilight existence with nothing very clear or very bold, or more one thing than another, like all her brothers and sisters, except perhaps Herbert—they were all the same poor water-veined creatures who did nothing. Then in the midst of this creeping, crawling life suddenly she was on the crest of a wave. That wretched fly—where had she read the story that kept coming into her mind about the fly and the saucer?—struggled out. Yes, she had those moments. But now that she was forty, they might come more and more seldom. By degrees she would cease to struggle any more. But that was deplorable! That was not to be endured! That made her feel ashamed of herself!

She would go to the London Library tomorrow. She would find some wonderful, helpful, astonishing book, quite by chance, a book by a clergyman, by an American no one had ever heard of; or she would walk down the Strand and drop, accidentally, into a hall where a miner was telling about the life in the pit, and suddenly she would become a new person. She would be absolutely transformed. She would wear a uniform; she would be called Sister Somebody; she would never give a thought to clothes again. And forever after she would be perfectly clear about Charles Burt and Miss Milan and this room and that room; and it would be always, day after day, as if she were lying in the sun or carving the mutton. It would be it!

So she got up from the blue sofa, and the yellow button in the looking-glass got up too, and she waved her hand to Charles and Rose to show them she did not depend on them one scrap, and the yellow button moved out of the looking-glass, and all the spears were gathered into her breast as she walked towards Mrs. Dalloway and said, "Good night."

"But it's too early to go," said Mrs. Dalloway, who was always so charming.

"I'm afraid I must," said Mabel Waring. "But," she added in her weak, wobbly voice which only sounded ridiculous when she tried to strengthen it, "I have enjoyed myself enormously."

"I have enjoyed myself," she said to Mr. Dalloway, whom she met on the stairs.

"Lies, lies, lies!" she said to herself, going downstairs, and "Right in the saucer!" she said to herself as she thanked Mrs. Barnet for helping her and wrapped herself, round and round and round, in the Chinese cloak she had worn these twenty years.

KATHERINE MANSFIELD

Katherine Mansfield (1888-1923) was born and reared in New Zealand. After attending New Zealand schools she spent three years, 1902-05, at Queen's College, London. Returning to New Zealand she wrote articles and stories for *The Native Companion.* But colonial life dissatisfied her, and in 1908 she went to live in London where she served for several years as a book reviewer for *The Westminster Gazette.* In 1913 she married the writer and critic J. Middleton Murry. During the remaining ten years of her life she worked with great intensity on the short story, always striving for more subtlety, accuracy, and perception in her writing. She traveled from place to place on the Continent in search of a climate that would bolster her failing health. Her final illness overtook her while she was living at Fontainebleau, in France. Collections of her stories are *Bliss, The Garden Party,* and *The Dove's Nest.* In 1937 *The Short Stories of Katherine Mansfield* was published.

The Stranger

IT SEEMED to the little crowd on the wharf that she was never going to move again. There she lay, immense, motionless on the gray crinkled water, a loop of smoke above her, an immense flock of gulls screaming and diving after the galley droppings at the stern. You could just see little couples parading—little flies walking up and down the dish on the gray crinkled tablecloth. Other flies clustered and swarmed at the edge. Now there was a gleam of white on the lower deck—the cook's apron or the stewardess perhaps. Now a tiny black spider raced up the ladder onto the bridge.

In the front of the crowd a strong-looking, middle-aged man, dressed very well, very snugly in a gray overcoat, gray silk scarf, thick gloves, and dark felt hat, marched up and down, twirling his folded umbrella. He seemed to be the leader of the little crowd on the wharf and at the same time to keep them together. He was something between the sheep-dog and the shepherd.

But what a fool—what a fool he had been not to bring any glasses! There wasn't a pair of glasses between the whole lot of them.

"Curious thing, Mr. Scott, that none of us thought of glasses. We might have been able to stir 'em up a bit. We might have managed a little signaling. *Don't hesitate to land. Natives harmless.* Or: *A welcome awaits you. All is forgiven.* What? Eh?"

Mr. Hammond's quick, eager glance, so nervous and yet so friendly and confiding, took in everybody on the wharf, roped in even those old chaps lounging against the gangways. They knew, every man-jack of them, that Mrs. Hammond was on that boat, and he was so tremendously excited it never entered his head not to believe that this marvelous fact meant something to them too. It warmed his heart toward them. They were, he decided, as decent a crowd of people— Those old chaps over by the gangways, too—fine, solid old chaps. What chests—by Jove! And he squared his own, plunged his thick-gloved hands into his pockets, rocked from heel to toe.

"Yes, my wife's been in Europe for the last ten months. On a visit to our eldest girl, who was married last year. I brought her up here, as far as Salisbury, myself. So I thought I'd better come and fetch her back. Yes, yes, yes." The shrewd gray eyes narrowed again and searched anxiously, quickly, the motionless liner. Again his overcoat was unbuttoned. Out came the thin, butter-yellow watch again, and for the twentieth—fiftieth—hundredth time he made the calculation.

"Let me see, now. It was two-fifteen when the doctor's launch went off. Two-fifteen. It is now exactly twenty-eight minutes past four. That is to say, the doctor's been gone two hours and thirteen minutes. Two hours and thirteen minutes! Whee-ooh!" He gave a queer little half-whistle and snapped his watch to again. "But I think we should have been told if there was anything up—don't you, Mr. Gaven?"

"Oh, yes, Mr. Hammond! I don't think there's anything to—

anything to worry about," said Mr. Gaven, knocking out his pipe against the heel of his shoe. "At the same time–"

"Quite so! Quite so!" cried Mr. Hammond. "Dashed annoying!" He paced quickly up and down and came back again to his stand between Mr. and Mrs. Scott and Mr. Gaven. "It's getting quite dark, too," and he waved his folded umbrella as though the dusk at least might have had the decency to keep off for a bit. But the dusk came slowly, spreading like a slow stain over the water. Little Jean Scott dragged at her mother's hand.

"I wan' my tea, mammy!" she wailed.

"I expect you do," said Mr. Hammond. "I expect all these ladies want their tea." And his kind, flushed, almost pitiful glance roped them all in again. He wondered whether Janey was having a final cup of tea in the saloon out there. He hoped so; he thought not. It would be just like her not to leave the deck. In that case perhaps the deck steward would bring her up a cup. If he'd been there he'd have got it for her–somehow. And for a moment he was on deck, standing over her, watching her little hand fold round the cup in the way she had, while she drank the only cup of tea to be got on board. . . . But now he was back here, and the Lord only knew when that cursed Captain would stop hanging about in the stream. He took another turn, up and down, up and down. He walked as far as the cab-stand to make sure his driver hadn't disappeared; back he swerved again to the little flock huddled in the shelter of the banana crates. Little Jean Scott was still wanting her tea. Poor little beggar! He wished he had a bit of chocolate on him.

"Here, Jean!" he said. "Like a lift up?" And easily, gently, he swung the little girl onto a higher barrel. The movement of holding her, steadying her, relieved him wonderfully, lightened his heart.

"Hold on," he said, keeping an arm round her.

"Oh, don't worry about *Jean*, Mr. Hammond!" said Mrs. Scott.

"That's all right, Mrs Scott. No trouble. It's a pleasure. Jean's a little pal of mine, aren't you, Jean?"

"Yes, Mr. Hammond," said Jean, and she ran her finger down the dent of his felt hat.

But suddenly she caught him by the ear and gave a loud scream.

"Lo-ok, Mr. Hammond! She's moving! Look, she's coming in!"

By Jove! So she was. At last! She was slowly, slowly turning round. A bell sounded far over the water and a great spout of steam gushed into the air. The gulls rose; they fluttered away like bits of white paper. And whether that deep throbbing was her engines or his heart Mr. Hammond couldn't say. He had to nerve himself to bear it, whatever it was. At that moment old Captain Johnson, the harbor-master, came striding down the wharf, a leather portfolio under his arm.

"Jean'll be all right," said Mr. Scott. "I'll hold her." He was just in time. Mr. Hammond had forgotten about Jean. He sprang away to greet old Captain Johnson.

"Well, Captain," the eager, nervous voice rang out again, "you've taken pity on us at last."

"It's no good blaming me, Mr. Hammond," wheezed old Captain Johnson, staring at the liner. "You got Mrs. Hammond on board, ain't yer?"

"Yes, yes!" said Hammond, and he kept by the harbor-master's side. "Mrs. Hammond's there. Hul-lo! We shan't be long now!"

With her telephone ring-ringing, the thrum of her screw filling the air, the big liner bore down on them, cutting sharp through the dark water so that big white shavings curled to either side. Hammond and the harbor-master kept in front of the rest. Hammond took off his hat; he raked the decks—they were crammed with passengers; he waved his hat and bawled a loud, strange "Hul-lo!" across the water; and then turned round and burst out laughing and said something—nothing—to old Captain Johnson.

"Seen her?" asked the harbor-master.

"No, not yet. Steady—wait a bit!" And suddenly, between two great clumsy idiots—"Get out of the way there!" he signed with his umbrella—he saw a hand raised—a white glove shaking a handkerchief. Another moment, and—thank God, thank God!—there she was. There was Janey. There was Mrs. Hammond, yes, yes, yes—standing by the rail and smiling and nodding and waving her handkerchief.

"Well, that's first class—first class! Well, well, well!" He positively stamped. Like lightning he drew out his cigar-case and offered it to old Captain Johnson. "Have a cigar, Captain! They're pretty good. Have a couple! Here"—and he pressed all the cigars in the case on the harbor-master—"I've a couple of boxes up at the hotel."

"Thenks, Mr. Hammond!" wheezed old Captain Johnson.

Hammond stuffed the cigar-case back. His hands were shaking, but he'd got hold of himself again. He was able to face Janey. There she was, leaning on the rail, talking to some woman and at the same time watching him, ready for him. It struck him, as the gulf of water closed, how small she looked on that huge ship. His heart was wrung with such a spasm that he could have cried out. How little she looked to have come all that long way and back by herself! Just like her, though. Just like Janey. She had the courage of a— And now the crew had come forward and parted the passengers; they had lowered the rails for the gangways.

The voices on shore and the voices on board flew to greet each other.

"All well?"

"All well."

"How's mother?"

"Much better."

"Hullo, Jean!"

"Hillo, Aun' Emily!"

"Had a good voyage?"

"Splendid!"

"Shan't be long now!"

"Not long now."

The engines stopped. Slowly she edged to the wharf-side.

"Make way there—make way—make way!" And the wharf hands brought the heavy gangways along at a sweeping run. Hammond signed to Janey to stay where she was. The old harbor-master stepped forward; he followed. As to "ladies first," or any rot like that, it never entered his head.

"After you, Captain!" he cried genially. And, treading on the old man's heels, he strode up the gangway on to the deck in a bee-line to Janey, and Janey was clasped in his arms.

"Well, well, well! Yes, yes! Here we are at last!" he stammered.

It was all he could say. And Janey emerged, and her cool little voice—the only voice in the world for him—said,

"Well, darling! Have you been waiting long?"

No; not long. Or, at any rate, it didn't matter. It was over now. But the point was, he had a cab waiting at the end of the wharf. Was she ready to go off? Was her luggage ready? In that case they could cut off sharp with her cabin luggage and let the rest go hang until tomorrow. He bent over her and she looked up with her familiar half-smile. She was just the same. Not a day changed. Just as he'd always known her. She laid her small hand on his sleeve.

"How are the children, John?" she asked.

(Hang the children!) "Perfectly well. Never better in their lives."

"Haven't they sent me letters?"

"Yes, yes—of course! I've left them at the hotel for you to digest later on."

"We can't go quite so fast," said she. "I've got people to say good-bye to—and then there's the Captain." As his face fell she gave his arm a small understanding squeeze. "If the Captain comes off the bridge I want you to thank him for having looked after your wife so beautifully." Well, he'd got her. If she wanted another ten minutes— As he gave way she was surrounded. The whole first-class seemed to want to say good-bye to Janey.

"Good-bye, *dear* Mrs. Hammond! And next time you're in Sydney I'll *expect* you."

"Darling Mrs. Hammond! You won't forget to write to me, will you?"

"Well, Mrs. Hammond, what this boat would have been without you!"

It was as plain as a pikestaff that she was by far the most popular woman on board. And she took it all—just as usual. Absolutely composed. Just her little self—just Janey all over; standing there with her veil thrown back. Hammond never noticed what his wife had on. It was all the same to him whatever she wore. But today he did notice that she wore a black "costume"—didn't they call it?—with white frills, trimmings he supposed they were, at the neck and sleeves. All this while Janey handed him round.

"John, dear!" And then: "I want to introduce you to—"

Finally they did escape, and she led the way to her stateroom. To follow Janey down the passage that she knew so well—that was so strange to him; to part the green curtains after her and to step into the cabin that had been hers gave him exquisite happiness. But—confound it!—the stewardess was there on the floor, strapping up the rugs.

"That's the last, Mrs. Hammond," said the stewardess, rising and pulling down her cuffs.

He was introduced again, and then Janey and the stewardess disappeared into the passage. He heard whisperings. She was getting the tipping business over, he supposed. He sat down on the striped sofa and took his hat off. There were the rugs she had taken with her; they looked good as new. All her luggage looked fresh, perfect. The labels were written in her beautiful little clear hand—"Mrs. John Hammond."

"Mrs. John Hammond!" He gave a long sigh of content and leaned back, crossing his arms. The strain was over. He felt he could have sat there forever sighing his relief—the relief at being rid of that horrible tug, pull, grip on his heart. The danger was over. That was the feeling. They were on dry land again.

But at that moment Janey's head came round the corner.

"Darling—do you mind? I just want to go and say good-bye to the doctor."

Hammond started up. "I'll come with you."

"No, no!" she said. "Don't bother. I'd rather not. I'll not be a minute."

And before he could answer she was gone. He had half a mind to run after her; but instead he sat down again.

Would she really not be long? What was the time now? Out came the watch; he stared at nothing. That was rather queer of Janey, wasn't it? Why couldn't she have told the stewardess to say good-bye for her? Why did she have to go chasing after the ship's doctor? She could have sent a note from the hotel even if the affair had been urgent. Urgent? Did it—could it mean that she had been ill on the voyage—she was keeping something from him? That was it! He seized his hat. He was going off to find that fellow to wring the truth out of him at all costs. He thought he'd noticed just something. She was just a touch too calm—too steady. From the very first moment—

The curtains rang. Janey was back. He jumped to his feet.

"Janey, have you been ill on this voyage? You have!"

"Ill?" Her airy little voice mocked him. She stepped over the rugs, and came up close, touched his breast, and looked up at him.

"Darling," she said, "don't frighten me. Of course I haven't! Whatever makes you think I have? Do I look ill?"

But Hammond didn't see her. He only felt that she was looking at him and that there was no need to worry about anything. She was here to look after things. It was all right. Everything was.

The gentle pressure of her hand was so calming that he put his over hers to hold it there. And she said:

"Stand still. I want to look at you. I haven't seen you yet. You've had your beard beautifully trimmed, and you look—younger, I think, and decidedly thinner! Bachelor life agrees with you."

"Agrees with me!" He groaned for love and caught her close again. And again, as always, he had the feeling he was holding something that never was quite his—his. Something too delicate, too precious, that would fly away once he let go.

"For God's sake let's get off to the hotel so that we can be by ourselves!" And he rang the bell hard for someone to look sharp with the luggage.

Walking down the wharf together she took his arm. He had her on his arm again. And the difference it made to get into the cab after Janey—to throw the red-and-yellow striped blanket round them both—to tell the driver to hurry because neither of them had had any tea. No more going without his tea or pouring out his own. She was back. He turned to her, squeezed her hand, and said gently, teasingly, in the "special" voice he had for her: "Glad to be home again, dearie?" She smiled; she didn't even bother to answer, but gently she drew his hand away as they came to the brighter streets.

"We've got the best room in the hotel," he said. "I wouldn't be put off with another. And I asked the chambermaid to put in a bit of a fire in case you felt chilly. She's a nice, attentive girl. And I thought now we were here we wouldn't bother to go home tomorrow, but spend the day looking round and leave the morning after. Does that suit you? There's no hurry, is there? The children will have you soon enough. . . . I thought a day's sightseeing might make a nice break in your journey—eh, Janey?"

"Have you taken the tickets for the day after?" she asked.

"I should think I have!" He unbuttoned his overcoat and took out his bulging pocketbook. "Here we are! I reserved a first-class carriage to Cooktown. There it is—'Mr. *and* Mrs. John Hammond.' I thought we might as well do ourselves comfortably, and we don't want other people butting in, do we? But if you'd like to stop here a bit longer—?"

"Oh, no!" said Janey quickly. "Not for the world! The day after tomorrow, then. And the children—"

But they had reached the hotel. The manager was standing in the broad, brilliantly lighted porch. He came down to greet them. A porter ran from the hall for their boxes.

"Well, Mr. Arnold, here's Mrs. Hammond at last!"

The manager led them through the hall himself and pressed the elevator-bell. Hammond knew there were business pals of his sitting at the little hall tables having a drink before dinner. But he wasn't going to risk interruption; he looked neither to the right nor the left. They could think what they pleased. If they didn't understand, the more fools they—and he stepped out of the lift, unlocked the door of their room, and shepherded Janey in. The door shut. Now, at last, they were alone together. He turned up the light. The curtains were drawn; the fire blazed. He flung his hat on to the huge bed and went toward her.

But—would you believe it?—again they were interrupted. This time it was the porter with the luggage. He made two journeys of it, leaving the door open in between, taking his time, whistling through his teeth in the corridor. Hammond paced up and down the room, tearing off his gloves, tearing off his scarf. Finally he flung his overcoat on to the bedside.

At last the fool was gone. The door clicked. Now they *were* alone. Said Hammond: "I feel I'll never have you to myself again. These cursed people! Janey"—and he bent his flushed, eager gaze upon her—"let's have dinner up here. If we go down to the restaurant we'll be interrupted, and then there's the confounded music" (the music he'd praised so highly, applauded so loudly last night!). "We shan't be able to hear each other speak. Let's have something up here in front of the fire. It's too late for tea. I'll order a little supper, shall I? How does that idea strike you?"

"Do, darling!" said Janey. "And while you're away—the children's letters—"

"Oh, later on will do!" said Hammond.

"But then we'd get it over," said Janey. "And I'd first have time to—"

"Oh, I needn't go down!" explained Hammond. "I'll just ring and give the order . . . you don't want to send me away, do you?"

Janey shook her head and smiled.

"But you're thinking of something else. You're worrying about something," said Hammond. "What is it? Come and sit here—come and sit on my knee before the fire."

"I'll just unpin my hat," said Janey, and she went over to the dressing-table. "A-ah!" She gave a little cry.

"What is it?"

"Nothing, darling. I've just found the children's letters. That's all right! They will keep. No hurry now!" She turned to him, clasping them. She tucked them into her frilled blouse. She cried quickly, gaily: "Oh, how typical this dressing-table is of you!"

"Why? What's the matter with it?" said Hammond.

"If it were floating in eternity I should say 'John!'" laughed Janey, staring at the big bottle of hair tonic, the wicker bottle of eau-de-Cologne, the two hair-brushes, and a dozen new collars tied with pink tape. "Is this all your luggage?"

"Hang my luggage!" said Hammond; but all the same he liked being laughed at by Janey. "Let's talk. Let's get down to things. Tell me"—and as Janey perched on his knees he leaned back and drew her into the deep, ugly chair—"tell me you're really glad to be back, Janey."

"Yes, darling, I am glad," she said.

But just as when he embraced her he felt she would fly away, so Hammond never knew—never knew for dead certain that she was as glad as he was. How could he know? Would he ever know? Would he always have this craving—this pang like hunger, somehow, to make Janey so much part of him that there wasn't any of her to escape? He wanted to blot out everybody, everything. He wished now he'd turned off the light. That might have brought her nearer. And now those letters from the children rustled in her blouse. He could have chucked them into the fire.

"Janey," he whispered.

"Yes, dear?" She lay on his breast, but so lightly, so remotely. Their breathing rose and fell together.

"Janey!"

"What is it?"

"Turn to me," he whispered. A slow, deep flush flowed into his forehead. "Kiss me, Janey! You kiss me!"

It seemed to him there was a tiny pause—but long enough for him to suffer torture—before her lips touched his, firmly, lightly—kissing them as she always kissed him, as though the kiss—how could he describe it?—confirmed what they were saying, signed the contract. But that wasn't what he wanted; that wasn't at all what he thirsted for. He felt suddenly, horribly tired.

"If you knew," he said, opening his eyes, "what it's been like—waiting today. I thought the boat never would come in. There we were, hanging about. What kept you so long?"

She made no answer. She was looking away from him at the fire. The flames hurried—hurried over the coals, flickered, fell.

"Not asleep, are you?" said Hammond, and he jumped her up and down.

"No," she said. And then: "Don't do that, dear. No, I was thinking. As a matter of fact," she said, "one of the passengers died last night—a man. That's what held us up. We brought him in—I mean, he wasn't buried at sea. So, of course, the ship's doctor and the shore doctor—"

"What was it?" asked Hammond uneasily. He hated to hear of death. He hated this to have happened. It was, in some queer way, as though he and Janey had met a funeral on their way to the hotel.

"Oh, it wasn't anything in the least infectious!" said Janey. She was speaking scarcely above her breath. "It was *heart*." A pause. "Poor fellow!" she said. "Quite young." And she watched the fire flicker and fall. "He died in my arms," said Janey.

The blow was so sudden that Hammond thought he would faint. He couldn't move; he couldn't breathe. He felt all his strength flowing—flowing into the big dark chair, and the big dark chair held him fast, gripped him, forced him to bear it.

"What?" he said dully. "What's that you say?"

"The end was quite peaceful," said the small voice. "He just"—and Hammond saw her lift her gentle hand—"breathed his life away at the end." And her hand fell.

"Who—else was there?" Hammond managed to ask.

"Nobody. I was alone with him."

Ah, my God, what was she saying! What was she doing to him! This would kill him! And all the while she spoke:

"I saw the change coming and I sent the steward for the doctor, but the doctor was too late. He couldn't have done anything anyway."

"But—why *you*, why *you?*" moaned Hammond.

At that Janey turned quickly, quickly searched his face.

"You don't *mind*, John, do you?" she asked. "You don't— It's nothing to do with you and me."

Somehow or other he managed to shake some sort of smile at her. Somehow or other he stammered: "No—go—on, go on! I want you to tell me."

"But, John darling—"

"Tell me, Janey!"

"There's nothing to tell," she said, wondering. "He was one of the first-class passengers. I saw he was very ill when he came on board. . . . But he seemed to be so much better until yesterday. He had a severe attack in the afternoon—excitement—nervousness, I think, about arriving. And after that he never recovered."

"But why didn't the stewardess—"

"Oh, my dear—the stewardess!" said Janey. "What would he have felt? And besides . . . he might have wanted to leave a message . . . to—"

"Didn't he?" muttered Hammond. "Didn't he say anything?"

"No, darling, not a word!" She shook her head softly. "All the time I was with him he was too weak . . . he was too weak even to move a finger. . . ."

Janey was silent. But her words, so light, so soft, so chill, seemed to hover in the air, to rain into his breast like snow.

The fire had gone red. Now it fell in with a sharp sound and the room was colder. Cold crept up his arms. The room was huge, immense, glittering. It filled his whole world. There was the great blind bed, with his coat flung across it like some headless man saying his prayers. There was the luggage, ready to be carried away again, anywhere, tossed into trains, carted on to boats.

. . . "He was too weak. He was too weak to move a finger." And yet he died in Janey's arms. She–who'd never–never once in all these years–never on one single solitary occasion–

No; he mustn't think of it. Madness lay in thinking of it. No, he wouldn't face it. He couldn't stand it. It was too much to bear!

And now Janey touched his tie with her fingers. She pinched the edges of the tie together.

"You're not–sorry I told you, John darling? It hasn't made you sad? It hasn't spoilt our evening–our being alone together?"

But at that he had to hide his face. He put his face into her bosom and his arms enfolded her.

Spoilt their evening! Spoilt their being alone together! They would never be alone together again.

Katherine Anne Porter was born at Indian Creek, Texas, in 1894. A descendant of Daniel Boone, she shows in her stories a denial of convention and a liking for primitive people—

KATHERINE ANNE PORTER

qualities which perhaps indicate the frontier influence in her family tradition and in her own experience. After a childhood in the South she lived for years in Europe. The scenes of her stories vary widely, but she repeatedly returns to treatment of the Southwest and Mexico. In 1944 she was a Fellow of Regional American Literature in the Library of Congress. Her stories have been brought together in *Flowering Judas, Noon Wine, Hacienda, The Leaning Tower,* and *Pale Horse, Pale Rider.* In 1952 she published *The Days Before,* a collection of nonfiction writings.

The Jilting of Granny Weatherall

SHE FLICKED her wrist neatly out of Doctor Harry's pudgy careful fingers and pulled the sheet up to her chin. The brat ought to be in knee breeches. Doctoring around the country with spectacles on his nose! "Get along now, take your schoolbooks and go. There's nothing wrong with me."

Doctor Harry spread a warm paw like a cushion on her forehead where the forked green vein danced and made her eyelids twitch. "Now, now, be a good girl, and we'll have you up in no time."

"That's no way to speak to a woman nearly eighty years old just because she's down. I'd have you respect your elders, young man."

"Well, Missy, excuse me." Doctor Harry patted her cheek.

"But I've got to warn you, haven't I? You're a marvel, but you must be careful or you're going to be good and sorry."

"Don't tell me what I'm going to be. I'm on my feet now, morally speaking. It's Cornelia. I had to go to bed to get rid of her."

Her bones felt loose, and floated around in her skin, and Doctor Harry floated like a balloon around the foot of the bed. He floated and pulled down his waistcoat and swung his glasses on a cord. "Well, stay where you are, it certainly can't hurt you."

"Get along and doctor your sick," said Granny Weatherall. "Leave a well woman alone. I'll call for you when I want you. . . . Where were you forty years ago when I pulled through milk-leg and double pneumonia? You weren't even born. Don't let Cornelia lead you on," she shouted, because Doctor Harry appeared to float up to the ceiling and out. "I pay my own bills, and I don't throw my money away on nonsense!"

She meant to wave good-by, but it was too much trouble. Her eyes closed of themselves, it was like a dark curtain drawn around the bed. The pillow rose and floated under her, pleasant as a hammock in a light wind. She listened to the leaves rustling outside the window. No, somebody was swishing newspapers: no, Cornelia and Doctor Harry were whispering together. She leaped broad awake, thinking they whispered in her ear.

"She was never like this, *never* like this!" "Well, what can we expect?" "Yes, eighty years old. . . ."

Well, and what if she was? She still had ears. It was like Cornelia to whisper around doors. She always kept things secret in such a public way. She was always being tactful and kind. Cornelia was dutiful; that was the trouble with her. Dutiful and good: "So good and dutiful," said Granny, "that I'd like to spank her." She saw herself spanking Cornelia and making a fine job of it.

"What'd you say, Mother?"

Granny felt her face tying up in hard knots.

"Can't a body think, I'd like to know?"

"I thought you might want something."

"I do. I want a lot of things. First off, go away and don't whisper."

She lay and drowsed, hoping in her sleep that the children would keep out and let her rest a minute. It had been a long day. Not that she was tired. It was always pleasant to snatch a minute now and then. There was always so much to be done, let me see: tomorrow.

Tomorrow was far away and there was nothing to trouble about. Things were finished somehow when the time came; thank God there was always a little margin over for peace: then a person could spread out the plan of life and tuck in the edges orderly. It was good to have everything clean and folded away, with the hair brushes and tonic bottles sitting straight on the white embroidered linen: the day started without fuss and the pantry shelves laid out with rows of jelly glasses and brown jugs and white stone-china jars with blue whirligigs and words painted on them: coffee, tea, sugar, ginger, cinnamon, allspice: and the bronze clock with the lion on top nicely dusted off. The dust that lion could collect in twenty-four hours! The box in the attic with all those letters tied up, well, she'd have to go through that tomorrow. All those letters—George's letters and John's letters and her letters to them both—lying around for the children to find afterwards made her uneasy. Yes, that would be tomorrow's business. No use to let them know how silly she had been once.

While she was rummaging around she found death in her mind and it felt clammy and unfamiliar. She had spent so much time preparing for death there was no need for bringing it up again. Let it take care of itself now. When she was sixty she had felt very old, finished, and went around making farewell trips to see her children and grandchildren, with a secret in her mind: This is the very last of your mother, children! Then she made her will and came down with a long fever. That was all just a notion like a lot of other things, but it was lucky too, for she had once for all got over the idea of dying for a long time. Now she couldn't be worried. She hoped she had better sense now. Her father had lived to be one hundred and two years old and had drunk a noggin of strong hot toddy on his last birthday. He told the reporters it was his daily habit, and he owed his long life to that. He had made quite a scandal and was very pleased about it. She believed she'd just plague Cornelia a little.

"Cornelia! Cornelia!" No footsteps, but a sudden hand on her cheek. "Bless you, where have you been?"

"Here, Mother."

"Well, Cornelia, I want a noggin of hot toddy."

"Are you cold, darling?"

"I'm chilly, Cornelia. Lying in bed stops the circulation. I must have told you that a thousand times."

Well, she could just hear Cornelia telling her husband that Mother was getting a little childish and they'd have to humor her. The thing that most annoyed her was that Cornelia thought she was deaf, dumb, and blind. Little hasty glances and tiny gestures tossed around her and over her head saying, "Don't cross her, let her have her way, she's eighty years old," and she sitting there as if she lived in a thin glass cage. Sometimes Granny almost made up her mind to pack up and move back to her own house where nobody could remind her every minute that she was old. Wait, wait, Cornelia, till your own children whisper behind your back!

In her day she had kept a better house and had got more work done. She wasn't too old yet for Lydia to be driving eighty miles for advice when one of the children jumped the track, and Jimmy still dropped in and talked things over: "Now, Mammy, you've a good business head, I want to know what you think of this? . . ." Old. Cornelia couldn't change the furniture around without asking. Little things, little things! They had been so sweet when they were little. Granny wished the old days were back again with the children young and everything to be done over. It had been a hard pull, but not too much for her. When she thought of all the food she had cooked, and all the clothes she had cut and sewed, and all the gardens she had made—well, the children showed it. There they were, made out of her, and they couldn't get away from that. Sometimes she wanted to see John again and point to them and say, Well, I didn't do so badly, did I? But that would have to wait. That was for tomorrow. She used to think of him as a man, but now all the children were older than their father, and he would be a child beside her if she saw him now.

It seemed strange and there was something wrong in the idea. Why, he couldn't possibly recognize her. She had fenced in a hundred acres once, digging the post holes herself and clamping the wires with just a Negro boy to help. That changed a woman. John would be looking for a young woman with the peaked Spanish comb in her hair and the painted fan. Digging post holes changed a woman. Riding country roads in the winter when women had their babies was another thing: sitting up nights with sick horses and sick Negroes and sick children and hardly ever losing one. John, I hardly ever lost one of them! John would see that in a minute, that would be something he could understand, she wouldn't have to explain anything!

It made her feel like rolling up her sleeves and putting the whole place to rights again. No matter if Cornelia was determined to be everywhere at once, there were a great many things left undone on this place. She would start tomorrow and do them. It was good to be strong enough for everything, even if all you made melted and changed and slipped under your hands, so that by the time you finished you almost forgot what you were working for. What was it I set out to do? she asked herself intently, but she could not remember. A fog rose over the valley, she saw it marching across the creek swallowing the trees and moving up the hill like an army of ghosts. Soon it would be at the near edge of the orchard, and then it was time to go in and light the lamps. Come in, children, don't stay out in the night air.

Lighting the lamps had been beautiful. The children huddled up to her and breathed like little calves waiting at the bars in the twilight. Their eyes followed the match and watched the flame rise and settle in a blue curve, then they moved away from her. The lamp was lit, they didn't have to be scared and hang on to mother any more. Never, never, never more. God, for all my life I thank Thee. Without Thee, my God, I could never have done it. Hail, Mary, full of grace.

I want you to pick all the fruit this year and see that nothing is wasted. There's always someone who can use it. Don't let good things rot for want of using. You waste life when you waste good food. Don't let things get lost. It's bitter to lose things.

Now, don't let me get to thinking, not when I am tired and taking a little nap before supper. . . .

The pillow rose about her shoulders and pressed against her heart and the memory was being squeezed out of it: oh, push down the pillow, somebody: it would smother her if she tried to hold it. Such a fresh breeze blowing and such a green day with no threats in it. But he had not come, just the same. What does a woman do when she has put on the white veil and set out the white cake for a man and he doesn't come? She tried to remember. No, I swear he never harmed me but in that. He never harmed me but in that . . . and what if he did? There was the day, the day, but a whirl of dark smoke rose and covered it, crept up and over into the bright field where everything was planted so carefully in orderly rows. That was hell, she knew hell when she saw it. For sixty years she had prayed against remembering him and against losing her soul in the deep pit of hell, and now the two things were mingled in one and the thought of him was a smoky cloud from hell that moved and crept in her head when she had just got rid of Doctor Harry and was trying to rest a minute. Wounded vanity, Ellen, said a sharp voice in the top of her mind. Don't let your wounded vanity get the upper hand of you. Plenty of girls get jilted. You were jilted, weren't you? Then stand up to it. Her eyelids wavered and let in streamers of blue-gray light like tissue paper over her eyes. She must get up and pull the shades down or she'd never sleep. She was in bed again and the shades were not down. How could that happen? Better turn over, hide from the light, sleeping in the light gave you nightmares. "Mother, how do you feel now?" and a stinging wetness on her forehead. But I don't like having my face washed in cold water!

Hapsy? George? Lydia? Jimmy? No, Cornelia, and her features were swollen and full of little puddles. "They're coming, darling, they'll all be here soon." Go wash your face, child, you look funny.

Instead of obeying, Cornelia knelt down and put her head on the pillow. She seemed to be talking but there was no sound. "Well, are you tongue-tied? Whose birthday is it? Are you going to give a party?"

Cornelia's mouth moved urgently in strange shapes. "Don't do that, you bother me, daughter."

"Oh, no, Mother. Oh, no. . . ."

Nonsense. It was strange about children. They disputed your every word. "No what, Cornelia?"

"Here's Doctor Harry."

"I won't see that boy again. He just left five minutes ago."

"That was this morning, Mother. It's night now. Here's the nurse."

"This is Doctor Harry, Mrs. Weatherall. I never saw you look so young and happy!"

"Ah, I'll never be young again—but I'd be happy if they'd let me lie in peace and get rested."

She thought she spoke up loudly, but no one answered. A warm weight on her forehead, a warm bracelet on her wrist, and a breeze went on whispering, trying to tell her something. A shuffle of leaves in the everlasting hand of God, He blew on them and they danced and rattled. "Mother, don't mind, we're going to give you a little hypodermic." "Look here, daughter, how do ants get in this bed? I saw sugar ants yesterday." Did you send for Hapsy too?

It was Hapsy she really wanted. She had to go a long way back through a great many rooms to find Hapsy standing with a baby on her arm. She seemed to herself to be Hapsy also, and the baby on Hapsy's arm was Hapsy and himself and herself, all at once, and there was no surprise in the meeting. Then Hapsy melted from within and turned flimsy as gray gauze and the baby was a gauzy shadow, and Hapsy came up close and said, "I thought you'd never come," and looked at her very searchingly and said, "You haven't changed a bit!" They leaned forward to kiss, when Cornelia began whispering from a long way off, "Oh, is there anything you want to tell me? Is there anything I can do for you?"

Yes, she had changed her mind after sixty years and she would like to see George. I want you to find George. Find him and be sure to tell him I forgot him. I want him to know I had my husband just the same and my children and my house like any other woman. A good house too and a good husband that I loved and fine children out of him. Better than I hoped for even. Tell him I was given back everything he took away and more. Oh, no, oh, God, no, there was something else besides the house and the man and the children. Oh, surely they were not all? What was it? Something not given back. . . . Her breath crowded down under her ribs and grew into a monstrous frightening shape with cutting edges; it bored up into her head, and the agony was unbelievable: Yes, John, get the Doctor now, no more talk, my time has come.

When this one was born it should be the last. The last. It should have been born first, for it was the one she had truly wanted. Everything came in good time. Nothing left out, left over. She was strong, in three days she would be as well as ever. Better. A woman needed milk in her to have her full health.

"Mother, do you hear me?"

"I've been telling you—"

"Mother, Father Connolly's here."

"I went to Holy Communion only last week. Tell him I'm not so sinful as all that."

"Father just wants to speak to you."

He could speak as much as he pleased. It was like him to drop in and inquire about her soul as if it were a teething baby, and then stay on for a cup of tea and a round of cards and gossip. He always had a funny story of some sort, usually about an Irishman who made his little mistakes and confessed them, and the point lay in some absurd thing he would blurt out in the confessional showing his struggles between native piety and original sin. Granny felt easy about her soul. Cornelia, where are your manners? Give Father Connolly a chair. She had her secret comfortable understanding with a few favorite saints who cleared a straight road to God for her. All as surely signed and sealed as the papers for the new Forty Acres. Forever . . . heirs and assigns forever. Since the day the wedding cake was not cut, but thrown out and wasted. The whole bottom dropped out of the world, and there she was blind and sweating with nothing under her feet and the walls falling away. His hand had caught her under the breast, she had not fallen, there was the freshly polished floor with the green rug on it, just as before. He had cursed like a sailor's parrot and said, "I'll kill him for you." Don't lay a hand on him, for my sake leave something to God. "Now, Ellen, you must believe what I tell you. . . ."

So there was nothing, nothing to worry about any more, except sometimes in the night one of the children screamed in a nightmare, and they both hustled out shaking and hunting for the matches and calling, "There, wait a minute, here we are!" John, get the doctor now, Hapsy's time has come. But there was Hapsy standing by the bed in a white cap. "Cornelia, tell Hapsy to take off her cap. I can't see her plain."

Her eyes opened very wide and the room stood out like a picture she had seen somewhere. Dark colors with the shadows rising toward the ceiling in long angles. The tall black dresser gleamed with nothing on it but John's picture, enlarged from a little one, with John's eyes very black when they should have been blue. You never saw him, so how do you know how he looked? But the man insisted the copy was perfect, it was very rich and handsome. For a picture, yes, but it's not my husband. The table by the bed had a linen cover and a candle and a crucifix. The light was blue from Cornelia's silk lampshades. No sort of light at all, just frippery. You had to live forty years with kerosene lamps to appreciate honest electricity. She felt very strong and she saw Doctor Harry with a rosy nimbus around him.

"You look like a saint, Doctor Harry, and I vow that's as near as you'll ever come to it."

"She's saying something."

"I heard you, Cornelia. What's all this carrying-on?"

"Father Connolly's saying—"

Cornelia's voice staggered and bumped like a cart in a bad road. It rounded corners and turned back again and arrived nowhere. Granny stepped up in the cart very lightly and reached for the reins, but a man sat beside her and she knew him by his hands, driving the cart. She did not look in his face, for she knew without seeing, but looked instead down the road where the trees leaned over and bowed to each other and a thousand birds were singing a Mass. She felt like singing too, but she put her hand in the bosom of her dress and pulled out a rosary, and Father Connolly murmured Latin in a very solemn voice and tickled her feet. My God, will you stop that nonsense? I'm a married woman. What if he did run away and leave me to face the priest by myself? I found another a whole world better. I wouldn't have exchanged my husband for anybody except St. Michael himself, and you may tell him that for me with a thank you in the bargain.

Light flashed on her closed eyelids, and a deep roaring shook her. Cornelia, is that lightning? I hear thunder. There's going to be a storm. Close all the windows. Call the children in. . . . "Mother, here we are, all of us." "Is that you, Hapsy?" "Oh, no, I'm Lydia. We drove as fast as we could." Their faces drifted above her, drifted away. The rosary fell out of her hands and Lydia put it back. Jimmy tried to help, their hands fumbled together, and Granny closed two fingers around Jimmy's thumb. Beads wouldn't do, it must be something alive. She was so amazed her thoughts ran round and round. So, my dear Lord, this is my death and I wasn't even thinking about it. My children have come to see me die. But I can't, it's not time. Oh, I always hated surprises. I wanted to give Cornelia the amethyst set—Cornelia, you're to have the amethyst set, but Hapsy's to wear it when she wants, and, Doctor Harry, do shut up. Nobody sent for you. Oh, my dear Lord, do wait a minute. I meant to do something about the Forty Acres, Jimmy doesn't need it and Lydia will later on, with that worthless husband of hers. I meant to finish the altar cloth and send six bottles of wine to Sister Borgia for her dyspepsia. I want to send six bottles of wine to Sister Borgia, Father Connolly, now don't let me forget.

Cornelia's voice made short turns and tilted over and crashed. "Oh, Mother, oh, Mother, oh, Mother. . . ."

"I'm not going, Cornelia. I'm taken by surprise. I can't go."

You'll see Hapsy again. What about her? "I thought you'd never come." Granny made a long journey outward, looking for Hapsy. What if I don't find her? What then? Her heart sank down and down, there was no bottom to death, she couldn't come to the end of it. The blue light from Cornelia's lampshade drew into a tiny point in the center of her brain, it flickered and winked like an eye, quietly it fluttered and dwindled. Granny lay curled down within herself, amazed and watchful, staring at the point of light that was herself; her body was now only a deeper mass of shadow in an endless darkness and this darkness would curl around the light and swallow it up. God, give a sign!

For the second time there was no sign. Again no bridegroom and the priest in the house. She could not remember any other sorrow because this grief wiped them all away. Oh, no, there's nothing more cruel than this—I'll never forgive it. She stretched herself with a deep breath and blew out the light.

D. H. LAWRENCE

D. H. Lawrence (1885-1930) was born in a coal-mining town in the English Midlands. In his famous novel *Sons and Lovers* (1913) he gave a vivid picture of his father, who worked in the mines, and his mother, a gifted and strong-spirited woman who was determined that her son should have a better life than her own. At sixteen Lawrence became a clerk, and a year later he began teaching in an elementary school. Despite poverty and depressing surroundings, he educated himself by wide and thoughtful reading. His first published writing was verse, but he soon turned to fiction. When his health began to fail he traveled in search of a salubrious climate, living for various periods in Australia, Mexico, Italy, the southwestern United States, and rural France. These settings allowed him to observe primitive society, in which he discovered more vitality than he had found in the industrial and intellectual culture of England. Some of his best stories appear in *The Tales of D. H. Lawrence* (1934).

Odor of Chrysanthemums

THE SMALL locomotive engine, Number 4, came clanking, stumbling down from Selston with seven full wagons. It appeared round the corner with loud threats of speed, but the colt that it startled from among the gorse, which still flickered indistinctly in the raw afternoon, outdistanced it at a canter. A woman, walking up the railway line to Underwood, drew back into the hedge, held her basket aside, and watched the footplate of the engine advancing. The trucks thumped heavily past, one by one, with slow inevitable movement, as she stood insignificantly trapped between the jolting black wagons and the hedge; then they curved away towards the coppice where the withered oak leaves dropped noiselessly, while the birds, pulling at the scarlet hips beside the track, made off into the dusk that had already crept into the spinney. In the open, the smoke from the engine sank and cleaved to the rough grass. The fields were dreary and forsaken, and in the marshy strip that led to the whimsey, a reedy pit-pond, the fowls had already abandoned their run among the alders, to roost in the tarred fowl-house. The pit-bank loomed up beyond the pond, flames like red sores licking its ashy sides, in the afternoon's stagnant light. Just beyond rose the tapering chimneys and the clumsy black head-stocks of Brinsley Colliery. The two wheels were spinning fast up against the sky, and the winding-engine rapped out its little spasms. The miners were being turned up.

The engine whistled as it came into the wide bay of railway lines beside the colliery, where rows of trucks stood in harbor.

Miners, single, trailing and in groups, passed like shadows diverging home. At the edge of the ribbed level of siding squat a low cottage, three steps down from the cinder track. A large bony vine clutched at the house, as if to claw down the tiled roof. Round the bricked yard grew a few wintry primroses. Beyond, the long garden sloped down to a bush-covered brook course. There were some twiggy apple trees, winter-crack trees, and ragged cabbages. Beside the path hung dishevelled pink chrysanthemums, like pink cloths hung on bushes. A woman came stooping out of the felt-covered fowl-house, halfway down the garden. She closed and padlocked the door, then drew herself erect, having brushed some bits from her white apron.

She was a tall woman of imperious mien, handsome, with definite black eyebrows. Her smooth black hair was parted exactly. For a few moments she stood steadily watching the miners as they passed along the railway: then she turned toward the brook course. Her face was calm and set, her mouth was closed with disillusionment. After a moment she called:

"John!" There was no answer. She waited, and then said distinctly:

"Where are you?"

"Here!" replied a child's sulky voice from among the bushes. The woman looked piercingly through the dusk.

"Are you at that brook?" she asked sternly.

For answer the child showed himself before the raspberrycanes that rose like whips. He was a small, sturdy boy of five. He stood quite still, defiantly.

"Oh!" said the mother, conciliated. "I thought you were down at that wet brook—and you remember what I told you—"

The boy did not move or answer.

"Come, come on in," she said more gently, "it's getting dark. There's your grandfather's engine coming down the line!"

The lad advanced slowly, with resentful, taciturn movement. He was dressed in trousers and waistcoat of cloth that was too thick and hard for the size of the garments. They were evidently cut down from a man's clothes.

As they went slowly toward the house he tore at the ragged wisps of chrysanthemums and dropped the petals in handfuls along the path.

"Don't do that—it does look nasty," said his mother. He refrained, and she, suddenly pitiful, broke off a twig with three or four wan flowers and held them against her face. When mother and son reached the yard her hand hesitated, and instead of laying the flower aside, she pushed it in her apron-band. The mother and son stood at the foot of the three steps looking across the bay of lines at the passing home of the miners. The trundle of the small train was imminent. Suddenly the engine loomed past the house and came to a stop opposite the gate.

The engine-driver, a short man with round gray beard, leaned out of the cab high above the woman.

"Have you got a cup of tea?" he said in a cheery, hearty fashion.

It was her father. She went in, saying she would mash. Directly, she returned.

"I didn't come to see you on Sunday," began the little gray-bearded man.

"I didn't expect you," said his daughter.

The engine-driver winced; then, reassuming his cheery, airy manner, he said:

"Oh, have you heard then? Well, and what do you think—?"

"I think it is soon enough," she replied.

At her brief censure the little man made an impatient gesture, and said coaxingly, yet with dangerous coldness:

"Well, what's a man to do? It's no sort of life for a man of my years, to sit at my own hearth like a stranger. And if I'm going to marry again it may as well be soon as late—what does it matter to anybody?"

The woman did not reply, but turned and went into the house. The man in the engine-cab stood assertive, till she returned with a cup of tea and a piece of bread and butter on a plate. She went up the steps and stood near the footplate of the hissing engine.

"You needn't 'a' brought me bread an' butter," said her father. "But a cup of tea"—he sipped appreciatively—"it's very nice." He sipped for a moment or two, then: "I hear as Walter's got another bout on," he said.

"When hasn't he?" said the woman bitterly.

"I heered tell of him in the 'Lord Nelson' braggin' as he was going to spend that b—— afore he went: half a sovereign that was."

"When?" asked the woman.

"A' Sat'day night—I know that's true."

"Very likely," she laughed bitterly. "He gives me twenty-three shillings."

"Aye, it's a nice thing, when a man can do nothing with his money but make a beast of himself!" said the gray-whiskered man. The woman turned her head away. Her father swallowed the last of his tea and handed her the cup.

"Aye," he sighed, wiping his mouth. "It's a settler, it is—"

He put his hand on the lever. The little engine strained and groaned, and the train rumbled towards the crossing. The woman again looked across the metals. Darkness was settling over the spaces of the railway and trucks: the miners, in gray somber groups, were still passing home. The winding-engine pulsed hurriedly, with brief pauses. Elizabeth Bates looked at the dreary flow of men, then she went indoors. Her husband did not come.

The kitchen was small and full of firelight; red coals piled glowing up the chimney mouth. All the life of the room seemed in the white, warm hearth and the steel fender reflecting the red fire. The cloth was laid for tea; cups glinted in the shadows. At the back, where the lowest stairs protruded into the room, the boy sat struggling with a knife and a piece of whitewood. He was almost hidden in the shadow. It was half-past four. They had but to await the father's coming to begin tea. As the mother watched her son's sullen little struggle with the wood, she saw herself in his silence and pertinacity; she saw the father in her child's indifference to all but himself. She seemed to be occupied by her husband. He had probably gone past his home, slunk past his own door, to drink before he came in, while his dinner spoiled and wasted in waiting. She glanced at the clock, then took the potatoes to strain them in the yard. The garden and fields beyond the brook were closed in uncertain darkness. When she rose with the saucepan, leaving the drain steaming into the night behind her, she saw the yellow lamps were lit along the high road that went up the hill away beyond the space of the railway lines and the field.

Then again she watched the men trooping home, fewer now and fewer.

Indoors the fire was sinking and the room was dark red. The woman put her saucepan on the hob, and set a batter pudding near the mouth of the oven. Then she stood unmoving. Directly, gratefully, came quick young steps to the door. Someone hung on the latch a moment, then a little girl entered and began pulling off her outdoor things, dragging a mass of curls, just ripening from gold to brown, over her eyes with her hat.

Her mother chid her for coming late from school, and said she would have to keep her at home the dark winter days.

"Why, mother, it's hardly a bit dark yet. The lamp's not lighted, and my father's not home."

"No, he isn't. But it's a quarter to five! Did you see anything of him?"

The child became serious. She looked at her mother with large, wistful blue eyes.

"No, mother, I've never seen him. Why? Has he come up an' gone past, to Old Brinsley? He hasn't, mother, 'cos I never saw him."

"He'd watch that," said the mother bitterly, "he'd take care as you didn't see him. But you may depend upon it, he's seated in the 'Prince o' Wales.' He wouldn't be this late."

The girl looked at her mother piteously.

"Let's have our teas, mother, should we?" said she.

The mother called John to table. She opened the door once more and looked out across the darkness of the lines. All was deserted: she could not hear the winding-engines.

"Perhaps," she said to herself, "he's stopped to get some ripping done."

They sat down to tea. John, at the end of the table near the door, was almost lost in the darkness. Their faces were hidden from each other. The girl crouched against the fender slowly moving a thick piece of bread before the fire. The lad, his face a dusky mark on the shadow, sat watching her who was transfigured in the red glow.

"I do think it's beautiful to look in the fire," said the child.

"Do you?" said her mother. "Why?"

"It's so red, and full of little caves—and it feels so nice, and you can fair smell it."

"It'll want mending directly," replied her mother, "and then if your father comes he'll carry on and say there never is a fire when a man comes home sweating from the pit. A public-house is always warm enough."

There was silence till the boy said complainingly: "Make haste, our Annie."

"Well, I am doing! I can't make the fire do it no faster, can I?"

"She keeps wafflin' it about so's to make 'er slow," grumbled the boy.

"Don't have such an evil imagination, child," replied the mother.

Soon the room was busy in the darkness with the crisp sound of crunching. The mother ate very little. She drank her tea determinedly, and sat thinking. When she rose her anger was evident in the stern unbending of her head. She looked at the pudding in the fender, and broke out:

"It is a scandalous thing as a man can't even come home to his dinner! If it's crozzled up to a cinder I don't see why I should care. Past his very door he goes to get to a public-house, and here I sit with his dinner waiting for him—"

She went out. As she dropped piece after piece of coal on the red fire, the shadows fell on the walls, till the room was almost in total darkness.

"I canna see," grumbled the invisible John. In spite of herself, the mother laughed.

"You know the way to your mouth," she said. She set the dust-pan outside the door. When she came again like a shadow on the hearth, the lad repeated, complaining sulkily:

"I canna see."

"Good gracious!" cried the mother irritably, "you're as bad as your father if it's a bit dusk!"

Nevertheless she took a paper spill from a sheaf on the mantel-piece and proceeded to light the lamp that hung from the ceiling in the middle of the room. As she reached up, her figure displayed itself just rounding with maternity.

"Oh, mother–!" exclaimed the girl.

"What?" said the woman, suspended in the act of putting the lamp glass over the flame. The copper reflector shone handsomely on her, as she stood with uplifted arm, turning to face her daughter.

"You've got a flower in your apron!" said the child, in a little rapture at this unusual event.

"Goodness me!" exclaimed the woman, relieved. "One would think the house was afire." She replaced the glass and waited a moment before turning up the wick. A pale shadow was seen floating vaguely on the floor.

"Let me smell!" said the child, still rapturously, coming forward and putting her face to her mother's waist.

"Go along, silly!" said the mother, turning up the lamp. The light revealed their suspense so that the woman felt it almost un-bearable. Annie was still bending at her waist. Irritably, the mother took the flowers out from her apron-band.

"Oh, mother–don't take them out!" Annie cried, catching her hand and trying to replace the sprig.

"Such nonsense!" said the mother, turning away. The child put the pale chrysanthemums to her lips, murmuring:

"Don't they smell beautiful!"

Her mother gave a short laugh.

"No," she said, "not to me. It was chrysanthemums when I mar-ried him, and chrysanthemums when you were born, and the first time they ever brought him home drunk, he'd got brown chrysanthemums in his buttonhole."

She looked at the children. Their eyes and their parted lips were wondering. The mother sat rocking in silence for some time. Then she looked at the clock.

"Twenty minutes to six!" In a tone of fine bitter carelessness she continued: "Eh, he'll not come now till they bring him. There he'll stick! But he needn't come rolling in here in his pit-dirt, for *I* won't wash him. He can lie on the floor– Eh, what a fool I've been, what a fool! And this is what I came here for, to this dirty hole, rats and all, for him to slink past his very door. Twice last week–he's begun now–"

She silenced herself, and rose to clear the table.

While for an hour or more the children played, subduedly intent, fertile of imagination, united in fear of the mother's wrath, and in dread of their father's homecoming, Mrs. Bates sat in her rocking-chair making a "singlet" of thick cream-colored flannel, which gave a dull wounded sound as she tore off the gray edge. She worked at her sewing with energy, listening to the children, and her anger wearied itself, lay down to rest, opening its eyes from time to time and steadily watching, its ears raised to listen. Sometimes even her anger quailed and shrank, and the mother suspended her sewing, tracing the footsteps that thudded along the sleepers outside; she would lift her head sharply to bid the children "hush," but she recovered herself in time, and the footsteps went past the gate, and the children were not flung out of their play-world.

But at last Annie sighed, and gave in. She glanced at her wagon of slippers, and loathed the game. She turned plaintively to her mother.

"Mother!"–but she was inarticulate.

John crept out like a frog from under the sofa. His mother glanced up.

"Yes," she said, "just look at those shirt-sleeves!"

The boy held them out to survey them, saying nothing. Then somebody called in a hoarse voice away down the line, and suspense bristled in the room, till two people had gone by outside, talking.

"It is time for bed," said the mother.

"My father hasn't come," wailed Annie plaintively. But her mother was primed with courage.

"Never mind. They'll bring him when he does come—like a log." She meant there would be no scene. "And he may sleep on the floor till he wakes himself. I know he'll not go to work tomorrow after this!"

The children had their hands and faces wiped with a flannel. They were very quiet. When they had put on their nightdresses, they said their prayers, the boy mumbling. The mother looked down at them, at the brown silken bush of intertwining curls in the nape of the girl's neck, at the little black head of the lad, and her heart burst with anger at their father who caused all three such distress. The children hid their faces in her skirts for comfort.

When Mrs. Bates came down, the room was strangely empty, with a tension of expectancy. She took up her sewing and stitched for some time without raising her head. Meantime her anger was tinged with fear.

II

The clock struck eight and she rose suddenly, dropping her sewing on her chair. She went to the stairfoot door, opened it, listening. Then she went out, locking the door behind her.

Something scuffled in the yard, and she started, though she knew it was only the rats with which the place was overrun. The night was very dark. In the great bay of railway lines, bulked with trucks, there was no trace of light, only away back she could see a few yellow lamps at the pit-top, and the red smear of the burning pit-bank on the night. She hurried along the edge of the track, then, crossing the converging lines, came to the stile by the white gates, whence she emerged on the road. Then the fear which had led her shrank. People were walking up to New Brinsley; she saw the lights in the houses; twenty yards further on were the broad windows of the "Prince of Wales," very warm and bright, and the loud voices of men could be heard distinctly. What a fool she had been to imagine that anything had happened to him! He was merely drinking over there at the "Prince of Wales." She faltered. She had never yet been to fetch him, and she never would go. So she continued her walk toward the long straggling line of houses, standing blank on the highway. She entered a passage between the dwellings.

"Mr. Rigley?—Yes! Did you want him? No, he's not in at this minute."

The raw-boned woman leaned forward from her dark scullery and peered at the other, upon whom fell a dim light through the blind of the kitchen window.

"Is it Mrs. Bates?" she asked in a tone tinged with respect.

"Yes. I wondered if your Master was at home. Mine hasn't come yet."

"'Asn't 'e! Oh, Jack's been 'ome an' 'ad 'is dinner an' gone out. 'E's just gone for 'alf an hour afore bedtime. Did you call at the 'Prince of Wales'?"

"No—"

"No, you didn't like—! It's not very nice." The other woman was indulgent. There was an awkward pause. "Jack never said nothink about—about your Mester," she said.

"No!—I expect he's stuck in there!"

Elizabeth Bates said this bitterly, and with recklessness. She knew that the woman across the yard was standing at her door listening, but she did not care. As she turned:

"Stop a minute! I'll just go an' ask Jack if 'e knows anythink," said Mrs. Rigley.

"Oh, no—I wouldn't like to put—!"

"Yes, I will, if you'll just step inside an' see as th' childer doesn't come downstairs and set theirselves afire."

Elizabeth Bates, murmuring a remonstrance, stepped inside. The other woman apologized for the state of the room.

The kitchen needed apology. There were little frocks and trousers and childish undergarments on the squab and on the floor, and a litter of playthings everywhere. On the black American cloth of the table were pieces of bread and cake, crusts, slops, and a teapot with cold tea.

"Eh, ours is just as bad," said Elizabeth Bates, looking at the woman, not at the house. Mrs. Rigley put a shawl over her head and hurried out, saying:

"I shanna be a minute."

The other sat, noting with faint disapproval the general untidiness of the room. Then she fell to counting the shoes of various sizes scattered over the floor. There were twelve. She sighed and said to herself, "No wonder!"—glancing at the litter. There came the scratching of two pairs of feet on the yard, and the Rigleys entered. Elizabeth Bates rose. Rigley was a big man, with very large bones. His head looked particularly bony. Across his temple was a blue scar, caused by a wound got in the pit, a wound in which the coal-dust remained blue like tattooing.

" 'Asna e come whoam yit?" asked the man, without any form of greeting, but with deference and sympathy. "I couldna say wheer he is—'e's non ower theer!"—he jerked his head to signify the "Prince of Wales."

" 'E's 'appen gone up to th' 'Yew,' " said Mrs. Rigley.

There was another pause. Rigley had evidently something to get off his mind:

"Ah left 'im finishin' a stint," he began. "Loose-all 'ad bin gone about ten minutes when we com'n away, an' I shouted, 'Are ter comin', Walt?' an' 'e said, 'Go on, Ah shanna be but a'ef a minnit,' so we com'n ter th' bottom, me an' Bowers, thinkin' as 'e wor just behint, an' 'ud come up i' th' next bantle—"

He stood perplexed, as if answering a charge of deserting his mate. Elizabeth Bates, now again certain of disaster, hastened to reassure him:

"I expect 'e's gone up to th' 'Yew Tree,' as you say. It's not the first time. I've fretted myself into a fever before now. He'll come home when they carry him."

"Ay, isn't it too bad!" deplored the other woman.

"I'll just step up to Dick's an' see if 'e *is* theer," offered the man, afraid of appearing alarmed, afraid of taking liberties.

"Oh, I wouldn't think of bothering you that far," said Elizabeth Bates, with emphasis, but he knew she was glad of his offer.

As they stumbled up the entry, Elizabeth Bates heard Rigley's wife run across the yard and open her neighbor's door. At this, suddenly all the blood in her body seemed to switch away from her heart.

"Mind!" warned Rigley. "Ah've said many a time as Ah'd fill up them ruts in this entry, sumb'dy 'll be breakin' their legs yit."

She recovered herself and walked quickly along with the miner.

"I don't like leaving the children in bed, and nobody in the house," she said.

"No, you dunna!" he replied courteously. They were soon at the gate of the cottage.

"Well, I shanna be many minnits. Dunna you be frettin' now, 'e'll be all right," said the butty.

"Thank you very much, Mr. Rigley," she replied.

"You're welcome!" he stammered, moving away. "I shanna be many minnits."

The house was quiet. Elizabeth Bates took off her hat and shawl, and rolled back the rug. When she had finished, she sat down. It was a few minutes past nine. She was startled by the rapid chuff of the winding-engine at the pit, and the sharp whirr of the brakes on the rope as it descended. Again she felt the painful sweep of her blood, and she put her hand to her side, saying aloud, "Good gracious!—it's only the nine o'clock deputy going down," rebuking herself.

She sat still, listening. Half an hour of this, and she was wearied out.

"What am I working myself up like this for?" she said pitiably to herself, "I s'll only be doing myself some damage."

She took out her sewing again.

At a quarter to ten there were footsteps. One person! She watched for the door to open. It was an elderly woman, in a black bonnet and a black woollen shawl—his mother. She was about sixty years old, pale, with blue eyes, and her face all wrinkled and lamentable. She shut the door and turned to her daughter-in-law peevishly.

querulously

"Eh, Lizzie, whatever shall we do, whatever shall we do!" she cried.

Elizabeth drew back a little, sharply.

"What is it, mother?" she said.

The elder woman seated herself on the sofa.

"I don't know, child, I can't tell you!"—she shook her head slowly. Elizabeth sat watching her, anxious and vexed.

"I don't know," replied the grandmother, sighing very deeply.

"There's no end to my troubles, there isn't. The things I've gone through, I'm sure it's enough—" She wept without wiping her eyes, the tears running.

"But, mother," interrupted Elizabeth, "what do you mean? What is it?"

The grandmother slowly wiped her eyes. The fountains of her tears were stopped by Elizabeth's directness. She wiped her eyes slowly.

"Poor child! Eh, you poor thing!" she moaned. "I don't know what we're going to do, I don't—and you as you are—it's a thing, it is indeed!"

Elizabeth waited.

"Is he dead?" she asked, and at the words her heart swung violently, though she felt a slight flush of shame at the ultimate extravagance of the question. Her words sufficiently frightened the old lady, almost brought her to herself.

"Don't say so, Elizabeth! We'll hope it's not as bad as that; no, may the Lord spare us that, Elizabeth. Jack Rigley came just as I was sittin' down to a glass afore going to bed, an' 'e said, ''Appen you'll go down th' line, Mrs. Bates. Walt's had an accident. 'Appen you'll go an' sit wi' 'er till we can get him home.' I hadn't time to ask him a word afore he was gone. An' I put my bonnet on an' come straight down, Lizzie. I thought to myself, 'Eh, that poor blessed child, if anybody should come an' tell her of a sudden, there's no knowin' what'll 'appen to 'er.' You mustn't let it upset you, Lizzie—or you know what to expect. How long is it, six months—or is it five, Lizzie? Ay!"—the old woman shook her head—"time slips on, it slips on! Ay!"

Elizabeth's thoughts were busy elsewhere. If he was killed—would she be able to manage on the little pension and what she could earn?—she counted up rapidly. If he was hurt—they wouldn't take him to the hospital—how tiresome he would be to nurse!—but perhaps she'd be able to get him away from the drink and his hateful ways. She would—while he was ill. The tears offered to come to her eyes at the picture. But what sentimental luxury was this she was beginning? She turned to consider the children. At any rate she was absolutely necessary for them. They were her business.

"Ay!" repeated the old woman, "it seems but a week or two since he brought me his first wages. Ay—he was a good lad, Elizabeth, he was, in his way. I don't know why he got to be such a trouble, I don't. He was a happy lad at home, only full of spirits. But there's no mistake he's been a handful of trouble, he has! I hope the Lord'll spare him to mend his ways. I hope so, I hope so. You've had a sight o' trouble with him, Elizabeth, you have indeed. But he was a jolly enough lad wi' me, he was, I can assure you. I don't know how it is. . . ."

The old woman continued to muse aloud, a monotonous irritating sound, while Elizabeth thought concentratedly, startled once, when she heard the winding-engine chuff quickly, and the brakes skirr with a shriek. Then she heard the engine more slowly, and the brakes made no sound. The old woman did not notice. Elizabeth waited in suspense. The mother-in-law talked, with lapses into silence.

"But he wasn't your son, Lizzie, an' it makes a difference. Whatever he was, I remember him when he was little, an' I learned to understand him and to make allowances. You've got to make allowances for them—"

It was half-past ten, and the old woman was saying: "But it's trouble from beginning to end; you're never too old for trouble, never too old for that—" when the gate banged back, and there were heavy feet on the steps.

"I'll go, Lizzie, let me go," cried the old woman, rising. But Elizabeth was at the door. It was a man in pit-clothes.

"They're bringin' 'im, Missis," he said. Elizabeth's heart halted a moment. Then it surged on again, almost suffocating her.

"Is he—is it bad?" she asked.

The man turned away, looking at the darkness:

"The doctor says 'e'd been dead hours. 'E saw 'im i' th' lamp-cabin."

The old woman, who stood just behind Elizabeth, dropped into a chair, and folded her hands, crying: "Oh, my boy, my boy!"

"Hush!" said Elizabeth, with a sharp twitch of a frown. "Be still, mother, don't waken th' children: I wouldn't have them down for anything!"

The old woman moaned softly, rocking herself. The man was drawing away. Elizabeth took a step forward.

"How was it?" she asked.

"Well, I couldn't say for sure," the man replied, very ill at ease. " 'E wor finishin' a stint an' th' butties 'ad gone, an' a lot o' stuff come down atop 'n 'im."

"And crushed him?" cried the widow, with a shudder.

"No," said the man, "it fell at th' back of 'im. 'E wor under th' face, an' it niver touched 'im. It shut 'im in. It seems 'e wor smothered."

Elizabeth shrank back. She heard the old woman behind her cry:

"What?—what did 'e say it was?"

The man replied, more loudly: " 'E wor smothered!"

Then the old woman wailed aloud, and this relieved Elizabeth.

"Oh, mother," she said, putting her hand on the old woman, "don't waken th' children, don't waken th' children."

She wept a little, unknowing, while the old mother rocked herself and moaned. Elizabeth remembered that they were bringing him home, and she must be ready. "They'll lay him in the parlor," she said to herself, standing a moment pale and perplexed.

Then she lighted a candle and went into the tiny room. The air was cold and damp, but she could not make a fire, there was no fireplace. She set down the candle and looked round. The candlelight glittered on the luster-glasses, on the two vases that held some of the pink chrysanthemums, and on the dark mahogany. There was a cold, deathly smell of chrysanthemums in the room. Elizabeth stood looking at the flowers. She turned away, and calculated whether there would be room to lay him on the floor, between the couch and the chiffonier. She pushed the chairs aside. There would be room to lay him down and to step round him. Then she fetched the old red tablecloth, and another old cloth, spreading them down to save her bit of carpet. She shivered on leaving the parlor; so, from the dresser-drawer she took a clean shirt and put it at the fire to air. All the time her mother-in-law was rocking herself in the chair and moaning.

"You'll have to move from there, mother," said Elizabeth. "They'll be bringing him in. Come in the rocker."

The old mother rose mechanically, and seated herself by the fire, continuing to lament. Elizabeth went into the pantry for another candle, and there, in the little penthouse under the naked tiles, she heard them coming. She stood still in the pantry doorway, listening. She heard them pass the end of the house, and come awkwardly down the three steps, a jumble of shuffling footsteps and muttering voices. The old woman was silent. The men were in the yard.

Then Elizabeth heard Matthews, the manager of the pit, say: "You go in first, Jim. Mind!"

The door came open, and the two women saw a collier backing into the room, holding one end of a stretcher, on which they could see the nailed pit-boots of the dead man. The two carriers halted, the man at the head stooping to the lintel of the door.

"Wheer will you have him?" asked the manager, a short, white-bearded man.

Elizabeth roused herself and came from the pantry carrying the unlighted candle.

"In the parlor," she said.

"In there, Jim!" pointed the manager, and the carriers backed round into the tiny room. The coat with which they had covered the body fell off as they awkwardly turned through the two doorways, and the women saw their man, naked to the waist, lying stripped for work. The old woman began to moan in a low voice of horror.

"Lay th' stretcher at th' side," snapped the manager, "an' put 'im on th' cloths. Mind now, mind! Look you now—!"

One of the men had knocked off a vase of chrysanthemums. He stared awkwardly, then they set down the stretcher. Elizabeth did not look at her husband. As soon as she could get in the room, she went and picked up the broken vase and the flowers.

"Wait a minute!" she said.

The three men waited in silence while she mopped up the water with a duster.

"Eh, what a job, what a job, to be sure!" the manager was

saying, rubbing his brow with trouble and perplexity. "Never knew such a thing in my life, never! He'd no business to ha' been left. I never knew such a thing in my life! Fell over him clean as a whistle, an' shut him in. Not four foot of space, there wasn't —yet it scarce bruised him."

He looked down at the dead man, lying prone, half naked, all grimed with coal-dust.

"'Sphyxiated,' the doctor said. It *is* the most terrible job I've ever known. Seems as if it was done o' purpose. Clean over him, an' shut 'im in, like a mouse-trap"—he made a sharp, descending gesture with his hand.

The colliers standing by jerked aside their heads in hopeless comment.

The horror of the thing bristled upon them all.

Then they heard the girl's voice upstairs calling shrilly: "Mother, mother—who is it? Mother, who is it?"

Elizabeth hurried to the foot of the stairs and opened the door: "Go to sleep!" she commanded sharply. "What are you shouting about? Go to sleep at once—there's nothing—"

Then she began to mount the stairs. They could hear her on the boards, and on the plaster floor of the little bedroom. They could hear her distinctly:

"What's the matter now?—what's the matter with you, silly thing?"—her voice was much agitated, with an unreal gentleness.

"I thought it was some men come," said the plaintive voice of the child. "Has he come?"

"Yes, they've brought him. There's nothing to make a fuss about. Go to sleep now, like a good child."

They could hear her voice in the bedroom, they waited whilst she covered the children under the bedclothes.

"Is he drunk?" asked the girl, timidly, faintly.

"No! No—he's not! He—he's asleep."

"Is he asleep downstairs?"

"Yes—and don't make a noise."

There was silence for a moment, then the men heard the frightened child again:

"What's that noise?"

"It's nothing, I tell you, what are you bothering for?"

The noise was the grandmother moaning. She was oblivious of everything, sitting on her chair rocking and moaning. The manager put his hand on her arm and bade her "Sh—sh!!"

The old woman opened her eyes and looked at him. She was shocked by this interruption, and seemed to wonder.

"What time is it?"—the plaintive thin voice of the child, sinking back unhappily into sleep, asked this last question.

"Ten o'clock," answered the mother more softly. Then she must have bent down and kissed the children.

Matthews beckoned to the men to come away. They put on their caps and took up the stretcher. Stepping over the body, they tiptoed out of the house. None of them spoke till they were far from the wakeful children.

When Elizabeth came down she found her mother alone on the parlor floor, leaning over the dead man, the tears dropping on him.

"We must lay him out," the wife said. She put on the kettle, then returning knelt at the feet, and began to unfasten the knotted leather laces. The room was clammy and dim with only one candle, so that she had to bend her face almost to the floor. At last she got off the heavy boots and put them away.

"You must help me now," she whispered to the old woman. Together they stripped the man.

When they arose, saw him lying in the naïve dignity of death, the women stood arrested in fear and respect. For a few moments they remained still, looking down, the old mother whimpering. Elizabeth felt countermanded. She saw him, how utterly inviolable he lay in himself. She had nothing to do with him. She could not accept it. Stooping, she laid her hand on him, in claim. He was still warm, for the mine was hot where he had died. His mother had his face between her hands, and was murmuring incoherently. The old tears fell in succession as drops from wet leaves; the mother was not weeping, merely her tears flowed. Elizabeth embraced the body of her husband, with cheek and lips. She seemed to be listening, inquiring, trying to get some connection. But she could not. She was driven away. He was impregnable.

She rose, went into the kitchen, where she poured warm water into a bowl, brought soap and flannel and a soft towel.

"I must wash him," she said.

Then the old mother rose stiffly, and watched Elizabeth as she carefully washed his face, carefully brushing the big blond moustache from his mouth with the flannel. She was afraid with a bottomless fear, so she ministered to him. The old woman, jealous, said:

"Let me wipe him!"—and she kneeled on the other side drying slowly as Elizabeth washed, her big black bonnet sometimes brushing the dark head of her daughter-in-law. They worked thus in silence for a long time. They never forgot it was death, and the touch of the man's dead body gave them strange emotions, different in each of the women; a great dread possessed them both, the mother felt the lie was given to her womb, she was denied; the wife felt the utter isolation of the human soul, the child within her was a weight apart from her.

At last it was finished. He was a man of handsome body, and his face showed no traces of drink. He was blond, full-fleshed, with fine limbs. But he was dead.

"Bless him," whispered his mother, looking always at his face, and speaking out of sheer terror. "Dear lad—bless him!" She spoke in a faint, sibilant ecstasy of fear and mother love.

Elizabeth sank down again to the floor, and put her face against his neck, and trembled and shuddered. But she had to draw away again. He was dead, and her living flesh had no place against his. A great dread and weariness held her: she was so unavailing. Her life was gone like this.

"White as milk he is, clear as a twelve-month baby, bless him, the darling!" the old mother murmured to herself. "Not a mark on him, clear and clean and white, beautiful as ever a child was made," she murmured with pride. Elizabeth kept her face hidden.

"He went peaceful, Lizzie—peaceful as sleep. Isn't he beautiful, the lamb? Ay—he must ha' made his peace, Lizzie. 'Appen he made it all right, Lizzie, shut in there. He'd have time. He wouldn't look like this if he hadn't made his peace. The lamb, the dear lamb. Eh, but he had a hearty laugh. I loved to hear it. He had the heartiest laugh, Lizzie, as a lad—"

Elizabeth looked up. The man's mouth was fallen back, slightly open under the cover of the moustache. The eyes, half shut, did not show glazed in the obscurity. Life with its smoky burning gone from him, had left him apart and utterly alien to her. And she knew what a stranger he was to her. In her womb was ice of fear, because of this separate stranger with whom she had been living as one flesh. Was this what it all meant–utter, intact separateness, obscured by heat of living? In dread she turned her face away. The fact was too deadly. There had been nothing between them, and yet they had come together, exchanging their nakedness repeatedly. Each time he had taken her, they had been two isolated beings, far apart as now. He was no more responsible than she. The child was like ice in her womb. For as she looked at the dead man, her mind, cold and detached, said clearly: "Who am I? What have I been doing? I have been fighting a husband who did not exist. *He* existed all the time. What wrong have I done? What was that I have been living with? There lies the reality, this man." And her soul died in her for fear: she knew she had never seen him, he had never seen her, they had met in the dark and had fought in the dark, not knowing whom they met nor whom they fought. And now she saw, and turned silent in seeing. For she had been wrong. She had said he was something he was not; she had felt familiar with him. Whereas he was apart all the while, living as she never lived, feeling as she never felt.

In fear and shame she looked at his naked body, that she had known falsely. And he was the father of her children. Her soul was torn from her body and stood apart. She looked at his naked body and was ashamed, as if she had denied it. After all, it was itself. It seemed awful to her. She looked at his face, and she turned her own face to the wall. For his look was other than hers, his way was not her way. She had denied him what he was—she saw it now. She had refused him as himself. And this had been her life, and his life. She was grateful to death, which restored the truth. And she knew she was not dead.

And all the while her heart was bursting with grief and pity for him. What had he suffered? What stretch of horror for this helpless man! She was rigid with agony. She had not been able to help him. He had been cruelly injured, this naked man, this other being, and she could make no reparation. There were the children—but the children belonged to life. This dead man had nothing to do with them. He and she were only channels through which life had flowed to issue in the children. She was a mother—but how awful she knew it now to have been a wife. And he, dead now, how awful he must have felt it to be a husband. She felt that in the next world he would be a stranger to her. If they met there, in the beyond, they would only be ashamed of what had been before. The children had come, for some mysterious reason, out of both of them. But the children did not unite them. Now he was dead, she knew how eternally he was apart from her, how eternally he had nothing more to do with her. She saw this episode of her life closed. They had denied each other in life. Now he had withdrawn. An anguish came over her. It was finished then: it had become hopeless between them long before he died. Yet he had been her husband. But how little!

"Have you got his shirt, 'Lizabeth?"

Elizabeth turned without answering, though she strove to weep and behave as her mother-in-law expected. But she could not, she was silenced. She went into the kitchen and returned with the garment.

"It is aired," she said, grasping the cotton shirt here and there to try. She was almost ashamed to handle him; what right had she or any one to lay hands on him; but her touch was humble on his body. It was hard work to clothe him. He was so heavy and inert. A terrible dread gripped her all the while: that he could be so heavy and utterly inert, unresponsive, apart. The horror of the distance between them was almost too much for her—it was so infinite a gap she must look across.

At last it was finished. They covered him with a sheet and left him lying, with his face bound. And she fastened the door of the little parlor, lest the children should see what was lying there. Then, with peace sunk heavy on her heart, she went about making tidy the kitchen. She knew she submitted to life, which was her immediate master. But from death, her ultimate master, she winced with fear and shame.

Graham Greene, born in England in 1904, was educated at Birkhamsted School and at Balliol College, Oxford. For fifteen years he was a London journalist; he began as a staff writer on *The Times* and became literary editor of *The Spectator*.

GRAHAM GREENE

In these years he wrote his first novels and short stories. In 1938 he traveled in the United States and Mexico. During World War II he served in the Foreign Office and was sent on a tour of special duty to West Africa. His novels include *The Man Within* (1929), *The Name of Action* (1930), *The Power and the Glory* (1940), *The Ministry of Fear* (1943), *The Heart of the Matter* (1948), and *The End of the Affair* (1951). His short stories are collected in *The Basement Room* and *Nineteen Stories*.

Across the Bridge

"THEY SAY he's worth a million," Lucia said. He sat there in the little hot damp Mexican square, a dog at his feet, with an air of immense and forlorn patience. The dog attracted your attention at once; for it was very nearly an English setter, only something had gone wrong with the tail and the feathering. Palms wilted over his head, it was all shade and stuffiness round the bandstand, radios talked loudly in Spanish from the little wooden sheds where they changed your pesos into dollars at a loss. I could tell he didn't understand a word from the way he read his newspaper—as I did myself, picking out the words which were like English ones. "He's been here a month," Lucia said. "They turned him out of Guatemala and Honduras."

You couldn't keep any secrets for five hours in this border town. Lucia had only been twenty-four hours in the place, but she knew all about Mr. Joseph Calloway. The only reason I didn't know about him (and I'd been in the place two weeks) was because I couldn't talk the language any more than Mr.

Calloway could. There wasn't another soul in the place who didn't know the story—the whole story of the Halling Investment Trust and the proceedings for extradition. Any man doing dusty business in any of the wooden booths in the town is better fitted by long observation to tell Mr. Calloway's tale than I am, except that I was in—literally—at the finish. They all watched the drama proceed with immense interest, sympathy, and respect. For, after all, he had a million.

Every once in a while through the long steamy day, a boy came and cleaned Mr. Calloway's shoes: he hadn't the right words to resist them—they pretended not to know his English. He must have had his shoes cleaned the day Lucia and I watched him at least half a dozen times. At midday he took a stroll across the square to the Antonio Bar and had a bottle of beer, the setter sticking to heel as if they were out for a country walk in England (he had, you may remember, one of the biggest estates in Norfolk). After his bottle of beer, he would walk down between the money-changers' huts to the Rio Grande and look across the bridge into the United States: people came and went constantly in cars. Then back to the square till lunch-time. He was staying in the best hotel, but you don't get good hotels in this border town: nobody stays in them more than a night. The good hotels were on the other side of the bridge: you could see their electric signs twenty stories high from the little square at night, like lighthouses marking the United States.

You may ask what I'd been doing in so drab a spot for a fortnight. There was no interest in the place for anyone; it was just damp and dust and poverty, a kind of shabby replica of the town across the river: both had squares in the same spots; both had the same number of cinemas. One was cleaner than the other, that was all, and more expensive, much more expensive. I'd stayed across there a couple of nights waiting for a man a tourist bureau said was driving down from Detroit to Yucatan and would sell a place in his car for some fantastically small figure—twenty dollars, I think it was. I don't know if he existed or was invented by the optimistic half-caste in the agency; anyway, he never turned up and so I waited, not much caring, on the cheap side of the river. It didn't much matter; I was living. One day I meant to give up the man from Detroit and go home or go south, but it was easier not to decide anything in a hurry. Lucia was just waiting for a car going the other way, but she didn't have to wait so long. We waited together and watched Mr. Calloway waiting—for God knows what.

I don't know how to treat this story—it was a tragedy for Mr. Calloway, it was poetic retribution, I suppose, in the eyes of the shareholders he'd ruined with his bogus transactions, and to Lucia and me, at this stage, it was pure comedy—except when he kicked the dog. I'm not a sentimentalist about dogs, I prefer people to be cruel to animals rather than to human beings, but I couldn't help being revolted at the way he'd kick that animal—with a hint of cold-blooded venom, not in anger but as if he were getting even for some trick it had played him a long while ago. That generally happened when he returned from the bridge: it was the only sign of anything resembling emotion he showed. Otherwise he looked a small, set, gentle creature with silver hair and a silver moustache, and gold-rimmed glasses, and one gold tooth like a flaw in character.

Lucia hadn't been accurate when she said he'd been turned out of Guatemala and Honduras; he'd left voluntarily when the extradition proceedings seemed likely to go through and moved north. Mexico is still not a very centralized state, and it is possible to get round governors as you can't get round cabinet ministers or judges. And so he waited there on the border for the next move. That earlier part of the story is, I suppose, dramatic, but I didn't watch it and I can't invent what I haven't seen—the long waiting in anterooms, the bribes taken and refused, the growing fear of arrest, and then the flight—in gold-rimmed glasses—covering his tracks as well as he could, but this wasn't finance and he was an amateur at escape. And so he'd washed up here, under my eyes and Lucia's eyes, sitting all day under the bandstand, nothing to read but a Mexican paper, nothing to do but look across the river at the United States, quite unaware, I suppose, that everyone knew everything about him, once a day kicking his dog. Perhaps in its semi-setter way it reminded him too much of the Norfolk estate—though that too, I suppose, was the reason he kept it.

And the next act again was pure comedy. I hesitate to think what this man worth a million was costing his country as they edged him out from this land and that. Perhaps somebody was getting tired of the business, and careless; anyway, they sent across two detectives, with an old photograph. He'd grown his silvery moustache since that had been taken, and he'd aged a lot, and they couldn't catch sight of him. They hadn't been across the bridge two hours when everybody knew that there were two foreign detectives in town looking for Mr. Calloway—everybody knew, that is to say, except Mr. Calloway, who couldn't talk Spanish. There were plenty of people who could have told him in English, but they didn't. It wasn't cruelty, it was a sort of awe and respect: like a bull, he was on show, sitting there mournfully in the plaza with his dog, a magnificent spectacle for which we all had ringside seats.

I ran into one of the policemen in the Bar Antonio. He was disgusted; he had had some idea that when he crossed the bridge life was going to be different, so much more color and sun, and—I suspect—love, and all he found were wide mud streets where the nocturnal rain lay in pools, and mangy dogs, smells and cockroaches in his bedroom, and the nearest to love, the open door of the Academia Comercial, where pretty mestizo girls sat all the morning learning to typewrite. Tip-tap-tip-tap-tip—perhaps they had a dream, too—jobs on the other side of the bridge, where life was going to be so much more luxurious, refined and amusing.

We got into conversation; he seemed surprised that I knew who they both were and what they wanted. He said, "We've got information this man Calloway's in town."

"He's knocking around somewhere," I said.

"Could you point him out?"

"Oh, I don't know him by sight," I said.

He drank his beer and thought a while. "I'll go out and sit in the plaza. He's sure to pass sometime."

I finished my beer and went quickly off and found Lucia. I said, "Hurry, we're going to see an arrest." We didn't care a thing about Mr. Calloway, he was just an elderly man who kicked his dog and swindled the poor, and who deserved anything he got. So we made for the plaza; we knew Calloway would be there, but it had never occurred to either of us that the detectives wouldn't recognize him. There was quite a surge of people round the place; all the fruit-sellers and boot-blacks in town seemed to have arrived together; we had to force our way through, and there in the little green stuffy center of the place, sitting on adjoining seats, were the two plainclothes men and Mr. Calloway. I've never known the place so silent; everybody was on tiptoe, and the plainclothes men were staring at the crowd looking for Mr. Calloway, and Mr. Calloway sat on his usual seat staring out over the money-changing booths at the United States.

"It can't go on. It just can't," Lucia said. But it did. It got more fantastic still. Somebody ought to write a play about it. We sat as close as we dared. We were afraid all the time we were going to laugh. The semi-setter scratched for fleas and Mr. Calloway watched the U.S.A. The two detectives watched the crowd, and the crowd watched the show with solemn satisfaction. Then one of the detectives got up and went over to Mr. Calloway. That's the end, I thought. But it wasn't, it was the beginning. For some reason they had eliminated him from their list of suspects. I shall never know why.

The man said, "You speak English?"

"I *am* English," Mr. Calloway said.

Even that didn't tear it, and the strangest thing of all was the way Mr. Calloway came alive. I don't think anybody had spoken to him like that for weeks. The Mexicans were too respectful—he was a man with a million—and it had never occurred to Lucia and me to treat him casually like a human being; even in our eyes he had been magnified by the colossal theft and the world-wide pursuit.

He said, "This is rather a dreadful place, don't you think?"

"It is," the policeman said.

"I can't think what brings anybody across the bridge."

"Duty," the policeman said gloomily. "I suppose you are passing through."

"Yes," Mr. Calloway said.

"I'd have expected over here there'd have been—you know what I mean—life. You read things about Mexico."

"Oh, life," Mr. Calloway said. He spoke firmly and precisely, as if to a committee of shareholders. "That begins on the other side."

"You don't appreciate your own country until you leave it."

"That's very true," Mr. Calloway said. "Very true."

At first it was difficult not to laugh, and then after a while there didn't seem to be much to laugh at; an old man imagining all the fine things going on beyond the international bridge. I think he thought of the town opposite as a combination of London and Norfolk—theaters and cocktail bars, a little shooting and a walk round the field at evening with the dog—that miserable imitation of a setter—poking the ditches. He'd never been across, he couldn't know that it was just the same thing over again—even the same layout; only the streets were paved and the hotels had ten more stories, and life was more expensive, and everything was a little bit cleaner. There wasn't anything Mr. Calloway would have called living—no galleries, no book-shops, just *Film Fun* and the local paper, and *Click* and *Focus* and the tabloids.

"Well," said Mr. Calloway, "I think I'll take a stroll before lunch. You need an appetite to swallow the food here. I generally go down and look at the bridge about now. Care to come too?"

The detective shook his head. "No," he said, "I'm on duty. I'm looking for a fellow." And that, of course, gave *him* away. As far as Mr. Calloway could understand, there was only one "fellow" in the world anyone was looking for—his brain had eliminated friends who were seeking their friends, husbands who might be waiting for their wives, all objectives of any search but just the one. The power of elimination was what had made him a financier—he could forget the people behind the shares.

That was the last we saw of him for a while. We didn't see him going into the Botica Paris to get his aspirin, or walking back from the bridge with his dog. He simply disappeared, and when he disappeared, people began to talk, and the detectives heard the talk. They looked silly enough, and they got busy after the very man they'd been sitting next to in the garden. Then they too disappeared. They, as well as Mr. Calloway, had gone to the state capital to see the Governor and the Chief of Police, and it must have been an amusing sight there too, as they bumped into Mr. Calloway and sat with him in the waiting-rooms. I suspect Mr. Calloway was generally shown in first, for everyone knew he was worth a million. Only in Europe is it possible for a man to be a criminal as well as a rich man.

Anyway, after about a week the whole pack of them returned by the same train. Mr. Calloway traveled Pullman, and the two policemen traveled in the day coach. It was evident that they hadn't got their extradition order.

Lucia had left by that time. The car came and went across the bridge. I stood in Mexico and watched her get out at the United States Customs. She wasn't anything in particular but she looked beautiful at a distance as she gave me a wave out of the United States and got back into the car. And I suddenly felt sympathy for Mr. Calloway, as if there were something over there which you couldn't find here, and turning round I saw him back on his old beat, with the dog at his heels.

I said "Good afternoon," as if it had been all along our habit to greet each other. He looked tired and ill and dusty, and I felt sorry for him—to think of the kind of victory he'd been winning, with so much expenditure of cash and care—the prize this dirty and dreary town, the booths of the money-changers, the awful little beauty parlors with their wicker chairs and sofas looking like the reception rooms of brothels, that hot and stuffy garden by the bandstand.

He replied gloomily, "Good morning," and the dog started to sniff at some ordure and he turned and kicked it with fury, with depression, with despair.

And at that moment a taxi with the two policemen in it passed us on its way to the bridge. They must have seen that kick; perhaps they were cleverer than I had given them credit for, perhaps they were just sentimental about animals, and thought they'd do a good deed, and the rest happened by accident. But the fact remains—those two pillars of the law set about the stealing of Mr. Calloway's dog.

He watched them go by. Then he said, "Why don't you go across?"

"It's cheaper here," I said.

"I mean just for an evening. Have a meal at that place we can see at night in the sky. Go to the theater."

"There isn't a chance."

He said angrily, sucking his gold tooth, "Well, anyway, get away from here." He stared down the hill and up the other side. He couldn't see that that street climbing up from the bridge contained only the same money-changers' booths as this one.

I said, "Why don't *you* go?"

He said evasively, "Oh—business."

I said, "It's only a question of money. You don't *have* to pass by the bridge."

He said with faint interest, "I don't talk Spanish."

"There isn't a soul here," I said, "who doesn't talk English."

He looked at me with surprise. "Is that so?" he said. "Is that so?"

It's as I have said; he'd never tried to talk to anyone, and they respected him too much to talk to him—he was worth a million. I don't know whether I'm glad or sorry that I told him that. If I hadn't, he might be there now, sitting by the bandstand having his shoes cleaned—alive and suffering.

Three days later his dog disappeared. I found him looking for it, calling it softly and shamefacedly between the palms of the garden. He looked embarrassed. He said in a low angry voice, "I *hate* that dog. The beastly mongrel," and called "Rover, Rover" in a voice which didn't carry five yards. He said, "I bred setters once. I'd have shot a dog like that." It reminded him, I *was* right, of Norfolk, and he lived in the memory, and he hated it for its imperfection. He was a man without a family and without friends, and his only enemy was that dog. You couldn't call the law an enemy; you have to be intimate with an enemy.

Late that afternoon someone told him they'd seen the dog walking across the bridge. It wasn't true, of course, but we didn't know that then—they'd paid a Mexican five pesos to smuggle it across. So all that afternoon and the next Mr. Calloway sat in the garden having his shoes cleaned over and over again, and thinking how a dog could just walk across like that, and a human being, an immortal soul, was bound here in the awful routine of the little walk and the unspeakable meals and the aspirin at the *botica*. That dog was seeing things he couldn't see—that hateful dog. It made him mad—I think literally mad. You must remember the man had been going on for months. He had a million and he was living on two pounds a week, with nothing to spend his money on. He sat there and brooded on the hideous injustice of it. I think he'd have crossed over one day in any case, but the dog was the last straw.

Next day when he wasn't to be seen I guessed he'd gone across, and I went too. The American town is as small as the Mexican. I knew I couldn't miss him if he was there, and I was still curious. A little sorry for him, but not much.

I caught sight of him first in the only drug-store, having a Coca-Cola, and then once outside a cinema looking at the posters; he had dressed with extreme neatness, as if for a party, but there was no party. On my third time round, I came on the detectives—they were having Coca-Colas in the drug-store, and they must have missed Mr. Calloway by inches. I went in and sat down at the bar.

"Hello," I said, "you still about?" I suddenly felt anxious for Mr. Calloway, I didn't want them to meet.

One of them said, "Where's Calloway?"

"Oh," I said, "he's hanging on."

"But not his dog," he said, and laughed. The other looked a little shocked, he didn't like anyone to *talk* cynically about a dog. Then they got up—they had a car outside.

"Have another?" I said.

"No, thanks. We've got to keep moving."

The man bent close and confided to me, "Calloway's on this side."

"No!" I said.

"And his dog."

"He's looking for it," the other said.

"I'm damned if he is," I said, and again one of them looked a little shocked, as if I'd insulted the dog.

I don't think Mr. Calloway was looking for his dog, but his dog certainly found him. There was a sudden hilarious yapping from the car and out plunged the semi-setter and gamboled furiously down the street. One of the detectives—the sentimental one—was into the car before we got to the door and was off after the dog. Near the bottom of the long road to the bridge was Mr. Calloway—I do believe he'd come down to look at the Mexican side when he found there was nothing but the drugstore and the cinemas and the paper shops on the American. He saw the dog coming and yelled at it to go home—"home, home, home," as if they were in Norfolk—it took no notice at all, pelting toward him. Then he saw the police car coming and ran. After that, everything happened too quickly, but I think the order of events was this—the dog started across the road right in front of the car, and Mr. Calloway yelled, at the dog or the car, I don't know which. Anyway, the detective swerved—he said later, weakly, at the inquiry, that he couldn't run over a dog, and down went Mr. Calloway, in a mess of broken glass and gold rims and silver hair, and blood. The dog was on to him before any of us could reach him, licking and whimpering and licking. I saw Mr. Calloway put up his hand, and down it went across the dog's neck and the whimper rose to a stupid bark of triumph, but Mr. Calloway was dead—shock and a weak heart.

"Poor old geezer," the detective said, "I bet he really loved that dog," and it's true that the attitude in which he lay looked more like a caress than a blow. I thought it was meant to be a blow, but the detective may have been right. It all seemed to me a little too touching to be true as the old crook lay there with his arm over the dog's neck, dead with his million between the money-changers' huts, but it's as well to be humble in the face of human nature. He had come across the river for something, and it may, after all, have been the dog he was looking for. It sat there, baying its stupid and mongrel triumph across his body, like a piece of sentimental statuary. The nearest he could get to the fields, the ditches, the horizon of his home. It was comic and it was pitiable; but it wasn't less comic because the man was dead. Death doesn't change comedy to tragedy, and if that last gesture was one of affection, I suppose it was only one more indication of a human being's capacity for self-deception, our baseless optimism that is so much more appalling than our despair.